The Prior fixed Kurruné with a steady eye. "So you know not what dance is being danced, or which piper plays the tune? I would not have Hársan hurt, Kurruné. I know that you are not accountable for this transfer to the capital, nor can I exact the compensation of Shámtla blood-money if he is brought low through some scheming. Yet I do beg of you, as we both love the Lord of Wisdom, to keep ear clapped to earth and eye to door-crack, as I know you do in any case, and warn the lad of ill portents. This much I ask of you out of old friendship."

"You have my oath on it." Kurruné solemnly stretched forth his right palm, and Haringgáshte pressed his own to it. Together the two men moved down the aisle between the looming, black-shadowed shapes.

Behind them a tapestry rustled. It might have been the "Silent Walker of the Night."

The Man Of Gold

M.A.R. Barker

Published by Tékumel Foundation
www.tekumelfoundation.org

The first publication of *The Man of Gold* was by DAW Books; it was published as a "DAW Superstar" paperback in 1984. This edition includes several minor changes, most notably diacritical marks, which were left out in the DAW edition.

ISBN: 978-0-9864323-1-6

Cover art Giovanna Fregni. Cover design and interior design by Knotted Road Press. Interior map by Jeff Dee. Used with permission.

Manuscript preparation by Theresa Jarosz Alberti, Stephen Hearn, Kathryn Hearn, and Victor Raymond.

The Man of Gold

M.A.R. Barker

Tékumel Foundation
www.tekumelfoundation.org

Also by M.A.R. Barker

Flamesong
Lords of Tsamra
Prince of Skulls
A Death of Kings

The Man of Gold

M·A·R· Barker

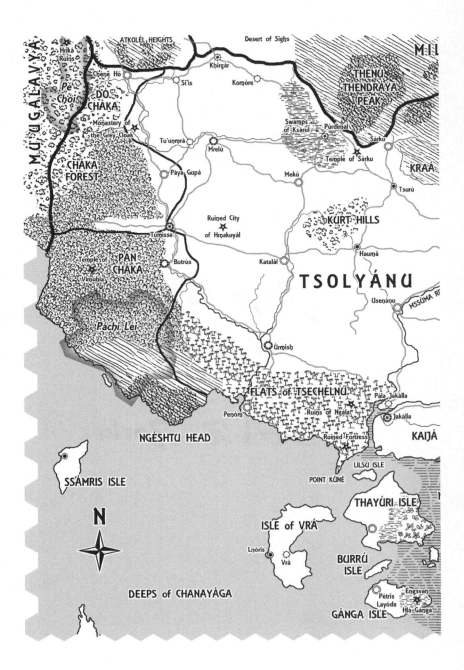

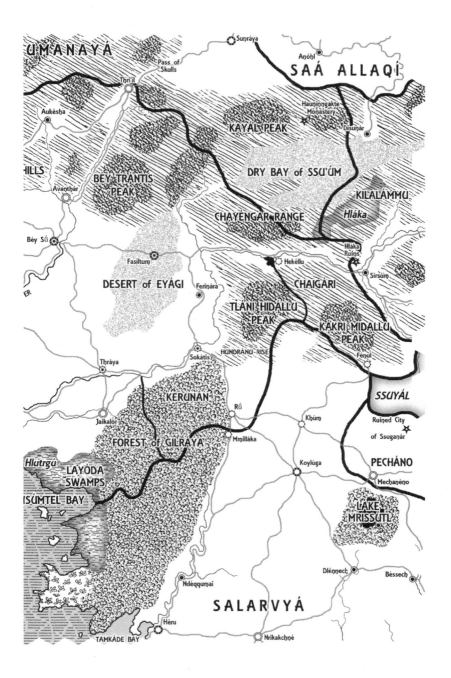

Chapter One

For upwards of half an hour now they had watched the runner on the road below the single watchtower of the monastery. Nothing at first but a tiny fleck of azure on the heat-shimmering horizon, he became a species of insect, all coppery brown legs beneath a carapace of brilliant blue, then a tiny manikin moving with jerky puppet strides along the dusty, empty roadway. The younger of the two watchers on the parapet made the Pé Chói gesture-language symbol for "half" to his comrade.

The other man shook his shaven head and applied a box-like device to his eye. "Not so, Hársan, not this time. I make no more wagers. I still think he will take another *Kirén* to reach our gates, but I'll not bet upon it. You have impoverished me already."

The younger man hitched up his grey priestly kilt and carefully clambered back down from the dizzy height of the embrasured wall. "Let me look again through your invention, Zarén. I cannot imagine what an Imperial messenger desires here."

The older priest handed over his device, a square box in which several small mirrors and lenses had been inserted and held in place with bits of wax, wood, and fibre. Hársan held it to his eye, squinted, and fiddled with the adjustment.

"By our Lord Thúmis, Patron of Savants, this fellow springs up at me like a beast from its lair! Without your box all I can see is a pen-flick of blue and a splotch of skin. With it, I can even make out the golden cord that binds his headdress! You must submit this to the Adepts as one of your Labours of Reverence, Zarén. Surely you will make Fifth Circle – or even Sixth."

Zarén smiled lopsidedly. "Not so. The principles underlying my box are all laid down in the 'Book of the Visitations of Glory,' written some four thousand years ago. All I did was to take them, cook them together, and putter until I got to a logical result. I am nothing but a tinkerer, Hársan. My skull is a pot in which other men's ideas may be boiled. Our good Lord Prior will pat me on the head, but that will be all."

The younger priest pushed wavy shoulder-length black hair away from his face and raised the instrument to focus upon the horizon. Behind the toiling messenger the stone causeway wound down across sere, dusty fields, a brown-grey rivulet, to join with its parent, the *Sákbe*-road on the eastern horizon. This mighty highway marked the visible presence of the Imperium of Tsolyánu; its three levels of roadway, crenellated and parapeted like some citadel wall, marched away south to the little city of Páya Gúpa, and thence on to Tumíssa and the southern provinces of the Empire.

Turning to the north, Hársan inspected the chalky peaks of the Cháka Range, upon the easternmost spur of which the Monastery of the Sapient Eye of Thúmis stood. Eleven hundred *Tsán* to the north these fastnesses would descend through crumpled foothills and valleys into the alluvial plains bordering the northern sea, the lands of the hostile lords of Pijéna and Yán Kór. To the south, beyond Páya Gúpa, the green coverlet of jungle ran another thirteen hundred *Tsán* to the southern ocean, of which most of the priests of the monastery had heard no more than travellers' tales.

Yet it was not there that the young priest's eyes lingered but on the hazy blue-green ranges behind the monastery to the west where slender ropes of smoke upon the sky marked the places of villages beneath the jungle roof.

Zarén followed his gaze. "Not even my invention can pierce the forest, Hársan. The Pé Chói villages lie beyond its reach. Leave off looking, my friend. Why do you always turn to thinking of your Pé Chói foster parents – great insects and no kin of ours – when you are now amongst your own kind?"

The younger man did not turn. "It was they who found and raised me, Zarén. My heart wishes me once more amongst them, though they have six limbs to our four."

Zarén would have said something, but Hársan went on. "Had it not been for those 'insects,' my life were ended before it had begun. How shall I not think of the Pé Chói? My own human parents, my clan, my origins – I know none of them. Nor do I love those who left me there to die in the forest. Lá, man, shall I not yearn for T'kék who raised me, and for Ch'bê who taught me, and for Lkét who hunted with me? In my dreams shall I not return to Htíqkkú, the only clan-village I knew until T'kék brought me to this monastery when I was thirteen? I was used better by those 'insects' than by my own kind." He lapsed into moody silence, stroking his lower lip with a gesture that struck Zarén as more characteristic of a Pé Chói than of one of humankind.

Zarén sighed and shuffled his plump bulk around to the narrow stair leading down from the eyrie. "Come, we have been over these matters as often as a peasant ploughs his field. – An accident, a babe lost from a merchant's caravan, an unwed maid fleeing the vengeance of her clan – Thúmis knows what brought you to the Pé Chói, and He alone may reveal it to you if it is so written in your Skein of Destiny. In the meantime you had best dash down and inform Prior Haringgáshte of the arrival of our guest. Go now, speed! Otherwise our noble Prior will count his rosaries upon your backside with his knotted thong."

Hársan pulled himself up for one last look over the parapet. The runner was now almost directly below, long legs pumping rhythmically, arms outflung, flanks gleaming with perspiration, blue cloth headdress bobbing with the final effort of the steep incline just below the monastery gates. In his right hand, clearly visible, was the tasselled blue and white baton of an Imperial courier. This was indeed a visitor of significance.

The narrow stair circled down within the monastery's prow-like eastern wall and emerged in the Hall of Instruction. Here, high up under the roof, lighted by tall recessed windows glazed with cloudy-grey glass, several dozen aspiring priests, a scattering of female acolytes, and a few scions of the local Chákan nobility sat struggling with the intricacies of Tsolyáni calligraphy. Hársan's old preceptor Charéshmu sat upon the dais, meticulously dissecting one of the Seventy-Seven Specimens of Dirrésa the Copyist, traditional in priestly schools for the past thousand years. Hársan grinned. Charéshmu had all of the enthusiasm for his art of an addict for his drug, yet all of the lecturing talent of a stone idol. Heads lifted at the intrusion; pens stopped in mid squiggle. Hársan bowed perfunctorily in the old teacher's direction, sketched the symbol of Thúmis in the air, and ducked out, feeling Charéshmu's baneful glare all the way across the room like a fire upon his back. Someone would suffer now – probably poor Kru'óm, whose earnest pothooks resembled tangled tree branches more than they did the graceful Tsolyáni script.

Hársan entered a pillared arcade, thence down a staircase painted with murals of Thúmis bestowing the Orb of Eternal Light upon Hrúgga, the hero of the Epics. Here the deity held out many-rayed hands towards the kneeling warrior king; there Thúmis in his Aspect of the Jewelled Serpent strode at Hrúgga's back, protecting him from the Demon Qu'ú. Farther on, the god's many-faced, many-armed figure overspread marching columns of Classical Tsolyáni script which related Hrúgga's victory over Missúm, Lord of the Dead, on Dórmoron Plain. Hársan gave these patched and peeling paintings only a bare glance. He had spent many hours here as a boy, copying each glyph under the shadow of Charéshmu's quizzical eye and all too active rod.

The staircase debouched into the colonnade surrounding the outer precincts of the Hall of Divine Supplication. Here scribes swarmed, drawing up documents, copying devotional texts for sale to the pious, and tending to the myriad tasks of temple administration.

The monastery was charged with more than just religious obligations, of course: the district capital, Páya Gúpa, lay some two hundred *Tsán* to the south. This place thus served as both shrine and local administrative centre. The Prior and his officers were empowered to settle land disputes, register claims, maintain records, license merchants, regulate trade, and even deal with criminal cases of a minor sort.

Hársan picked his way between low tables piled with scrolls, inkpots, and pen cases, dodged perspiring copyists squatting crosslegged over their dry grass-smelling sheets of fibrous paper, and narrowly avoided collisions with young acolytes buried beneath armloads of record scrolls. The great bronze gates of the Hall of Divine Supplication stood ajar, and Hársan slipped into its shadowy gloom, fragrant with incense but deserted until the ceremony of Purifying the Lips of Thúmis at sunset. From this chamber a half-hidden door of worn, black *Tíu*-wood opened onto a covered balcony overlooking the temple's Hall of Enactments. Here Prior Haringgáshte was wont to sit, watching all that transpired under his jurisdiction with a beady eye. He was not present today.

Hársan leaned over the age-blackened railing to peer down into the hubbub of scribes, peasants, landowners, merchants, and priests. Three pyramidal daises occupied the centre of the hall, the middle one standing three man-heights above the chipped grey marble pavement, the other two somewhat lower. From these, narrow gangways ran down to still lower platforms; short stairs, runways, ramps, and little wooden bridges travelled thence to still lower, broader daises, and finally to the floor. So great was the Tsolyáni love for the visible display of all abstract relationships that one could almost trace the structure of the temple's administration from the heights, arrangements, and interconnections of these daises.

All of the levels were occupied by shaven-headed, ink-stained priests of the Second and Third Circles, men and women who had devoted their lives to the neat rows of entries of fields and produce, the ciphering of columns of tithes and taxes, and the recording of markets and trade. Here one entry announced the arrival of an infant into this world of Tékumel; there another line of script indicated his or her clan, profession, and status; a further squiggle noted the person's marriage; other registers recorded the payment of taxes and tithes, the ownership of lands and goods, the growth of a family, children, servants, and concubines; and still another entry marked the citizen's departure from this life and the final journey into the Halls of Belkhánu, the Lord of the Excellent Dead. All of the events of a thousand, thousand lifetimes were here in these scrolls, tossed carelessly back and forth from one careless sacerdotal hand to another.

Lamps for the melting of sealing wax burned blue with the pitchy redolence of *Vrés*-wood. Young children did futile battle with cloth whisks against clouds of bottle-green *Chrí*-flies. Older boys and girls carried brass trays of earthen cups brimming with *Chumétl*, the traditional daily drink of watered and salted buttermilk, to this outstretched hand or that. Clay waterjugs spread wet stains of welcome coolness over the soiled matting of the daises. Servitors in once-grey kilts bustled up from the lower platforms to pass some document to those higher up; others bore officiously sealed decrees down again to the petitioners waiting below.

Today the Hall of Enactments was crowded. The place thronged with villagers and the local gentry of the Chákas. Hársan noted the presence of Lord (– if one could dignify him with so lofty a title –) Sé'eqel, the richest landowner of the district, surrounded by his little entourage of servants and bully-boys. There stood an awkward group of Kachór chiefs from the Inner Range, gaudy in their sleeveless tunics of *Hmá*-wool and *Khéshchal*-feather headdresses. Townsmen in open vests and pleated kilts ostentatiously embroidered with their clan symbols milled around the scribes of the lower levels, jostling with traders in stained leather kilts, particoloured overcloaks, and laced travel leggings. Peasants of both sexes, nude save for brief clouts of *Dáichu*-bark cloth, strove for the attention of the rows of bored petition-writers seated crosslegged along the back wall of the chamber.

Slightly apart from the rest, in a circle of their own, four graceful Pé Chói communed together like dancers before a performance. Hársan's gaze lingered upon these: the six slender limbs, the upper pair of which ended in tiny skeletal hands, the middle pair used now for grasping and now for standing, and the two heavier rear limbs spread in a perpetual grasshopper-like crouch; the shiny black chitinous integument (these were males — females would be bone-white); the long, segmented tail switching restlessly to emphasise some point made by its owner; the delicate black-to-grey shading of the ear-ridges of the long, sleek heads; the lambent green eyes; the dainty jaws filled with peg-like teeth. For a moment Hársan's perspective did a sudden somersault: these Pé Chói were the *Ntú-ntík*, "the People," and the soft-fleshed, hairy humans were again the *Tkík-ntík*, "the Outsiders." One of these Pé Chói he recognised as old Tná-Chú, the *Pqá E'étk*, "the One to Be Consulted"— as much as human speech could match the connotations of the many-layered Pé Chói term, and as nearly as a human tongue and lips could reproduce the clicking, whispering, hooting language — of the nearest Pé Chói village some twenty *Tsán* into the forest to the west.

A stir in the chamber below brought Hársan back to his mission. A man dressed in the grey-lacquered *Chlén*-hide armour of the temple gate guards had thrust his way through the throng and was speaking earnestly with the scribes on the lower daises. Even as Hársan turned towards the staircase at the far end of the balcony he realised that he could never reach the highest dais before the guard did.

"Now," said Hársan to himself, "I shall receive the 'leather rosary.' Damned Ferrúga will announce this messenger to our beloved Prior before I can get there." Nevertheless he adopted a fiercely dutiful look, drew five deep breaths to show that he had run all the way, and plunged down the steps three at a time. As he had predicted, he was too late.

Chapter Two

The summons from Prior Haringgáshte did not come until after the
lector priests had completed the nightly adoration of Lord Thúmis,
and the jewelled image, attired in robes of deepest purple-grey, had
been conveyed upon its gilded litter by forty chanting bearers from the Hall
of Divine Supplication to the upper shrine, the Gallery of Gazing Forth by
Night. Here sat the priests of the Sixth and Seventh Circles, surrounded by
their astrolabes and ephemerides, to ponder the skeins of past, present, future,
might-be and might-have-been, in the movements of Tékumel's two moons
and four sister planets. As a newly anointed Scholar Priest of the Second
Circle, Hársan had perforce to attend upon chubby old Vríshmuyel, chief of
the astrologers, whose interests lay more in dozing than in the imparting of
celestial mechanics to his brood of students.

With a sinking sensation, Hársan accepted the little plaque of dyed *Chién*-
hide, embossed with the symbol of Thúmis upon one side and the Prior's
personal glyph upon the other, from the hand of the pretty girl acolyte who
had brought it.

The Prior's apartments were in the eastern wing, almost directly opposite
the Gallery of Gazing Forth by Night across the east-west axis of the
monastery. Hársan arrived slightly out of breath and paused to collect himself
and to ascertain the Prior's mood from the *Méshqu*, the little silver hook at eye-

height beside the door, upon which coloured plaques of *Chlén*-hide were hung to indicate the current humour of the occupant within. To Hársan's surprise, the symbol that hung there tonight was green striped with red: "The Badge of Solemn Contemplation," rather than the red and black chequered "Fist of Stern Retribution." With somewhat higher spirits he rattled the wooden clappers hanging from the door lintel.

Qumál, the Prior's flat-faced, unsmiling body-servant, admitted Hársan to the empty anteroom, led him past the dining chamber, where three children were stacking up the many little golden bowls of the evening's repast (and surreptitiously stuffing their cheeks with left-overs), and opened the bronze-studded door into Haringgáshte's audience hall.

This chamber was furnished in the simple style preferred by the austere temple of Thúmis: grey-washed walls covered with painted devotional texts in black and red, coloured vignettes of the god, a tessellated marble floor overspread with a single carpet of cloud-grey *Mnór*-fur, several ascending daises, each with its low table set upon legs carven in the shapes of comical *Kurukú*-beasts, and a larger table in one corner heaped with scrolls, books, inkpots, jars of pigments, and vessels of unknown contents. A single branching candelabrum held twelve tiny oil-lamps. High up beneath the beamed ceiling four small clerestory windows admitted the cool evening breeze that blew nightly down off the Inner Range.

Prior Haringgáshte sat alone upon the highest dais at the far end of the room. As with many from his native city of Tumíssa, his physique had developed like that of the *Choqún*-plant: reed-slender in his youth, in his latter years he had become almost bottle-shaped. His small and delicate head joined his sloping chest with little pause for shoulders, and his rotund pot-belly overhung his rounded, almost feminine hips in testimony to his love of sedentary habits — and of good food. The grey vestments of Thúmis did little to conceal his girth, nor did the black skullcap of the priesthood hide his bald and mottled scalp. He watched Hársan's approach with a steady and not overly baneful gaze, from which the latter derived some faint comfort. His first words took Hársan by surprise.

"It is related, priest Hársan, that you have been anointed a Scholar Priest of the Second Circle. What was the Labour of Reverence that brought you to this exalted status?"

"My — my Prior, it was a study of the language of the ancient Empire of Llyán of Tsámra…"

"Would you then become a grammarian?"

8

"Languages come as easily to me, Sire, as swimming to a fish. I know not why. Yet I would also study history, doctrines, and other —"

The Prior put forth a soft hand, palm down, two fingers extended, to show that he wished to continue. "How go your studies of Llyáni?"

The younger priest swallowed, started to speak, and tried again. "My Lord, as is known to you, the Empire of Llyán perished some twenty-five thousand years ago — nay, more, if the Livyáni scholars are correct. We lack material — I have studied rubbings of the one hundred and fifty-eight stone inscriptions in Llyáni, and I have had access to five of the seventeen most authentic books in the language. Yet this is so little. As my Lord knows, the centre of Llyán's empire lay not within our own land of Tsolyánu but rather in the plains between Mu'ugalavyá and Livyánu to the southwest. All that we have are the later records of the Three States of the Triangle, some works of the Time of the Dragon Lords..." He trailed off, cursing himself for a babbler, well aware that the Prior knew all that he was telling him. But what did the man want?

Prior Haringgáshte pulled himself to his feet and extracted a worn leathern case of map-symbols from the litter of documents on his work table.

From this he took out a small pyramid of blue lapis lazuli. Tiny knobs and loops of gold had been affixed here and there upon its surface, and flecks of other minerals glinted from within. This, Hársan knew, symbolised the Empire of Tsolyánu, and each protuberance, curve, subtle shading, and texture told its tale of cities, roads and distances, populations, products, villages and towns, and other data, readable only by those skilled in High Cartography. Next emerged an oblong of sand-yellow jasper: the desert lands of Milumanayá to the north of Tsolyánu. Beyond this he set out a faceted rhomboid of smooth green serpentine; this stood for the hostile lands of Baron Áld of Yán Kór. Above this a tablet of wavy blue slate was placed to indicate the crag-coasted northern sea, each serration, curve, and change of texture marking a harbour, a cove, an island, a distant settlement — even reefs and tides. Three smaller polyhedrons of carnelian, agate, and red porphyry were arranged to the left of this to represent the little northern states of Pijéna, Ghatón, and N'lüss. The Prior then brought forth a cloudy wine-red dodecahedron of bloodstone which stood for the sprawling empire of Mu'ugalavyá, Tsolyánu's sometimes hostile western neighbour beyond the Cháka Range. Below this he added a curiously twisted moon-shaped symbol of rippling fire opal: the far-off land of Livyánu. A final plaque of wavy slate to the right of the symbol for Livyánu and beneath that of Tsolyánu signified the southern ocean, the Deeps of Chanayága. The rest of the symbols he left in the case.

"Can you read these, then, priest Hársan?"

"Only the rudiments, my Lord. I am more comfortable with the maps drawn upon paper by merchants – not with these of the High Cartography."

The Prior's lips sketched a thin smile. "These tell much more. To see, to touch, to feel – so much more than flat lines upon a page. Come, show me where the Empire of Llyán of Tsámra once lay."

Wondering, Hársan put forth a tentative finger and touched the empty space between the symbols for Mu'ugalavyá and Livyánu. "Here, my Lord."

The Prior reached into the welter of materials on the table, picked up a small casket of dun-red metal, and extracted another map symbol. With the air of a mother setting a morsel of sugary *Dmí*-root before a child, he laid this in the space marked by Hársan's finger. "This was found in a tomb of the Bednálljan Dynasty near our city of Úrmish. The casket is *Fulát* – steel – alas, now one of the rarest metals on Tékumel and one of the most costly therefore. Go ahead, examine it."

Slowly the younger man stretched forth his hand to caress the faceted crystal. The symbol was translucent, as deeply green as the Chákan forests; it resembled beryl, yet it was softer and somehow warm to the touch. Within it tiny motes of living gold and ruby-red and jet-black swam lazily like little fishes. Hársan's fingers seemed to travel of themselves from knobbly protuberance to tiny gold boss to miniature intaglio. As he did so, he realised that he was hearing snatches of speech at the very outer limits of his hearing: diminutive pygmy voices talking, lecturing, reciting, shouting, declaiming, singing – all in a language he could not make out and so faint as to seem but the echo of his own blood beating within his temples.

He snatched his hand away.

"It is a thing of the old ones, priest Hársan." The Prior reached out to take the symbol. "Once when I travelled with our late High Priest, Hukétláyu hiTánkolel (– may Thúmis commend him to the gate-guards of Belkhánu's paradise! –) to the Imperial citadel at Avanthár, I saw others of these things in the cabinets of Lord Qorúma, the High Princeps of the Omnipotent Azure Legion. Most of these map symbols are still and cold, like the poor copies made now by our artisans, but he had one or two which glowed like this and seemed to speak as this one does, though no one living knows the magic needed to bring the voices of these ghosts clearly to us." Prior Haringgáshte turned the map symbol over. "Look here, priest Hársan."

10

Hársan peered and then suddenly bent closer. The crisply incised characters on the symbol's base were the convoluted whorls and ornate floral arabesques of the artists of Llyán's empire, and in the midst of these were the squarish, squat characters of the Llyáni syllabary. In an awed voice he read:

"The Ever-Glorious and Most Puissant – three characters I do not know – Empire of Llyán, God-King, Ruler of Tsámra, and – another glyph I cannot read – Master of – hmm – and Holder of the Power of –" he paused and finished on a questioning note, "– the Man of Gold?"

As he looked up his eyes met the hard gaze of the Prior. For a moment the silence held. Then the older man blinked, took the map symbol from Hársan's hand, and said, "There is more, priest Hársan. – Tell me, is your analysis of the structure of the Llyáni language complete?"

Hársan wrenched his attention away from the green-glowing map symbol. "My Lord, it was accepted as my Labour of Reverence. I mean, Lord Thúmis deemed it worthy – there are only details…Even now Chushél the Glassmaker blows the final matrices for the elaboration of the syntax…"

"Come, I will look upon it." Haringgáshte rose and slipped knobbly feet into worn sandals of woven reed.

Chapter Three

P rior Haringgáshte led the way through the night-shadowed halls of the sleeping monastery to the north wing where the Scholar Priests had their quarters. Beyond this in what was called the New Annex, built half a millennium ago, was the Hall of Mighty Tongues. This was unique to the Monastery of the Sapient Eye, a showplace that even the Temple of Eternal Knowing in Béy Sü, the capital, lacked. Many learned pilgrims made the detour from the north-south *Sákbe*-road to trudge up into the foothills and gaze up at the marvels wrought by Thúmis' priests. Here, in keeping with the Tsolyáni love of depicting everything visually, the Scholar Priests had striven to reduce the complex patterns of language itself to visible, tangible models, comprehensible to those who had mastered the symbolism.

A single torch guttered in its bracket just within the door of the long L-shaped gallery. Inside in the place of honour stood Vringayékmu's rendition of the phonology and syntax of Mu'ugalavyáni, the tongue of Tsolyánu's mighty rival to the west. Twisting spirals of smoky red glass rose from a foliated plinth of black onyx; these were the features that made up Mu'ugalavyáni's twelve vowels. Farther up, these joined, separated, and joined again with convolutions of emerald, ochre, and violet, representing the consonants and the syllabic patterns of the language. Above this, skeins of other colours of glass, crystal, and precious metals danced in the torchlight: the complexities of the noun system and the Mu'ugalavyáni verb. Then, like the boughs of some great petrified crystalline tree, these networks entwined, reached out, met, parted, rose and fell together, branched away, and interlocked far overhead to form the intricate patterns of the syntactic structure. Hársan had learned to read it all, could drink it in through every pore, could almost sense spiritually the final mingling of all of these many strands to form at the very apex of the model the first couplet of the Third Ode of Bi'isúmish, the Blind Poet of Ssa'átis:

'Wherefore seekest thou, O sage? Tarry, for lo,
The spring, the autumn, the rains – all come round to thee again.'

Beyond Vringayékmu's creation stood a massive tower of soft, mottled, green stone, dark velvet, grating pebbles, and thin lacquered strips of *Chlén*-hide. This was priestess Fssu'úma's analysis of Ghatóni, the tongue of the fisherfolk who dwelt along the western shores of the northern sea. Its three major dialects were each represented by a towering pinnacle reaching up into the gloom. Still farther down the gallery the long-dead priest Hórri's squat pyramid of black glass, set with winking garnets and looped with silver strands, symbolised the language of Salarvyá, the great feudal empire bordering Tsolyánu to the southeast. In spite of his present concerns, Hársan could not help but feel a momentary twinge of envy: how beautifully had Hórri treated the two hundred and fourteen conjugations of the obstreperous Salarvyáni verb! No pilgrim from Salarvyá had ever looked upon this masterpiece without gasping in admiration, and indeed, some scholars had even been known to shed tears before its perfection.

More recent constructions lay around the corner of the room to the left, among them Hársan's own analysis of Llyáni. Now he saw that a stranger sat before his work, crosslegged upon a study-mat. A five-wick oil lamp flickered beside him, washing his right arm and his sharp profile with yellow-ruddy light. It was the messenger.

The Prior stopped before him, sketched a bow of greeting. "Auspicious messenger Kurruné, this is priest Hársan, who made this."

The man seemed to unfold as he got to his feet. He towered over Hársan by a handspan, yet he was slender as a new sapling, fine-boned, of early middle years, with the axe-edged features of eastern Tsolyánu and the indefinable air of the far traveller about him. Now he wore a grey guest-robe of the monastery. His blue courier's headdress lay beside him upon the flagstones.

"I greet you, priest Hársan. I was pondering your creation." His voice was deep, grave, and slow. Hársan recognised the flat accent as belonging to the desert city of Fasíltum in the north-eastern corner of Tsolyánu.

"It is insufficient, my Lord." Indeed, Hársan's truncated pillar of amber and gold filigree could never match the glory of Vringayékmu's creation not even the slighter work of Fssu'úma. Too little was known; there were too few sources, no living speakers of Llyáni. The curving, spiralling filaments were bare, deficient in detail. The model's amber spheres were simple, lacking the nuances of curve, colour, and texture which should have revealed the inner systems of the language: the relationships of its grammar and syntax to its semantics and thence to a depiction of the Llyáni world-view. To the practiced eye the model was a good yet introductory sketch, clearly the work of a student, albeit one whose insights showed promise.

The messenger paced slowly around the construction, looking, feeling, touching, gently rubbing. The smooth warmth of the amber and the russet-yellow highlights of the dark gold seemed to fascinate him. He paused finally before the two priests.

This was no unlettered bearer of messages. Hársan ventured, "My Lord, you comprehend...?"

The other gave him a slight smile. "Who I am concerns you not. What you have made here does concern me. You may address me as *Tusmikétlan*, the 'You of Polite Anonymity.' In return I shall call you *Tusmingáru*, the 'You of Honourable Youth.' Let me look upon the creator of this work."

The messenger bent and lifted the lamp. Its light revealed a serious-appearing young man attired in the knee-length grey kilt, stiffened *Firyá*-cloth collar, and reed sandals of a junior priest of Thúmis. Hársan was perhaps twenty years of age, slim of build, yet clearly strong as a new tent-rope is strong, with light coppery-gold skin, high cheekbones set in a sharply triangular face, perhaps a bit over-long in the jaw, eyes set a trifle aslant above a typical Tsolyáni eagle nose, yet with the wide and generous mouth of the peoples of the western Empire. Hársan's brows were now a straight line of furrowed puzzlement beneath his cap of black hair.

Kurruné considered. It was clear that the boy had not yet so totally committed him-self to the temple as to shave his head and don the black skullcap. Two braids hung down to Hársan's collar in front of his ears, their ends caught up with twists of silver wire, and the hair at the back of his head was cut to three fingers' length, all in the rural fashion of the Chákas. A rustic. Yet a young man with talent – and some burgeoning skill.

The messenger nodded and turned to the Prior. "Have you shown him the object I brought?"

"I have. He read most of the inscription."

"Then I shall show him another item." The courier took something from a wallet at his belt, unwrapped it, and held it out to Hársan.

Wondering, Hársan took it – and almost dropped it. The object was a human hand!

"Fear not," Kurruné said in an amused tone. "What you hold is but a waxen cast of a piece of sculpture. The original is of gold. Have a care lest the heat of your fingers blur the writing upon the palm. That is what I wish you to see."

Hársan turned it over, holding it gingerly by the carven fingers. The hand was excellently modelled. At first glance it did appear to be a waxy-pale human hand, severed at the wrist, the thumb and four fingers extending straight out and touching one another. Yet it was clear that this was but a carving: the fingers were too long, the workings of the joints and the creases of the knuckles stylised. And strangest of all, there were only conventionalised depressions where the nails should have been. Holding it near the light, Hársan saw that the palm was indeed covered with script. Two writings were here, however, one horizontal band across the palm, and another, vertical column that led down from the finger-tips to the wrist.

The vertical column was again Llyáni.

There was a long, intense silence. At length Hársan raised his head.

"My Lord, this is a religious relic. A pilgrim's copy of some powerful talisman. People can purchase trinkets like this at any of the great shrines." He drew a breath and pulled at his lip. "There are two inscriptions. The horizontal one is in N'lüssa, the tongue of the Dragon Warriors, that dynasty which ruled after the fall of the Three States of the Triangle. I am not much versed in it." He shot an apologetic glance at the Prior, "but I did study it somewhat in order to use the Llyáni grammar of Tlu'én of Ssa'átis, which is written in N'lüssa. In any case the text is not difficult: prayers for the buyer of the talisman. It was added later, for you can see that it partially covers the Llyáni writing. 'High' Llyáni was nigh a forgotten tongue by the time of the Dragon Warriors."

"And you can read the Llyáni inscription?" The messenger's gaze was keen.

"Not all, my Lord. I should consult my notes on the syllabary, and also the dictionary of Homón Tnéqqu of Khéiris, which we have here in the library. It is an incantation, and it speaks of several things. This much I can

15

read. There is mention of a 'Place of Iron Scales,' and there is the name of a Llyáni goddess called *Kúù Tép* – followed by the classifier glyph for 'original structure.' I cannot make much of that. Then comes the classifier for 'tool' or 'instrument,' and the words 'cube of flint' – obsidian. Then it speaks of the defeat of this goddess and her – minions? – the – umm – *He'ésa*, 'Those Who Are Always Seen and Yet Remain Unseen' – whatever that means – at a city called Shóshche, together with the dismantling – or walling up? – or sealing off? – of her 'cube' by the 'Man of Gold,' the same glyphs as were upon the map symbol. Then there are two columns of incantations addressed to this 'Man,' but they are meaningless without the sorcerous skill to unlock them – and there are some signs here at which I cannot even guess."

"Is not this 'Shóshche' the modern Mu'ugalavyáni city of Ch'óchi?" the Prior interjected.

"Even so, my Lord, or at least a site nearby in the jungle there. As for the name, as you know, the Llyáni fricative 'sh' became a glottalised affricate 'ch' during the Bednálljan dynasty, and though the Mu'ugalavyáni no longer pronounce the glottalised series as such, they still write certain archaic names with those symbols. The medial 'shch' first became 'chch,' then this simplified to –"

The messenger raised an impatient hand. "Peace! There will be time for such mysteries later! I am off to Tumíssa at sunrise and require my sleep." He paused, then said, "There is yet one important cask to be broached. Priest Hársan, the two items you have seen tonight are only a part of a trove discovered in the old Bednálljan cemetery at Úrmish. I would describe the other pieces to you, but I was myself not permitted to see them. They are… important…"

He retrieved the waxen hand from Hársan's fingers. "Your analysis of Llyáni was reported, of course, to the Temple of Eternal Knowing in Béy Sü. I imagine your good Prior Haringgáshte keeps the High Council abreast of all that transpires here at the monastery, eh? Well, the bare bones of it are these: when this tomb was opened at Úrmish, the High Council only needed to poke into their records, and, Ohé! – there's a priest Hársan at our monastery in the Chákas who reads Llyáni. I had business in Chéne Hó, Páya Gúpa, and Tumíssa, and the High Council deputed me to pass by and sniff at you and your work. If you can read these ancient squiggles, then I am to ask you if you would undertake the study of the hand – and the other items as well?"

Hársan could only nod. The successful completion of such a temple-backed project would open doors to dizzying heights within the hierarchy. For a young man with no clan and no wealth, this was better than the best!

Kurruné hitched up his kilt. "I cannot claim to read your language-model well. It shows promise. Prior Haringgáshte knows me from of old, and he'll vouch that though I possess but a pinch of knowledge, I do own a handful of judgment." He shot a half-humourous glance at the Prior, who remained impassive.

The messenger dug again into his wallet and produced a scrap of brownish parchment. "I can thus complete my task here by handing this over to friend Haringgáshte. It is a writ for the transfer of this priest Hársan to the Temple of Eternal Knowing in Béy Sü. You have a six-day to prepare, and then they want you there within two or three months: say, the first of Drenggár."

This opened one door too many and too fast. Hársan shook his head involuntarily as thoughts leaped to his lips. "My Lord Kurruné – this means leaving my service here, and –" he cast about for some objection that would make sense, "– and – but – why ME? I am not a known scholar of Llyáni. What of Kuruktén of Jakálla, the Arch Scholar Grunéshu, the Priestess Dlessúna of the temple of Hnálla, the Lord Búretl hiChuvrén…?"

Kurruné waved a hand, palm up to show that he did not know. "I am not privy to the doings of your High Council. It's not my business. Gossip has it, however, that this Kuruktén died some two months back. And Grunéshu is an ancient dodderer, as I can attest with my own eyes. I know nothing of the others. I was sent to look at your model and see if you're really as clever as your kindly Prior keeps reporting. …And, as our proverb in Fasíltum has it, 'the main course does not much care what else is for dinner.' All I can suggest is that your youth and this," he waved at the model, "make you more useful now than the fusty pedantry of all your other greybeards. You'd best get your feet hardened for a long journey. It's twelve hundred *Tsán* or so to Béy Sü."

"Hold, now, Kurruné," Prior Haringgáshte interposed smoothly. "You come at the boy teeth snapping like a charging *Zrné!* Give us time to gather our wits, and then we shall see what reply to give the High Council. I, for one, do not wish to see Hársan leave his studies as yet. Even Zarén, Hársan's comrade here, knows nearly as much Llyáni as Hársan does. His talents have always been more practically directed, of course, but –"

"My Lord Prior, the writ is there." Kurruné leaned down to pick up his headdress and pinch out the lamp. Shadows leaped forth to take possession of Hársan's model. "There is no answer other than compliance. You do have time – if you have both daring and high connections in the capital. Delay, then, and fire off such protests as you will. Or bargain Hársan for funds for a new image of Lord Thúmis, or the rebuilding of the dormitory for your guests. The present one is full of biting *Karái*-beetles. Or as you will. The High Council is not immune to string-pulling. More than this I do not say." He yawned. "In any case, the night demons befog my wits and whisper to me of sleep."

The Prior pursed his lips and bent to roll up the mat Kurruné had used. "Hársan, you may leave us now. We shall see what is to be seen." As the younger priest turned to go, he added, "Sleep now, but do not fail to call upon Qumál tomorrow. He will supply you with five strokes of the 'leather rosary.' How else to repay you for failing to announce Kurruné's arrival before that ill-visaged and latrine-breathed Ferrúga burst in upon my nap? As it is written, 'the hide of a young man is like that of a *Chlén*-beast; peel it, and it grows back ever thicker and stronger.'"

The Prior smiled lopsidedly and turned back to his guest.

Chapter Four

The two men waited in silence until the receding slip-slap of Hársan's sandals and the click of the door closing told them that he had left. Above them the high clerestory windows were etched in the eldritch green luminescence of Gayél, Tékumel's second moon. The torch at the entrance, around the corner of the narrow L-shaped gallery, had long ago collapsed into dark coals within its sconce, and now only the faintest scattering of Gayél's light dusted the ghostly upper pinnacles of Fssu'úma's towering work and picked out veins of gleaming gold from among the twisted boughs of Vringayékmu's masterpiece. At the far end of the chamber, behind Hársan's model of Llyáni, the wall tapestries fluttered in response to the "Silent Walker of the Night," as the men of the Chákas named the chill night breeze from the Inner Range.

The Prior rounded upon Kurruné and spoke with fierce intensity. "And now you can unravel me this skein, my friend! When you asked me to show the boy the map symbol I had no idea you came to take him from us! I had hoped to see him complete his work – attain the Third Circle at least, before sending him out to jig to the pipers of temple politics!"

The other shrugged, held out a hand cupped palm up in mute deprecation. "Old friend, what can I say? I am but a talking *Küni*-bird, fluttering here and there to squawk my simple words, and am gone again..."

The Prior snorted. "Nonsense. I know you from of old. Did we not sweat out a miserable ten years together in the temple school at Tumíssa? Tell me, honestly, as Hnálla, Lord of Light, loves you: how many masters now do you serve?"

Kurruné smiled, not in the least put out. "Currently I think it is six – three of which are here, here, and here." He touched his stomach, his heart, and his forehead. "The remaining three are less troublesome." He held out his blue courier's headdress. "You know that I am a messenger for our good Lord, the sixty-first Seal Emperor of Tsolyánu. You know also that I favour our Lord of Wisdom, great Thúmis. And the sixth of my masters you must guess at, for I may not reveal the name."

"Tell me what you know of this matter at least!"

Kurruné sighed. "'Sow seeds in the desert and reap only sand,' as we say in Fasíltum. The High Council of the temple does not confide in such as I. But this, good Haringgáshte, may be the shoot from which the tree sprouts: not only is Hársan young, not only does he unravel Llyáni as easily as a maiden weaves garlands for her lovers, but is it not also true that he speaks the tongue of the insects – the Pé Chói?"

"Ohé, I had guessed as much." The Prior licked thin lips. "The boy is clanless, brought to us by the Pé Chói from the inner valleys. For Thúmis knows what reason they had kept him instead of handing him over to the nearest human settlement when they found him abandoned in the forest. None knew his parents, nor had we any record of him. When he came to us, he spoke only Pé Chói, a language no human has ever learned before. He whistled, he hooted, he trilled, he snapped his fingers and clapped his hands – and the insects understood him. He lacked the organs needed to make all of their strange sounds, yet he had developed substitutes. It was three summers before he could speak freely with the other children here in the monastery. Even now there are times when he strikes me as odd: a difference of idiom, a sense of attitude, who can say?"

The messenger glanced over to Hársan's model. "You tell me that he is the only human ever to learn the tongue of the Pé Chói. Why did he not make it the subject of his Labour of Reverence? There are many who know Llyáni."

"We had thought the same," the Prior replied, "but he said that there are no symbols – in glass, metal, or any other substance – for the sounds of the insects' speech. More, he denies that our symbologies can truly represent their conceptual framework. Who knows, he may be right...

"Perhaps he would keep his knowledge to himself? Later, when he grows more skilled, he may submit it as a Labour of Reverence for admission to a higher Circle?"

The Prior made a sour face. "Another unanswerable riddle. In any case, Llyáni has status, prestige as a 'high tongue' of the ancients. It is also likely that the other acolytes in our school had much to do with his choice — teased him about his jungle origins, his lack of clan, lineage, and parentage — and made him miserable enough to select the most noble, most difficult, and most esoteric of all of the ancient languages."

"Lá, friend Haringgáshte, you now answer your own question. Why send for this one lowly novice, as fresh as a *Dlél*-fruit from the tree? Here is a reason as good as any: a clever young fellow, talent visible within him as light within a lamp, a love of picking apart your ancient grammatical puzzles, a background of alien strangeness — something that provides him with a new perspective upon his studies. Why should the High Council not whistle him up when a bagful of old bones and trinkets comes to light?" He tapped his wallet.

"Because it is not enough! If there is one lesson I've learned in fifty years in the priesthood, it's to follow a skein until I get back to the first knot. When Hársan spoke of Grunéshu and the others, his bolt did not miss its mark. Other scholars of Llyáni exist, greater ones by far. Every temple of the twenty deities has some duffer or other who can riddle the language." He scraped a hand across his small, shaven chin. "— And these relics have naught to do with the Pé Chói. There's no hint of Pé Chói manufacture in the two you showed me. We lack a theorem sufficient to explain the data, as our old teacher Chayánu used to tell us in his logic lectures. The boy is clanless — not a good sign, for it means that he is expendable, and none to ask after him. He is naive, unlettered in the intrigues of the temple, vulnerable as a fish on the shore…"

Kurruné lowered his eyes. "Old friend, I really speak words of wind. I know nothing of this. About other matters I could fill you as a river fills a bucket. But not this. I swear it to you." His tone softened. "My sources do bring me a drop here, a driblet there, and from all of these trickles I can often make a pond. They say of me that all gossip flows to Kurruné the Messenger, as a river enters the sea. Were you to ask, I could tell you how the Royalist Party fiddles and the priesthoods dance; how the Military Party sings sweetly in our Emperor's ear of conquests in Yán Kór and the re-establishment of the halcyon days of the Bednálljan kings; how the Imperialist Party in Avanthár sulks and waits to pounce upon posts closer to the Petal Throne; how the royal Prince Eselné diddles and dallies with Misénla, High Priestess of Hriháyal in Béy Sü; how his brothers pout and glower, and the youngest, Dhich'uné, yearns to call up all the undead demons of accursed Sárku and give the land over to the Mysteries of the Worm. I could whisper of certain heirs to the throne who are as yet unrevealed, kept secret by the Emperor and his Omnipotent Azure Legion until the time is ripe for them to be brought forth…All of these things I can tell and more; yet of this present instance I have less knowledge than an eel-fisher in the swamps of Tsehélnu."

The Prior fixed Kurruné with a steady eye. "So you know not what dance is being danced, or which piper plays the tune? I would not have Hársan hurt, Kurruné. I know that you are not accountable for this transfer to the capital, nor can I exact the compensation of *Shámtla* blood-money if he is brought low through some scheming. Yet I do beg of you, as we both love the Lord of Wisdom, to keep ear clapped to earth and eye to door-crack, as I know you do in any case, and warn the lad of ill portents. This much I ask of you out of old friendship."

"You have my oath on it." Kurruné solemnly stretched forth his right palm, and Haringgáshte pressed his own to it. Together the two men moved down the aisle between the looming, black-shadowed shapes.

Behind them a tapestry rustled. It might have been the "Silent Walker of the Night."

Chapter Five

The Great Council of the Temples had been summoned to meet in the Palace of the Priesthoods of the Realm at one hour after sunrise. As usual, it began most tardily. The square-pillared portico at the eastern end of the chamber had first let in the cool, ruddy light of dawn to finger the blue and gold traceries of the ceiling. Now the hot, pale glare of midday pressed through the gauze curtains lowered by the attendants, and sunlight lay upon the flags nearest the columns like puddles of molten brass. The parched odour of summer hung upon the air, underlaid by the darker effluvia of the Missúma River. Here, high above Béy Sü, the breeze brought the clean smells of ripening crops from beyond Patyél's Walls, and these mingled with the fragrances of woodsmoke, charcoal, cooking spices, incense, the vast markets, and the less-pleasing redolences of sewers and open gutters and crowded humanity, all baking together under the midsummer sun.

Humidity streamed up from below, too, where the jumbled wharves on the western bank of the river extended out through the yellow mudflats like the fingers of a drowning man through quicksand. Legions of slaves toiled there upon their dredges, endlessly clearing the channels for the galleys and the many-sailed ships that brought trade – and life itself – down from Avanthár in the north and up from Jakálla and the great ocean far to the south. Even through the gauzy drapes the heat shimmered from the blue slate roofs of the city, from the high spires of the temples, each set upon its pyramid above the stews below, from the long colonnades and the offices of the Imperial bureaucracies, from the domes and cupolas of the mansions of the nobles and the high clans, and from the distant walls and turrets of the governor's palace, set like a gem in a ring within its preciously cool trees and parks, outside the city to the north.

Lord Dúrugen hiNáshomai, the High Adept of the Temple of Thúmis in Béy Sü, was already hot. The rustling robes of grey *Güdru*-cloth were stifling enough, but the ceremonial headdress of lacquered *Chlén*-hide and gold slowly drove a spike of dull pain down through his forehead. The Gods must love suffering to see their devotees tortured so! But, then, why involve the Gods? Man was marvellously expert at creating pain for himself.

The stiff brocade of the coif of his headdress prevented him from turning his head unless he twisted his entire torso. He did so, hoping that his colleagues in the High Council were all present and ready for the business that had summoned them here. The sooner done, the sooner back within the cool depths of the Temple of Eternal Knowing. The sooner a cup of dewy, chilled *Chumétl*, the sooner a nap.

Along the northern wall of the chamber stood five daises: stepped pyramids blazoned with the colours and insignia of the *Tlomitlányal*, the Five Lords of Stability. There was the white of Hnálla, the grey of his own good Lord Thúmis, the scarlet and gold of the war-god Karakán, the sky-blue of the goddess Avánthe, and the yellow of Belkhánu. Across the mosaic floor five identical daises lined the southern wall. These bore the blazons of the *Tlokiriqáluyal*, the Five Lords of Change, the counterparts of the *Tlomitlányal*: the deep purple of Hrü'ü, the flame-orange of Vimúhla, the black of Ksárul, the earth-brown of Sárku, and the emerald green of Lady Dlamélish. The High Adept of the Temple of Lord Ksárul, directly opposite Lord Dúrugen, had taken off his ritual silver mask in the heat. They nodded to one another with exaggerated courtesy. Lá, two rival suitors for the same maiden, Lord Dúrugen thought wryly.

He shifted to look down at the lower daises of the *Hlimékluyal*, the "Cohorts," lesser deities who each served one of the Great Gods. Directly below Lord Dúrugen, the sunlight made a bronze helmet of the bald pate of Elkhóme hiBriyénu, the High Priest Of Thúmis' Cohort, Lord Keténgku. The priests and scribes of Keténgku's dais wore grey and white. Those of the other Cohorts of the Lords of Stability similarly wore white bordered with the colour of the deity their master served – all except for Drá the Uncaring, Cohort of Lord Hnálla, whose dais was decked in an indifferent white and tan. The five Cohorts of the Lords of Change were blazoned similarly in purple joined with the colour of their particular divine Master or Mistress.

In the deeper shadows at the far western end of the hall a single dais rose above all the rest. This was draped with the royal blue and gold of the Second Imperium, the dynasty ruled by Hirkáne Tlakotáni, the Sixty-First Emperor of Tsolyánu. A golden disc, the replica of the Seal of the Imperium, hung like a miniature golden sun near the ceiling there. Today the Imperium would be represented by Lord Murésh hiQolyélmu, Prefect of the Omnipotent Azure Legion in Béy Sü. Lord Dúrugen was relieved to see that this worthy was already in place. Trust that the special servitors of the Emperor were never late!

A chamberlain sat on the topmost step of the Imperial dais, just below Lord Murésh. His duty was to speak for his superior, for Lord Murésh, like all members of the higher Circles of the Omnipotent Azure Legion, was a deaf-mute, made so in infancy in order that he might better devote himself to his Emperor – and speak no secrets of the Golden Tower at Avanthár. Thus had been the custom since the founding of the Empire some 2,358 years ago.

Lord Murésh spoke with his chamberlain through an intricate code of finger gestures. The chamberlain turned back to the room and struck two clappers of wood together. Lord Dúrugen sighed and rubbed his long, ascetic fingers. Now, at the age of sixty-two years, his extremities sometimes remained cold even when the summer heat danced upon the land like the nimbus of fire above an alchemist's crucible. The helmet was a crown of stones upon his skull.

The susurrus of conversation died away. The scribes and functionaries on the lower daises ceased their gossip. Attendants and lesser priests moved silken-footed along the central aisle between the two rows of daises, down the narrow passages between them, and around to the back of the chamber where knots of lesser folk stood to listen and to ogle the mighty. Over all, high up under the inlaid roof beams, hung the hum of the ever-present *Chrí*-flies.

There was no introductory ceremony – a relief. Lord Murésh, it was said, disliked lengthy rituals. The chamberlain consulted a document and signalled with his clappers to Lord Miriggá hiDulumésa, High Adept of the Temple of Hrü'ü, he of the purple dais.

Lord Miriggá was a small, gnomish man, almost buried in his stiff, richly worked robe of purple, his features concealed by the black velvet mask decreed by his sect for state occasions. He stood up.

"My Lords, let us open the matter for which we come, and let us close it as speedily. We all have other business." He was totally motionless, except for one slender, ivory-hued hand which made chopping gestures in the air to emphasise each point. His words were abrupt and precise, snapped off as a man bites off sections of sweet *Mnósa*-root. Lord Dúrugen had disliked him roundly for a score of years – and never remembered quite why.

Lord Miriggá now raised both arms, a histrionic gesture meant to stress his thesis. "The issue is a simple one: the Temple of Thúmis holds certain ancient artifacts found at Úrmish. We of the Temple of Lord Hrü'ü have submitted our case in writing to the Imperium to demonstrate that they belong not to Thúmis but to us, You have seen our arguments – and the proofs thereof. Let the Imperium decide this, so that we may all go home."

This was much too fast a dance! Lord Dúrugen struggled to his feet, silently cursing his elaborate vestments and all of the ornaments and pectorals that jingled and dangled from them. He stretched out his arms for recognition, hoping that no one else managed to get the chamberlain's attention first. The clappers clacked at him.

"My Lord! Eye of the Imperium! We protest! I urge that we look to precedent, upon which all our laws are founded, and without which we should be drowned in a clamour of yeas and nays! Has it not always been the custom that the finders of the things of the ancients should retain them? Saving, of course, occasions of great exigency, when the Imperium itself may demand them? We came by this present lot honourably: workers digging in the City of the Dead at Úrmish came upon these artifacts, my Lord, and being worshippers of our good Lord of Wisdom, they turned them over to us. Our request to retain them is both proper and usual. We are distressed at the holding of this council here today."

He would have gone on – and the High Priest of Keténgku had been primed to follow him with further urgings – but Lord Miriggá, still on his feet, interrupted. "Let the Temple of Thúmis curb its eagerness, great Lord! The road is not so smooth. It is true that the contents of ancient tombs are customarily the property of him who finds them, for good or for ill. Yet the walls of this tomb bore the insignia and icons of the Fifth Form of Gyánu, a deity of the Bednálljans now acknowledged in our doctrine as a precursor and hence a Greater Aspect of our Lord Hrü'ü. The articles of this burial chamber thus belong to Lord Hrü'ü and to none other. We invoke the Concordat!"

"You, of all the temples, invoke the Concordat?" Lord, Dúrugen cried. He spread a hand before his face to mime astonishment. "What offence has been given to the Temple of Hrü'ü? We do not breach the Concordat but only retain what is our –"

The chamberlain's accursed clappers cut him off. He had gone a step too far, perhaps, but the point was made. And it left room for later appeasement of his visibly righteous anger. Thus far, the ship sailed smoothly.

Lord Murésh gestured, and the chamberlain now pointed to another, the occupant of the yellow-draped dais at the far eastern end of the hall, Lord Sünúm hiMráktine, newly appointed Grand Adept of the Temple of Belkhánu, Lord of the Excellent Dead. Here was an ally. A fool, no doubt, but a friend. Lord Dúrugen hoped he had his lines right.

Lord Sünúm waved a heavy, hairless hand, beringed with stones of amber and topaz. His voice was smooth and mellifluous. "My Lords, let us consider what transpires after death. Our faith states that the soul of a man requires precisely 1,326 years to traverse the Isles of Dead, thence to pass on to the Paradises of Teretané, or to emerge into the Heavens of the Gods there to be joined with their supernal essences. It is thus as our colleague, Lord Dúrugen, opines: whatever may have been the faith of the occupant of this tomb in this sphere, uncounted millennia have since elapsed, and he has passed beyond our ken. The shelter of the Fifth Form of Gyánu, and hence that of great Hrü'ü, is now unneeded and inoperative." He paused to wipe his fingers fastidiously upon his brocaded yellow robe, then picked out a saffron-dyed document from those before him. "According to the Sayings of Chi'utléna of Khéiris, therefore, 'Such spirits are of no consequence to the living, and their worldly goods revert to their inheritors, or if long concealed from the view of these, then to those who later come upon them.' The clause at the end is of significance here." He sat down. He had actually done quite well.

Lord Dúrugen extended a hand for permission, but the clappers snapped again at Lord Miriggá. He began softly, a logician patiently explaining a point to his students. "Specious, my Lords, not worthy of rebuttal! Once the shadow of Lord Hrü'ü falls upon a thing, it is his for all eternity! The portrayals upon the walls of the tomb chamber are there for just this purpose: to show the faith of the occupant and to command the attention of the patron deity for all time to come! The texts, the symbols, the prayers – all are there to call upon the protection and holy sanctity of Lord Gyánu, and hence of Lord Hrü'ü, whose Aspect He is! No, we must appeal to the Concordat, my Lord, which stipulates that no temple may attach or confiscate the goods of another. Without this, we would soon return to the Time of the Wrath of the Gods, when priest slew priest, and the land ran scarlet with blood." The extended hand made a sharp slashing motion, and his voice rose. "If we are wronged in this, shall we not once again see such days?"

This time it was Lord Dúrugen who was allowed to interrupt.

"Were this to become precedent, my Lord, chaos would rise up like an *Akhó*, 'the Embracer of Ships,' from the ocean deeps! We know of things emblazoned with the emblems of Thúmis in the treasure-houses of the temples of Change." He smiled and pointed a rhetorical finger. "Ohé, then, would the priests of Sárku give up the trove they uncovered in the ruins of the city of Hmakuyál?" The occupant of the earth-brown dais bent down to confer urgently with those below him. "Would the priesthood of Vimúhla, Lord of Fire, hand over the booty they excavated from the catacombs beneath Tumíssa?" Now it was the turn of the priest on the flame-orange dais to mutter with his subordinates. "No? Then I think my point is made, my Lord." He resumed his seat with the pleasant air of one who has just relished a good dinner. "When one bird flies up, all others look to their own nests," he thought. That ought to toss Miriggá's specious arguments out upon the dungheap! Too many pots belonging to others would be broken if the Temple of Hrü'ü were allowed to smash this one!

Several others were on their feet. The chamberlain singled out the woman who sat upon the emerald green dais of Lady Dlamélish, Mistress of Demons.

Until now Lady Timúna hiReretlésa, High Priestess of the Goddess in Béy Sü, had seemed to pay no attention to the debate, instead extending a slender foot to caress the bare back of the pretty priestess on the step below her, or to rub the shaggy upcurving ears of the great doglike beast that squatted by her side. Lady Timúna wore little to conceal her middle years: a girdle of silver chain about her thickening waist, from which depended strips of silky green *Güdru*-cloth. Some of these latter were attached by links to her jingling wristlets. Her thick, oiled, black hair was bound with silver wire, and its braids hung down over her broad collar of green jade and her heavy, rouged breasts.

What, Lord Dúrugen wondered, could she have to add? Her Goddess served the ephemeral, physical pleasures of the moment, the hedonism of the "now." She had no more place in this debate than her *Rényu*-beast did!

"The *Túnkul*-gongs will call us all to the noon rituals – and to lunch – if we do not make an end of this." Her voice was a throaty whisper. "Let those who wish be convinced of precedents, theology, and learnedly logicked arguments. We of the Goddess agree with our colleague, Lord Miriggá; yet the rule-parsers of the temples of Stability raise such a storm of paper and quotations that naught can be come at. Let us therefore propose a compromise. Lord

Dúrugen's precious relics relate to the Llyáni and thus to the powers of the ancients: things of import to the Imperium and hence to all of us, for it is from the breast of the Empire that we suckle the milk of prosperity." (The priestess below her strove to repress a giggle.) "Therefore, as in the tale of the *Kurukú*-beast and the *Rényu*" (she reached back to caress the tapering snout of the beast on the dais) "let us throw the bone to neither but give it to the third party, the *Mnór* of the story – in this case, the Imperium. Give over these relics to the High Chancery at Avanthár!"

Lord Dúrugen was on his feet. Who, by all the Pearl-Grey Aspects, had put this into her head? He doubted whether she had the wit to come to it herself. Was it the Imperialist Party in Avanthár, mayhap? The Temple of Dlamélish was no bedfellow – Lord Dúrugen repressed a smile at his own unspoken gibe – of Prince Mridóbu. Not unless the Temple of Lord Ksárul, the backers of that Prince, was in league with Dlamélish' sensuality-loving devotees! As unlikely as rain in the month of Firasúl! Lord Ksárul's doctrines centred upon the acquisition of knowledge, much like those of his counterpart, Lord Thúmis, save that the black-robes wanted that wisdom for themselves alone, to gain personal power and mastery, and not for the prosperity of the land. No, Lady Dlamélish would not sit willingly at Lord Ksárul's feasting. There was something else here!

Lady Timúna's argument had to be refuted, of course. The Imperium could not be allowed to gain the right to confiscate temple properties whenever the Emperor so decreed!

"What have the purveyors of the pleasures of the body to do with this?" he asked. "Were we to hand over to the Imperium all those items in our treasuries which might be of interest, we should all be paupers in a trice! Moreover, it is through our study and our scholarship that these things are made useful; a curio-cabinet at Avanthár is no place for artifacts that may contain knowledge otherwise lost to us since the Time of Darkness!"

"Then go to Avanthár and study them there." This, dryly, from Lady Timúna.

"Such has never before been demanded of us!" This was becoming ridiculous. She'd have him tricked out as a traitor to the Emperor if this went on! "Oh, it is true that the Imperium does at times request items of import from private persons – but never from the temples or the clans! Precedent –"

Voices drowned him out. There were others whose ships would founder if the woman brought this one of hers into port!

The chamberlain clacked his billets once, twice, thrice, before silence was restored. Ignoring those who had spoken before, he pointed now at the occupant of the green and purple dais in front of that of the Goddess Dlamélish: a woman little more than a girl, Misénla hiQurródu. High Priestess of Hriháyal, the Dancing Maiden of Temptation, Dlamélish' Cohort.

Like the Lady Timúna, she was clad in a girdle of silver chain, but her diaphanous skirt was of emerald and purple. Her face was round, fine-boned and small-chinned, with high cheekbones and long eyes made even longer by the artful application of black *Tsúnu*-paste. Her small, hard nipples were brushed with iridescent green powder. A line of tattooed glyphs ran down each sinuous arm from shoulder to wrist, and similar lines followed her youthful curves from bare hip to braceleted ankle.

"My Lord, let me show Lord Dúrugen that we of the 'fleshly persuasion' can con these casuistries as well as he." She extended a delicate hand, thumb touching index fingertip. "Firstly, the issue begins with certain relics found in a tomb bearing the icons of one of the Greater Aspects of Lord Hrü'ü, and hence under his protection."

Thumb to middle finger. "Secondly, they are discovered by those who serve Thúmis. His priests – and their allies – make their case for retention upon grounds of theology and precedent."

Thumb to ring finger. "Thirdly, – and now I mince no words but say plainly what our sources report to be so – the temple of Thúmis has winnowed its harvest for someone who can comprehend the use and meaning of these relics, and all they have come up with is a beardless boy from their monastery in the Chákas." She flashed a cool glance at Lord Dúrugen. "Scholars there are aplenty in other temples, but the wise men of Thúmis entrust this task to a youth who has just submitted his Labour of Reverence for admission to the Second Circle." On the grey-draped dais of Thúmis faces turned up to look at Lord Dúrugen. He sat impassive and silent; she must come out into the open before he could pounce.

Thumb now to little finger. "Fourthly, we are also informed – as all of you must be, if your agents are not as brainless as *Chlén*-beasts – that the Baron Áld of Yán Kór intrigues with the Red-hats of Mu'ugalavyá and with the Ebon Palace of Salarvyá to invade this land, and his spies are thick as *Chrí*-flies upon a honeypot. Have we not heard rumours of his 'Weapon Without Answer?' Indeed, which faction here has not had reports of the great black-swathed box being trundled along the Mákhis road from the Baron's fortress of Ke'ér to the city of Hlíkku? Might not his servants seek to purloin such items as hold ancient powers of use to us? – And the temple of Thúmis is no guard-girt fortress immune to such as they may send: men – and others – who can scale its walls like a *Chnéhl*, or wriggle through holes like slippery *Nenyélu*-fish."

Misénla spread her hand, tapered fingers outstretched. "No, my Lord; agree with the Lady Timúna and command the giving over of these relics to Avanthár." She resumed her seat, smoothing the swinging strips of her skirt about her thighs.

It was now as clear as Lord Hnálla's Purest Light. Lady Timúna had been well schooled in her little song; it was no more than a prelude for Lady Misénla's concert. And why? Lord Dúrugen had to admire the pretty melody – and the choice of musicians! This Misénla hiQurródu was mistress to Prince Eselné, the Emperor's second son, the shining protégé of the Military Party and of the temples of the war-gods, both Lord Karakán of Stability and Lord Vimúhla of Change.

The generals, the war-gods' clergy, and the old aristocratic clans had their hopes set upon Eselné's becoming Emperor – and upon the glorious conquest of Yán Kór, Milumanayá, and the rest of the smaller states of the north, lost hundreds of years ago through the foolishness of a weak ancestor of the present Emperor. If the relics discovered at Úrmish were weapons (and Lord Dúrugen had seen nothing yet to indicate that they were), or if they led to further caches containing weapons of the ancients, then Prince Eselné and his Legions would desire them more than any other faction here. If given to the Imperium gracefully, they might gain the Temple of Thúmis some consideration from the Prince's adherents. But to hand the relics over as meekly as a clan-girl gives her hand in marriage violated every tradition, every precedent!

Perhaps it would be best to compromise, at least for now. The Temple of Thúmis bore no ill will toward the adherents of Karakán – nor toward Prince Eselné – although certain political manoeuvrings must come later, and these might not sit so well with the Prince! Lord Dúrugen could not help but glance down at his entourage. His master-sorcerer there turned to face him and shook his head; no spells or mental probings were being attempted – or if they were, his wardings still held. Lord Dúrugen smiled with outward cordiality. He signalled to the chamberlain that he wished to say no more.

No more speakers arose. Several conferred with those below them; some looked to the occupants of other daises. The buzz of conversation drowned out the humming of the *Chrí*-flies. Attendants sped from dais to dais bearing hastily scrawled notes. Outside, the great droning boom of the *Túnkul*-gong of the temple of Karakán announced the midday rituals, and this was answered from across the river by the higher, sweeter note from the *Túnkul*-tower of the temple of Avánthe. On his dais Lord Murésh spoke with earnest hand gestures to his chamberlain. At length the latter turned back to the room and called for quiet with his clappers.

"Worthy priests! The Ever-victorious, Ever-living Emperor, Seizer of Kingdoms, Follower of the Paths of Glory, He of the Petal Throne, the mighty Lord Hirkáne Tlakotáni, speaks through me, his humble mouthpiece in this place!" He paused to clear his throat. The long Classical Tsolyáni formula demanded stamina as well as eloquence. "It is our decree that the items found at Úrmish shall remain within the precincts of the Temple of Thúmis, for such is ancient custom and precedent." (This was much better than might have been expected after Misénla's charming performance. There were smiles and soft finger-snappings upon Lord Dúrugen's dais; silence upon the purple.) "Yet here do we break with tradition. We further command that these articles shall be guarded by soldiers of the Imperium, men of the military arm of our Omnipotent Azure Legion. Furthermore, these relics shall be open to study by those properly deputed by the other temples of this realm." (Now it was Lord Dúrugen's turn to be still, but there were excited whispers among the black-masked priests upon the purple dais.) "As we have decreed, so let it be." The chamberlain struck his clappers together.

Lord Murésh arose and swept down from the blue and gold dais, followed by his retinue of scribes, servants, and officials.

Lord Dúrugen, frozen-faced, descended from his seat too, briefly saluted the priests of Hnálla and the High Priestess of Avánthe, who would have stayed him, and slipped away through the rear passage. Across the room, the knot of purple around the dais of Hrü'ü mingled first with the black and silver of Ksárul, then the flame-orange of Vimúhla, and finally with the brown of the priesthood of Sárku. The centre of the chamber was bedlam as scribes, priests, and attendants all strove to gather up their papers and paraphernalia and depart. Of the emerald of Dlamélish and the green and purple of Hriháyal there was no sign, for those delegations had left immediately in the wake of Lord Murésh.

It was clear that the compromise had settled nothing and pleased no one.

As he stalked through the gilded hallways of the Palace of the Priesthoods of the Realm, miserable in his stuffy grey vestments, Lord Dúrugen fumed. This had not been a total defeat, of course – there was that consolation – but it had been no victory either! Lord Miriggá had been discomfited, a matter of considerable satisfaction, but to have rival temples sending their scholars into the Temple of Eternal Knowing was not a pleasant prospect! To have them prying into the relics – within his own sacred precincts – was unbearable! The Temple of Thúmis would have to break up this cluster of plottings. Nothing less than the hammer of a real revelation could do that, and one was needed that would take all of Thúmis' foes by the ears! A certain hidden Imperial heir might have to be revealed, somewhat in advance of what they had planned for him.

It was worth considering. It was Tsolyáni custom for a Prince or a newly enthroned Emperor to proclaim the existence of only some of his progeny. Others were sent away to be raised in secret by the temples, the high clans, and various important patrons, under the aegis of the Omnipotent Azure Legion. Lord Dúrugen had seen the documents; the Temple of Thúmis had been granted one such Imperial stepchild. Now might be the time to play him, as a black counter is brought onto the board in the game of *Dén-den*. Then there would be another Imperial Prince – a Prince devoted to Lord Thúmis. The crop seemed ripe for cutting – no, overripe, after this morning's merry fiasco – and Lord Dúrugen vowed to himself that the matter would be brought up just as soon as he could convene the other Adepts of the temple and bring the Grand Adept, Lord Gámulu, from his estate in distant Páya Gúpa to Béy Sü and get him to agree.

That would cut certain knots!

Another minor matter prodded at the edge of his consciousness: the boy they had summoned to inspect the relics. The Lady Misénla had known of him! He must be guarded now, reinforced with another, more senior scholar, and watched. There would be danger for the young man, whoever he was – the temple's scribes would have the details – and he should be warned.

Or should he? After all, the youth was but a pawn, useful if he could reach Béy Sü and decipher the wretched Llyáni relics. But he was quite expendable. There were others who could perform that task, though perhaps not as well. Prior Haringgáshte had submitted very enthusiastic reports. The original plan had been to summon a scholar who would attract no attention, squeeze all useful information from the relics, and spirit them off quickly to some remote temple treasury. This was no longer feasible; half the Empire seemed to know the fellow was coming!

Another possibility made Lord Dúrugen pause, and his entourage dutifully halted behind him: the young man might lure any who wanted trouble into the open, a juicy haunch of *Hmélu*-meat to snare the *Zrné*. The priests of both Ksárul and Sárku had been suspiciously silent throughout this morning's proceedings. Lord Vimúhla's people had also sat all too snugly upon their flame-orange dais. Whoever was not satisfied with Lord Murésh' decision might attempt to alter it by various extraordinary methods. Much could be made of a captured spy; a breach of the Concordat and the culprits' ensuing disgrace alone were worth a dozen young priests!

Lord Dúrugen grumbled a ritual catechism to himself. The long staircase was hard on his legs, and the lappets of his heavy golden pectoral banged against his thighs. All of these matters required more information and study. For now, however, he must be satisfied with the thought that each laboured step brought him ever nearer to his midday cup of thick *Chumétl*. He pulled off his towering headdress, heedless of the breach of traditional propriety, and plodded on.

Chapter Six

From the Monastery of the Sapient Eye the *Sákbe*-road wound south through familiar country. The rumpled green foothills of Dó Cháka lay like old friends along the way on the right hand, the west, and the dun-coloured patchwork fields of ripening grain swept off to the horizon and beyond to mighty Béy Sü and the centre of the Empire on the left. This was the landscape Hársan knew well.

The first two days produced the expected crop of aches and blisters, but thereafter Hársan found his muscles hardening and his body becoming road-wise. Farmers and women might ride in the agonisingly slow *Chlén*-carts, and the aristocracy sat high in palanquins borne by trotting slaves; aside from one's feet these two were the only methods of transportation on Tékumel. Hársan needed neither. Being able to march at the same rate as the booted traders and hard-faced soldiers, somehow exhilarated him. This was the first time he had really used his limbs in all the years since the Pé Chói had brought him to the monastery, and he began to luxuriate in the rhythmic cadences of walking.

The *Sákbe*-road thrust out before him like a triple-tongued blade of grey stone. Hársan perforce used the lowest level, a paved thoroughfare wide enough for fifteen men to march abreast. The eastern parapet stood a good two man-heights above the sunbaked fields below, while the western side was a solid wall that rose up to the next higher level, five handspans beyond Hársan's tallest reach. The second level was narrower but smoother, and its western wall in turn ascended another spear-length up to the third and highest tier. The lowest roadway was used by anyone: merchants, peasants, work-gangs, caravans of slaves bearing the goods of the Empire, the great trundling *Chlén*-carts which creaked their leisurely way from city to city laden with heavier items, and common travellers such as Hársan. The middle level was reserved by custom – and by harsh Tsolyáni law – for members of the aristocracy, troops, officials, and priests of the higher Circles. The uppermost level belonged to the great nobles, the highest clergy, and couriers upon the Emperor's business.

Every few *Tsán* these triple roadways were blocked by a squat guard tower. Many of these were dark and empty in these days of relative peace, used by sojourners as convenient places to unroll sleeping mats and spend the night. Some were occupied by detachments of blue-armoured soldiery. These paid but perfunctory attention to a lone, grey-robed priest, and after a bored glance at Hársan's writ, they let him be off upon his way. It had not always been so. There, where the mist-wreathed peaks of the Inner Range actually lay within the borders of Mu'ugalavyá, the outer parapet of the third and highest level, buttressed and embattled like a fortress, always faced to the west, a line of defensible fortifications stretching from north to south along the frontier of the Empire. There was no war now – and had not been for over three hundred years – but there were rumblings along the border and whispers of an alliance between the "Red-Hats" of Mu'ugalavyá and Baron Áld of Yán Kór.

At first he met few travellers. Most of these were peasants or townsmen, carrying goods on their backs or in *Chlén*-carts to some nearby market or fair. They saluted Hársan respectfully and held out a hand for him to touch in blessing. In these parts it was thought good luck to meet a priest of Thúmis, or one of Thúmis' Cohort, Keténgku, the Patron of Physicians.

On the second day he passed a tax collector, a thin-lipped old man, borne in a litter by ten slaves. This august personage ignored Hársan's greeting, though some of his retinue of scribes, record-keepers, and guards called out jocular salutations. On the second day, also, two parties of merchants overtook Hársan, their heavily laden burden-slaves jogging along at a fast trot that he could only envy.

On the third morning he encountered two cohorts of soldiers in blue-lacquered *Chlén*-hide armour. Some of these leaned down from the middle roadway to shout obscene but friendly greetings, and a junior officer, resplendent in helmet and breastplate, tossed down a small skin of Tumíssan wine for good luck. These were troops on their way north to reinforce the Tsolyáni forces on the Yán Koryáni border near Khirgár.

He even met a party of Páchi Léi. This was another of the eight friendly non-human species which shared Tékumel with humankind. Hársan had not been this close to one of these creatures before. They were pear-shaped, soft-skinned beings, greyish-green in hue, a hand taller than a man, with four curiously articulated lower limbs for locomotion and four more, longer upper limbs for swinging in the trees of the forests of the Pán Chákan Protectorate that lay to the south of Hársan's own Dó Chákan hills. The Páchi Léi wore little more than cross-belts of untanned hide, and their leader carried a thick, short spear tipped with a barb of white bone. Hársan stared at them, and they stared back from round, platter-sized eyes, greeting him pleasantly enough in oddly accented Tsolyáni and chattering amongst themselves in their own burbling tongue.

On the sixth day, footsore but nevertheless pleased with his growing stamina, Hársan reached Páya Gúpa – not PA-ya Gu-PA, as the Tsolyáni called it, wrongly accenting the last vowel, but PA-ya GU-pa. The name meant "Red Mountain" in the older dialect of Dó Cháka, and thus it appeared: walls and towers of rufous sandstone heaped along the summit of a low hill spurring out of the Chákan forests. The houses behind the walls were whitewashed, tiled with reds and tans, and scattered like children's blocks around the summit upon which the palace of the local governor stood.

Hársan's writ obtained lodging at the temple of Thúmis. The sect of the Master of Wisdom was very powerful here, and Lord Gámulu hiBeshyéne, the Grand Adept of the Temple, made his summer headquarters in the old, grey shrine that clambered down the hill to the west.

The Proctor of the Dormitories arranged for Hársan to continue on to Tumíssa and thence to Béy Sü in the company of a party of merchants. This was in itself somewhat daunting, for the capital still lay over a thousand long *Tsán* away. Even though Hársan felt himself capable of making thirty to forty *Tsán* a day, he wondered if he could keep up.

He need not have worried. Much of the cargo carried by the thirty-odd slaves of the little caravan consisted of fine pottery and the crimson crystal goblets and ewers of Mu'ugalavyá. Mnésun hiArkúna, the chief of the party and owner of most of its merchandise, fussed over the packing of each reed basket and the balancing of every slave's burden in the morning and then again over its unloading at night while the other merchants dawdled over their food and the tasks of the camp. They made little more than twenty-five *Tsán* a day. Hársan guessed that it would take seven days to reach Tumíssa, one day more than if he had travelled alone. Yet he found the bustling routine comforting and the company of the others a reassurance.

Besides Mnésun, squat and thick-set as a river *Ghár*-beast, there were six in the party, not counting the slaves. Two of these were twin brothers, Mu'ugalavyáni, whose goods included rare earths, perfumes, and scented oils from distant Khéiris. The third, a Salarvyáni named Bejjéksa, was a trader of much experience and self-proclaimed cunning. He was now returning home with bales of finely-figured cloth and chests of soapstone carvings, products of Livyánu, the land to the south of Mu'ugalavyá. The next, Helé'a of Ghatón, brought wares concealed within stoppered jars. Of these he said nothing, nor did he speak much otherwise: a small, tight, hard, little man as grey as the seas of his northern homeland. The fifth man was Sa'aráz, a Livyáni who affected all the airs and niceties of that nation's aristocracy, though none could actually attest to his antecedents. He had neither chests nor bales but carried whatever it was he sold in a worn leathern wallet affixed to his belt with a stout chain of rare iron.

The sixth member of the group was a nonhuman, a hulking reptilian Shén, native to the hot lands south of Livyánu, half a continent away. He traded in the flame opals of Pán Cháka and in garnets, commodities which the Shén knew were valued by humans and other races, but which they themselves held in no particular esteem. Although the Shén was friendly enough, his guttural name was unpronounceable – something between a hiss and a snarl. Hársan made do with calling him "companion," which seemed to please the creature greatly.

It was the afternoon of the seventh day before they saw Tumíssa. Once the guardian of the western marches of the Tsolyáni frontier, its ponderous bastions and serried battlements had seen no fighting since the two Protectorates, Dó Cháka and Pán Cháka, had been wrested from Mu'ugalavyá in the great war some three hundred years before. Hársan looked upon the looming rings of concentric walls inlaid with marching rows of serpentine glyphs in the old Classical Tsolyáni script, the tier upon tier of red-tiled roofs, and the dizzy turrets of the prow-like fortress which crowned the city's westernmost hill, and would have greatly liked to spend a few days here. Others in the monastery had had much praise for Tumíssa: its goods and shops, its rich palaces and mansions, its great library of hoary fame, the image called "Thúmis Ascending to the Sun," carved long ago by Márya of Tsámra, and many other wonders. They had also spoken of entertainments and displays more to the tastes of a young man – and of pretty clan-girls and courtesans and a dozen things more. But Mnésun gruffly stated that the caravan would journey forth in the morning. Lodgings were arranged outside the walls in the clanhouse of the People of the White Pebble, a mercantile clan allied by both blood and marriage to Mnésun's own Clan of the Green Reed.

When the party gathered at dawn in the cramped courtyard to curse and coax the caravan's slaves into wakefulness, Hársan discovered that another small group had been added. A score of bearers and servitors in an unfamiliar clan livery stood stamping and yawning around a blue-curtained covered litter.

"We are joined by a lady," Mnésun announced to all within hearing, "one Eyíl hiVriyén, of the Green Kirtle Clan of Tumíssa, who is on her way to marry her clan-cousin in Béy Sü."

There was no sign of the occupant of the litter, and thus it remained for a six-day. The party now took the *Sákbe*-road which branched off directly to the east, an endless three-step staircase, the highest level of which faced north towards hostile, distant Yán Kór. The foothills were left behind, dust storms lay ever along the flat horizon, and heat lightning flickered there throughout the summer evenings. All of the visible world consisted of endless fields of standing grain, plots of yellow-brown earth, lone *Vrés*-trees, olive-drab and drooping like lost wayfarers in the tawny yellow desolation, and occasional villages of baked brick, where naked dusty peasants lifted their heads from the perpetual round of toil to watch them pass by.

The lady made but few appearances. Hársan had occasional glimpses of a tall, boyishly slender girl, attired in the embroidered open vest and slit-sided skirt preferred by the women of the western provinces. The Lady Eyíl did not come to sit by their fire in the evenings but instead sent her attendant, a grim-faced peasant woman named Tsátla, to get her dinner from the common cookpots.

It had gradually come to be understood that, as the only priest in the party, Hársan would offer the prescribed libation before each meal. This he did with care, choosing words that would give no offence to worshippers of other gods than his. One evening when supper was finished and his comrades had retired to drink wine and gamble or to seek sleep, the woman Tsátla came to Hársan and said that the Lady Eyíl would speak with him.

The litter lay in darkness, one curtain thrown back all along one side, forming a little three-sided room. The ochre-red glow of Káshi, Tékumel's smaller, second moon, turned the gilded orbs of the four corner-posts into ruddy copper coins. Two of Lady Eyíl's attendants dozed upon their haunches nearby, while a little farther away her bearers lay sprawled in shadowed huddles, asleep.

"Worthy priest?" The voice was low and musical, the accent the purring, slurred speech of Tumíssa. "I have troubled you that I may ask a question."

"My lady?"

"You are a servitor of Thúmis and not of my Goddess Avánthe. Yet both are of the Lords of Stability. Advise me, therefore, upon a matter of propriety." A silhouetted hand moved within the blackness of the litter. "I grow bored riding in this conveyance day after day. My limbs ache with its jouncing, and the heat within these curtains is enough to melt even the Shield of Vimúhla, Lord of Fire." (Hársan thought: the woman is educated, as glib as any temple priestess.) She continued, "Now tell me this: is it fitting for me to join your circle for the morning and evening meals? I wish no dishonour to my clan nor inconvenience to your merchants, yet I do yearn for a chance to move about..."

Hársan hesitated. Some northern Chákan clans, he knew, guarded their womenfolk as zealously as any heap of gold in a treasure-vault, hemming them all about with veils and guards and eunuchs. Those of the south, on the other hand, paid little heed when their ladies walked abroad bare-breasted and bold amongst strange men. Nor, it was said, did they care overmuch about the paternity of the inevitable results. Custom in Tumíssa and the western cities lay somewhere betwixt these two extremes.

He temporised. "My Lady, this must depend upon the practice of one's clan. While some see nothing amiss in allowing a clan-daughter to exercise her limbs on a long journey and to alleviate the tedium with conversation, others find such behaviour brazen and ill-omened. Surely the tradition of your clan is better known to you than to an outsider such as myself."

"True, but in this matter I have little to guide me. At home we girls are granted considerable liberty. But this is the first time in my memory that one of us has been married outside Tumíssa, and I recall no precedent."

"What commandments, then, were given to your attendants by your father or clan patriarchs when you set forth?"

"Why, to serve me, to protect me from harm, and to see me safe into the house of my clan-cousin, noble Retlán hiVriyén of Béy Sü." There was a hint of what sounded like suppressed amusement in the girl's voice.

Priestly dialectics came to Hársan's aid. "If these are the precise words, then the first and last clauses have no application. The second injunction, too, is of little relevance. You are certainly 'protected from harm' by your clan's travel contract with the merchant Mnésun. He and his colleagues will do all possible to honour their agreement, for to act otherwise would bring shame upon their clans; they would be open to a lawsuit and demands for *Shámtla* – money paid to satisfy a grievance or to compensate for a crime – would follow. None would trust them thereafter. Barring the untoward, thus, there is no question of ill befalling you in this company."

"Then?"

"Ah – surely the needs of a healthy person for exercise and the desire for decorous and instructive conversation cannot be classified as 'ill.'" Hársan knew not quite where this path led, but logic seemed to point in this direction.

"I see, I see. My thanks for having unriddled the matter so clearly, wise priest. Henceforth I shall join you for meals, and you shall enlighten me further in questions of ethics and theology, areas in which I lamentably lack instruction."

The Lady Eyíl clapped her hands, and Hársan had a fleeting glimpse of slender wrists encircled by golden bangles. One of the attendants rose – the woman Tsátla – and bowed Hársan back to his sleeping mat beside the greying coals of the cook-fire.

All night long he kept seeing images of lithe wrists, tapering fingers, and narrow gold bangles.

Thereafter the Lady Eyíl graced their meals. Attired in a voluminous overcloak of blue *Güdru*-cloth, she sat demurely to one side of the circle, gruff and silent Tsátla ever just behind her. (As one of the Mu'ugalavyáni brothers put it: "Like the demon Tusu'ú, who hovers ever at the shoulder of the Goddess Dlamélish…") Lady Eyíl took little part in their conversations but listened with apparent interest to their recountings of profits and losses, goods and caravans, cities and peoples. She was unfailingly courteous, using the "you of perfect piety" to Hársan, as was fitting for a priest much more learned than he, and the "you of pleasant dealings" to the merchants, even including the Shén, upon whom such niceties may well have been lost. The thirty-four pronouns for "you" of the Tsolyáni language made the maintenance of such social distinctions easy.

None could dispute that the Lady Eyíl was a Tumíssan. She had the heart-shaped face, pointed chin, wide and mobile mouth, and long, heavy-lashed eyes of the women of the west. She was as long-legged and lithe as Hársan himself, small-breasted, and perhaps a trifle narrow through the hips for Tsolyáni tastes. Her mane of black hair often escaped the confines of her cloak, and she restrained it with a headband of blue, proclaiming her allegiance to the goddess Avánthe.

Day pursued day across the hot, fertile plains of the Tsolyáni heartland. Hársan walked more and more beside the litter of the Lady Eyíl, or, better yet, tramped with her upon the grey river of the *Sákbe*-road. Their discussions grew ever longer. She knew little of theology and the arts Hársan had been taught in the Monastery of the Sapient Eye, but she bubbled like a cookpot with the doings of the clans and lower nobility of Tumíssa.

Hársan was intrigued. He was no stranger to women. The monastery contained both male and female clerics and acolytes, and there was no objection to friendly couplings, experimentation, or to marriage. Yet most of the girls of his experience had been fellow students involved in the same studies and pursuits, or else had been the village girls of the Chákas, unlettered, earthy, and quite unabashed before the mysteries of sexuality. Here, however, was a girl who cut her meat daintily with a tiny knife, who never put more than the first knuckles of her right hand into her food, who quoted romantic verses gleaned from the ladies of the governor's court, and who chattered of etiquette and formalities as alien to Hársan as the sun is to the black depths of the sea.

At times she asked Hársan questions which betrayed her ignorance of even the most fundamental matters of knowledge and religion. This unsettled him somewhat. Was her religious training then no more than a veneer? What was education in the Empire coming to? He put it down to the well-known apathy to abstract wisdom prevalent amongst the better clans and the aristocracy and answered her questions as simply and faithfully as he could.

"Priest Hársan," she asked one day, "in our great temple of Avánthe at Tumíssa there are shrines to many of the Goddess' Greater Aspects: Sunrudáya the Young Bride, Ngachání the Patroness of Mothers With Babes, and a score of others. Why is it that the Goddess appears in so many forms if She is but one person? Once, when I was a child, I asked our clan's house-priest, but he replied with such weighty words that I understood him not."

"My Lady, it is because your Goddess holds sway over all that concerns women in their relation to society," he replied. "She is the newborn baby girl, the innocent who suffers the first coming of the blood, the maiden in the ecstasy of love, the new-married girl who goes in to her husband for the first time, the wife, the mother, the sister, and finally the clan-mother wise in years and great in honour in her household. Avánthe is all of these and more: the fertility of the crops, the forces of nature, the creatures of the forests, the fish of the rivers. We who are unable to conceive of her oneness all at once can perceive her better through her diversity."

"Then what of Dilinála, her Cohort? Is she not 'woman' as well?"

"Yes, but in different spheres. Dilinála does not participate in home, children, and clan. She is ever-virginal, ever-chaste, celibate, free from the eternal duality of woman and man. She is woman focussed inward upon herself. She is separate from Avánthe, yet a part of the whole."

"I am not intrigued by Dilinála." Lady Eyíl pushed back her thick, heavy tresses, a pleasingly feminine gesture that Hársan did not fail to note. "Further, then, if Avánthe and Dilinála make up 'woman,' tell me what functions are served by the Goddess Dlamélish and her Cohort, Hriháyal?"

"My Lady, these are not of the illumined side but of the dark. Just as a silver mirror held to the sun blazes and reflects its light, so is the back of it in shadow. Dlamélish is woman as wanton, as destroyer, as the violence of the female soul; just as the Fire Lord, Vimúhla, signifies the cruelty and ferocity that dwell within the heart of a man. Dlamélish is woman as a selfish individual; Avánthe is woman as a builder of society and the smooth running of the cycles of life and of the world. So does Lord Karakán, the Brave God of Noble War, oppose Lord Vimúhla. Both stand for violence, but Lord Karakán represents violence in the cause of stability and the preservation of order: fighting for one's home, for the Imperium, for the doing of noble actions and the establishment of glory…

"And Hriháyal?"

"She governs only lust, sensuality with no purpose beyond hedonism, the gratification of the body with no thought of what is beyond. All these things exist in every soul. If the balance tilts one way, then that person devotes herself to Avánthe or to Dilinála. If it tips the other, then she serves Dlamélish or Hriháyal."

"If these Goddesses are all 'woman' in some form or other, how and why, then, do men – priests and clansmen – serve them?"

"Why, Avánthe requires both male and female for procreation and for the operation of the natural order of things. Dlamélish and Hriháyal appeal to the more lustful side of a man just as to a woman, and some of their Greater Aspects are said to be male – I know little of their doctrines. As for Dilinála, she is indeed solely the patroness of females, and her hierarchy admits no males."

She gave him an arch look. "If all these qualities are found in some measure or another in every woman – and in men as well – then why not argue that all four of the Goddesses are naught but Greater Aspects of just one goddess? Nay, say even that Karakán and Vimúhla and all the rest are parts of one supreme godhead as well? Just as the front and the back of a mirror are only parts of the same object? Lá, priest Hársan, see how I have just reduced all the Gods and Goddesses of Tsolyánu to just one! What a saving on temples and priests!"

Shock tumbled over horror to Hársan's lips. "Lady Eyíl, this is the gist of the Heresy of Chú'inur, discredited and refuted now for over three thousand years! The great Priest Pavár, who discovered the existence of our twenty deities – and who, it is recorded, spoke to them as I now speak to you – unequivocally states that these entities, are separate and distinct beings. The Scrolls of Pavár –"

She did not let him finish but was off on another tack. "I have often wondered how it would be to serve Dlamélish or Hriháyal. I have seen the spring rites of our Lady Avánthe, and they are…very frank. But must the sensuality condoned by our Goddess always end in some dullard clan-cousin's bed? A brood of brats for a husband who has other wives, and whose interests lie not in me but in his male pursuits: his friends, his enemies, his plots, his status, and his post in some petty bureaucratic hierarchy?"

Hársan strove for an answer. At length he said, "My Lady – one may serve the body and its lusts for perhaps a score of years. Yet what thereafter? Once beauty is fled, the priestess of Dlamélish or Hriháyal has naught to comfort her old age but her empty rituals – and an emptier bed. The clan-mother, on the other hand, is honoured by her children and those of her clan-sisters, and her last years are peaceful and secure."

Eyíl made a face. "Many of the priestesses of Dlamélish and Hriháyal declare themselves *Aridáni*. Under the law a woman may thus pronounce herself independent of, clan and family strictures and enjoy the same legal status as a man. Though she retains her clan, she cannot be married off, as you see happening to me. Nor can she be commanded and cozened by her husband or her clan-elders. She may become a priestess, an administrator, even a warrior, as she wills. I have met one such: the Lady Avéya hiBurútla of the Clan of the Jade Diadem. In her youth she served Lady Dlamélish and became an *Aridáni*. Later, through certain of her lovers, she obtained a post at the governor's court, and now she is Magistrate of the Markets in the Palace of the Realm in Tumíssa. She has five husbands and a score of slave lovers as well. What, then, of that life?"

Hársan had regained his composure. Surely the girl was mischievously testing him. He said, "If she is satisfied, then she is blessed. But to give up the security of clan and husband is assuredly a hard step. And those who do often seem hard and uncompromising, different from other women, and yet not men. You do not seem such a person." Two could play at word-games!

"Oh, Hársan, you do not know me yet! I am serious! If I were an *Aridáni* and held an Imperial or temple post, I could support husbands and do as I pleased! – Or perchance I could serve in the army. Are not my breasts small enough to squeeze within a soldier's breastplate?"

Hársan saw the perils of this question and struggled to change the topic. "There are many paths, and who are we to speak ill of the life-skeins of others? We of the Temple of Thúmis see knowledge as the surest road to an understanding of existence. All things have purpose, and all help to maintain the balance beloved of our Lords of Stability ..."

She would not be diverted and went on. "You are perhaps right about me. It would be difficult to become an *Aridáni* and abandon the solace of my clanspeople. Yet the idea of becoming the bride of a man I have never seen, and whom I hear is thrice my age – and who probably has other wives and stinks of the cloying *Purú*-oil so dear to those of Béy Sü –!" She stopped, leaned upon the coping of the parapet, and turned to face him. "Oh, Hársan, I am not at all eager to follow my own Skein of Destiny. I long for my home and my own people. Already I am well into the age of marriage – I am almost eighteen summers – but yet I cannot take cheer from these pretty songs you sing me of family, children, household chores, and a – a – a boring old age."

She appeared to be upon the verge of tears, and Hársan knew not how to console her. In an effort to distract her he began to describe his own strange childhood, at first haltingly, and then pouring out the story in a rush of words: his life with the Pé Chói, his loneliness and the bitter sense of loss and betrayal when gentle T'kék took him to the Monastery of the Sapient Eye, his misery in those surroundings, his boyhood friendship with Zarén, his slowly burgeoning confidence among his new human comrades, his pride in his model of the Llyáni language, then the sudden wrenching separation of this mission – as grievous as hers, he thought – and over all else his yearning for a clan and the security of knowledge of his origins, more precious in Tsolyáni society than gold and lands and slaves.

When he had done, she took his hand and pressed it to her cheek. Then she wept indeed, and all he could think of to comfort her was to put an arm around her shoulders and to try, quite inexpertly, to stroke her hair.

The brazen yellow afternoon had distilled itself into the ale-coloured twilight of midsummer before Tsátla finally found her charge, lagging far behind the caravan, hand in hand with the young priest and uncaring of the amused stares of peasant workmen and other passersby.

Tsátla was properly irate, Lady Eyíl appropriately contrite. Hársan, however, heard Tsátla's acrid remonstrances no more than a boulder hears the rippling of the stream. Nor did he heed the banter of his companions at dinner that night – nor, for that matter, for many days thereafter.

Chapter Seven

The four hundred-odd *Tsán* from Tumíssa to Katalál took them nearly twenty days. It was now the month of Langála, the first month of summer and the fourth of the Tsolyáni year. Next would come Fésru, then Drenggár, and after that dread Firasúl, "when the earth melts, and the air itself is aflame." Mnésun hoped to reach Béy Sü before the first day of Drenggár, and in this he was abetted by Bejjéksa and the two Mu'ugalavyáni, who planned to hurry on eastward to spend the hottest part of the year in Sokátis in the cooler Chaigári foothills.

They thus took to travelling in the dim hours just before dawn, then resting in an unoccupied guard tower or in the shade of the great roadway itself while the sun blazoned its golden brand upon the fields. In the evening they moved on again until it grew too dark to see one's footing. At first Mnésun marched whenever there was light from both the moons, but after a slave, confused by the double red and green shadows, slipped and went asprawl, breaking most of his load of glassware – a loss of seven hundred *Káitar*s – he resigned himself to a slower pace.

At last Katalál lay before them, a splash of green upon a dust-yellow canvas. Its ornate gables, peaked roofs, and pyramided temples rose above a tiny blue lake, fed from an underground spring that nourished not only the city but also long avenues of *Gapúl*-trees beyond the red-and-black-chequered walls. Katalál was justly famed for its roof gardens. As in many of the cities of the plains, it was customary to cultivate cool grottoes of exotic foliage in urns upon the flat roof of one's house. From a distance, thus, Katalál looked like nothing more than some great jungle ruin, all overgrown with vines, creepers, shrubs, and garish flowers. In the midst of the city the governor's palace shimmered pearl-white above the lake, and just beyond the temples of Vimúhla and Karakán faced one another across the square like two behemoths before a wrestling match. Here many folk espoused the faith of the Fire God and of his Cohort Chiténg, He of the Red-Spouting Flame. The Lords of Stability, too, had their shrines in Katalál, but of these only warlike Karakán and his Cohort Chegárra were popular.

For all their militant gods, the people of Katalál seemed singularly peaceable. They wore knee-length kilts of red and black chequers and stripes, flat wide-brimmed hats of enamelled *Chlén*-hide, and short cloaks of gauzy *Thésun*-cloth. This, Hársan was told, was woven from the silk of the *Dnélu*, a fierce six-legged insect-like creature half the size of a man. These predators built underground dens from whence they leaped out upon smaller game and occasionally even upon unwary humans. The eggs of the *Dnélu* came wrapped in skull-sized cocoons of flossy grey fibre, and the braver youths of the city vied with one another in provoking the creatures into an attack while others stole their eggs.

The folk of Katalál were less receptive to a priest of Thúmis than those of the Chákas, but Hársan found his way without difficulty to the unpretentious temple of his sect in a side street off the main plaza. Here his writ again got him food and lodging. That evening he carefully cut the stitching of his grey robe and brought forth the three gold *Káitar*s which Prior Haringgáshte had advanced him. He then undid his bedroll and contemplated the farseeing device given him by Zarén. There were also his notes on the Llyáni language, a painstakingly copied manuscript of the Llyáni grammar of Tlu'én of Ssa'átis, and two leaves bearing reproductions of the glyphs upon Kurruné's map symbol and the waxen hand. He kept the money out, but the rest he bound up in the roll once more.

In the morning he found a merchant in the marketplace and surrendered half of a precious *Káitar* for a delicate blue faience amulet of the Goddess Avánthe in her Aspect of Tahelé, the Maid of Beauty. When Mnésun's caravan set forth again on the following day he chose an occasion and presented this to the Lady Eyíl. She received it with pleasure and kissed him for it, but she did not wear it much thereafter, much to his hidden disappointment.

Now Hársan walked regularly with the Lady Eyíl. Bejjéksa, the Salarvyáni trader, made a wager with the Shén that Hársan would abandon his sleeping mat near the fire for another and more enticing bed before they reached Katalál. In this he was the loser, and he paid up with ill grace, muttering about inexperienced boys who could not see when a warm female bosom yearned to receive them.

The Lady Eyíl continued to plague Hársan with arguments about theology, but now more of her queries were purely personal, as was the way of a girl attended by an earnest suitor in Tsolyánu – and probably other lands as well.

Her feet, she complained, hurt her and were a misfortune: "big enough to thresh out all the crops in the Empire in the harvest dances." Hársan gazed upon the supple limb extended for his inspection and demurred strongly.

The Lady Eyíl smiled.

The following day she said, "Hársan, think you that my eyes are too large for my face?" Hársan did not and said so volubly.

Still later, she said, "My clan-sisters say my breasts are really too small for my height." Hársan, who even now had one of these criticised objects pressed warmly against his side as they walked, disagreed.

The next evening, after Tsátla had been summarily dismissed into a silently protesting huddle on the far side of the litter, the Lady Eyíl used the "thou of heart's desire," as befitted the occasion, and whispered, "Hársan, think you my knees are too close together to accord with the Twenty-seventh Criterion of Beauty enjoined by my Goddess?" Hársan had never heard of these standards, but he knelt now looking down at the delicious length of her within the shadowed litter, and he gladly would have sung an ode to her knees or to any other part she cared to name, if only he had had even a smidgin of versifying. He berated himself for having studied ancient epics instead of love sonnets.

Then, when the fire had died away to a memory of redness, the Lady Eyíl turned her head upon Hársan's shoulder, touched lip to lip, and said, "There are those who might say my teeth are uneven and not worthy of the canon of the Goddess…" Hársan explored the matter for himself with his tongue and pronounced the unknown critics to be fools.

Thus did Bejjéksa win his second wager with the Shén.

Even so, the path to the Lady Eyíl was not without its thorny patches. One of the Mu'ugalavyáni brothers was an accomplished flute-player who often entertained the party in the evenings with the wistful melodies of his own land. He began to seek out the Lady Eyíl's company, and for a time she walked both with him and with Hársan, much to the latter's pent-up despair. But then she made a clever pun upon flutes and flute-players, almost certainly within the man's hearing, and he called upon her no more.

More troublous was the matter of the Livyáni, Sa'aráz, who fancied himself a courtier. He paid her elaborate compliments in his lisping, accented Tsolyáni. One evening he showed her the contents of his leathern wallet: gleaming chrysoberyls, amethysts, carnelians, and opals of milky pearl and green inner fire. Some of these, he hinted, might well grace the throat of a noble lady. She fingered them longingly, asked their qualities and prices, and spoke fair words to Sa'aráz, who made her a gift of one of his smaller stones. The affair might have been more serious if the Livyáni had not been a man of indefinite age and unprepossessing appearance. She smiled upon him and exchanged courtly banter, a game in which he easily outmatched her. But she admitted privately to Hársan that Sa'aráz' polished urbanities and his ageless, smooth skin did not enchant her. His eyes, too, repelled her, she said, being flat and expressionless, looking upon her as though she were but one more glittering gem. Sa'aráz soon saw where this road led and contented himself with pretty words and an occasional subtle gibe at Hársan.

One evening, six days out of Katalál and two days before they were to reach the town of Haumá, they stopped beneath one of the watch towers. This one had a small garrison of soldiers. A broad, low, stone platform had been built out from the lowest level of the roadway, and half a dozen parties of merchants, townsmen, and other travellers were encamped upon it. There were several rude stalls where provisions and fuel might be had, a well of good water, and a gaggle of tents filled with singers, dancers, jugglers, and harlots. The caravan-master had his slaves pitch his dun-coloured tent near the wall on the platform.

The mood was almost that of a village fair, and Mnésun purchased a bundle of *Kháish*, long white tubers as sweet as honey. Sa'aráz then outdid him by obtaining three *Jakkóhl*, small edible beasts indigenous to these plains and devilishly hard to catch. Helé'a of Ghatón contributed a clay jug of *Ngálu* wine and the Lady Eyíl added another. The Shén bought a basket of sugary blue *Dlél*-fruit, which he himself did not fancy but which he knew would please his human comrades. Bejjéksa and the Mu'ugalavyáni brothers walked half a *Tsán* to the nearest village and returned with fresh-baked loaves of coppery-red bread of *Dná*-flour. Hársan alone had no money to spare, but he contributed his forest-learned skills by skinning and dressing the *Jakkóhl,* and no one grumbled.

The feast in Mnésun's tent was a pleasant success. Afterwards the squat trader would have sent for singers, dancers, and even for harlots to cheer the slaves. All of the entertainers had been reserved already by others, however.

The evening seemed yet incomplete. The Mu'ugalavyáni trilled a bright roundelay on his flute, and his brother sang the words in their own staccato language. Then, to the surprise of all, the Lady Eyíl sent Tsátla to rummage through her baggage and bring a *Sra'úr*, a potbellied little instrument with six strings. She slipped silver plectra over nimble fingertips and proceeded to draw forth a Tumíssan air. After a moment the flute-player joined in, and she sang the lyric in her low, throaty voice. Hársan would gladly have exchanged his life for the Isles of the Excellent Dead on the spot, had only mighty Belkhánu promised him an aeon or two more of the Lady Eyíl and her singing.

She finished, and all snapped their fingers in applause in the Tsolyáni fashion. The Shén, whose forelimbs ended in scaled three-fingered claws, contented himself with hissing like a blazing iron plunged into water.

Hársan's pleasure was interrupted by the merchant Sa'aráz, who had seated himself nearby on a bale of cloth. "Worthy priest," he began, "during our days together you have enlightened us with wisdom and with tales of your Tsolyáni gods. Yet never have we heard what you will do when we reach the capital."

Hársan hesitated. He had wondered when Prior Haringgáshte had forbidden him to speak of the Llyáni artifacts or of his mission in Béy Sü. Not even the Lady Eyíl had been told. Now he replied, "I go to serve as Thúmis wills."

Sa'aráz was not satisfied. "I have friends in the Temple of Eternal Knowing and may assist you there. You, on the other hand, can introduce me to your colleagues and thus aid me. 'Steel and flint make fire together.'"

"I know little yet of my duties in Béy Sü." That was true enough. "I do whatever the Weaver has woven into my Skein of Destiny. 'A rock rolls downhill until it stops.'" He finished, answering Sa'aráz' proverb with one from the Chákas.

"Perhaps Hársan goes to make water in the well of wisdom," interjected Bejjéksa in his gruff, guttural accent. He looked flustered when the group burst into laughter. "Is it not the idiom? Is it not to be said thus?"

"Perhaps, Oh learned savant of Salarvyá, someone should make water in your ear and thus inject wisdom into it!" This from Mnésun.

"If someone would proffer me one more sip of wine," Hársan laughed, "I would let the sleep-demons have my soul for the night."

The conversation turned back to the interminable talk of wares, brokers, and profits. Hársan wandered outside. He hoped that the Lady Eyíl would follow, but she sat now on the other side of the fire, all ruddy with its light, eyes sparkling as she related something to Mnésun.

He picked his way through the maze of tents, bundles, chests, and sleeping bodies towards the parapet. From inside a tent a woman giggled, and a man's voice guffawed in return. Music shrilled from one of the encampments, and there came the rhythmic clashing of wrist and ankle bells. Slaves sat about a fire under the bored watch of a caravan guard. Some played at *Dén-den*, moving the rough-cut wooden pieces from square to square of a board scratched in charcoal upon the stones. Others slept.

He reached the coping at last; drew a breath of smoke-tinged air, and gazed down into the velvet darkness beyond the platform. A rushlight betrayed the presence of peasant huts at the base of the access ramp. Neither moon was up as yet, and the guard tower loomed black upon black, orange light sketching a window upon its massive flanks. From below a baby cried, and a woman's tired voice sounded a plaintive reply.

"Worthy priest…"

Hársan started and turned to see the thin, bowlegged form of Helé'a of Ghatón behind him.

"Good priest, I mean no fear to you." The oddly accented syllables whispered forth in a breathy rush. "What you do is of peril, and there are those who are opposed. Do you know this?"

Hársan stared. Helé'a was silhouetted against the campfires. and his features could not be seen. "What —?"

"I am one sent. Be assured."

"What is this you tell me?" Hársan was still numb with surprise.

"I perceive…feelings. I am — how is it spoken? — a sensitive. I lack the power to see minds, as some priests and scholars do, yet I can see feelings. When you spoke just now, I sensed hatred, worthy priest."

"From — from whom?"

"In a group I cannot tell. My ability is not directional. But I know that hatred was there." The shadowed head seemed to twist this way and that.

"Of what use this warning, then, if you cannot see where the danger lies?"

"The one who hates guards his mind. Only if you, were to speak to each in turn, alone, might the enmity leak past the barriers and be plain to me."

A thrill of apprehension crept along Hársan's limbs. Prior Haringgáshte had never hinted that this mission could involve danger. For a moment he wondered if Helé'a's warning had to do with the Lady Eyíl: jealousy from Sa'aráz or the Mu'ugalavyáni. Moreover, who was this Helé'a anyway? A madman? One who would extract nonexistent money from him?

Helé'a continued. "I feel your doubts. Yet I must protect you if I can. This hatred has naught to do with the girl. It is cold and without pity, a dagger in its sheath, hidden from the eye. Two days remain before we reach Haumá, and my feelings tell me that it will leap forth before then."

"I have seen nothing to make me think your words are true. But if so, I should go at once to the captain of the tower, sleep there this night, and continue on alone tomorrow." He knew not whether he was serious or was simply humouring the man. But in his stomach a cold ball grew ever larger.

"Not so. Again, it is only my…feeling. But I sense that this is not the path of safety." Dry, skeletal fingers brushed his arm, and something hard, round, and cold was pressed into his palm. "What I give you now will protect you. Do you know what an 'Eye' is?"

"I do. They are devices made by the ancient sages, long before Llyán of Tsámra ruled, and before the Time of Darkness which preceded him. I have seen an 'Eye of Raging Power,' as my tutor named it, in the vaults of our monastery. He told me that its magic was gone, however –"

"Good, then. I must not tarry, for some may watch. What I give you now is the 'Unimpeachable Shield Against Foes.' Can you feel it – carefully now – the little stud on the back?"

Hársan fumbled the device in his fingers. It was of the size and shape of a river pebble – or of a human eye – a shallow, circular depression on one side, a tiny squarish protuberance on the other. "I feel it."

"If you are endangered, face the iris – the circle – towards yourself and depress the square projection. No weapon can then strike you. The power does not last long, however. Do you comprehend?"

"Yes, but – what does it do precisely? I –"

"We cannot speak further. It will keep you safe from any weapons not charged with enchantments of their own. Now I go, priest Hársan."

Another figure was picking its way past the huddles of sleeping slaves. A foot grated against a chest of goods, and there was a muffled curse in some foreign tongue. Hársan turned back to Helé'a, but the Ghatóni had gone.

"Good evening to you, priest Hársan." It was one of the Mu'ugalavyáni brothers, the flute-player. "A night without moons is of good omen, eh?"

Hársan found himself sidling away along the parapet, the 'Eye' clutched tightly in his fist.

"Is there aught amiss? The Lady Eyíl asks after you." Was there sardonic malice in the man's tone?

"I thank you for the message. I have just completed my evening devotions and must bid you goodnight." Hársan's eye had picked out an unobstructed path back to the comparative security of their campfire. The flute-player was left to stand gazing perplexedly after him.

The Lady Eyíl teased him about his preoccupation, complained that the wine must have washed away his lovemaking, pouted, and ended sleeping with her back to him. All that night Hársan lay with the 'Unimpeachable Shield Against Foes' but a finger's breadth away, hidden under a cushion of her litter. He slept little and was relieved when he heard Mnésun barking at his recalcitrant slaves to arise and begin the new day's journey.

No attack came that day, or the next. Helé'a did not approach Hársan again, nor, for that matter, did anyone else in the party.

They were only a *Tsán* or so from the town of Haumá when it happened.

It was blazing midday, and a haze of dust hung hot and stifling over the land. Mnésun had chosen to press on, however, saying that the arcaded caravanserai at Haumá offered more relief than an awning spread by the side of the baking *Sákbe*-road.

Hársan had stopped to pick at a blister on his foot. A slave bearing one of Mnésun's tall baskets chanced to pass close to him, and before Hársan could react, twisted so as to dump his burden of red crystal ewers over onto the surprised priest.

As Hársan fell the man plucked a slender dagger from his breechclout and slashed at him. Taken unawares, Hársan could only sprawl backward into the welter of broken glassware. Biting streaks of pain told him that the jagged shards were taking their toll upon his back. The slave, a burly youth with the tattooes of the Mu'ugalavyáni lowlands livid upon his cheeks, hurled himself upon Hársan again.

There was no time to dig the 'Eye' from his pouch. Hársan moved as he had learned in his rough childhood games with the nimble Pé Chói. Their chitinous arms might be weaker than a man's, but they had four of them with which to grapple, and they were as graceful as dancers. He feinted to the left, rolled to the right, struck out with his left hand to seize the slave's dagger wrist, and brought up a knee for defense.

The man was an experienced brawler. The wrist flipped out of reach, the roll was rewarded by a heavy kick to Hársan's left side, and the upcoming knee was swiftly dodged. Hársan had to keep rolling, and a blazing line of white pain ran down his left shoulder toward his spine. Glass crunched beneath him. The next thrust would be fatal. He fetched up hard against the parapet, on his back, and kicked out with both feet. The slave took the kick glancingly and jumped back out of range. Time had been gained, and Hársan's muscles cracked as he threw himself to his feet. He felt the sticky wetness of his own blood slide upon the scorching stones as his wounded shoulder scraped against the parapet.

The entire battle had been fought in silence. Other slaves had stopped to watch, but none made any effort to assist either fighter. Now, however, there was hubbub from behind. Hársan dared not take his eyes from the circling needle point of the dagger. The man feinted – and leaped.

There was a thin twanging sound. The slave opened his eyes and mouth wide, and a gout of blood spurted forth as though he shouted words of vivid scarlet. Then he fell, heavily, upon Hársan. A flanged, red-drenched rod of metal protruded from his throat.

Mnésun stepped forward from behind him, a stubby brown crossbow in his hands.

Hársan tried to push the slave aside, but the circle of openmouthed faces shimmered and danced before him. He felt hands grasping, supporting, probing at him, and somehow he was lying down. Then the babble of voices dwindled away and down a long, white corridor of pain.

He woke again to feel the cushions of the Lady Eyíl's litter lumpy and strangely sticky beneath him. Mnésun was there, and Eyíl, and others whom he could not see.

"– He was my slave," the caravan-master was saying, "but why he attacked the priest –? I never heard him speak a word to Hársan."

The Lady Eyíl said something unintelligible, and Mnésun replied, "Yes, against animals, brigands, runaway slaves – even disgruntled customers. We merchants must know a little of weapons…"

"I shall give him a drug, a pain-killer…" The voice sounded like one of the Mu'ugalavyáni brothers. Something bitter touched his lips.

Hársan wanted to speak with Helé'a, tried to look for him, but then the long hallway unrolled before him once more, and pain reverberated along it like the drums of a temple pageant.

He opened his eyes to find himself looking up at a lacework of geometric designs. These resolved themselves into the ribbed and groined arches of a vaulted ceiling. Cords creaked, and a great sweep-fan swung to and fro overhead through the honey-thick, still air of the room. The pain seemed mostly gone, but when he would have risen a hundred daggers ripped at his shoulders, and he fell back gasping.

A pale oval of a face looked down at him: no one he knew. It said, "Be at peace, priest Hársan. Your wounds are not serious and have been tended. I am Nusétl hiZayávu, priest of Thúmis of the Fourth Circle, and you lie in our temple at Haumá." Something cool and damp touched his face. "Your companions are here and may see you presently."

The long corridor stretched out before him again, however, and he slept.

It was three days before he could move about the little sleeping room he had been given, just off the temple dispensary. The Lady Eyíl sat with him daily, bandaged him, exclaimed softly over the network of lurid but superficial slashes upon his shoulders ("like the back of a man who has been flogged," she said, and Hársan thought to detect a thrill of fascination in her voice), and promised to wait until he was ready to travel again.

Mnésun also came each day when the temple's sonorous *Túnkul*-gong had ceased to call the faithful to the midday ceremonies. The grizzled caravan-master was almost obsequiously apologetic. He insisted upon presenting Hársan with a new grey tunic, much finer than the one he had had, and vowed to make a triple offering to Thúmis in the Temple of Eternal Knowing upon their safe arrival in Béy Sü. The two Mu'ugalavyáni brothers, Bejjéksa, and even the Shén paid him visits as well, each offering some little gift and their commiserations. When Hársan asked after Helé'a, however, he was told that the Ghatóni had pleaded urgent business and departed for Béy Sü alone.

On the last day of his stay in Haumá the physician priest Nusétl hiZayávu sought him out.

"Priest Hársan, you resume your journey tomorrow?"

"I do. My companions have suffered enough delay awaiting me."

"It would be a shame to their clans if they did not." The priest bobbed his long, shaven head. "Before your arrival, one came and left this for you with the guard at our gates." Gravely he extracted a rolled tube of parchment from within the folds of his tunic.

Wondering, Hársan unrolled it and saw two lines of vertical glyphs: the prickly, sword-edged curlicues of ancient N'lüssa! Each was printed in a careful, amateurish hand, as though by one who knew little of the language. Hársan recognised the text as a couplet from Tyélqu Dyáq's "Song of the Sky-Singers of Nakomé." It read:

'One has come, O Lord, to grasp thy hand,
From a foreign land, from the greater dark; more I know not.'

Hársan studied the parchment in bewilderment. Was the glyph for "hand" not a little larger and bolder than the rest? He turned me scroll over. There was no signature, but on the back he saw a stylised sketch of a long-beaked, plume-tailed bird. He puzzled a moment. Then he knew.

The bird was the literal meaning of the archaic Tsolyáni word *Kurruné*.

He quite startled the physician-priest by demanding to see his bedroll and other possessions at once. Nusétl hiZayávu produced these from a chest near his sleeping mat, and Hársan tore the roll open. Zarén's farseeing device was there, as were his notes and the Llyáni grammar. And, yes, there were the two leaves with his copies of the glyphs upon Kurruné's map symbol and the waxen hand.

But these last Hársan had left folded. Now they were rolled, like a scroll.

Chapter Eight

The Temple of Eternal Knowing swallowed Hársan up as a minnow is engulfed by the *Akhó*, "the Embracer of Ships." The tall bronze-barred gates swung to behind him, and he found himself once more in a world like that he had left behind in the Monastery of the Sapient Eye. Within the blue basalt walls, three man-heights high, one first encountered a stone causeway; on both sides of this lay a veritable maze of geometrically perfect, formal gardens overflowing with the grey and green *Tetél*-flowers sacred to Lord Thúmis. To the left, a ramp ran off towards the dim pillared halls and porticoes of the temple schools and colleges, and to the right, another, broader paved avenue led to the colonnades of the administrative offices. Directly ahead, the central causeway carried the worshipper on above the gardens to the temple proper, rising like some slaty leviathan of the forest, a sloping pyramidal platform surmounted by vertiginous crags of plinths and buttresses, with smaller domes, cupolas, and rotundas hugging its steep sides as foothills cling to the skirts of a mountain. Out of sight behind the temple were the dormitories, cookrooms, magazines, storehouses, workshops, and all of the more mundane periphera of sacerdotal life.

Everywhere there were carvings and bas-reliefs and murals and images: Lord Thúmis was here in all of his Forty-Seven Greater Aspects, and also in many of his minor forms: teaching, guiding, writing, aiding, admonishing, and contemplating. Bands of black porphyry glyphs, each over a man-height tall, proclaimed the greater glories of the Lord of Wisdom all around the upper flanks of the temple between marching rows of sculptured heroes and demons. Each carven and gilded gable, every blue slate roof, and each pavilion cornice and capital bore the intricate oval medallion of Lord Thúmis, Knower of Arts and Sage of the Gods.

Within, throngs of worshippers swirled among the ubiquitous grey robes of the clergy. Here one trod upon black and white marble mosaics, there upon hieroglyphs of glittering pegmatite set into tiles of greyish-blue riband jasper, there again upon tessellations of ashen steatite and pearly chalcedony. The devout moved in hushed groups from one shrine to the next, awed by the rich gold, the high dim altars, and the incense-heavy air. The peasant deposited his *Tetél*-flower or yellow *Dzíya*-melon upon the altar tray and stood openmouthed to watch the passing of the daily processions and pageants and tableaux. The townsman offered a silver *Hlásh* or a handful of copper *Qirgál* and had the satisfaction of hearing his presence announced to the God to the singing of a silver gong. Old women knelt in the cool silence of the shrine of Chaishólen the Imparter to plead for the success of an aspiring grandchild in the temple schools; occasionally a noble attired in pleated floor-length kilt, short overcloak of white *Güdru*-cloth blazoned with clan emblems, head cloth of light gauze bound with strips of iridescent brocade, and sandals of gilded *Chlén*-hide swept haughtily into one of the inner shrines to be admitted by bowing priests, there to offer a larger sum – and to receive proportionately greater favours from the Lord of Wisdom.

The Temple of Eternal Knowing was a universe of its own, a world cut off both by walls and by function from the humdrum city without. It was a place Hársan un-derstood at once and into which he fitted as a favourite hammer fits the carpenter's hand.

The last stages of the journey had been accomplished without incident. Hársan had ridden part of the way in the litter of the Lady Eyíl (and often her panting bearers had had to carry a double load). When they camped for the last night on Berenánga Plain with the myriad lamps of Béy Sü a twinkling heap of red gems upon the dark silver throat of the great river, the Lady Eyíl had wept and kissed him copiously. She swore that she would indeed become an *Aridáni* and send her clan-cousin, Retlán hiVriyén, off to the Halls of Hell to beg for another wife. As they talked, however, grey reality began to push in along with the cold light of dawn. If she abandoned clan and household how would she live? She had no profession, no training, no calling. She could, of course, cast herself upon the mercy of her temple and become an acolyte, but she seemed to have little patience with the cloistered ways of ritual and prayer. She was too slight to become a warrior, and too unlettered to become a scribe. The flame of this fancy had no more died than she began another: could not Hársan run away with her and the two of them find a new life in some distant land beyond her clan's certain revenge?

Yet even as they spoke of it both knew that this, too, was only another "rainbow bridge": all beauty but without substance.

At last the sun thrust up through the spires of the city's pyramids and palaces. It was clear that nothing could be done. They bid one another a tearful goodbye, and Eyíl promised to see him again if her new husband did not keep her mewed up too close. For Hársan's part, he wavered between the pangs of separation and a surreptitious sense of relief. He told himself that he loved her, romantically and eternally, as the heroes of the epics always loved their paramours; yet mingled in this adoration he could sense little worms of ugly doubt: life with Eyíl would be tempestuous at best, dangerous if her husband turned out to be a man of power and clan-pride, and certainly an obstacle to Hársan's progress within the temple. For these doubts he hated himself.

Thus they parted. Mnésun came to touch Hársan's hand and wish him good fortune, and the others also bid him farewell, each according to his custom. To these merchants this was just the end of one journey and the start of another.

To Hársan it was a return to reality.

He soon found, however, that he was of little interest to the hierarchy of the Temple of Eternal Knowing. He showed his writ and was questioned by a bored scribe, who copied down his account of the incident upon the *Sákbe*-road – and who also carried off Helé'a's 'Eye' to see what wiser heads might make of it.

Then Hársan was shown to a cramped stone cell in a dormitory at the rear of the temple, where he cooled his heels for four long days, besieged in the morning by odours of spices and roasting meat from the nearby kitchens, and assailed at night by redolences of latrines and midden-heaps emanating from ponderous *Chlén*-carts driven along beneath his window by masked members of one of the sweeper clans, the lowest of the low. Béy Sü indeed had its sewer system, but many houses were not connected to it, and all larger items of waste had to be carried beyond the walls to be dumped and burned.

At length he was summoned to the Hall of the Diffusion of Radiance, a cluttered annex apparently added as an afterthought to the shrine of Chuhárem the Diviner, the Thirteenth Aspect of Thúmis. There he was directed to one Znaqülu hiGúrika, a peppery little bureaucrat entrusted with all those Labours of Reverence involving matters of the ancients. This person handed him on to a younger priest, a pasty-faced youth whose nasal drawl identified him as a native of Sokátis on the eastern frontier of the Empire.

"I am Siyún hiDaigán, priest of the Fourth Circle." Sharp eyes, set close beneath hairy black brows hinting at Salarvyáni ancestry, flicked up and then down over Hársan. "So you're the miracle of wisdom we were told to expect? You're not as full of years as I had anticipated."

Siyún had employed the "You of Honourable Youth," although he looked to be no older than Hársan. The latter was careful not to let his irritation show and replied carefully, "I am here because I have done some introductory study of the Llyáni language."

The other turned away, picking a path between the crosslegged scribes, pencases, and documents that littered the stained floor matting. "Many have come and many have departed, all at the whim of some exalted high priest or other…You'll probably be forgotten here for years – and then be hauled forth to deliver a report you hadn't known you must prepare."

This was unpleasant news. Hársan said, "I thought my – mission – was of some interest to somebody. Else why summon me all the way from Dó Cháka?"

"How did you conclude that? – Oh, because someone told you that the high lords of the temple had seen fit to squabble over the Llyáni relics with certain other mighty temples I could name? And the bickering ending with them being made as open as a prostitute's parlor, all sorts of people wandering in to poke at them, and a handful of Legion bravos standing about picking their arses to boot?"

Hársan had heard none of this and admitted as much.

"Never mind, then. Keep out of the way of the priests of the Lords of Change. Give no information and leave nothing written for them to read!" They were out of the Hall of the Diffusion of Radiance, moving down a zigzag corridor. "The soldiers won't bother you. They play at guarding the relics, play at Dén-den, and play with our girl acolytes who bring them their food. I've laid a wager with one of the rogues that both he and I will be here to celebrate the Five Feast Days at year's end together. Once the great lords have settled their wrangling, it's easy to mislay the likes of us until we're all ready to board Belkhánu's barque for the Isles of the Dead."

Now they passed through a stout wooden door, descended a winding stone staircase, and emerged into a high vaulted room. This was lit by tiny brass oil lamps, set near clever ducts that took the smoke up through the massive heart of the temple above. They must now be well below the level of the pyramid that supported the upper structure.

Two men wearing only light *Firyá*-cloth kilts sat crosslegged on the flagging. An oblong *Dén-den* board lay between them and a heap of counters beside it. A jumble of armour and rolled sleeping mats proclaimed this room to be a temporary guardroom. Siyún saluted the two soldiers, who muttered greetings in return. He then picked up an oil lamp from a niche beside the door, lit it, and plunged off again into another dim passageway. This was constructed of massive stone blocks, hand-hewn and fitted together with the meticulous precision of the ancients. Moisture ran from the walls and trickled silently along a runnel in the centre of the floor.

The corridor wound downward, turned, branched, went down more stairs, and emerged into another lamplit chamber. Two more guards sat on their haunches by the door. These were attired in blue-lacquered *Chlén*-hide breastplates, the flaring shoulder guards of the Tsolyáni regular army, and kilts like those of their comrades above. Two crested helmets bearing the insignia of the Omnipotent Azure Legion lay in a comer, and curved, scallop-edged swords leaned against a wall. One rose to greet Siyún, who said a word or two in reply and jerked a thumb at Hársan. The other guard seemed lost in some reverie of his own.

They passed through the chamber beyond, where a table stood covered with a grey cloth. On it lay the golden hand and the map symbol. There were other items as well: three roundish lumps of crumbling red rust, a rod of some silvery-blue metal perhaps as long as a man's forearm, and a heap of manuscript leaves. These last were obviously fragile with age, mouldering, stained, and rotten.

A glance took in all of this. Then Hársan's gaze shifted to the other occupant of the room and he stared.

It was a Pé Chói.

But yet what a Pé Chói! Instead of the sleek, dully-gleaming black nudity of the Pé Chói of Dó Cháka, this specimen was decked out in an odd-fitting copy of a human's kilt, a gorget of *Chlén*-hide all chased and set with winking blue stones, and most ludicrous of all – a hat! Rising up between the delicate grey-shadowed ear-ridges was a loaf-shaped bonnet of embroidered cloth-of-gold, a style currently fashionable among the young aristocrats of Béy Sü.

Hársan repressed a wild impulse to laugh, then a strong surge of revulsion. No Pé Chói of the Chákas would ever have worn this foppish travesty of human costume! This was a parody, a caricature. It was like the *Küni*-bird a trader had once brought to the monastery; it had been garbed in a tiny grey priest's tunic and black skullcap, and the man had made it say preposterously pontifical things in its shrill little voice.

Siyún was saying, "I can't pronounce his name, but this is a priest of our Lord Thúmis' Cohort, Keténgku. Here is priest Hársan, the language scholar we were told to expect."

The Pé Chói minced forward on his two powerful rear legs, articulated tail swaying in unconscious imitation of a dandy's walk. "I am Chtík p'Qwé, Scholar Priest of the Fourth Circle." He spoke almost perfect Tsolyáni with only a trace of a whistle to mar the sibilants. "I have heard that you come from near my home in Dó Cháka?"

Hársan had not yet recovered from his surprise and could only nod in affirmation.

Siyún said indifferently, "I leave you to your tasks. Our great *Túnkul-*gong can be heard even at these depths, so you'll probably know when it is dinner time."

The two were left to stare at one another. The Pé Chói almost certainly sensed Hársan's distaste and reticence and was the first to break the silence.

"Since our two temples are so close, we may find it profitable to work together. I can show you what my techniques have uncovered, and you in turn can aid by analysing the writings." He bent his long oddly-jointed neck closer to Hársan. "Two more will return – they are gone to the midday rituals at their own temples. They serve the Lords of Change, and we are told in be wary of them. They are here only upon the direct permission of the Imperium, as you may have heard by now."

He led Hársan to the table and pointed to the relics. "This is a religious icon, a hand of gold made in imitation of that of some more ancient idol, named *Tgá'a Nmémsu*, 'the Man of Gold.'" Hársan gave no sign that he had heard of this before. "Next, there is a map symbol showing the Empire of Llyán of Tsámra. It cannot be used without certain devices now lost to us, and indeed, which we did not know still were workable as late as Llyáni times." The map symbol? Kurruné the Messenger must have run hard to carry it back, or perhaps he had sent it by some other courier.

Chtík p'Qwé picked up a blob of rust. "These lumps also contain artifacts, but their iron caskets have rusted away. The manuscripts are in Llyáni, but in a difficult and cryptic hand – perchance you can help there. And this rod may be a power source similar in function to the 'Eyes' made by the savants who preceded Llyán's empire, even as he precedes ours. I have not been able to puzzle out its use, and mayhap its force is now gone. As with similar devices, it probably drew upon the energies of the Planes Beyond, which fill the gaps between each bubble of reality."

"I have studied only the rudiments of that theory," Hársan murmured.

"It is so? The 'Layers of Reality' were my specialty in our temple, and I submitted a treatise upon the topic as my Labour of Reverence for the Fourth Circle."

"I fear I am not so far advanced." He felt uncomfortable.

"No matter. I shall explain." The Pé Chói raised a thin hand in unwitting imitation of the statues of Féshmu'un, Tutor of the Gods, the Ninth Aspect of Thúmis. "What we perceive is only the exterior of reality, like the bark upon a section of *Mnósa*-root. Beneath the bark run the fibres which contain the sweetness. Thus it is here: below the surface of the world we see, touch, smell, taste, and feel there are networks of invisible forces. Where these come together they create 'nexus points,' and there the power is stronger, mightier. Where no force lines run, there are 'bare' areas in which no sorcery operates. Long before Llyán of Tsámra the ancients learned to 'reach through' to this network with instruments and shape this power to their needs. Their wisdom created devices which pull, push, focus, and mould this energy to many purposes."

"I have heard that the devices of the ancients are similar in their powers to the magical spells employed by the higher Circles of the Sorcerer Priests within the temples."

"So it is. The ancients performed their wonders with instruments, but later our savants learned to produce similar effects with no more than the strength of their minds. It may be for this reason that the arts of making these devices are forgotten. That knowledge was lost before the Time of Darkness, though a few maintained it even into the Latter Times which preceded all of our historical empires. Now those who have the talent use their minds to 'reach through,' employing such aids as mnemonic words, gestures, thought attitudes, and even substances. This is what is called 'magic' by those who know not the truth."

"I have seen such spells. On the day of the Visitations of the Wise the senior priests of our monastery create mighty illusions to entertain the populace: ancient sages who stride forth from the high altar chamber bearing books and scrolls and emblems. Some of these phantasms are even made to speak learned words and give moral instruction; others scatter fantastic flowers over the crowd, and these turn into bright *Khéshchal*-birds and fly away —"

The Pé Chói opened his long, toothed beak in a copy of a human smile. "As you say. But all is not illusion. There are ways of 'reaching through' and turning energy into substance – or substance into nothingness." He took up a reed pen from the table. "Observe."

The skeletal fingers made a twisting gesture, and the Pé Chói hummed a single sonorous syllable deep in his throat. The pen appeared to turn over in his hand. Then it was gone.

Hársan was intrigued. The supercilious Sorcerer Priests of the monastery had performed such tricks, but he had not been considered advanced enough to study these arts. "Can you make it return?"

"Certainly. It is just a sort of 'reaching around the corner.'"

The Pé Chói made a second gesture, and the pen was back in his hand again. Hársan put out a finger to touch it – and jerked back in surprise. The pen was now deathly cold.

"One must be cautious; an object thus brought back cannot be held long in soft human fingers! 'Around the corner,' as I call it, is not a place for the living. I have heard that certain sages have put their heads there to see what is to be seen, and have been dragged back with eyes burst and blood running from their noses and frozen upon their cheeks. Dead as stones, and all within a trice!"

"Can you teach me to do this thing?"

The lambent green eyes came near, and the yellow-slit pupils looked full into Hársan's own brown eyes. "I can try, if you are so willed, and if you have the talent. Teach me Llyáni, and I shall teach you this."

"Agreed." In spite of himself Hársan felt himself warming to this strange travesty of a Pé Chói.

They spent the better part of the afternoon at it. The two priests of the Lords of Change did not return, and none came to disturb them until they heard the evening guard detail clattering down the corridor to relieve their comrades. By this time Hársan had at least touched the terrible cold of "around the corner" twice or thrice, although he had no success at making anything travel to or from that curious, alien space.

Chapter Nine

Four sat together in a room that was not a room, in a place that was not a place, and in a time that was timeless. Sparks of colourless light swam lazily to and fro, fish in a pool that had never known water.

The first was a man attired in the silver-chased, engraved armour of the city of Dháru, the Forge of Yán Kór. He was in his early middle years, massive as the plinth of a fortress, heavy through the shoulders and upper arms, and almost without a neck, his shaven head seeming to sit directly upon his torso. His breastplate, pauldrons, and gorget of fine steel exaggerated this massiveness. His was an imposing figure of physical power, although if one looked closely, certain softnesses of cheek and jowl revealed concessions made to age. Two creases ran down from his broad-winged nose past shaven lips to a square-cut black beard shot with silver, as ravines run down from a headland to the foam-tipped waves of the sea. Yet his most arresting feature, perhaps, was his eyes: green-glinting black, level, stern beneath the jutting eaves of his brows – and possibly a trifle mad.

The second was also a man, but cast by a different potter upon another wheel. Earth-hued robes hid his body, and he might thus have been slender or stout, old or young. Somehow, even so, he had the air of one who is young but who has never experienced youth. This man sat motionless as an idol of clay, corpse-hued hands folded before him upon his knees, the nails like chips of ochre flint. His features were concealed by a sombre cowl, but the light from above – which had no source and cast no shadow – touched a jaw painted bone-white, the colour of a skull.

The third who sat in that group might have been a man – and might have been something quite other. He was reed-thin, of no age determinable, sallow-saffron of skin, with a cap of dead black hair held by a curiously wrought fillet of silver and obsidian. He wore a slashed tunic of purple and ebon and russet which was cut loose and might thereby hide any number of anomalies of form. No pupils were visible in his eyes, and these glinted now black, now red, like marbles of translucent glass.

The fourth was most definitely not a man. Rich coppery-brown skin and sepia-hued fur rippled in the pallid light. A fanged animal snout, up-tilted ears, and a heavy-ridged brow made the creature a demon out of legends old before man had walked upon Tékumel. Save for a harness of studs and links and bosses, the being was nude. Scarlet eyes, like rich rubies, stared down at a luminous blue-glowing orb cupped between six-fingered paw-like hands.

The first man spoke in a grating, foreign voice. "You sought this council. Why?"

The second replied in a higher, mellower tone, a voice without emphasis or intonation, like the base-note of some sad threnody. "They near the goal. If more is not done, what was concealed will be opened."

"You are resourceful. Why call upon us?"

"Several players play this game. My pieces can be identified. Should this occur, more than one will be the loser."

The first man swore casually in a harsh, crackling tongue. "What would you of us?"

"You have pawns still unplayed, even in Béy Sü. If one or two are dashed from the board, it will be no more and no less than others expect. On the other hand, if even one of my pieces is clearly seen, both our games are speedily done."

"What difficulty do you apprehend?" The armoured man shifted his weight, leather and metal harness creaking. "So the priest-boy has reached Béy Sü; there is little chance he will come upon the prize!"

The second man paused, then went on. "You know that the 'Book of Changing into Dust' is in my possession. It contains the records of the necropolises of the Bednálljan Dynasty from the reign of Queen Nayári up through the age of the Great Decline. Amongst the entries for Úrmish there is one for the tomb of a certain Ha'akosún, who was governor of that city, a scholar, and an antiquarian of some skill. The list of contents for his tomb is… quite interesting, if true. There is power – real power – in some of the objects interred there. Perhaps even the power to halt certain mighty forces…"

The third man now spoke for the first time, his voice a sibilant hiss as though made with organs other than a human tongue and lips. "We know of that power. There is little chance that the priest-boy – or others who seek it – will find the key of it."

"True. It may require an historian to know what it is and where it is, a scholar to unlock it, and a sorcerer to use it. But there are those who would aid the priest-boy. What is lacking may be supplied."

"Unlikely," the first man snapped. "Your temples squabble over the relics; the relics themselves may be false or inoperative – after so many millennia the latter is probable. Should they be real – and useful – the priest-boy must still reach the treasure to which they point. And learn its use! A series of tasks as incredible as the legend of Súbadim the Sorcerer!"

"Has the priest-boy yet discovered the place of the power?" The third man broke in. "There is the map symbol."

"Yes, and well you know whither it points. Still, certain of my sources hint at subterfuge." The bone-white lips opened in a soundless smile. "The ancients were as devious as they are now dead! It would be like them to lead the would-be tomb robber a long dance half across the world."

"If so, then we have even less cause for concern! Why risk our agents to halt such an unlikely project? As well wear a helmet to protect one's head from falling lightning bolts!" The first man turned his entire upper body to face the third. "What think you, Lord Fú Shi'í? Counsel me."

"My Lord, we should not act, and well our colleague here knows it. There are watches and wards upon all connected with this affair, and our hand would be as plain as milk in wine. Let him move his own pieces. They are better placed and better hidden than ours."

The third man was silent. The first shifted again, impatiently, and the second sat as though carved from dull clay. The fourth being said not a word but continued to gaze into the lustrous blue orb.

At length the second spoke again, upon a higher, tenser note. "If I act and others come to know, it will be as though a summer flood has swept across all our lands! My brothers – and my sister – would delight to see me stumble."

"Stumbling is always possible for those who would ascend to dizzy heights." The third man made a convoluted gesture in the air. "Your minions are many, and your nets are spread wide. 'The *Shqá*-beetle makes tunnels within tunnels.'"

"My success is your success. If I fail, then I go onto the impaler's stake for the 'high ride.' And all of your long-laid plans go with me."

"You will not fail." The third spoke again. "If any has the talent and the ambition to win to mighty goals, it is you. Remember the sum wagered upon this throw, my Lord: an empire —"

"Enough." The first man waved a blunt hand. "Our compact is firm. We will aid you, but now is not the time. Make use of the others: the factions within the temples, the nobles you control, the dark ones whom you alone can summon. But you are the one who can — and should — act. It is premature for us to move. Call our help only if you see defeat before you as a *Zrné* sees the hunters' pit."

The second man did not move, but his smooth, creaseless fingers were knotted upon his knees before him. "What if instead I were to aid the priest-boy in his lessons? What if I were the hero who brought about your fall? There would be lamentation in many places beyond Tsolyánu."

The first man made an abrupt movement to rise. "We own more than one jug for our wine, Prince. You may break this one, but there are others fired in the kiln. No, I do not think you would betray our bargain, for it gives us each more than either can achieve alone. At the proper time we shall see that you do indeed have certain royal siblings to mourn. And the Petal Throne to sit upon. We —"

"You, Baron, stand to gain lands and cities which were part of the Imperium since the first Tlakotáni Emperor sat upon the Petal Throne over two thousand years ago!" The colourless voice dropped to a whisper. "Once you were great within Tsolyánu, Baron Áld. You served as general of one of my father's armies, and you could have risen yet higher, even to stand at the right hand of the God-Emperor himself! Now you would snatch from us what is anciently ours! You know that I join you in this only because —"

One thick fist smashed down into the palm of the other hand. "— Only because you cannot alone win the Petal Throne for yourself, Prince Dhich'uné! When your father dies, you will face the *Kólumejàlim*, 'the Rite of Choosing of Emperors,' as is the custom in your land. You would certainly best your eldest brother, Rereshqála, in those trials, for he dallies in pleasant lethargy in his villa in Jakálla with his whores and cronies, drunk or drugged, perhaps even by your doing! Your second brother, Eselné, could cleave you in twain with no more than a table-knife. And even your sister, Ma'ín Krüthái, has more swordsmanship than you. But your three permitted champions may defeat them, and you would easily overthrow them in the tests of sorcery and magic. No, it is your third brother, Mridóbu, whom you fear, he who sits in the High Chancery at Avanthár and cons the arts of administration and statecraft even as you pore over your tomes of wormy runes! Without our bargain, Mridóbu – or some princeling as yet unrevealed by the Omnipotent Azure Legion – will sit upon the Petal Throne. It will be *your* shade that will go howling down into the crypts of Sárku's many hells!"

The second man extended a dun-coloured hand, palm up, and his voice dropped to a gentle, almost dulcet note. "Let us not fall out, Baron. Our alliance is delicate enough as it is. We only weaken both our lands through war. Instead, I propose an even greater sweetening to our bargain. Join with me in more than just blood and pillage! Why should Yán Kór and Tsolyánu not be united under our rule? I as Emperor in Avanthár, and you as First General of the Empire? If our present scheme does succeed, then I am Emperor, and you seize Khirgár and parts of our north by force of arms. Yet you know that I must then put on a show of repelling you, whatever we may agree here, and much would be lost to flame and plunder. Others would rejoice as well: the Salarvyáni yearn for our southeastern Protectorates of Kerunán and Chaigári; the Red-Hats of Mu'ugalavyá would swoop to take back their lost Chákas – and mayhap parts of your little allies, Pijéna and Ghatón, which border their lands. Is it not said that, 'when water meets fire, both turn to harmless vapour'?"

"Our alliance rests upon our mutual benefit, Prince. Yet your sweetening is still not sweet enough. You know my reasons."

"I am well aware. But for both our sakes put aside those offences which Tsolyánu certainly offered you. With me in Avanthár and yourself as my First General, you will gain more wealth and power than a hundred, a thousand, lootings of Khirgár could ever bring. Forget Káidrach Field –"

The fist came crashing down again. "Speak not to me of that place, Prince! It was your conniving aristocrats and their puppet generals who left me there to defend a hopeless position! Do you accuse me of treachery that I then kissed Yán Koryáni gold? After all, who was I to your Empire – a hired mercenary, a wild warrior from Saá Allaqí? What mattered a little army and a loyal fool who was naught but a northern tribesman and a half-cousin to the men of Yán Kór?" His voice dropped to a deadly whisper. "Though I was betrayed, still I bore you Tsolyáni no great ill will, for I knew that such are the vagaries of politics and men. Even after I had climbed to my present station over the heads – and blood – of Yán Kór's squabbling chieflings, still I would have been your father's friend. But then he dispatched his legions to take me, as huntsmen take a *Jakkóhl*, and his accursed general, Kéttukal, sent his officer, Bazhán, to seize my lady Yilrána from my citadel of Ke'ér. Bazhán did her to a shameful death! And so did he suffer for it." White ridges of pain drew downward from the thin lips. "If you speak to me of power and wealth, Prince, then I spurn them! I seek blood payment – my own kind of *Shámtla* – for all that was done to me and to mine, and this shall I have though I have to raise all the myrmidons of the many hells to do it! No, make me no offers and plot me no plots! Our bargain gives you the Petal Throne; I take Khirgár, Chéne Hó, and the northlands. I have sworn before my mountain gods to end our blood feud only when these cities are delivered up to my vengeance. – And note well that this debt is not paid until General Kéttukal is also in my hand, even as was Lord Bazhán!"

"Kéttukal hiMráktine is at Chéne Hó, and there I shall try to detain him until you can come to collect him. You shall have him, for I have almost the same love for him as you."

The first man shifted restlessly and looked away. The second said softly, "Beware, Baron Áld, that you do not raise myrmidons who will not serve you but master you instead. You do not summon maidens to a summer's frolic! There are hints of forces beyond all that we know – and can control. The relics –"

He would have continued, but the third man interrupted. "Our Miháli colleague grows weary. The globe dims, and our contact must soon be dissolved. Let us make an end to it. Come, Prince, agree to action: block the plots of the temple of Thúmis and seize the Llyáni relics. Keep them if you wish, an assurance against any threat of our duplicity. This should satisfy you."

"You do not fear that they may contain power? That you do not hand me a sword too sharp for your own liking?"

"It is possible," the third man said, "but there are many Skeins. One is drab: the possibility that the relics are lost, false, or inoperative. The second Skein is brighter: you halt the priests of Thúmis, seize the relics, and find that your interests are better served by cooperation with us than by using them against us – for which we also have further counters. Unlikely are weavings that take you on to success in your land and victory over us – or, conversely, our defeat of you. Such chances we must take. No, Prince Dhich'uné, the best course is for you to join with us, use your agents now to frustrate your rivals, and aid us in creating a Skein that leads you to the Petal Throne – and my master here to his rightful vengeance. A denouement you can easily afford. Agreed?"

"I protest. As I said, my agents are all too soon seen: bright-plumaged *Khéshchal*-birds sitting upon a leafless branch! If they are caught, we are undone! My sources hint that the relics may be of very great importance to you indeed: it is possible that they can give your foes the means to halt your 'Weapon Without Answer' – and to slay the *He'ésa*, the minions of the Goddess Who Must Not Be Named! Even to drive Her from this Plane! Would you have that? The end of your schemings because you now underestimate the danger? Use one of Her *He'ésa* to destroy the priest-boy and those who aid him!"

"As well shoot a *Dri*-ant with a ballista!" the first man growled. "Your lesser folk can take care of the Thúmis priest. I see no need to involve my own people at all. The Goddess' creatures are still more valuable: they are undetectable by sorcery, and they have other, longer-term uses, including the removal of certain of your Imperial siblings, Prince. No, we will watch – and we will act when we must. This – and only this – do I promise you."

"Hold to our alliance most carefully, then, Baron. It is a vial of thin crystal that can spill much poison if broken." The second man rose, flinging earth-hued robes about his thin shoulders.

"Agreed," grunted the first. Armour clattered as he stood up.

The fourth raised red-ruby eyes from the smoke-blue globe. It flickered, pulsated, and went dark.

The place that was not a place was empty, a featureless void, as it had always been since time's first eternal moment …

Chapter Ten

In the days that followed his first attempts at spell-casting, Hársan began
work in earnest upon the Llyáni relics. The golden hand and the map
symbol he examined carefully but soon discarded as containing little new
information. Instead, he turned to the pile of crumbling manuscript leaves.
The temple apothecaries provided him with the dried bark of the *Voqu'ó*-plant
and certain other substances, and he boiled these into a sticky syrup with
which he painted each fragment, as he had learned to do in the library of the
Monastery of the Sapient Eye. The fibres of the ancient *Hruchán*-reed paper
took on new life. The tattered shreds became strong enough to be separated.
The tomb-damp and the deterioration of the glazing had taken their toll, but
some of the text slowly started to return to near-readable condition.

The Pé Chói continued to dissect the three lumps of rust in order to
free any artifacts inside. Each day he laid out his chest of knives, picks, and
files that were almost too delicate for human fingers and chipped away at
the aeons-old corrosion. He also sometimes coached Hársan in the elements
of spell-casting, and the latter started to show progress. Small objects now
usually went "around the corner" with ease, though larger ones still defied
his efforts. Some returned; others did not. At times, as he told Chtík p'Qwé,
he could almost feel the strange power of the Planes Beyond throbbing just
beyond his fingertips.

Hársan also requested and got permission to move from the noisome dormitory cell to the upper chamber within the pyramid. He was thus both closer to his work and also cooler. It was the middle of Drénggar, and the heat of the plains swathed the city in a blazing, suffocating blanket of misery.

He soon regretted this move, however, for the off-duty troopers who slept in this room were not slow to perceive the virtues of cool underground quarters. First they took to bringing in jugs of heady Ngálu-wine, then their comrades from the sweltering barracks, and finally their mistresses and courtesans to go with it all.

They were joined by not a few of the temple's female acolytes, for who might not appreciate the cool relief, liquid refreshment, and ever-festive company? The attractions of a brawny soldier's embrace, instead of those of the scholars of the Lord of Wisdom, also probably had something to do with it. The noise and ribaldry rapidly grew insupportable. Had the temple maidens been caught, they would have paid for their pleasures with the coin of some considerable physical discomfort, but dagger-tongued Znaqülu hiGúrika rarely frequented the nether regions, and others of the temple personnel either joined in or winked at the matter. As long as the girls chewed Lisútl-root and produced no unwanted priestlets, complaints would not be made. Are not soldiers to be soldiers, after all, and girls to be girls?

Hársan took little part in these diversions. Some of the priestesses were lissome enough, and two or three there were who cast sidelong glances at his not unhandsome figure. But the barracks room atmosphere was not to his taste. He requested further permission to move his sleeping mat to the antechamber below, where the night guards stood watch. Thereafter at the end of the day's labours, he had only to wait for the laconic trooper Réshmu to seal the Llyáni relics into their stone and metal cabinet and lock up the papers and notes in the chest at the back of the inner room. Then Réshmu and his companion, Guténu, took up their posts in the corridor outside the antechamber (this being the two guards' concession to Hársan's desire to sleep rather than to talk or play at Dén-den), and Hársan was left alone in the outer chamber. It was both lonely and oppressive, with the silent weight of the great temple pressing down upon him as Sru'rúm Peak had tried to crush Súbadim the Sorcerer in the legend. Nevertheless it was peaceful.

In due course the two priests of the Lords of Change put in an appearance. One wore the particoloured purple and mauve vestments and the black velvet hood of the sect of Wurú, the Cohort of Lord Hrü'ü. He introduced himself as Heshélu hiDaishúna and said little thereafter, going about his examinations of the golden hand and the map symbol with secretive care. The second was attired in the black robes, flattish square headgear, and ever-smiling silvery mask of the priesthood of Lord Ksárul, called the Doomed Prince of the Blue Room, Thúmis' counterpart amongst the servitors of Change and just as interested in the acquisition of knowledge – though for the glory of his minions alone. Lord Ksárul's interests were purely selfish: power and authority for Him amongst the Gods, and naught but the dregs for humanity as a whole.

This latter individual, Keréktu hiKhánmu, was more talkative, and the silver mask was soon laid aside to reveal ivory features of an almost inhuman beauty, pale and still as the deathmask of a god. Hársan knew he was male only because of his name, Keréktu, which could not belong to a woman.

The priest of Ksárul lost no time in approaching Hársan. "Scholar of Thúmis," he said, "we are all boxed up here like *Étla*-crabs in a fishmonger's basket. Let us at least agree to be civil, though we may disagree upon the proper way for the gods to rule the universe. You would have the cosmos a stagnant pool of changelessness, while we would make it a rippling stream. Yet for us to be hostile in this dungeon profits neither of us, nor our faiths."

"'Civility is the livery of the man of noble honour,'" Hársan quoted from his childhood lessons. He cast a sidelong glance at Chtík p'Qwé to see what the Pé Chói's reaction might be. He seemed to be totally engrossed in scraping verdigris from around a tantalising glint of coppery metal in his blob of rust.

"'And noble action is the first step on the stairway to godhood,'" Keréktu finished the quotation. "If you would listen, I might propose that we climb even farther than the first step." The delicate, over-full lips curved up in a smile like that of his mask. "Perhaps we could even agree to a modicum of cooperation. Nothing, naturally, that would compromise anyone. But why should we each do the same work as the other? It is a waste of time for each of us to translate that heap of mouldering pages only to come up with a well-nigh identical translation. Of course, we need not – and should not – share our conclusions."

"Your point is well taken. As we say in Dó Cháka, 'One stomach needs but one mouth.' Yet I doubt that I can add anything worthwhile to your knowledge."

The priest of Ksárul gave him another smile, radiant, almost loving. "Another perspective, another approach. All is of value. We shall also avoid duplication of effort, finish, and be out of this catacomb all the faster. More, the contents of our temple libraries may well complement one another. What you lack, we may supply – and conversely."

The offer seemed both attractive and harmless. Yet Hársan temporised, saying, "We shall see. Let me first judge the scope of the work."

Keréktu hiKhánmu bowed gracefully and said no more. The priest of Wurú turned enigmatic eyes upon them both from behind his black hood. And later when Hársan mentioned the matter to the Pé Chói, the latter only gave him another Dó Chákan proverb: "The most appetising prey is the hunter's best bait."

Thus the days drifted by, almost unremarked in the lamplit stillness below the temple. Work became routine. Chtík p'Qwé got the first lump of corrosion open, revealing no more than a handful of gleaming gems of no great value, contained in the remnants of a copper casket and a leather pouch. These were examined by all, declared to be of no interest, and were placed in the storage cabinet to be sealed by the guards. Undaunted, the Pé Chói applied his tools to the second chunk of oxidised metal.

Hársan was jolted one day from his humdrum round of manuscript analysis by the arrival of the priest Siyún.

"Priest Hársan, I bear you two gifts! The first comes from our learned savants above." He tossed a small object toward Hársan, who automatically reached up and caught it. It was Helé'a's "Eye," the "Unimpeachable Shield Against Foes."

"Alas, I am to tell you that your mighty device has all the magical power of a heap of *Chnéhl* droppings!" Siyún laughed. "One can buy better fakes from the wandering peddlers in the marketplace."

Hársan could only stare at him in stunned confusion. What had happened? Had Helé'a known the thing was useless? If so, the little Ghatóni would answer several pressing questions if ever he saw him again!

"The second gift is perhaps more to your taste." Siyún produced a folded scrap of paper with a flourish. "Some swooning admirer, it seems, would speak to you of talents other than Llyáni conjugations."

Hársan glared but opened the note. It contained a crudely sketched clan emblem, that of the People of the High Pillar, a local winemakers' clan. Below this was the next day's date and the single word "sunset." It bore no signature but ended with a crude and girlish drawing of a litter.

He hardly knew whether he was overjoyed or dismayed. All that night he pondered the matter, his memories of the Lady Eyíl pitting themselves like soldiers against his present absorption in his work and the warm cocoon of temple security in which he was so much more at ease. To go to her would be wonderful but might involve him in unforeseen entanglements. Not to go…well, not to go would certainly be the wiser; safer course, the way to avoid imbroglios, possibly to make strides in his work, and to achieve rank and prestige in his temple…

Of course he went.

He found the clanhouse of the People of the High Pillar easily. It was a landmark in the city's teeming commercial section, a place of tall stone walls, rambling storehouses, many courtyards, and dark cellars from which *Chlén*-carts rumbled forth groaning under their cargoes of sweet wine for all corners of the Empire. A rugged giant of a servitor admitted him to the outer portico where the common folk stood to purchase their clay jugs from the rows of perspiring clerks. A busy clan official asked his name, consulted a list, and had him ushered on into the warren of rooms within the building. Here chambers could be rented for short periods by those who preferred to hold their parties at a public – but discreet – place, rather than take their purchases home to drink. A silver *Hlásh* or two bought privacy, and the vintners' clans had connections with others who would provide food, music and dancing, and various entertainments.

The room he entered was long and pleasant, smelling of sharp wine and wooden casks and new cordage. The nearer end opened onto a veranda hung all about with vines and waxy-orange *Sauqún*-flowers. Screens of grass matting were suspended along the farther walls, and these had been splashed with water to provide coolness. A sweep-fan stirred the turgid air overhead. The cords that drew it ran clucking along little pulleys to an aperture high up in the wall, behind which sat the fan-boy, unable to see or interfere with the activities within. Rumour had it that fan-boys had oversize ears, however, and a winemakers' clanhouse was no place for meetings demanding real secrecy. The best of these establishments provided servitors who were deaf – and sometimes mute as well.

The Lady Eyíl sat upon a dais beside the dripping grass mats, a little table before her spread with viands and bronze goblets. Hársan gazed upon her for a long moment, for she was much changed. Her Tumíssan costume had been cast aside for the fashions of the capital. She wore a flounced floor-length skirt of gauzy blue *Güdru*-cloth, sandals of silvered leather with buckles shaped like laughing little *Rényu* faces, and a wide collar of stiff gold wire all decorated with filigree work and set with tiny stones. Her thick black hair was done in a single heavy tress bound about with ribbons of gold and blue, and this now hung down over one smooth, bare shoulder. Her breasts (not so small that they were not shapely, for all her apprehensions!) were painted with little curlicue designs in many colours, and their dark nipples were rouged and touched with glittering mica dust. A street-cape of dark blue lay crumpled at her feet.

"Do I address a certain Hársan, priest of Thúmis of the Second Circle?" She laughed, low in her throat, as he well remembered her. "You stare at me as if I'd grown four arms, grey skin, and a sword, like the Enemy of Man, the Ssú!"

"I had thought to meet a noble lady from Tumíssa." It grew easier as he spoke. "But all I see is someone from Béy Sü. The little brown egg has hatched out into a many-hued *Khéshchal*-bird!"

"Do you like the transformation?" She slipped to her feet and turned before him, displaying a length of graceful calf through the clever slashes of her skirt.

"Indeed." He let himself admire her openly and was surprised to see that his fingers appeared quite steady as he poured himself a goblet of wine. "I did not hear – I thought of you –"

"Lá, you thought I would not keep my sworn oath? To break a promise is ignoble, and to deceive a priest is to offend the Gods! Would you have had me anger your mighty Thúmis?"

He laughed but made no reply. More important matters came to mind.

"You are married?" he asked.

"Oh, no, not yet…or perhaps I should say that I am as much married now as I shall ever be. Our clan-elders have set our nuptials for the third month hence, Halír, when all the harvests are done. My noble clan-cousin is a busy man and will be married only after all the crops are in, the accounts made, and tithes and taxes paid –" She was still smiling, but her lips trembled. "I am much valued, Hársan. Lord Retlán is a kindly and important person. He gives me everything –" Her voice broke a little. "I am valued, valued as a *Khéshchal*-bird is valued, or talking *Küni*-bird….He dresses me and sees that his slaves make me beautiful. He commands me to eat and become sleek. And he has given me over to his third wife, the Lady Gíu, for training in the arts of etiquette, for he is popular at the governor's court –" Her voice, broke entirely, and she took a step towards him.

Hársan did what seemed to be expected and took her in his arms. He comforted her as he had done upon the *Sákbe*-road, held her, and touched her as he knew she wished to be touched. Soon the black *Tsúnu*-paste upon her eyelids was all tear-washed and kissed away, and the designs upon her breasts were rubbed and blurred beyond repair.

The sun had sunk below the horizon when they arose, but its vermilion and magenta banners still filled the western sky. Lady Eyíl stood and stretched before him, ruddy light gleaming off the supple lines of breast and buttock and thigh. She bent to pick up her skirt from the floor, but she twisted away when Hársan would have reached for her.

"Oh, no, my love, not again! My dear Lord Retlán hiVriyén cares little where I go and whom I see, as long as I do not dishonour him by public display. But if I am late for supper the Lady Gíu will purse her vinegary lips and vent her bile upon me. No. Wait for my message. I will send to you again within the six-day. Though you may forget me for love of your wise, cold God, yet I am not so fickle as to abandon you!"

That night the cool darkness of the underground antechamber seemed lonelier and more oppressive than ever.

Thereafter they met more and more frequently. Always Eyíl arranged the place and the time, usually at the clanhouse of the People of the High Pillar, occasionally at the establishment of one of the other winemakers' clans, and once even at a caravanserai in the Quarter of Foreign Persons. Each time they ate and drank, made love together, and then parted.

At first Hársan was apprehensive of her clan's possible surveillance and displeasure, but she quickly disabused him of this.

"Oh, lá, Hársan! My noble fiancé desires only that I become a suitable companion for him at the governor's feasts. Lord Retlán is a mild man, perhaps thrice my age, going bald and wrinkled. He is too old – and dried up – to beget more children. His first and second wives have borne him sons, and the oldest of these is already an officer in the Legion of Káikama –" She broke off and gave him an sidewise look before continuing. "The Lady Gíu attends to his personal needs. He has even offered to buy me a slave lover and a plentiful supply of *Lisútl*-root to keep me content. You see, my love, I am being groomed as a pet *Rényu* is groomed – all for show! Were it not for my clan-elders' greed for ties with our wealthier brethren here in Béy Sü, I would now be safe at home in Tumíssa."

"And more than likely betrothed to some provincial popinjay!" Hársan drew a teasing finger along the silky thigh pressed so pleasantly against his own. "Were you in Tumíssa, you would never have met me on the road."

"You have no faith in the Weaver of Skeins!" She ruffled his hair. "Let me summon my barber-slave and have him rid you of that Dó Chákan coiffure, my love. It is time you joined the world of greater Tsolyánu! There are feasts and fetes and festival in the harvest season, and I can take you with me, so long as Lord Retlán does not care to go himself. It's all the fashion now for noble women to be attended by at least one suitor to sing her praises – nowadays even matrons too old to waddle appear with a troupe of swains to fawn upon them. Oh, please let me show you these things, Hársan!"

He laughed and protested. In truth, he did not much like the idea of appearing at functions with her as her adoring gallant. In the end, however, he gave in and allowed the temple barber (and not her slave!) to shear off his forebraids and trim his locks to a more fashionable length. When the old man muttered something about it being more proper for a priest of Thúmis to get his head shaved, rather than to have his hair done like a dandified noble, Hársan silenced him with a sharp word – and then added a silver *Hlásh* as an apology. It disturbed him, nevertheless. At times he felt rather like a huge, dumb *Chlén*-beast, led by its halter willy-nilly wherever its master willed. Yet the Lady Eyíl was here, she was beautiful, and she was full of love for him.

Chapter Eleven

The month of Firasúl came to bestride the land, ravaging all with its heat and dust and baking winds. During the day the wealthy retreated to suites of underground apartments below their clanhouses; the nights were spent amidst the greenery of their lofty roof-gardens. The poor sweltered, cursed, sweated – and laboured – as the poor have always done in all times and places everywhere since the Age of the Immortal Gods.

Pardán at last took the place of Firasúl, and all the world heaved a sigh of relief at the passing of yet another summer. The grain now stood tall in the fields, and men spoke of crops, harvests, prices, rates, and the autumn festivals of the month of Halír to come.

The Lady Eyíl had said truly. In the intricate society of the capital none thought it strange to see a pretty daughter of a good middle class clan (or, to be charitable, a clan of the lower aristocracy) in the company of a grey-robed priest of Thúmis. The mighty lords of the city went about with retinues of cronies, courtesans, slaves, and hangers-on. Their wives and concubines likewise surrounded themselves with suitors: foppish courtiers, soldiers pricked out in fancy armour, and delicately mannered bravos whose hands were quicker to the wine-cup than to the sword. Indeed, the richest dowagers competed with one another for variety: one must have a warrior, a poet, a musician, an artist, a tall youth, a short one, a jolly one, a pensive one – and onward unto the limits of one's purse! Those who favoured the Lords of Change sought oddities, nonhumans, misfits, and sports. The most extreme of these were the devotees of Lady Dlamélish and her Cohort Hriháyal, who delighted in escorts of unclad girls and boys, great-thewed gladiators from the *Hirilákte* Arena (who might just as well have been nude for all that their brief kilts concealed), dwarves, giants, and a host of other aberrations.

All during Firasúl and the first days of Pardán the Lord Retlán hiVriyén remained closeted with his field-stewards and accountants, so the Lady Eyíl said. She thus took Hársan with her to the *Hirilákte* Arena and to the salons of certain nobles famous for their feasts and ever-changing rounds of fashionable partying. The name of Retlán hiVriyén seemed to get her into almost any clanhouse or mansion she chose.

The pageantry and colour of the Arena were exciting, but Hársan disliked the noise, the heat, and the stink of the crowd. He took no pleasure, moreover, in watching the endless spilling of blood, for, unlike some others of the twenty Tsolyáni deities, Lord Thúmis accepted only the sacrifice of flowers, fruit, and incense.

The diversions of the noble households, on the other hand, were very much to Hársan's taste. There were mimes and dances, presented by slave performers or by various lower clans specialising in these things, and there were also recitals of poetry and music. He became almost a connoisseur of the *Ténturen*, the huge twelve-stringed instrument favoured in central Tsolyánu. Almost a man-height in length, the *Ténturen* had two resonance chambers and several layers of sympathetic strings. Two persons were needed to play it: one to press the frets, and the other to pluck the melody. Accompanied by tiny drums and gongs, the instrument was perfect, Hársan thought, for the evocation of the deep, slow compositions of the classic modes. Indeed, it often served as the background for slave singers who wore masks and costumes representing the legend-cycle being performed. A new world opened out before Hársan when he discovered that musical and dramatic presentations of the epics were infinitely superior to reading or chanting them by oneself. He took much pleasure in attending performances of the Epic of Hrúgga, the Hymn of Mü'ükané, and the majestic Lament to the Wheel of Black, as well as many of the modern classics, some less than a thousand years old.

In these things he easily overmatched Eyíl, for she had no training in the music and literature of the past. For her part, she made no secret of the fact that the gaiety and exhilaration of the festivals were more to her liking than the solemn atmosphere of the private musicales. Therefore, when the Feast of Boats was celebrated on the seventh day of Pardán, she cajoled and teased Hársan into attending.

This night commemorated the Going Forth from Death into Life. The canine-masked priests of Qón, the Guardian of the Gates of Hell and Cohort of Lord Belkhánu, sailed in a splendid torchlit regatta down the Missúma River to portray the journey through the Underworld to the Isles of Excellent Dead. Children lined the banks of the river to push little yellow paper boats out into the current, each bearing a waxen candle and a carefully penned letter to some deceased relative or friend. The mighty voices of the *Túnkul*-gongs boomed and roared up and down the river, dancers filled all the market plazas, and the streets overflowed with celebrants.

Hársan and the Lady Eyíl mingled with the crowds eddying through the outer gates of the governor's palace. Inside, long tables were piled with Belkhánu's saffron-dyed pastries, heaps of fruits, and wooden casks of wine and bitter *Dná*-grain beer. Roasts of *Hmélu* and whole haunches of the giant *Tsi'íl*-beast sputtered aromatic fat into a dozen fires, and sweating cooks hacked off chunks of meat and thrust them into greedy hands. All was free, the largesse of Lord Khámiyal hiSayúncha, Imperial Governor of Béy Sü.

The gates of the second ring of crenellated walls were manned by halberdiers in the blue and gold livery of the Imperium. A plump chamberlain noted the Lady Eyíl's clan and status and pointed them to one of the daises that marched up the long slope amidst trees and shrubbery toward the lamplit towers of the palace. Holding tight to Hársan's hand, she wended her way up through the swarming lower levels. Each step of the shallow staircase of daises was only a hands-breadth high, Hársan noted sardonically, yet it represented all of those jealously guarded distinctions that humankind makes between man and man: clan and class, rank and office, and wealth, and prestige. It took no more than the lifting of a foot to progress from dais to dais, but to gain the *right* to do so might well cost a man a lifetime of ambition, toil, and intrigue.

At last they halted, approximately a third of the way up the ladder of layered platforms. Hársan gazed at those still above them. There, many tiers beyond theirs, sat the chiefs of the mercantile clans; still higher were the places reserved for the old noble clans, those descended from the aristocracy of the Bednálljan kings and from the Engsvanyáli Empire that followed: the Golden Sunburst, the Sea Blue, the Vríddi of Fasíltum, the Might of Gánga, the Citadel of Glory, the Cloak of Azure Gems, the Blade Raised High, and a dozen others. Still more elevated were the daises of the lords of Béy Sü, the generals of the legions, and the high priests of the temples. A row of armoured troopers stood below the even loftier station of the governor and his train.

At the very top, set higher than all the rest just below the frowning battlements of the inner palace, a single tall pillar draped with gold-banded blue brocade upheld the intricate, convoluted glyph which bespoke the invisible presence of the Seal Emperor, he who dwelt inviolate in the Golden Tower at Avanthár and who never set foot upon these vast lands over which he ruled as a god rules. For, as Hársan knew, once an Emperor was crowned, ancient law decreed that he might never again emerge from the Golden Tower. Provided with all he might wish by the deaf-mute Servitors of Silence, the highest branch of the Omnipotent Azure Legion, the Seal Emperor governed Tsolyánu as an omniscient but unseen presence until he, too, embarked upon Belkhánu's ship for the Isles of the Excellent Dead.

They found space at a low table on their dais, and a servitor brought a platter of *Hmélu* meat, dishes of tiny fish cooked in vinegar and spices, a bowl of savoury grubs fried in batter, reddish *Dná*-bread, and wine.

"Oh, Hársan, look there!" He followed Eyíl's pointing finger to see a slender, young-old man climbing towards the governor's dais. This person wore rich robes of black trimmed with azure and gold, but he was otherwise indistinguishable from the throngs of courtiers, warriors, and officials following along in his wake. For a moment the man turned to gaze down at those below, and Hársan caught a glimpse of a thin, ascetic face and the glitter of cool, appraising eyes.

"It is Mridóbu, the third Prince of the Empire! Is he not splendid?" The Lady Eyíl's eyes were alight and her cheeks flushed. "They say it is he who will ascend the Petal Throne next – the Imperial Party at Avanthár prefers him to any of his brothers, or to his sister!" She stood to gain a better look, but further sight of the man was cut off by the governor's retinue which had arisen to receive him.

"I would never have known," Hársan said... and wondered briefly how *she* recognised the Prince. Another thought struck him. "I had heard that the Temple of Avánthe – and that of Dilinála as well – support Prince Eselné, the Emperor's second son. Is not Prince Mridóbu a follower of one of the Lords of Change? Lord Ksárul? Why so enthused?"

She gave him a very odd look and sat down. Any further reply was drowned by the sudden cacophony of drums and horns. The gates of the inner palace were opening. Yellow-clad priests and priestesses of Belkhánu and Qón bore forth a towering palanquin upon which stood an obelisk of gilded wood and paper, its sides inscribed with glyphs.

The drums went silent. The priests chanted a litany, censed the tall obelisk with the smoke of fragrant *Vrés*-wood, and held up ritual emblems and insignia the meaning of which Hársan did not know. Two of the priestesses led out a naked girl, little more than a child. A masked officiant put a torch into the child's hand, and with this she set the obelisk alight. It must have been soaked in oil, for it flared up at once. Two of the yellow-robes then came forward to drape the girl in vestments of shimmering gold, exchanged her torch for a jewelled sceptre, and lifted her up so that she might touch this to the face of the Imperial Seal upon its pedestal. Those on the highest dais arose to embrace the child and thrust rich gifts into her hands.

"She is the Virgin of the Gods," the Lady Eyíl said in Hársan's ear. "Thus is death overcome and life renewed upon the land."

All remained standing and silent until the great blaze had died down to embers. Then the drums clamoured again, strident flutes and shrieking horns shouted defiance to the tyranny of mortality, and all in that concourse cheered and rejoiced and embraced one another. "Existence ends not with death!" the yellow-robes cried in unison, and nude priests and priestesses of Avánthe, Goddess of Life, poured forth from the palace to dance before the Seal of the Imperium. Eager hands reached forth to dash the torches out against walls or shrubbery, or to douse them in bowls of wine, and the uproar became pandemonium. The brazen-throated *Túnkul*-gongs of the temples rent the air with their bellowing metal voices.

All joined in the revelry, devotees of Stability and Change alike. The Lady Eyíl was in his arms, thrusting hard against him and seeking his tongue with hers. Then she was torn away by exultant youths wearing the scarlet and white of Chegárra, the Hero-King, Cohort of warlike Karakán. Hársan was caught up in the crush. A matron seized him, kissed him soundly, and then she was in turn caught and kissed by a soldier in blue-lacquered breastplate and towering *Chlén*-hide helmet.

Hársan looked about for Eyíl, but she was gone. Hands snatched at him and he stumbled over unseen bodies lying locked together in fierce embrace amidst the scattered goblets and dishes. A priestess of Avánthe fled by, laughing, her taut young body daubed with depictions of humanity's oldest preoccupation, the organs of procreation, and Hársan was jostled aside by a throng of noble youths belling in pursuit. Faces swam up before him in the flickering gloom, bodies, jewelled ornaments, rich headdresses, dark robes pulled askew to reveal tawny-gleaming limbs. Over all hung the passionate thunder of the great drums, sonorous, sensuous, compelling, rhythmic, and as hypnotic as any drug.

Fingers found his lips, thrust a bit of sweet pastry within. He whirled to see a grinning face a finger's breadth before his nose. It was a young man, wirily handsome, attired in a kilt of overlapping metallic scales coloured in emerald and purple. An elaborately curved sword swung from a clip at the youth's waist.

"Will you not dance the Round of the Return to Life with me O priest of mighty Thúmis?"

"Back to your barracks, warrior of Káikama! He belongs to us and not to you!" Another face pushed forward, a girl's. Hársan saw wide eyes, an open scarlet mouth, dishevelled hair cut straight across a low-rounded forehead. She wore a girdle of chain links and a skirt made up of many green and purple strips; tiny bells tinkled at her wrists, ankles, and throat: a priestess of Hriháyal, he thought. She bore a tray filled with little brass bowls. In one of these she dipped a finger, touched it to Hársan's lips. He tasted something sweet, dark, and fiery.

"An offering to Thúmis – from one who knows not wisdom but loves folly! Come, worthy priest, show me whether your god is as stiff and upright as he is said to be!" She threw an arch look back at companions still in shadow.

There was no sign of the Lady Eyíl. Hársan found himself ringed by a circle of laughing faces, men, women, even an elegantly attired Shén, resplendent in copper-trimmed armour.

"Would you chew Hnéqu-weed with me? – Or taste the delights of my white powders – or of my blue? Alas, I have no grey powder for a grey priest of the Lord of Wisdom!" Her perfumed breath filled his nostrils, and a sharp little tongue flickered against his ear. "I might give you a bit of my green powder as well!"

The slim fingertips grazed his mouth again, and this time he tasted a bitter, pungent substance, strangely aromatic and as sharp as new wine. He jerked his head away, and the finger left a trace of powder upon his cheek.

"Taste, Hársan, Priest of Thúmis! It will not harm you but will prepare you for what I offer next!" Bare thighs wriggled urgently against his own.

"How – how do you know me?"

"Ohé! 'The breeze knows many roads,' as it is said!" She laughed. "Friends of mine have seen you in that underground dungeon where the soldiers play at Dén-den – and other pastimes. But you prefer fumbling with musty books to putting your hand to better things." Fingers caught his wrist and guided his hand down over the silken curve of her belly.

He would have let her have her way – was not this night devoted to all of those things that bespoke joy and the cycle of life? – but at that moment a great voice roared happily in his ear, "Hársan! Hársan! Is it not Hársan, the priest of our journey?" A black claw inserted itself between his jaw and the pretty face before him. It was a Shén. "It is I, Hársan –" a guttural-sounding name hissed in his ear, but he could not catch it, "– I travelled with you to Béy Su, with Mnésun –"

Memory came back. "You –?" The Shén merchant. "Where –?"

The powerful scaled arm had him by the shoulder, pulling him around involuntarily, away from the girl. Why did the creature have to reappear now of all times? Hársan stammered, "How came you here? I had thought you'd be on your way back to Shényu by now."

"Not so, my friend. I await a cargo. It is delayed somewhere up north, in Milumanayá, between here and Yán Kór. Nothing travels on time in the summer because you humans are not like us, at ease in the heat."

"Will you not come away, my priest?" The girl in the green and purple skirt swayed before him, her comrades a dark ring behind her.

"Leave him be, Sríya," one of them called, "I just saw Misénla go by. Let us not be late tonight of all nights!"

"Hársan, I would speak with you." The Shén's hard grip did not slacken upon his shoulder. The armoured tail switched slowly from side to side.

"Await me," he muttered to the girl, "there – where the dancers are. I shall join you in a moment."

Something was wrong with his eyes. There were two Shén. He blinked and squinted to see who the newcomer was.

"Hársan, I have business to discuss." Both Shén spoke marvellously in unison. "You humans buy our opals and our garnets, and a comrade from Thri'íl tells me that other gems are popular as well." Why were the Shén saying such irrelevant things? Why interrupt at such a stupid, inopportune moment? "Now, I have access to a shipment of cloudy green moonstones, down from the Dry Bay of Ssu'úm in Saá Allaqí…" The creature was babbling! "If I can find someone here whom I can trust to receive these gems while I make a trip south…" Something was assuredly wrong with the Shén: he (or was it they?) leaned forward at an impossible angle. It was taking him so long to say what he had to say. Each syllable took a month, each word a year…

Hársan pitched down a tunnel into blackness.

— And awoke to a blaze of red light.

Red light? Was he afire? Did he stare at the sun?

A voice whirled by on wings like those of a forest glider-fly. "– It is not a large enough amount. *Zu'úr* takes as much as you can put on the tip of a dagger to lock its hold upon the brain –"

Hársan saw a serpent-like dagger coiling itself around a helpless, struggling brain. He giggled.

"He joins us again." Another voice. But whose?

The scene snapped open as does a banner in the wind. The Shén was there, beloved friend that he was, and Eyíl, hair loose upon her shoulders, wrapped in her dark blue street cloak. Someone else leaned over him: the funny Pé Chói! Hársan laughed outright. And could not stop. Something wet and sour was dashed into his face. He choked.

"Ohé, our adventuresome merrymaker honours us with his attentions again!" Chtík p'Qwé held another cup of wine ready to send it splashing after the first. Behind him stood the Shén and Lady Eyíl, somewhat more real and solid this time. They were in the lamplit chamber beneath the Temple of Eternal Knowing. Two more puppet figures jigged and whirled in the flickering background: the two guards.

"Where –? How –?"

"You have played at *Dén-den* with Missúm, Lord of Death," the Pé Chói replied. "And he held all the counters and made all the throws. This Shén says that you were given a dose of *Zu'úr*, a drug so pernicious that but a flick of it is sufficient to turn the mind into fungus pudding!"

"*Zu'úr* is forbidden in Shényu as well as in your human lands," the Shén interrupted. "It is said that it is supplied by the Hlüss, or possibly the Ssú, both of whom hate mankind and all other nonhuman species with almost equal fervour. Thus do they wish to destroy us all, for they believe this world was originally theirs and that we – the Shén, humankind, Pé Chói, Páchi Léi, Ahoggyá, and some others came from the Home of the Gods and usurped it from them."

"We have the story too," the Pé Chói added, "the 'Round of Hkék Qtèn.'"

"But if it is known that this *Zu'úr* is meant for the harm of man, then who would be fool enough to take it?" That was the Lady Eyíl's voice.

"Certain of the more depraved servitors of the Lords of Change, particularly those of the voluptuary Hriháyal, acquire it somehow and employ it in tiny quantities. They say it heightens sexual prowess and ecstasy to a pitch not otherwise attainable."

"Pleasure indeed!" The Pé Chói sponged Hársan's forehead with a damp cloth. "The other side of that coin is that it addles the mind of a human. It slays us Pé Chói and you Shén straightaway! I have seen human victims after a month or two of this sensual 'joy': they are good for nothing but propping up a wall. – Until they die, perhaps in two or three more months."

"I cannot understand why anyone would bring such a terrible thing to Lord Belkhánu's festival," Eyíl said. "What a hideous trick to play upon an unsuspecting stranger."

The Shén's armoured shoulders rose in a shrug. "The mischief of those people is great – though they usually reserve it for those who have somehow offended their goddess. Hársan seems to have been unlucky enough to meet a woman who was just whimsically malicious. Had I not seen –"

Hársan opened his mouth to tell the Shén that the girl in green and purple had known him, had indeed called him by name. Instead of words, however, a stream of sparkling diamonds issued from his lips. Dazed, he watched them ascend lazily to the ceiling and vanish.

"Try not to speak now, Hársan. Rest. You will be as weak as watered wine for a time." The Pé Chói unrolled his sleeping mat and shooed the two staring guards from the room. He turned to the Shén. "He will be much in your debt when he awakes."

"I ask no favour in return. I shall come again when he is strong, for I really do have a matter of business to broach with him."

"Let me stay – please!" The Lady Eyíl took the dampened cloth from Chtík p'Qwe's fingers.

"There is no need." The Pé Chói's voice was abrupt. "What of your family? Your clan?"

"What of them? It is the Night of the Fête of Boats, and all will be at the festivities. Who will complain of me?" Her words were fading, growing muzzy, dying away as does the chant of rowers from a galley passing by upon a dark and windy river.

Hársan rolled over and slept. The world whisked away to a glimmering spot in the unlighted void and disappeared.

Chapter Twelve

The smell of food awakened him. He opened his eyes to see Chtík p'Qwé setting a tray down next to his sleeping mat. Steam arose from a bowl of reddish *Dná*-grain porridge, and Chumetl dripping from an earthen mug made white puddles of buttermilk around a pair of bluish *Dlél*-fruit. The idea of solid nourishment did unpleasant things to his stomach, however, and he waved it all away.

The Pé Chói curled his articulated tail beneath himself to serve as a stool. The great green eyes gazed upon Hársan for a time; then he said, "'The fish does not run in the same pack as the *Zrné*.'"

Hársan tried to think of an appropriate adage in the Pé Chói tongue, but his head still seemed to belong to someone else. He replied in Tsolyáni, "You are right, my friend. I shall forever abstain from all strange foods, drinks, substances – and maidens!" He reached for the mug of salted buttermilk, gripped it with fingers that still trembled, and sipped at it.

"Where is the Lady Eyíl?" he asked.

"She stayed the night. Then she came again the next day. Your soul wandered for two days and two nights, and we nearly despaired of you. The Shén came once, too, but he is gone upon some commercial journey. He left a packet of gems for you to keep for him. I have had Réshmu lock them up in the cabinet with the Llyáni artifacts."

"When will the Lady Eyíl return?" Hársan persisted.

"She said she would make some excuse to her clanspeople and come again in the evening." The dry, whispery voice held no enthusiasm.

This was a matter that seemed to demand plain speaking. Hársan said, "I think you do not approve of her."

"Who am I to approve or disapprove? 'The tree profits nothing from cursing the clouds.' Your human couplings are of no concern to me. Sleep with a *Ssú* if you wish! But —"

"But what?"

"Perhaps I have said enough."

Both were silent. Again Hársan was surprised to find that he did not want to look directly at his relationship with Eyíl. It seemed to be a tightly closed little packet within his heart, bound about with the cords of Tsolyánu's traditions of romantic love and sealed with the wax of youthful attitudes appropriate to such things as pretty girls. In some way he felt afraid to open this parcel. The more he let himself ponder it, the more he was disturbed by niggling little suspicions to which he could put no names: things she had said, things she had done… He needed reassurance. He put the empty mug back on the tray and looked squarely at Chtík p'Qwé.

"I have never had anyone for whom I cared as much, my friend. Do you think she does not care for me?"

"It is clear that she does. She wept with remorse at having left you alone at the feast. But —"

"Another 'but?'"

The Pé Chói waved all four hands helplessly in the air in a gesture that instantly took Hársan back to his childhood in the Dó Chákan forests. "A great many 'buts.' I am not sure – I sense… You know that we Pé Chói possess powers of empathy…"

"I know," Hársan said in the Pé Chói tongue.

"Ah, so you do speak my language; thus the priests told me before you arrived here! You can follow me and it will be easier to explain," Chtík p'Qwé replied in kind. "You have lived amongst us; you know us as well as any human has ever known us; and you are aware that we sometimes sense things for which there are no words – in any tongue. To be a Pé Chói is to be cursed with thoughts that can never be uttered. As the Teachings of Tkù Pnìi say, 'Can the mountain know of the diamond hidden within its heart?' – Oh, Hársan, I feel there is something amiss. But —"

"Again a 'but'?"

"Yes. Another. But this: I would lay this topic aside until I know more – or know that I know nothing."

Hársan gave up. "What of the girl, Sríya, or whatever her accursed name is?"

"No trace, as one might expect. The priesthood of Hriháyal says it has a Sríya in Katalál and another in Hekéllu, in the eastern mountains. The Temple of Thúmis wants no confrontation with those people now, and you have no clan to go banging on their gates demanding *Shámtla*."

"They lie, all of them. She was here –"

"I know. The Shén saw her, after all. But unless you have a powerful clan, a good reason for your superiors to get involved, or money to hire one of the assassins' clans, you can only sing in the wind."

"Oh, how I'd like to see some of their temple records for myself – or apply a spell or two to the heads of some of those deceitful pimps who pass for priests…!"

"Nothing is to be gained from wishing. We Pé Chói are a practical race, and my counsel is that you give the matter up – for now. I have another and more urgent issue to chew over with you." He scraped his four hands lightly over the ebon-gleaming chitin of his haunches. "I am not concerned with your female, nor really with the incident of the other night. They are clouds that drift past me in the sky. Instead, I think of the work we do here. I would have you prosper, just as I myself would prosper. And I tell you that the priests of the Lords of Change make strides that will leave us behind in the dust. Your skills are needed, Hársan. Now. No more of girls and feasts, but work."

He uncoiled himself gracefully. "Let me show you something." He went into the inner room. and returned with a lump of whitish metal. "This is what was within the second rusted container."

Hársan turned the object over in his hands. It was hemispherical, like one half of a *Dzíya*-melon. A small circular hole occupied the centre of the flat side to the depth of a finger-joint. The rounded exterior was pockmarked with tiny, squarish depressions.

"I can make nothing of it, though I am familiar with many of the artifacts made by both your ancestors and mine." The Pé Chói ran a hard, jointed finger over the stippled depressions. "These may be some form of writing."

Thus they seemed to be, although Hársan did not recognise them. They were aligned in neat rows all around the convex outer surface of the object, and they were of uniform height and width and depth as well. Some were the same while others differed. Letters? Magical runes? Hársan held the artifact tightly, but no miniature voices whispered in his brain. It was therefore probably not a map symbol, or at least not an active one.

"Can you see the little ridges and whorls on the flat surface as well?" Chitk p'Qwe asked. "They are almost invisible unless one slants the half-globe toward the light."

Hársan peered. Then he thought of something. He arose, shakily, and brought his packet of personal belongings from the storage chest. From this he took out a cloth-wrapped object.

"Let me try this." Zarén's farseeing device was quickly set up to face the enigmatic white hemisphere. He adjusted it this way and that, but all he saw was a pale blur.

"A friend made this," he answered Chtík p'Qwé's unspoken question. "It brings far away objects nearer. I had hoped it would do the same for a little thing seen from close by." The Pé Chói examined the contraption. "I have seen pieces of curved glass used to enlarge things. There is a priest in my temple whose sight is as weak as a babe's. He has a broken piece of a Mu'ugalavyáni bottle which he uses to magnify the letters of books. But it distorts everything. Still – something might be made of this."

"Zarén spoke of a text that gives the principles underlying this phenomenon." Hársan struggled with his memory. "I think it was the 'Book of the Visitations of Glory.'"

"Not a common treatise. Yet I have heard of it," Chtík p'Qwé mused. "Your temple may have it here, or mayhap it will be in my temple's library?"

"Or perhaps in mine." They both jumped and whirled to see Keréktu hiKhánmu standing in the doorway, smiling silver mask in hand. "May I see the artifact, please?"

The Pé Chói pushed it reluctantly across the table. Hársan moved to conceal Zarén's farseeing device behind himself, surreptitiously dropping its cloth wrappings back over the box and its lenses. Keréktu hiKhánmu either did not see or affected not to notice. Instead, he took up the proffered artifact, inspected it as Hársan had done, felt, shook it, smelled it. At length he laid it down again.

"'A worthy treasury is not opened easily,'" he quoted ruefully. "What of the third container?"

Chtík p'Qwé hesitated. "I am still at work upon it. Extreme care must be used in order not to break anything fragile inside."

"Of course, colleague." Keréktu hiKhánmu turned smoothly to Hársan. "You may be interested in a piece of news, my friend. I have learned that our library contains a copy of the Llyáni lexicon of Ssümúnish Krá of Ch'óchi."

"I had heard that it was a lost book." Hársan could not repress a flare of interest — and envy.

"A thing is only lost until it is found again." Small white teeth flashed in a generous smile. "If you would consult it, I can have it copied for you."

This was a major temptation. Ssümúnish Krá was almost contemporary with the end of Llyán's empire! "My Lord, you offer a great boon. What would you have in exchange?"

"Nothing that would distress your superiors, or mine. We could join in reading the manuscript texts. A copy for you and a copy for me, and knowledge — and perchance promotion accruing to us both."

Hársan found words of agreement ready upon his tongue but thought better of it. "I will think upon this."

The long-lashed, almond-shaped eyes turned regretfully downward. "Ponder not too long, dear colleague. Both our superiors grow bored with us. Rumour has it that if we do not soon set the Empire agog with the wonder of our discoveries, we shall all be sent packing. You might like to return to your monastery, of course, and eke out your days scrambling for coppers from nose-picking peasants, but I would be grieved to find my Skein of Destiny woven of such drab stuff."

Chtík p'Qwé raised his head from studying the whitish metal hemisphere. He surprised Hársan by saying sweetly, "Alas, for your Skein of Destiny! That such a fabric of beauty might be transformed into a country bumpkin's soiled breechclout! Lyricists shall compose laments upon this tragedy for generations to come! On the other hand, the bucolic life is said to have its compensations…"

The gently passive gaze focussed upon the Pé Chói. "Gibes ill become you, colleague. What I say is of benefit to all of us. How much will your scraping and scratching excite the High Council of the Temple of Keténgku? Any good jeweller can do as much — and carve those wretched blobs of rust with bas-reliefs of the Thirty-Two Unspeakable Acts of Hrihával at the same time! I urge only that we pool our talents."

"Indeed. 'The lair of the *Mnór* is comfortable, but it is no place to sleep!' Had your Lord Ksárul been willing to work together with the other Gods — even those of His own party of Change — there would have been no Battle of Dórmoron Plain, and He'd not now be imprisoned in the Blue Room!"

This banter was verging upon acrimony, and Hársan interrupted, "Peace, colleagues, peace! Leave religious disputation to the marketplace orators! How am I to work?"

Keréktu hiKhánmu's expression did not change. He said politely, "I only ask for a modicum of cooperation. Time is short. 'The worm who sleeps too long upon the rock is fried by the sun.' You must have heard that Chákan adage?"

Hársan nodded courteously in return but said no more. He motioned Chtík p'Qwé toward his tool chest, and himself picked up one of the manuscript leaves. The priest of Ksárul smiled, bowed, and brought out his penbox. The discussion was apparently over, for now. The priest of Wurú did not appear.

At length Keréktu hiKhánmu sighed graciously, put aside his copying, and arose saying something about lunch. Hársan would have followed after, but Chtík p'Qwé put a restraining hand upon his arm.

"I have heard you humans say that after love and fear, the next greatest torment is temptation. Do not be hasty to aid this black-robe, Hársan. Who knows whether he speaks the truth? It is possible that he would deceive you with some later, garbled recension of the lexicon of Ssümúnish Krá. Be assured that the followers of Change wish neither of us well."

"Yet what if he does not lie? The Temple of Ksárul is known for its ancient, secret libraries. They may well possess a copy of the lexicon. Oh, how I could use it!" He held up two manuscript fragments. "I am so close to the meaning of these pages. I have discovered that there are two separate books here. One is a common text of funerary invocations and rituals, but the other is almost certainly the 'Book of Sunderings,' which has not been seen since Éngsvan hla Gánga's libraries sank beneath the southern sea! Oh, Chtík p'Qwé, what an achievement if it be true! What a prize! I only need to separate these two books and complete my translation –"

The Pé Chói showed his excitement by wobbling his great head from side to side. "Splendid! I, too, may have something at least as important. Let me show you what I accomplished this morning – something I did not wish our black-robed friend to see quite yet." He picked up the third lump of rust from the table, held it in his delicate upper pair of hands, and gently pulled in opposite directions. It separated into two pieces, coming apart as prettily as two halves of a shellfish. A few crumbs of rust pattered down onto the table.

Nested inside was a second hemisphere of white metal, identical to the one that lay upon the table. Chtík p'Qwé removed it and handed it to him.

Wondering, Hársan took the object. It was the same as the first, save that instead of a hole in the flat side there was a circular peg.

The Pé Chói forestalled him. "I have already fitted the peg into the hole. The two halves fit together to make a neat fist-sized sphere. But nothing else occurs. See for yourself."

Chtík p'Qwé was correct. Hársan put the two hemispheres together, twisted and prodded them this way and that, but could see no purpose to them. The ancients were not simple with their puzzles!

Nothing seemed to make the matter clearer. At last the Pé Chói hissed to warn him of the return of the priest of Ksárul, and the second hemisphere went back into its shell of rust and metallic accretions.

Chapter Thirteen

The remainder of the afternoon passed slowly. The Pé Chói silently went about his picking and scraping, while Keréktu hiKhánmu copied glyphs onto a scroll. Hársan set out several manuscript fragments and juggled them this way and that to see if any fitted together. No one wanted to resume the previous conversation.

Eventually Chtík p'Qwé threw down his tools and left. An hour or two thereafter a temple slave brought Hársan's dinner on a tray, sent, apparently, by the Pé Chói. Hársan started up at every little sound in the outer corridor, thinking that it might be the Lady Eyíl. But she did not come. Keréktu hiKhánmu finally wiped his pen nibs and departed, leaving the two guards to seal away the artifacts for the night.

Hársan had thought of one more experiment, however. This must be tested when neither of the priests of Change was present.

"Would you not leave the relics with me for a little longer?" he asked Réshmu. "I am in the midst of something."

The guard shrugged, and black-browed Guténu yawned. Neither made objection.

Out came Zarén's farseeing device, and Hársan pried at one of the larger lenses with impatient fingers. It came free of its wax, and he carried it to the table where the first hemisphere lay. A moment of fumbling and adjustment, and then strange lines appeared in the glass, though much twisted and blurred. The tiny grooves on the flat side were circular, and his eye followed them dizzily from one edge of the glistening whitish surface to the other. There was something about them...

He saw what it was. The grooves nowhere crossed one another but ran in an ever-narrowing spiral round and round to a central point – which would have been in the very middle of the round hole. He followed them back again in the opposite direction and came to the outer rim of the hemisphere. Just there, on the convex exterior, below the starting point of the grooves on the flat side, an almost invisible triangle had been incised into the metal. The rows of squarish symbols seemed to begin at this triangle too, marching away around the outer surface until they ended in a glyph of some sort at the deepest point of the curved hemisphere.

Excited now, he pulled the third lump of rust apart. Bits of corrosion flaked away, and he would have some explaining to do to Chtík p'Qwé in the morning. A glance through the lens told him that the second hemisphere was identical: the same concentric circles on the flat side, the same spiralling to a central point. This, however, was marked upon the summit of the protruding peg with a triangle. Another triangle on the outer edge indicated the entrance to the whorl. There was one more difference: the concentric grooves ran in the opposite direction to those of the first hemisphere.

He held the two pieces gently, positioned them so that the two little outer triangles lined up, and pushed the pegged half down into the other's hole. Then he twisted them together in the direction of the concentric circles. The two halves revolved easily, moving almost of their own volition in his hands. Then they stopped. He could rotate them no further.

And he knew.

HE KNEW!

It was as though a fiery dagger slashed a path through his brain. Knowledge poured in, echoed, roared, broke down barriers of language and intellect and memory...!

He knew where the Man of Gold was! It was not in Ch'óchi; it lay beneath the ancient city of Púrdimal in north-western Tsolyánu, some eight hundred *Tsán* from Béy Sü.

He did not know exactly *what* it was, but he knew how to find its aeons-old tomb, how to operate it, how to make it do what it had done before in a time so remote that not one whisper of it had carried down into any of the living mythologies of Tékumel.

The Man of Gold was made to be used against the *Kúù Tép*. He knew now what those words meant and why they were followed by the classifier glyph for "original structure" in the Llyáni script. They were the name of the Goddess of the Pale Bone, a being or force so malevolent that even the savants who built the Man of Gold to combat her had not reckoned all of her powers. She and her minions from the Planes Beyond, the ghastly *He'ésa*, were the enemies of mankind and of the Gods alike.

The globe had been made during the Latter Times, the ages long before the Engsvanyáli priest Pavár first contacted the twenty deities of Tsolyánu's present pantheon, codified Them, analysed Their theologies, and stated the relationships obtaining between Them and the creatures of Tékumel's Plane. Some of the knowledge of the Ancients, those who had ruled Tékumel before the Time of Darkness, had passed on into the Latter Times, and at the very end of this epoch of unknown length some smatterings and scraps were handed on to the savants of Llyán's empire. Beyond this no more could be said.

Pavár's revelations had hinted of other, older, inimical beings who dwelt beyond the bubble of reality. The Pariah Gods, so he named them, existed outside of the pantheon. These beings held goals so opposed to mankind – indeed, to all creatures made of matter and energy – that they were anathema upon all of the infinite Planes of Reality. This was no mere matter of divine rivalry: the difference between cold, undead Lord Sárku and fiery Lord Vimúhla was nothing compared to this! The supernal Light of Lord Hnálla and the shifting Chaos of Lord Hrü'ü were one and the same when compared to the deadly purposes of the Pariah Gods. Lord Ksárul might do battle with His fellows and be condemned to sleep for all eternity in the Blue Room, but before the Goddess of the Pale Bone He and His opponents were only brothers who had fallen out over some childhood quarrel!

The Goddess of the Pale Bone was still known in Tsolyánu – Hársan had heard tales of her, both from his Pé Chói tutors and from the lector priests in the Monastery of the Sapient Eye, but her worship had been stamped out ruthlessly over the centuries, driven underground, purged, and exterminated as no other sect had ever been. There was excellent reason for this.

Much was still unclear – or perhaps incomprehensible to creatures with limited intellects, such as men, even with the burst of knowledge imparted by the white metal globe. Pavar's Gods seemed to desire a cosmos in which matter and energy and being (for want of a better term) existed, whatever forms these might take. The Goddess of the Pale Bone – and certain others like her – sought to suck the universe empty of *all* being, to take its force and substance into themselves, to render all of the many Planes Beyond empty and lifeless and void in a way that could not be imagined! The Gods might be harsh, imperious, and uncaring; They did as They did; but at least They permitted other beings to co-exist, and They did grant a measure of dignity, personal worth, and the self-realisation upon which the morality of all sentient races must be built. The Pariah Gods would have none of this; they would deny these things to any Plane in which they dwelt. Once the Goddess of the Pale Bone had gained a foothold within the cosmos, none could stand against her. Indeed, none could exist at all. She made death itself ignoble, meaningless, an end that held no glory.

Why would anyone worship such a being? For immediate, transitory gain, of course, for the splendours and pleasures she permitted in order to gain access to this Plane. Her gifts were transitory, dust and dross, nothing but tempting baubles held out to fools.

The globe told Hársan of the battle waged by mankind – and certain allies – so long ago. All of the goals, all of the ideals, all of the aspirations he had ever had were as toys of clay beside the single, urgent, desperate need to vanquish the Goddess of the Pale Bone and to keep her from entering the universe of man ever again!

He could not think. The white metal sphere rolled from his hands to come to a stop against the silvery-blue rod. He now knew what *that* was, too: the key with which the powers of the Man of Gold were unleashed.

Images whirled through his head like leaves in a storm. Vast armies of men and nonhumans and unknown creatures toiled toward one another over landscapes that were tapestries of destruction. Enigmatic machines moved there as well. Faces of men and other beings in strange costumes glared and shouted. Leaves of books in alien languages rose before him: maps, plans, diagrammes, charts that changed even as he glimpsed them. Over all, there were the ravages of death and dying and blood and ruin. Towers toppling. Seas boiling. Dust rising into a flame-driven sky. New, raw wounds gaping in the faces of the very mountains themselves.

Then there was the sky-tall figure of a golden being, manlike yet not a man, who brushed aside the machines and scattered the armies and reached through the wrack and desolation to seize and crush the *He'ésa*, the minions of the Goddess who dwelt not on this Plane but in some other, awful universe and who came hither as spies and assassins, undetectable by sorcerers or any other means until they chose to strike. The golden being reached forth also to seal off the great black cube from whence the Goddess drew her powers into this Plane, silenced it, and rendered it useless. When it had done, there were no entrances left for Her here. Judging from the Goddess' objectives, this was a result that would be desired by all of the creatures of this Plane: all of the creatures, and indeed, all of the Gods… And there was Eyíl's face, too…

Eyíl?

Hársan struggled to free himself from these awful visions of the dead and uninvited past. He clutched his forehead, threw himself backwards against the chamber wall. Dazed, he looked up to see that it was indeed Eyíl, night-blue cloak over one arm, a net bag of foodstuffs dangling from her other hand.

The fruit and loaves of bread scattered, and a jug of wine made a plocking sound upon the flagstones, purple stains spreading out all round. She was beside him, eyes fear-wide, fingers to his brow.

"Oh, Hársan! The drug –?"

"No," he got out, "not the drug. Something else –"

She held him to her. "Not the *Zu'úr*? Then –?"

"Nothing. Nothing to fear now…" Strange after-images still danced before him, but they were receding. "I'll be all right."

His eyes went to the sphere upon the table, and her glance followed.

"What is that, Hársan? Is it dangerous? Did it – was it –?"

He dared not tell her of the Man of Gold. That knowledge was for his superiors, and for Chtík p'Qwé. "No, no danger, I – I had just made a discovery…"

"A discovery? When I entered your face was like the visage of Shu'uré, the Eighth Aspect of Dlamélish! What frightened you so?"

A knot of puzzlement formed in Hársan's breast. He rose. Carefully, he said, "And when did you ever see Shu'uré? She is never carried in procession outside of the temples of the Emerald Goddess?"

Was that wariness or just concern upon Eyíl's face? "Why, at the house of the *Aridáni* lady in Tumíssa, she of whom I spoke when we travelled upon the road. When we were little, she used to frighten us, my clan-sisters and me, with stories. She showed us her house-gods."

It was possible, nay, plausible. He temporised, "I was not really afraid – more surprised by my – discovery." What to do but plunge into a lie? "I learned something from – from the manuscript. It was too powerful, too far advanced in sorcery, for a student of my Circle."

The lines of worry softened around her lips. "By your expression, it was very advanced indeed, my love! Your face – no great beauty that it is – was like a temple gargoyle."

He bent to pick up the shattered jug, holding it carefully to save whatever wine was still inside.

"I am only a grammarian. Sometimes a mastery of nouns and verbs does not qualify one to cope with what those words denote." He had now regained full control. He said, "Come, great lady, speak no more of my dry and dusty work. All will wait until tomorrow. We shall eat and drink, and then, mayhap, I shall show you some other magic more appealing to our liking."

They lay together upon his sleeping mat, but the acts of love did not come easily to him. Every time he closed his eyes he saw again those terrible visions of ancient death.

At length she rose, nude and supple in the lamplight, and glided over to the table. Before he could intervene she had picked up the white metal sphere. It came apart in her hands, and she made a surprised sound.

"It breaks in two! Oh, I hope I have not ruined it, Hársan!"

He saw from her face that she had received no message from the sphere. He made a reassuring gesture, and she put it down to examine the silvery rod. The manuscripts she did not touch, for it was plain that they had been carefully arrayed upon the table, ready for final ordering. She came back to him, knelt, and rubbed a rounded breast against his shoulder.

"You were holding that globe when I entered, Hársan. Did your manuscripts tell you what it is?" Was she prying now, or just curious?

"Ah – not entirely." That much was true. "The powers of the ancients are not so easily unravelled."

She stretched around to kiss him, and desire for her rekindled. "Oh, Hársan, this thing that you have learned – it will be worth a great Labour of Reverence, will it not? They will initiate you into some high Circle! Will they give you money as well?" Delightful fingers sketched caresses along his body. "If so, then you could pay compensation to my clan for me. Lord Retlán cares little about me, and he would let me go. I have lands of my own near Tumíssa, and we could go there and live." This was the first Hársan had heard of her personal lands, but it was not unlikely. She took his face between her palms. "Oh, my love, let me help you! I long to see you out of this dingy place. Together, we –"

There was a noise in the corridor beyond the anteroom. They both leaped apart. Hársan snatched up his kilt, and Eyíl her street-cloak.

"The guards," he began.

But it was not the guards. The door opened a crack, and a hand came through, open and reaching, as though feeling for the latch.

Then, to Hársan's thunderstruck surprise, the hand slid down the edge of the door. The fingers clutched spasmodically and lay inert upon the flagstones.

He flung the door wide. A figure huddled there upon the threshold. It wore neither the grey of Thúmis nor the blue armour of the guards.

A blue and gold headdress rolled at his feet.

"Réshmu! Guténu!" he shouted. There was something terribly wrong here.

He shot a swift glance up the corridor but saw no one. Then he bent and turned the body over.

He looked down into the sightless eyes of Kurruné the Messenger.

A bit of parchment protruded from the dead hand. Automatically Hársan retrieved it, opened it. His eyes refused to focus upon the words written there. He was stunned. Who had done this thing? Who dared to violate the temple? Where were the guards?

He threw a wild look back at Eyíl. She stood against the far wall of the inner chamber, wide-eyed, her cloak crumpled about her naked shoulders.

A weapon. He wanted a weapon. His eye fell upon the silvery metal rod. Better that than nothing. He snatched it up.

Now he heard a step in the corridor outside. A figure lurched toward him from the shadows, and he backed away. Then came a surge of relief, for it was the older guard, dark-visaged Guténu.

Yet there was something amiss with him. He seemed to drag himself along the wall as though swimming against an invisible current. Wetness trickled from his hand and left a splotchy trail upon the stones. Blood? No, it was transparent. Water –?

The man staggered forward, looking all the while at Hársan with huge, wondering eyes. He opened his mouth to speak, but pale, frothy, pink fluid gushed from it instead. Then he seemed to collapse inward upon himself, as a *Hmélu*-bladder filled with water is pricked by children. His features deflated, wrinkled, shriveled…

Guténu fell, still spewing liquid. He lay still.

Eyíl screamed and pointed. Hársan looked down at the body of Kurruné beneath his feet to see the man's mouth slowly opening. Perhaps the Messenger still lived? Then his tongue protruded. – But no, that was no tongue, for it glistened brown and waved this way and that, questing, in the air.

It was a great worm!

Another appeared in the man's eye-socket, pushing the staring eye aside as though it were a stopper in a bottle. Pustules burst forth here and there upon his limbs, and other ugly, blind heads emerged. The body seemed to dance with a macabre life of its own as one and then another flat, glutinous creature wriggled forth to lie gorged and squirming upon the flagging.

Hársan gave a wordless cry and leaped back. His teeth were clenched to keep them from chattering, and the silver rod shook in his fingers.

Now he saw another terrible thing. The body of Guténu lay sprawled where it had fallen, but all of the liquid from it had run together into a viscous pool. Before his horrified eyes this seemed to coagulate, congeal, and rise up into thin, reaching tentacles of translucent, pink-dripping water.

He slammed the door of the antechamber, smashed with the rod at a slimy brown worm which had somehow got through, rushed back into the inner room, and shut the door of that as well. The work table he dragged over as reinforcement. Eyíl huddled terrified in the corner.

He shouted, hoping that the little ducts that carried away the lamp smoke would bring his voice to those in the temple above. He knew even as he did so that this was useless. The place was as solid as a tomb.

He heard the outer door go. Then the inner door bulged inward as something ponderous thudded against it. A sheen of water seeped beneath, and a liquescent tentacle felt along the wall. Hársan seized one of the lamps, dashed its oil down upon the floor matting, and set it ablaze with the lamp wick. The tentacle withdrew. The door bulged in again, splintering and screeching.

The fire crackled along the doorsill, and for a moment there was silence. Eyíl stared at him with fear-wide eyes. Nothing moved. Then the door bowed in again with an explosive crack. Hársan held the table against it with all his strength, but his feet slipped backwards as inexorably as if he pitted himself against the rising of the sun.

The door gave at last. The ancient hinge plates screamed and then snapped off. The thick *Tíu*-wood panel crunched in against the table.

"Eyíl – help me! Help me hold the table!" Her strength would add but little, yet what else was there to do?

"Give them the relics, Hársan! The relics! That is what they seek – otherwise it is our lives!"

He flashed her a dark look. "How do you know what 'they' seek?"

"There is no time for that now. Believe only that this is no sending of mine! Give them what they desire or we are dead!"

Any reply was cut short. The top of the door leaned in, and then the whole panel was dragged backward out of its frame. The table, Hársan and Eyíl behind it, was sent skidding across the room.

They looked upon a creature of nightmare.

It was tall and manlike, but never had it been spawned by humankind. Rolls of mottled, pasty-white skin hung about its arms in doughy folds. The head was round, hairless, marked with blotches and nodules. Two huge, saucer-like eyes glared from beneath deep ridges of waxy-pale cartilage, and lappets of tissue hung down its cheeks like curtains of oily pudding. Instead of a nose, a greyish-white beak opened and closed in the middle of the thing's face, emitting a stench of nauseous decay.

"A *Thúnru'u*!" Eyíl squealed. "The servants of the Master of the Undead!"

The creature filled the doorway. Behind it was another being, smaller, manlike—

Helé'a of Ghatón!

Now the tendrils of the water-thing crept into the room again, past the smouldering matting on the floor. The creature Eyíl had named a *Thúnru'u* advanced silently upon creased, pudgy feet.

There could only be seconds left. Hársan never knew whether his next actions came from within himself or whether he was commanded by the powerful imperatives of the white sphere. All he knew was that the Man of Gold should never fall into the hands of those who sent forth such emissaries! His mind was icily clear, as happens sometimes in moments of mortal peril.

But was there time?

He strove to concentrate, to ignore the death that lumbered across the chamber. He had the metal rod in his hand. There, beneath a scattering of manuscript pages, was one half of the white sphere – and there on the floor by the table was the other half! He scrabbled for them. The rest of the relics he could not see. These were what mattered.

He shut his eyes, struggled for calm. And failed. A false start! He tried again –

– And reached "around the corner!"

The two halves of the sphere and the silvery rod flickered from sight.

Helé'a of Ghatón must have seen, for he cursed and shouted something in an unintelligible tongue. The *Thúnru'u* s thick, moist hands were upon Hársan, and his struggles were as nothing.

Pain shot through his wrists as the spongy fingers closed upon them. Helé'a was at the other side of the table, Eyíl writhing in his arms.

Two more entered the room. These were human, however, hard and efficient men in brown-lacquered mail of *Chlén*-hide.

"Get the relics," Helé'a panted.

One hurled the table aside. The other snatched up the golden hand and the map symbol, thrust handfuls of crackling manuscript pages into a cloth bag. He began to ransack the storage cabinet. "The rest?" Helé'a snapped at Hársan.

"Gone – where you shall never see them!" Hársan managed. The *Thúnru'u* began to bend him backward as a man bends a sapling.

"Lord –! Someone comes!" the first man cried.

"There is naught else here," the other said. The cabinet and the chest where they had kept their notes were empty, contents strewn upon the floor. The man had found the gems which Chtík p'Qwé had extracted from the first lump of rust. Now he tore open the packet left for Hársan by the Shén, exclaimed joyfully, and stuffed all into his belt-pouch.

"We must leave," Helé'a grated. "If my eyes served me aright, priestling, then I know what you have done with the other gewgaws. You shall suffer the more for that! Take them along!"

They were dragged out into the corridor and up the stairs. Near the top the body of the other guard, Réshmu, crouched in a shrivelled mass against the wall. Water still dripped from his gaping mouth. Helé'a hurried them on into one of the branching passageways that Hársan had never entered. They passed musty boxes of temple vestments, the wreck of an ancient palanquin, tall standards from which the *Khéshchal*-plumes had rotted away. At last they stopped before a broken section of wall. A black tunnel mouth yawned there, and fragments of stone lay all about, half dissolved in puddles of water as though melted into sand by the washing of the sea.

The ghastly water-creature stood there, looming almost manlike in the shadows.

Behind them came voices, racing footsteps, wildly dancing torchlight. Hársan had a glimpse of an ebon whirlwind of arms and legs: Chtík p'Qwé, closely followed by the priest Siyún and two of the guardsmen from the upper chamber.

Hársan cried out, and Eyíl screamed too. The Pé Chói drew up short, facing the two brown-mailed soldiers. The monstrous *Thúnru'u* did not pause but gathered Hársan up effortlessly and plunged forward into the dank, dripping tunnel. Helé'a followed with Eyíl. The two armoured men scrambled into the hole as well, the last holding his short, barb-edged sword back to menace the Pé Chói.

It profited him nothing. Chtík p'Qwé knocked the blade aside with one of his upper limbs, jerked it out of the man's grip with his lower pair of hands, and reached in with his other upper arm to drive chitinous claws into the warrior's face. Red splashed down over the brown armour.

Something glinted burnished gold in Helé'a's hand. He called, "Oh *Nshé*, One of Water! Flow into the stones and bring down the roof upon those who follow!"

There was a damp, sucking sound, and the water on the floor seemed to flow backward toward the tunnel entrance as the tide ebbs from a sandy shore.

Hársan still struggled in the *Thúnru'u*'s grasp and thus saw what happened next. Moist earth came slithering down into the tunnel. For a moment Chtík p'Qwé's arms waved wildly, and then the whole ceiling sagged. A torrent of mud and water and stones hid the Pé Chói from view, and all was dark.

Chapter Fourteen

Jutting teeth of sharp stone bit at Hársan's back and shoulders as the *Thúnru'u* wrestled him through the narrow tunnel. After a dozen paces the way opened out, and he sensed that they had entered a larger cavern. Their footsteps went echoing and racketing off i`nto invisible distances, and the shrill tinkle of dripping water came back to them from velvety silences.

Helé'a of Ghatón ordered a halt, gave Eyíl into the remaining soldier's keeping, and struck flint to tinder. Soon he had a length of waxed tow alight, and with this he lit a torch from a pile seemingly placed there for just this purpose. The crackling orange blaze revealed an immense hall. Ornately carved, monolithic columns rose above their heads to support the unseen ceiling and marched away into black vastnesses. The near wall, through which Helé'a's tunnel had been hacked, flowed and danced with graven gods, kings, and vertical blocks of twisting Engsvanyáli script. These inscriptions likely proclaimed the eternal power and glory of the long-dead lords of Éngsvan hla Gánga, the Golden Age that had succeeded the Priest Pavár and antedated the present Second Imperium of the Tlakotáni Emperors by fifteen thousand years or more.

Hársan jerked and wriggled in a sudden effort to escape, but the flabby paws of the *Thúnru'u* held him as easily as a smith holds a piece of rare iron in his tongs. Eyíl was conscious but dazed, limp in the soldier's arms.

Helé'a raised his torch and looked about. "Where is Shukkáino?"

The other man shrugged. "Dead, master, I guess. The Pé Chói slew him, and then the two of them were buried together when the *Nshé* brought down the roof."

"What of the bag?"

"I have it here. Shukkáino carried nothing."

"Let us see…" Helé'a rummaged through the cloth bag, making only a half-hearted attempt to avoid damaging the fragile manuscript leaves. He brought forth the rolled parchment that Hársan had taken from the dead hand of Kurruné the Messenger.

"What is this, priest Hársan?" he chuckled. "Another summons from the Emperor? Alas, no, just a clever couplet – this time taken from the 'Epic of Tháunü of Sokátis!' One must be a literary critic to keep up with this Kurruné. But then he could not very well commit all his warnings to paper, could he? I would guess that he was coming to give you more detailed admonitions himself when Lord Sárku's Worms of Death dropped upon him." He broke off and chortled. "Splendid! A warning indeed, but not against us! Rather a caution against certain others!" (Did the man's glance shift to Eyíl?) "How suitable! We'll leave this here for your grey-robes to find when they break through the wall. Then will they go galloping off in pursuit of the wrong prey!" He dropped the parchment to the floor and scuffed at it with his foot.

"Now," he continued, "if you are reasonable, young man, we shall have the other relics – and well I know where you have put them. Then we shall leave you and your naked lady to await the coming of the industrious priests of Thúmis, who are doubtless burrowing even now to find our trail."

Hársan knew better. Those who had not feared to violate the Temple of Eternal Knowing, breach the Concordat, and slaughter Imperial soldiers would hardly stick at two more lives.

He tried to temporise. "At least you can tell me why you have done this, Helé'a. Why the attempt upon me before, on the road – I was meant to die there, was I not? – and what does all this profit you tonight?"

Thin fingers came up to brush back sparse, greying hair and tug at an earlobe. "Alas, poor Metlúnish! Had you used my 'Unimpeachable Shield' upon him, your bones would now be decorating some peasant's field. But you fought well, young priest, and then that accursed merchant spitted him like a haunch of *Tsi'íl* with his crossbow bolt. You see, you should never have reached Béy Sü. I would then have had time to arrange for a different, more compatible scholar to study your Llyáni pothooks."

"But anyone could have access to the relics – any temple –?"

"Ohé, there are those who must *own* what they desire! My master is no simpleton to stand gawking and yearning for the fine tunics in the tailor-shop! He is a *Zrné* who charges straight upon his prey – if you will pardon a poor foreigner his mixed metaphors, which are such a sin in your Tsolyáni elocution…" He peered back into the tunnel. "Come, we cannot tarry here. Give me what you have concealed, and you shall have quit of us. – I can even sweeten your loss with a purse of gold heavy enough to buy three doxies as comely as this one here. Then you can return to your monastery and die an old man with a hundred grandchildren singing elegies to your sainted memory."

"I – I cannot. Slay me if you will." Hársan realised that he really did not desire this latter event and cast about for some means of staying alive, something the Ghatóni would believe. "I do not know how to bring the relics back from – from 'around the corner' where I sent them. They are too big, bigger than anything I ever magicked before."

The other pursed his lips in disgust. "Chá! Leave it to an untried bowstring to fire the war-arrow! I sense that you speak at least a part of the truth. There is nothing for it, then, but to take you along. My master'll have sorcerers who'll make you cough up those relics as easy as a baby pukes up its lunch." He turned to the warrior. "Give the girl over to me, Tluomé, and do you bind him neat and tight!"

The *Thúnru'u* held Hársan while the soldier produced a length of braided leather cord and secured his wrists tightly behind his back.

"The girl, master? Shall I do her off here?"

Helé'a flashed a swift glance at Hársan's stricken face. "I think not. She must go with us. If you slay her now our poor priest would grieve, and this would distract him from our purpose."

The man took Eyíl, wrapped her street-cloak tightly about her, and then wound more of the cord about her upper body so that her arms were pinioned to her sides. She made no protest but only averted her face.

Helé'a turned for a last look into the tunnel. He held up a gold-glinting disc, an amulet. "Oh *Nshé*," he called, "One of Water, return to your lair! My master will be grateful."

Was that the gurgling flow of the *Nshé* that Hársan heard, or was it the sound of distant digging in the tunnel? He tried again to delay. "At least tell me the why of this, Helé'a," he pleaded. "Let me understand!"

"So, the pawn must know why the game is played?" The Ghatóni struck off at a rapid pace across the murky, echoing hall, the *Thúnru'u* and the soldier propelling their captives along behind him. "Too high for you, too high! Do you play *Dén-den*? If you do, then know that you are only a white counter who has for the moment been promoted to a blue. Now greens and blacks appear on every side, each thrice as mighty as you!" He made a slashing gesture in the air. "Your player casts his throw – and loses! Chá! You are taken! – Now if you would give up those Llyáni relics, you return to being a simple white counter, and the proud greens and blacks pass you by. But no, you are all puffed up with your puny importance! So must you pay the score – or rather your player pays the wager, while you, poor pawn, are dashed from the board."

"My superiors laid a command upon me, and I cannot go against that." He knew this would mean nothing to Helé'a. "Now, even if I would, I cannot retrieve the accursed things!" This sounded convincing. Intuitively he realised that as long as the relics were beyond the Ghatóni's reach, he and Eyíl would continue to live.

The little man pursed his lips. "We shall see."

The great hall ended at last, and they entered a labyrinth of smaller rooms, galleries, passageways, staircases up and then down again, and wandering corridors. Some were embellished with the bas-reliefs and frescoes of the Golden Age, others were unadorned, and still others seemed hacked out of the living rock.

Helé'a raised his torch to consult a scrap of parchment. They clambered down a steep circular stair into a new series of vaults. Here the walls were incised with the dagger-sharp symbols of the Bednálljan monumental script, floor to ceiling, in endless horizontal bands. This part of the labyrinth was half a score millennia older than that above!

The little Ghatóni noted Hársan's involuntary interest and said sardonically, "If it be ancient things you would have, young scholar, you must join the Lords of Change. Only such as we have access here."

"I have read of such places."

"Then you will have read of *Ditlána*, the ritual of the 'Renewal of the Land Before the Faces of the Gods.' Every five hundred years or so, the ancients razed their cities, tore them down to the foundations, filled in the lower rooms, and built anew upon the old. There are layers and layers beneath the older cities of the Five Empires. Some parts are open; others are lost and sealed. Did your grey-robes never tell you why so many cities sit upon such high mounds?"

"I know of *Ditlána* – the last Seal Emperor to order it done in Béy Sü was Hejjéka IV, 'The Restorer of Dignities,' about eight hundred years ago. But I never guessed –"

The little man warmed to his topic. Hársan tried to push the horrors of the previous hour into some corner of his brain and lock them there. Any means of keeping Helé'a occupied would allow them to live a while longer.

"Some of the most sacred shrines of the Inner Circles of the temples are down here," the Ghatóni continued. "Age adds to sanctity. Many areas are filled with stones and rubble, of course; otherwise the new cities above would come tumbling down. And if you can find your way down to the lowest regions, you'll see whole sections that are tilted, torn asunder by earth-shakings, filled with ooze or black water, or are brimful of hardened flowing-stone, sent up by Vimúhla, Lord of Fire, from his incandescent hells beneath the world."

They turned a corner, and a muddy, wet smell assailed them. The torch guttered in a current of moist air. Helé'a sent the *Thúnru'u* lumbering ahead, and metal squealed. The captives were prodded forward again, and the party emerged through a barred grating of bronze onto a rickety quay, beyond which the velvet waters of the Missúma River glimmered before them in Káshi's reddish light. The place was deserted.

The *Thúnru'u* took charge of Hársan and Eyíl cuffing him lightly when he would have spoken to her. The other two dragged a small skiff out of the shadows and slid it over into the water.

Hársan again contemplated escape. His legs were free, even though his hands were bound behind him. If he could attract the attention of the River Watch, he could come back for Eyíl…The monstrous *Thúnru'u* seemed to divine his intentions and took that very moment to encircle his neck with its clammy fingers.

Someone returned from the boat. A black, fish-smelling cloak was thrown over Hársan's head, and a smart push sent him stumbling forward to tumble down into the little craft. Eyíl sprawled on top of him with a muffled cry. A foot found the small of his back and stayed there, pinning him flat. He heard the rattle of oars being run out. Thole-pins thumped home. Water gurgled and lapped up through the oily planking, and the boat heaved as a second person came aboard. There was a further exchange of muttered words, apparently Helé'a ordering the *Thúnru'u* back to its lair in the labyrinth.

For a time there was only the rhythmic *thump-swash* of the oars, mingled with a litany of muttered grunts and curses. The soldier was no boatman.

At last the hull grated against stone. Helé'a called out, and hands lifted Eyíl away. Others plucked Hársan up and carried him like a bale of cloth over echoing cobblestones. More conversation, and then a hollow metallic boom as a heavy gate bar shot back into its socket. Hársan was set roughly on his feet and half dragged, half pushed onward through what he sensed were hallways, down a stair, along another passage, into a room. He ended banging his shins upon a sharp-edged something.

The hands turned him about, raised him, and threw him down upon a hard, seamed surface. Wood? The cloak was jerked away, and his wrists were twisted painfully up to be affixed to a clanking metal link.

He lay on his side in semi-darkness. All he could see were the black silhouettes of men above him and chinks of red light from a lamp or a torch dancing upon armour. Booted feet shuffled away, and the shadows merged with the deeper blackness.

"Eyíl," he called, "Eyíl!"

But he was all alone.

Chapter Fifteen

Hársan squirmed about to make himself more comfortable. He found that he lay upon an ancient, rutted table or bed-frame of wooden beams. One torch guttered high up in a bracket on the wall to his left, and he made out the dim outline of a tunnel-like doorway there. The walls were of well-mortared masonry, the stones cut precisely and small in the style of the Emperors of a millennium ago. Above him the ceiling rose in a series of vaults and groinings into the smoky darkness. He caught the glint of metal up there, some sort of hoist, pulleys, chains…

A shiver went up his spine as he began to realise what sort of place this was.

He rolled over and saw another door to his right, studded with bronze bolt-heads, and closed now. By lifting his head and straining his arms, which were beginning to ache, he could see a third wall some three or four man-heights beyond his feet. An arched alcove had been let into the wall there, raised about two paces above the level of the chamber, and reached by a little stair. The alcove was perhaps a man-height tall and four or five paces in width. He craned his head around for a look at the wall behind him and succeeded in glimpsing something that almost turned his bowels to water: great beams, the glitter of metal, sharp implements ranged upon a shelf.

He thought furiously. On the eastern bank of the Missúma River there were few buildings: the vast complex of the Temple of Avánthe, that of Keténgku, a famous and ancient shrine to Sárku, Lord of Worms, and a few other, minor temples. There were no suburbs or palaces on that side of the river, for most of the area was reserved for the City of the Dead, where the Emperors of the past slept beneath their squat pyramids or the rounded, crumbling domes of the Bednálljan Dynasty. All around these crowded the myriad little mausoleums of the nobility and the shapeless mounds that hid the naked corpses of the poor. The only dwellings were the tenements of the embalmers, professional mourners, ferrymen, amulet-carvers, wreath-makers, prayer-writers, and the other clans connected with the necropolis and the world of the dead.

There were also the Tólek Kána Pits.

He had seen their blind, cold, fortress walls from a parapet of the Temple of Eternal Knowing: the dreaded Imperial prison, founded before the Empire had been united by the first Seal Emperor. These dungeons were built upon the site of ancient, swampy pits into which the criminals of old had been thrown to suffer the bites of noxious insects and vermin. In their fastnesses were housed those whom the Imperium decreed should be removed from society, but who were condemned to live – after a fashion – rather than to die upon the impaler's stake. There were filthy halls in which debtors prayed for some clan-relative to rescue them from the squalor and the disgrace; there were the barracks of the Legion of Kétl, those men in brown armour whose task it was to see that the will of the Imperium was done according to the laws of Tsolyánu; there, too, were pleasant apartments in which noble prisoners and political rivals dwelt until they were needed – or executed. There were also chambers such as that in which Hársan now found himself, buried beneath the earth where none might see, forever secret and silent concerning the fates of those whose Skeins of Destiny had been so tragically woven.

But why?

Why?

Whom did Helé'a serve? In this lay the answer.

Many knew of the accursed Llyáni relics: the Imperium, the temples, some of the clans, possibly certain foreign lands... Not only were there spies upon spies and factions within factions, he supposed, but every temple had its library and its archives, and these likely contained more knowledge about these matters than Hársan had himself. Helé'a's master could be no mere high priest or aristocratic intriguer, however, to be able to violate temples and command the use of one of the Empire's most dreaded prisons! All he could say with certainty was that his present captors were allied with the Lords of Change and that they made use of the half-legendary creatures of the underworld below Béy Sü as easily as a peasant drives his *Chlén*-beast.

He forced himself to lay this unanswerable riddle aside and turn his thoughts to Eyíl. It was now plain what she was about. It was possible for a good clan-girl to fall in love with a clanless priest of no rank or status, of course, but anything more than a brief dalliance was as unlikely as three moons in the sky! Oh, the interlude on the *Sákbe*-road was natural enough: the proper mixture of youth, naïveté, proximity, and physical pleasure. But for Eyíl to have sought him out later – when Béy Su was full to overflowing with handsome, wealthy, sophisticated young men of her own class…?

No, she was almost certainly an agent of somebody or other. There had been hints aplenty, but his subconscious mind had done its best to hide them from him. Now he was sure. Her plea to give the relics to "them" was more than sufficient. He cursed himself for a fool.

But did she then serve Helé'a or his unknown master? Did she stand now outside this room and laugh with the Ghatóni about poor Hársan, the dupe? This picture brought the bitterness of masculine pride up into his throat.

No. The more he considered it, the more he believed her visible fear and horror to be real. He decided that Eyíl was no friend of Helé'a's.

Then was she an ally of Kurruné the Messenger?

Possibly. But then why did the man couch his warnings in such veiled and literary terms? Had he worked in collusion with Eyíl, he could have employed her to take his warnings directly to Hársan.

Who was Kurruné? An agent for the Temple of Thúmis, for Prior Haringgáshte personally, for some other faction – even for the Imperium? A servant of two – or more – masters might well wish to conceal his identity with ciphers and quotations from the epics that could be understood only by the person concerned…

There were no clear answers. Whatever the truth, it was still possible that the Messenger and Eyíl had been allies. After all, it might be useful to maintain a double watch: Kurruné to serve as an outside source of information, Eyíl to hold Hársan with the age-old lure of her body? He would thus be unguarded with her, easy to control.

Somehow this rang false, as a copper coin in a handful of silver *Hlásh*. He could not think why.

Had Eyíl been set over him by his own temple to see that he did not fall prey to the blandishments of such as Keréktu hiKhánmu?

This, too, was possible, but a little far-fetched. Had a maiden been wanted to ensnare him, his superiors could have assigned any pretty acolyte from the Monastery of the Sapient Eye – or from the Temple of Eternal Knowing once he had reached Béy Sü. No, such surveillance was probably the duty of the Pé Chói – Hársan was struck with a sudden stab of remorse; he had not taken even a moment to grieve for his poor friend! – It was likely that Chtík p'Qwé had been commanded to watch over him, while he, in turn, could be counted upon to report any untoward actions of the Pé Chói to his superiors. Why else bring in someone who knew not only Llyáni but also the language and customs of the Pé Chói?

The problem went round and round in his head, like a *Chlén* upon the threshing floor. Eyíl was almost certainly an agent. But not for either Helé'a nor for the Temple of Thúmis. Keréktu hiKhánmu? He could see no connection at present between the glib priest of Ksárul and Eyíl…

He tried to think impersonally of Eyíl, as he had been taught in the logic classes of the monastery. He had a hard time blotting out memories of her, nude and lithe in the lamplight, her long, dark eyes looking up into his in the litter, the shadowy curve of her hip as she lay beside him… Chá!

He tried again. Look at her actions, he ordered himself: her ignorance of some of the basic doctrines of Lady Avánthe, her arguments which seemed ever so slightly contemptuous of Stability. Then there was her mention of Shu'uré and the supposed *Aridáni* woman who worshipped Dlamélish. Clues came clicking together like *Den-den* counters into their box!

Eyíl must serve either Dlamélish or Hriháyal!

But if this theory were true, then it meant that the temples of Change were split over the matter of the relics – or that there were factions within them, at least, which seesawed this way and that against one another.

What of the girl in the governor's garden – Sríya? She had been a devotee of Hriháyal, had she not? Eyíl had certainly not sent her to poison him with *Zu'úr*; she could have done that herself at any time. Did this imply that Eyíl was *not* on Hriháyal's side? Or did it indicate dissension between the Temple of Hriháyal and some other faction, possibly the Temple of Dlamélish? – Or was that incident no more than a coincidence?

He sighed. Wheels within wheels, tunnels within tunnels, as the old proverb about the *Shqá*-beetle said…

He vowed that he would deal with the Lady Eyíl hiVriyén if ever he got the chance.

Ruddy torchlight blazed through the door to his left. Men entered, bearing objects of dull yellow metal; others behind carried lumpy bundles of some sort; still others followed with parchments and penboxes. He squirmed up to a sitting position and saw the metallic things to be ewers, cups, and dishes. The bundles were large, rich cushions.

By all of the Aspects of Thúmis, was this going to be a feast with Hársan himself as the main course?

Some of the men inserted torches into brackets around the walls. Others climbed the little stair and arranged the utensils and cushions upon a low dais which he now saw occupied the centre of the alcove. The scribes spread out their paraphernalia on the floor below and sat down, muttering and joking in low tones.

The door to his right opened, and two men stood there. One was a greybeard, long-faced, and not a little unkempt. Whitish hair straggled down over his shoulders from beneath a dun-coloured skullcap which resembled an unfired clay bowl overturned upon his head. He wore the floor-length brown vestments of a lay-priest of Sárku, shabby and stained with use, and cut in a fashion popular amongst elderly men some twenty years before.

The other person was a decade or so younger, barrel-bellied, dressed in a saffron kilt ornamented with many little dags, fringes, and clan symbols worked in gold thread, and pleated in the style of a bureaucrat of the Palace of the Realm. A shawl of fine yellow cloth swathed one shoulder, and Hársan caught the glint of a circular golden pendant upon his breast. It was a replica of the Seal of the Imperium.

This second man stepped forward and leaned over Hársan. He brushed absently at a lick of greying hair which partially hid his balding pate and unfolded a document. He smelled strongly of flowery *Purú*-oil.

"You are Hársan, priest of the Second Circle, of the Temple of Thúmis? What is your lineage, please? You are Hársan *hi*-what?"

"I have no lineage name," Hársan muttered. "Who are you? Why –?"

A delicate hand emerged from the yellow shawl, palm down, two fingers extended, to show that no interruption would be brooked. "Then we must put you down as Hársan hiShahád – 'Hársan of Slave-Lineage.'"

"I am no slave!" Hársan cried. "My parents are unknown, but –"

Small, pouched eyes blinked at him. "'Two streams that join to one another become the same.'" A pen scratched upon parchment.

"Why am I here? You know that I am a priest of the Temple of Thúmis. I was seized illegally, dragged here with a lady, my comrade…"

Another blink. "Legality is my concern indeed. I am Arkháne hiPurúshqe, of the Clan of Sea Blue. The Petal Throne has honoured me with the post of Master of the Tólek Kána Pits. All that matters to me is legality, and what I seek now is to establish whether you are that Hársan whom this writ names."

"Writ? How can there be a writ? We were abducted from our rightful business – my temple was violated – Imperial soldiers were murdered – illegal –!" He struggled to get his thoughts together.

"Illegal? Not at all. Such a misconception shall shortly be dissipated, and you shall be satisfied that all is as it should be, in perfect order."

Hársan could only make a strangled sound in his throat.

The other did not smile, but little crinkles of kindly humour appeared at the corners of his eyes. "Ohé, I dabble not in politics! What is done is no affair of mine, any more than it is yours to orchestrate the courses of the moons. No, I only serve here, young man. Those who come to me are treated precisely as their writs command. If it be ordered that a man may have his family about him, then so it is done: there are those here whose children and grandchildren were born within their cells, and whole families that have not seen the light of day for three generations. On the other hand, if it be decreed that another is to have flowerpots and bolsters and fine viands, then do I provide these things most amply. And if a third person is remanded to the impaling stake to dance his last jig, then this is what is written in his Skein of Destiny. My ancestors have served here in this capacity through many reigns and a multitude of changes, and always have we performed our duties with acuity and circumspection. No, your rights shall not be violated here, young man, and you shall receive whatever honours and dignities are enjoined for you – or else suffer such other treatments as may be commanded."

Hársan bit his tongue in sheer frustration. "At least tell me why I am here! What does this writ say? Who has signed it?"

"It was signed by myself, priest Hársan."

Hársan wrenched himself around to see that the dais was now occupied. A figure in the brown robes and cowl of an Adept of the Temple of Sárku sat there.

"At this time I pray to be excused, mighty one." Arkháne hiPurúshqe bowed low.

"Your task is done. Stay or go as you will." The voice was soft and colourless, with no rise or fall of intonation.

The figure arose, and Hársan saw the skull-painted face of the man for the first time: features like a slab of dry and weathered wood in which two marbles of black glass had been set for eyes. The near-lipless mouth moved as though it had no connection with those terrible, empty orbs.

"Where is Helé'a? Let him be brought to us." A guard sketched a bow and hurried out.

"Who – who are you?"

"Silence!" The old man who had entered with the Master of the Pits spoke for the first time. "You address a Prince of the Imperium incorrectly."

"A Prince –!" Hársan choked. He tried again, employing the highest pronoun he had ever learned, the "You of Supernal Omnipotence."

"Mighty Prince, I – I knew you not."

"Your usage is still erroneous, priest. You do not address my father upon the Petal Throne in Avanthár. The appropriate pronoun for my rank is *Tòquntúsmidàlisa*, the 'You of Awed Wonder.'"

"I pray you –"

"Pray if you will. We are not immune to prayer, particularly if it be accompanied by the proper offerings. In this we humbly ape the almighty Gods." The lips did not smile, but the cowled head turned from side to side as if seeking the approbation of those who sat below the dais. No one laughed.

"Loose his bonds somewhat, Vridékka. I am not accustomed to discourse with the soles of a man's feet. Let him sit up."

Spidery fingers plucked at the knots behind his back, the metal link clattered, and Hársan found that he could now rub life back into his numbed hands, although they remained bound behind him.

"I am Dhich'uné, fourth Prince of the Imperium, priest. I am told that you possess certain items which are rightfully mine." The lips opened to reveal brown, chipped teeth, like shards of chert. "Just now you mentioned illegality to our useful Lord Arkháne. If you have studied anything of our laws, you know that all right and authority over every being and every thing within the Empire is vested in the Omniscient Emperor. From him do these prerogatives descend to us, his offspring, and thence to the proper agencies of our Imperial government."

"Great Prince – Lord – no one can question this. But I understood the Temple of Thúmis to have custody of the Llyáni relics, and all the temples were to study them there. Soldiers were set to see that this was done. Yet those soldiers were slain, Lord, and I – we – were kidnapped!"

"Lives, property, all within Tsolyánu belong to the Seal Emperor. If a peasant owns a *Hmélu*-beast, is it not his to slaughter whenever he requires its meat? Must he hold discourse with the animal like an advocate before he applies the knife?"

"No – I mean, of course not, my Lord. But could not a command have been given to our temple to relinquish the relics into your custody without murder, without –?"

"There are reasons why that was not done." A brown-swathed arm came up. "This discussion is at an end, young man. Now will I have those objects which you have concealed."

The old man whom the Prince had named Vridékka approached the dais.

"Great and powerful Prince, may I speak? I have used my talent of mind-seeing, as you desired, and I –"

"Come nigh, Vridékka, and tell me." The dark cowl bent down, and the greybeard whispered and gestured. The skull-face turned to Hársan again.

"My mind-seer, Vridékka, informs me that the artifacts are there, just 'around the corner,' as you think of it. Your motives in this affair are commendable – and common to many young men. To you this is still a sort of game, a comradely loyalty to your temple, a proscription against being a 'traitor' to your superiors, and an innocent adherence to what you conceive to be your faith. All of these things are naught but adolescent romanticism. This is no basket of *Dlél*-fruit to be concealed by a gang of temple acolytes from the dormitory-master!"

Helé'a had entered the room. He bowed before the dais and said, "My Lord Prince, the priest says that he is unable to bring the relics back – that they are too large for his elementary magical skills."

Prince Dhich'uné waved him back. "He lies, Helé'a. He can get them for us. Vridékka has seen into his mind."

"Shall we then progress to further ministrations?"

"If need be. First, however, good Vridékka shall make another attempt, deeper this time."

The seamed face of the old man swam before Hársan's vision. Two tangled curtains of grey hair swung out on either side of the jutting chin. What was the creature about to do to him? Hársan felt a slight dizziness.

Now there was no one above him! Surprised, Hársan peered this way and that. Vridékka was at the dais holding something up to Prince Dhich'uné in a fold of his robe. It was the white metal globe, smoking with frigid cold. How had that happened so quickly?

"This is what was immediately within, mighty Prince," Vridékka was saying, "two halves of a Globe of Instruction."

"The message within the Globe?"

"Gone, my Lord. It is blank. Someone has used it."

The Prince gave a muttered curse. "The priest?"

"Possibly. Nay, probably. I could not penetrate his mind to any great depth. It is as though a seal has been laid upon certain regions of his brain."

"Then?"

The old man mumbled again in the Prince's ear. The latter arose and descended from the dais, coming to stand beside the table upon which Hársan sat.

"Our conversation grows prolonged, priest. You still possess something that belongs to me. More, the important matter is not physical –" the two halves of the metal sphere were held before him "– but rather the information these once contained. I will have it of you."

"My Lord – mighty Prince, I – I cannot." Somehow he could not bring his tongue to say otherwise. And a secret part of him rejoiced that the silvery-blue rod still seemed to be safe within, somewhere "around the corner."

"I tire of your obduracy. Is this what is taught now in the Temple of Thúmis? If so, I will have it purged of heresy and treason! Know that I am your superior, more than ever was your lowly Prior, or even the Lord Dúrugen hiNáshomai, or the Grand Adept Gámulu himself." He drew back and seemed to sigh, the passionless voice dropping to a whisper. "Let me tell you, then, why I do as I do. Mayhap it will save us all time, and you much pain.

"Know that the Yán Koryáni are arrayed against us along our northern borders. You have heard of this in the city? Yet there are few to block their path. Those who should act are weak or vacillating. My older brother, Prince Eselné, plays at generalship, but he kicks his heels to the tune of General Kéttukal hiMráktine, who commands the First Legion, and who in turn dances for the traditionalists of the Military Party: men who can drill their troops upon the parade ground or fight a simple battle, but who have no more notion of high strategy than does a *Chlén*-beast of the Gods.

"The others? My eldest brother, Prince Rereshqála, feasts and diddles his whores in Jakálla, and Prince Mridóbu, who is next above me in age, sings songs of praise to our father in Avanthár. He cares for nothing so much as popping a toady of his into some rich Imperial post, and popping the toadies of others out. And my sister, pretty Ma'ín Krüthái? She holds court with dandies and foreigners in the governor's palace here in Béy Sü. They say that she has left the worship of placid Avánthe and has adopted the hedonism and bodily pleasures of Lady Dlamélish, a change that improves her not a whit were she to become our next Empress, may the Gods forfend!

"At this moment these are all of my siblings. Yet, as well you are aware, it is the custom of our land for an Emperor to conceal some of his offspring, to hand them over secretly through the Omnipotent Azure Legion to be brought up by important patrons: to the highest clans, the temples, even to lesser fosterings. The present situation may thus be changed in a trice. Some misguided clan or temple council may bring forth another princeling to add to my woes, and with the Yán Koryáni in the north and the Mu'ugalavyáni mouthing threats to the west –! It is now that I must act."

"The temples, mighty Prince – the good of the Imperium –?"

"The priesthoods? They are crusted over with immoveable tradition, precedent, and protocol – even those of my own sect. By the time all of these fools have been neutralised or replaced, the Baron Áld of Yán Kór will be having supper in Khirgár! For I tell you one more thing, priest Hársan, and that is that any war to come will be fought with more than swords and spears! We have learned that Baron Áld sends a great black box, nigh as large as this chamber and drawn by many teams of Chlén-beasts, down the road toward the city of Hlíkku. Our agents tell us that he calls it his 'Weapon Without Answer,' and that it holds powers of destruction greater than any army of men or any Sákbe-road wall can withstand. To obtain this device, our people tell us further, the Baron has made a compact with some secret force of the ancients. If we are to combat this deadly thing, we must seek sorcerous machines of our own. My sources further tell me that your Man of Gold – oh, yes, I know something of what your relics speak – is just such an instrument. All I ask is that you give over the knowledge you have to them who have the need and the skill and the courage to use it."

Every word struck Hársan as logical and reasonable. Prince Dhich'uné was supported by law, custom, and the traditions of authority drummed into every Tsolyáni child as soon as it was old enough to speak. This was also plainly beyond the ken of a simple priest. "Let those fly who have the plumage," as his Pé Chói tutors used to say.

He opened his mouth to speak, to tell all he knew of the Man of Gold, where it lay, how it was to be employed, what the silvery rod did. But something sealed his lips as tightly as though they belonged to a dead man! Did the orders of his superiors still constrain him? He did not think so any more. Why, then, could he not reveal what he possessed?

He strove to speak again but his tongue refused to move. How could this be? Was it the terrifying nature of this strange, emotionless man and the dark emissaries who served him? The violence and callous political pragmatism that the Prince evinced? All legal right was vested in Prince Dhich'uné, whatever the arguments of other factions or sects. Who was he, Hársan *hiShahád* "of Slave-Lineage"– to refuse? By all the Gods…

No words would come. Had he been magicked all unawares by those in the Temple of Eternal Knowing? Or was there some injunction inherent within the thing the Prince had named a Globe of Instruction itself?

Prince Dhich'uné was speaking again. "I can give you little time to plot your course, priest Hársan. You are still perhaps under the thrall of the hoary rivalry between your Lords of Stability and mine of Change? There is more at stake here than that!" The skull-face again approached Hársan's own. "I regret dealing with you so roughly, young man, but I am used to playing with opponents who can match me wager for wager and throw for throw – not against those who must pit their poor copper against my gold! If I have taken stringent measures, it is because I play to win. This game is no pastime from which we can all arise yawning and go off happily to our beds."

"Mighty Prince –"

"You would consider my arguments? You shall have the chance, though it must be brief. – Vridékka, remove his bonds, give him water or wine, food if he desires it, and the freedom of this chamber. We return later."

One more thought struck Hársan, and this his tongue uttered easily: "What of my companion, the Lady Eyíl hiVriyén?"

The pale, wooden features turned back to him. "Why, it is she whom I now go to visit."

The Prince's entourage swept from the room, and Hársan was left alone to ponder.

Chapter Sixteen

The racking screech of the metal door brought Eyíl to her feet. She thrust herself back against the rough stone of the wall of the cell. The braided leather cord had been removed, and she had been left her street-cloak. This she wrapped more tightly around her.

Two guards with torches ranged themselves on either side of the door and made way for a third man to enter. The smoky glare made her squint, but she recognised him at once and knelt before him upon the flagging, as was proper to a Prince of the Imperium.

"Mighty Prin`ce Dhich'uné…"

"Stand up, girl. This is no court ceremonial. You are the Lady Eyíl hiVriyén, of the Green Kirtle Clan of Tumíssa, priestess of the Fourth Circle of the Temple of Hriháyal. Why so surprised? My people uncovered hints of your Temple's plans, and thus my faithful Helé'a had some discourse with your maid servant Tsátla whilst you were on the road. Helé'a's net swept you up along with the other fish, unfortunately for you."

"Hársan? Where is he?"

"Presently well, having a cup of wine, and considering my eminently logical postulations, as should any good priest of the Lord of Wisdom. You shall see him soon. If all goes as I propose, neither of you will come to any harm."

She said nothing. Prince Dhich'uné took a turn around the little cell, affecting to inspect the walls, the filthy granite water basin set in the corner, the green-corroded water pipe, the bronze fittings of the door.

At length he said, "I hope that you have not been too discomfited by all of this. A sister-priestess of the Lords of Change should not suffer unduly at my hands."

Again Eyíl made no answer.

"So, then." He turned back to her, and she saw that he had the two halves of the white metal sphere in one hand. "You see, Lady, the race is over. The Globe is mine. Your High Priestess, the Lady Misénla hiQúrrodu, must now abandon her excursions into Imperial politics and go back to gulling fat old degenerates out of their gold. – Or return to my brother, Prince Eselné, and dream her dreams of becoming an Imperial Consort in the Golden Tower."

"Mighty Prince, I know nothing of this." She clutched her cloak to her in an instinctive, defensive gesture.

"Dissemble with me at your peril, priestess! My servant –" he gestured at a stooped, elderly man who stood peering in at her through the open doorway, "– tells me that you are no lover – in any sense of the term – of the Lady Misénla. You cling to the more moderate faction of your temple and are no member of her Clan of the Emerald and Silver Crown. She could not have known that when she commanded that a clever and resourceful woman be sent from Tumíssa to join this priest Hársan on the road and dazzle him into giving up his secrets! It is from this that your Skein begins to unravel: though Misénla does not work with me in this venture, yet we had warned her to keep her people far from the Temple of Eternal Knowing this night! Were you close in her councils, she would have told you. But she trusts you not, Lady. Ill luck for you!"

"A priest of Lord Ksarul – Keréktu hiKhánmu – met me in the street earlier – when I entered the Temple of Eternal Knowing in search of Hársan. He hinted that something was afoot. I – I ignored him."

"You should have listened. He is an ally of ours – a member of the Black Robes' secret Ndálu Clan, the faction of their faith that seeks political action and is hence closest to my own. We had warned them as well."

She rubbed a dirt-smudged hand across her cheek in puzzlement. "Mighty Prince, how – how do you know so much about my – loyalties?" She peered past him at the old man. "Ah. He –?"

"Aí, Vridékka. He sees into your mind." The thin lips split in an imitation of a smile. "Under these conditions it is impossible for one of your Circle to block him out. He spears your thoughts as easily as a Ghatóni spears fish. His skills are invaluable here in the Tólek Kána Pits, for else we should waste much time in prodding it all out of you with less pleasant methods."

Eyíl let her shoulders droop, most prettily she hoped. "What would you of me, mighty Prince?"

He resumed his restless pacing. "I shall be frank with you, girl, for time is short. Vridékka informs me that this Globe of Instruction contained not only information about a – a device of the ancients, but also a powerful spell, a Mind-Bar. Do you know what that is?"

She nodded mutely.

"Your Hársan does not know it himself, but he can no more tell me where this instrument is than he can swallow Thénu Thendráya Peak! Were every torment in the Five Empires to be applied to him, he would still remain as dumb as a *Káo*-squash. He cannot reveal what he knows – at least not to those whom he intuitively identifies as foes. The ancients wrought so skilfully that they have cost us both time and possibly certain counters but not yet the game."

"Then how will you overcome this thing?"

"You have been told what we seek? The Man of Gold?" He shot her a glance and nodded sardonically at the expression upon her face. "At least your superiors have enlightened you to that extent! If we cannot wriggle our way past this Mind-Bar, then the Man of Gold remains as safe in its hiding place as is my father in his Golden Tower at Avanthár."

Eyíl would have answered with yet another question, but the old man gave an apologetic cough. Prince Dhich'uné went to confer with him in tones too low for her hearing. After a moment the bone-white features turned back to her.

"I have further disquieting news for you, girl. Your petty priestling suspects your allegiance and your affections. Vridékka has also seen this in his mind. Your masquerade was not as perfect as you had imagined. Yet I believe that my original stratagem will work, notwithstanding. You see, I know you to be unsure, irresolute in your feelings – though you may not admit as much even to yourself. You do care for this Hársan, more than your superiors would wish, and likely more than you desire in your own mind. You are not immune to him any more than he is to you. Indeed, were it not for your training – and your passion for those fripperies which no lowly priest of Thúmis could ever buy you – you would mayhap be content to wander off and raise his dull brats on a farm somewhere. Eh, girl?"

She could not deny the gaze of those black marble eyes. She lowered her head and let her black tresses fall about her face. She did not push them away again.

"You are here, and you must choose. Will you swim with me, or will you sink with your emerald and purple Goddess?"

"I can never do Hársan ill, mighty Prince. Your mind-seer has already seen it in my heart."

"Join me in this, and he comes to none. Decide."

"What must I do, my Lord?"

"We have two arrows for our target, Lady. Vridékka claims that though this Mind-Bar prevents speech, it may not hinder actions – particularly those that are strongly willed and desired. While he may not be able to speak of the Man of Gold or even draw us a map of its location, he can assuredly be got to guide us to it and demonstrate its workings. The encouragement to do so will be potent enough, I think."

"And – I am to provide the – this motivation?"

"You have seen it, priestess. The most ancient and obvious measures will be attempted first. You shall appeal to his romanticism, his protectiveness, and his masculinity. These ideals have plagued humankind since before the Gods walked upon Tékumel, and well do you know how to compose pretty melodies with them! His affection for you will overcome all else, and he will guide us to the Man of Gold as prettily as the golden *Sahulén*-bird leads the hunters back to her nest."

"But if he has recognised me for – what I am – then what hold have I upon him? You say that Hársan must have a strong and conscious desire to guide you to the Man of Gold? Of what use, then, am I? He will turn his face away from me."

"Unlikely. He is young and sees himself as gallant. He is steeped in the chivalry of the epics; he yearns for the highminded demeanour of the ancient heroes. No, he will not fail you, girl. We have only to display you to him in what appears to be deadly peril, and he will jump to lead us to his precious relics. It will be hard even for the ancients' dusty Mind-Bar to compete with the hotblooded heroism of youth!"

"Still, if he refuses? The spells of the old ones are mighty…"

"We have not shot our second arrow as yet. There are ways and ways, my Lady. While he is bemused by your apparent plight, Vridékka here will again stab like a dagger into his mind. He will be distracted, and that in itself may be enough to penetrate the spell. Once we discover where the thing lies, we shall take you both there and see to it that he continues to have the will – nay, the heartfelt determination – to expound the secrets of the device."

"You – you speak of my apparent plight, mighty Prince. You will not –"

"Hurt you? Not unless I must. I am no slippery-eyed, wet-lipped pervert to take pleasure in the shrieks of little boys and slavegirls in the privacy of my bedchamber!" The strange eyes seemed to look right through her. "I do what I must to gain my goals and no more. The Lord of Worms cares nothing for the pleasures of this world, nor do we who serve him yearn for the paradises of the Gods. Rather do we prefer existence here, in this universe: life everlasting in the reality that lies in and beyond the tomb."

"But is not Lord Sárku the Master of the Undead?"

"Naively put, but true. We who follow Him seek to remain here, forever, in all our consciousness and powers. There is then no difference between this state of life and that of death. If you call existence beyond the end of life 'Undead,' then so be it. Its real meaning is the survival of the mind, the will, the personality. We of the faith of Lord Sárku prefer no journeys into the unknown Planes that lie beyond this one – no voyages to the Isles of the Excellent Dead, there to be shunted into paradise or hell at the whim of some unfathomable God! We would stay here, alive and conscious, upon this Plane. The grave may be an end for most, but for us it is only the beginning of true existence."

She thrust her fingers into her long tresses to press her temples. "Oh, my Lord Prince, you confuse me. The grave is dark and ugly – fearsome –!"

"Fearsome? Why? It is only another stage of being. There is no road that does not lead to the grave, girl! There is no story that has a happy ending. Let the singers chant the deeds of heroes; let Avánthe's followers prate of survival through one's children and the generations to come; let those of your persuasion forget the future and tumble together upon their couches of pleasure; let the priesthoods of Stability preach of light and purity and the joys of the Isles of the Excellent Dead! Nothing avails. Death is all. Life is fleeting, but death is eternal!" The horrible skull-mask leaned close to her. "Yet death can be made sweet; it can be made into life – of a most satisfactory sort – a life that can be prolonged, lengthened, made to last as long as the will exists."

"Oh yes, I know." Eyíl could not help herself. "But at the cost of joy – the death of pleasure – the end of delight." She shook her hair back from her face. "If these things be lacking, mighty Prince, then you speak not of life but of a travesty –!"

"Your teachers have taught you your catechisms well, girl. A travesty? Not so! What is life, after all, but the ability to retain one's intellect, to be conscious, to will, to act? Ohé, but you must think it through, little priestess! Consider that you, too, will dance for but a few short years more. Then your loveliness will fade, men will avert their eyes from your wrinkles, and in the end you will come back to Him – back to the Worm, as must all do who wear this shell of flesh. Are you wise in sacrificing eternity for those organs which you treasure there between your legs? Dead indeed will you be – and so forevermore – whilst I shall live and rule and go on to see generation upon generation of you transitory little creatures pass away before me into the dust! The lifetime of a summer moth instead of the eternal perpetuation of the intellect? A poor trade, girl! I have made sacrifices – terrible sacrifices – and I shall continue to make them, for the game is well worth the throw!"

He stood so close to her that she breathed in the cold, musty scent of his flesh. She drew away until the dank stones of the wall pressed into her back.

"I cannot believe – I can never agree that such an empty and passionless existence is to be desired!"

"Little I care for your desires, priestess!" He slashed the air with one corpse-painted hand. "Now I shall tell you precisely what you are to do. Cry out to your Hársan, cozen him, play upon his heart! He will respond. Even though he knows you false a thousand times over, yet he will surrender. His body calls out to you, just as yours does to him. No, he will not refuse you, Lady Eyíl."

"And if he guides you to this Man of Gold? You will slay him – us?"

"Did I not say that I gain no pleasure from harming small things? No, I shall command Vridékka to blur his mind for a time, so that he may not recall aught of this. Then I will see him placed in some rural temple, far away, where he can follow his own little Skein of Destiny. You may accompany him there, if you desire it." The hollow black eyes bored into her. "But mayhap your love of ease and pleasure is too strong? In that case you may return to your temple. I shall see that you do not go empty-handed, for I wish no lasting quarrel with your Lady Misénla. She will be pleased at your success in bedazzling the priest. Ohé, she will forgive you for your lack of zeal in her cause – take you into her Clan of Emerald and Silver, promote you, whatever you wish. And why? Because I shall give you certain real secrets to lay into her hands: things of interest, yes, but not the Man of Gold." He watched her carefully: her unconsciously artful pose, the loose tresses that swung beside the curve of her cheek, her long, wary, clever eyes. "You can then go on in your practice of the Thirty-Two Unspeakable Acts of your Goddess until you are too old to care – or until you achieve the final orgasmic self-immolation of the Thirty-Second Act itself! Your future will be assured until at last you go to join your ephemeral comrades in the tomb. Then indeed will it be too late to remember my words…"

"And if I refuse to join you in this thing? If I remain loyal to Hársan?"

"You know your own body better than that, Lady Eyíl."

"Then if I remain devoted to my temple?" she cried. "You must know, my Lord, that I serve my Goddess – in my way, if not in Lady Misénla's – just as you are obedient to your cold and undead master!"

A hand like that of a corpse smeared with oily clay came up to touch her chin, and she shrank away. "Then your pain will be real, girl, and my plan will progress all the same. As you see, it revolves around Hársan and not really about you. If you thwart me, then know that afterwards, when the Man of Gold is mine, the last embrace you will feel will be that of the impalers of the Legion of Kétl, and your final orgasm will be kicked out on high, there above the battlements of this place. Fail me not, my Lady."

She bowed her head and wept. "I shall do as you command."

Chapter Seventeen

Hársan sat upon the cold wooden table where they had left him. He had gladly drunk the wine the guards had brought, but he had refused the food. Now he must decide.

What was he to do?

What, indeed? He suspected that he could not resist for long against the forces Prince Dhich'uné could bring against him: "The leaf cannot swim against the current." So Zarén's old adage said.

He thought about pain. He had faced nothing more dreadful than Prior Haringgashte's "leather rosary" and the sudden wounding he had suffered there on the *Sákbe*-road. He had never so much as broken a bone, and when some years back he had had a painful tooth pulled, Zarén stuffed him with so much *Airá*-grass paste that he had no memory of the operation at all – nor of the day after! How would he withstand the blandishments of the Legion of Kétl?

Something within him told him that he could. He sensed a deep reservoir of en-durance somewhere inside himself, though he could not imagine why or whence it came.

But there was Vridékka. He was Prince Dhich'uné's real weapon. Hársan had heard of such as Vridékka: men whose skills were so valuable that they were paid fortunes – and were kept virtual prisoners by their masters, the lords of the Five Empires; men who could cast up defensive shields of magical substance, who could see through stone walls, who could defend their employers with bolts of ravening energy drawn from the Planes Beyond. Yes, Vridékka would catch him out in any lie, probe through any web of subterfuge, and pick his brain as clean as a pauper's plate!

What point, then in delaying or resisting at all?

Was it possible that the Temple of Thúmis could aid him? They would certainly have bored through the collapsed tunnel by now and discovered the body of Helé'a's henchman. The man had worn brown armour – perhaps that of the Legion of Kétl and was hence identifiable. (A thought intruded itself: poor Chtík p'Qwé!) His superiors would know the means of Kurruné's ghastly demise and of the deaths of the two soldiers.

But were these things traceable to the Temple of Sárku? It seemed that servants of the other Lords of Change had access to the labyrinths – and commerce with the strange creatures who dwelt there as well. The Temple of Ksárul, for example, was famed for its command of the darker mysteries. Some suspicion would thus fall upon Keréktu hiKhánmu. Or upon the velvet-masked priest of Wurú. Hársan liked neither of them, and he wished them no better than they deserved; yet in this affair they both appeared guiltless.

There were probably further clues that Hársan had overlooked, but even if these led to Lord Sárku as blatantly as a *Sákbe*-road leads to a city gate, how would his superiors know of the machinations of this Skull-Prince?

He suspected that very few within the hierarchy of the Lord Sárku, Master of Worms, would be aware of what had transpired tonight either.

There was still another pebble in the porridge. Suppose that the priests of Thúmis made all the right deductions; there was still that accursed message which Kurruné had had in his hand. Had not Helé'a said that it pointed toward some other player in this ugly game? Who?

He resolutely refused to think of Eyíl.

What, then, was to be gained through resistance? A little time, not enough to be of use. Hársan almost groaned aloud. All of his being cried out against meek surrender to this arrogant, white-painted Prince of demons and bones! Nevertheless, Hársan's training in priestly logic led him through the maze to the one inescapable conclusion: there was nothing to be had, in the end, by refusing Dhich'uné's demands. Between Vridékka and the Legion of Kétl, they would squeeze it all out of him as the vintners pressed *Másh*-fruit to make brandy.

His thoughts went round again to Prince Dhich'uné's arguments. A Prince of the Empire could clearly claim legal jurisdiction over the artifacts. He could be overruled, of course, by orders from Avanthár. But, in the name of Belkhánu's Seventh Isle, how long would THAT take? Even if the priesthood of Thúmis went howling like *Zrné*-beasts to the Great Council of the Temples, to the governor, to the Emperor himself, it would likely be days – nay, months – before any action might be taken. The Prince would have the Man of Gold, and Hársan's skull would be picked clean by the river fish before anyone would come to the Tólek Kána Pits to inquire.

Even as he thought of this, Hársan cursed himself for a moral coward. A person must base his life upon "noble action"; thus thundered the epics, the books of admonitions, and the age-old traditions of Tsolyáni society. The soldier, the official, the priest – even those who sacrificed lives each day to grim Vimúhla or Chiténg – behaved as they did because of a belief in their principles and a willingness to stand up for them. Anything else was "ignoble": weakness, sophistry, self-deception, indolence, or downright cowardice. "An honest tyrant is better than a hypocritical altruist," as it said in the Pandects of Psánkunel the Knower. Perhaps it was the strangely powerful imperative contained in the Globe of Instruction; perhaps it was something within Hársan himself. Yet he knew instinctively that such as Prince Dhich'uné must not – must never – attain the secrets of the Man of Gold.

Were the others who sought the Man of Gold really any better? a niggling little thought asked. The greedy priesthoods? The squabbling political factions? The other Imperial heirs who jockeyed for power and waited for their aging father to pass on to the Isles? No matter. This was not a choice between one *Rényu* and another, fighting over the same bone. This lay between Hársan and himself. He made up his mind.

He would resist.

Eventually torchlight bathed the chamber once more. The Prince had returned.

"What, then, have you thought, Priest Hársan?" Prince Dhich'uné asked amicably.

Hársan licked dry lips. "I – I can tell you nothing more, mighty Prince."

The Prince sighed and made a sign. "Alas for the courage of youth. Vridékka!"

Two men of the Legion of Kétl took hold of him and bound his wrists to the metal link once more, this time over his head so that he lay upon his back on the coarse wooden table. The mind-seer leaned over him and stood gazing down into his face. The rheumy eyes loomed larger and larger beneath their scraggly brows.

Dizziness –

"Great Prince, I see within his mind. But he cannot speak. Just below the surface there is a defense like a buckler of iron."

"Circumvent it."

"I shall try, my Lord. If I can discover where the Man of Gold lies, it may be possible to trick his unconscious mind into still further admissions."

Hársan hung in emptiness. Vertigo seized him for there was no up and no down in this place. Whichever way he turned two huge eyes confronted him, driving out all else, becoming the one, the all, the beginning, and the end of being...

A voice called from a great distance. "Hársan," it cried, "think not of the Man of Gold! You have concealed it well, Hársan, and you are successful." Relief flooded over him. "There is no need to fear; all is as it should be." Were those eyes before him, or the two moons of Tékumel?

"Hársan," the voice called again, "Hársan, priest of Thúmis! Have you ever been to the city of Ch'óchi? Have you seen Ch'óchi, Hársan?"

He was mildly surprised to hear his own voice replying, as though from some cavern lost at the bottom of the sea.

"No. Never..."

"Tumíssa," the voice persisted, "do you like Tumíssa?"

"Yes. I passed by it when I came to Béy Sü."

"Jakálla?"

"The great port city... I have never seen it."

The list went on interminably. Within the egg of emptiness Hársan first became bored, then tired. The two voices prattled on somewhere far away.

"And Púrdimal?" the strange voice asked, "What of Púrdimal?"

"An old city, in the north... The swamps there..."

A veil dropped over the two staring eyes. Hársan's Universe shook and went swooping off into darkness. He knew no more.

Vridékka approached the dais. "Mighty Prince, the blockage lies here, in connection with Púrdimal. When I mentioned the other cities his mind was as open and limpid as a summer blossom, but when I spoke of Púrdimal it snapped shut, and there was the buckler of iron."

"So." Prince Dhich'uné rubbed his bone-painted chin. "It is as I expected. The ancients lied when they set up guideposts pointing to Ch'óchi – or else the shrine at Ch'óchi may have been the place of the Man of Gold during the days of its use, and later it was taken to Púrdimal. What know you of Púrdimal, Vridékka?"

The mind-seer came close and whispered.

"Your musty tomes may have the answer. You may be right. I, too, have seen references to her, the Goddess of the Pale Bone, 'She Who Must Not be Named Aloud'. If this Man of Gold is hers – or connected to her – then we have too little information. A citation here, a hint there…"

"Ignorance is danger in this affair, mighty Prince. We know that worship of this goddess was banned, her shrines razed as if they had never been, her minions slain and scattered and driven from the very face of Tékumel. Worse than the Ssú and the Hlüss, who hate us more than –"

"But the power! The power! More than the world has seen in all the generations since the Time of the Gods! Now if the Man of Gold be a servitor of hers…!"   .

"Then we may well wreak our own doom, mighty Prince. My sources suggest that to loose her upon the world again may rock the very foundations of both Stability and Change! Not one of the Priest Pavár's twenty deities she! Instead, she is said to be as much anathema to Hrü'ü, Lord of Darkness, as she is to Hnálla, Lord of Light."

Prince Dhich'uné seemed not to hear. "Another thought, Vridékka: why, think you, does the Baron of Yán Kór find such fascination in these Llyáni relics? It cannot be their power alone, great though that may be. Scores of devices exist from the ages before the Time of Darkness, and from the Latter Times that followed. The vaults and treasuries of the Five Empires are stuffed full of such bric-a-brac. Only if the Man of Gold were urgent for his schemes would he take so much interest. He must own another piece of the puzzle. His 'Weapon Without Answer' –?"

"The Man of Gold may be an aid to it – or a hindrance?"

"If it be designed to assist the Baron's black box, then we can withhold it from him, or mayhap make him pay more dearly for it than he wishes. And if it be an instrument made to combat his 'Weapon,' then – then we may not have to give Khirgár and the north over to his blind vengeance after all. Indeed, the tree may be felled so as to crush Yán Kór and not us."

"Is it wise –?" the old man began.

"'To plough stones is foolish when fertile fields lie at hand.'" An earth-hued hand crept out of the brown sleeve, thumb touching index fingertip. "We know that the Man of Gold lies – or lay – at Púrdimal." Thumb to middle finger. "There was the last stronghold of those who served the Goddess of the Pale Bone." Thumb to ring finger. "The Man of Gold is therefore likely to be some device of hers, or an ally." The thumb moved to the little finger. "And since the Baron Áld is interested, we guess that either he needs this instrument, or dreads its coming forth – more probably the latter, judging by his comportment at our last council. Either way we stand to win the throw, if only we can come upon this Man of Gold!"

"As you say, mighty Prince." Vridékka drew himself up, his voice yet filled with doubt. "And now?"

"Awaken the priest. His cooperation is more necessary than ever."

Hársan blinked. No time had passed. But here was the skull face of the Prince gazing down at him from a hand's breadth away.

"You have aided us much, priest. You have our thanks." The toneless voice held no hint of irony. "We know that your Man of Gold is in Púrdimal –" the rigid mouth sketched a smile at Hársan's appalled look, "– and we have learned that it is bound to one who cannot be named aloud. Whisper the name in his ear, Vridékka."

Hársan heard, and felt defeat empty him as a slave does a waterjug. They had it all. He had done what he could. Still, it had been so easy for them, like a *Dáichu*-leaf trying to stand against the chill of autumn!

"Now you have only to guide us to it," the Prince continued smoothly. "This is your only course. Once the Man of Gold is within my hand, I shall use it to bring our enemies, the Yán Koryáni – and all who would oppose our Imperium – to their knees. Through it, we shall have her whom I shall not name to serve us –"

Hársan's heart gave a great leap inside him. Then the Prince really did not know!

"The Man of Gold – serves the – the goddess?" he managed.

Vridékka cursed and scuttled around to pluck at Prince Dhich'uné's arm. "Lord Prince! He suspects! He realises that we have only a part of the riddle. I see it in his mind. The Man of Gold is not her servant but must instead be her deadliest foe! He knows this, and his mind has gone shut against us!"

"Then do as you did before! Use your arts!"

"My probing tells me when something is or is not so. Whenever I touch upon the ancients' Mind-Bar I sense it. But this is not enough. He must aid us willingly. Otherwise we shall waste endless time badgering each step of the road from him! And there will assuredly be pitfalls that he will know and employ to frustrate us. My Lord –"

"You can accomplish no more?"

The bony shoulders rose high, helplessly. "Yes, yes, but it will be long – and dangerous. Others will have time to array themselves against us."

"Then I see no other path. Bring in the girl."

Chapter Eighteen

Two of the brown-armoured soldiers of the Legion of Kétl escorted Eyíl into the chamber. Helé'a went to her and drew away her cloak. Others dragged something forth from the shadows: a narrow wooden trestle with wide-splayed legs, angled so that one end was higher than the other. On this they laid her upon her back, made her ankles fast at the lower end on either side so that she straddled the thing, and then bound her wrists down to links on the upper legs similarly. She made no protest but permitted the troopers to handle her as though she were a sack of *Dná*-grain. All the while she gazed steadily at Prince Dhich'uné. She seemed not to see Hársan.

"Eyíl!" Hársan cried, "Eyíl –!"

She turned her head toward him, her black tresses falling away from her face. Her eyes were underscored with dark circles of weeping. He could not read her expression: fear, shame, remorse – a mixture of all three?

"Mighty Prince," he called, "Prince Dhich'uné! The Lady Eyíl hiVriyén has no part in this matter. She knows nothing of the Llyáni relics!"

The still features looked upon him. "Possibly. However, we would have you aid us, priest. You know my power already; yet you refuse me. One more lesson appears to be needed to make you zealous in my cause."

Hársan attempted to lie. "The Lady is of no real concern to me, mighty Prince – a girl with whom I made liaison upon the road..."

"Not so. Vridékka sees into your heart as easily as a maiden gazes into a mirror. Helé'a? The silver box."

The ugly little Ghatóni stood by the trestle upon which Eyíl lay. He extracted something from a little casket, no bigger than his thumb.

It was tiny, mottled brown and crimson. It wriggled in his fingers.

Eyíl gasped. Even from where Hársan lay he could see that the whites of her eyes showed all round, and her face had taken on a waxy pallor.

"One of the servitors of the Worm Lord," Helé'a announced. He bent and placed the little worm upon the satiny golden skin, of Eyíl's abdomen, just above the darkness between her thighs. "It seeks a home, a dark, warm place where it may eat and grow fat…"

Hársan's resolve crumbled. "I will tell you, mighty Prince – all – whatever I know!" He tried to say more but found that again his tongue would not move, and his lips refused to form the words.

"Tell on, then," Dhich'uné said implacably.

He struggled. All that the Globe of Instruction had contained lay like spring flood waters behind the dam of his lips. But the accursed dam would not break! He strove until the cords stood out in his neck, his teeth grated upon one another, and breath choked in his nostrils. He could utter no word related to what the Skull-Prince sought.

"You see, you are still obstinate," Prince Dhich'uné chided gently.

"Oh, my Lord – I try –"

Eyíl strained her head forward to watch the little red-brown worm crawling upon her belly. It left a thin trail of viscous slime.

She spoke for the first time. "Give them what they seek, Hársan," she pleaded. Her voice sounded somehow artificial, brittle and false.

The hideous worm threw back its sightless sucker-ringed mouth and then curved forward to touch her skin. There could have been little pain, but the horror and apprehension must have been great indeed. Eyíl choked and then shrieked. "Tell them, Hársan, tell them! It will kill me!" The sincerity of terror now rang in her words.

"Not there, not yet," Helé'a said, prodding the worm's questing head away with his finger. A spot of bright red stained her abdomen where the obscene little mouth had caressed her. Eyíl writhed upon the trestle, but the creature did not fall away. It continued its slow progress down over her belly.

Words, pleas, prayers, imprecations whirled through Hársan's mind. With the mind-seer beside him, he knew he could not lie. He opened his mouth and promises poured forth: he would serve as the Prince commanded, whatever the task!

All at once there was another violent onrush within his brain. The chamber faded, and he fell shrieking through emptiness again, dizzy, nauseous with vertigo. His thoughts, memories, yearnings – all were ransacked and pillaged by a callous, skillful plunderer: Vridékka! He could no longer hear Eyíl's pleas nor feel the agony in his own wrists as he jerked and tore at his bonds. Pictures arose unbidden before his eyes: the patient Pé Chói tutors of his forest childhood; the sprawling bulk of the Monastery of the Sapient Eye, the crumpled Inner Range drowsing green and gold behind it; Zarén at work upon one of his devices; the warm, reassuring gleam of the great golden image of Lord Thúmis within its sanctuary; Eyíl asleep in his arms upon the velvet cushions of her litter; the priest at Haumá (what was his name?); Chtík p'Qwé and Keréktu hiKhánmu deep in argument. Then a clear vision of a jagged, leaning black tower, wave-wrack pale around its sea-ringed skirts, where fangs of dark grey stone reached hungrily out into the crashing foam of a lead-hued ocean. Then a ritual of some sort: men and women – and others – doing incomprehensible and obscene things to one another, a tangled mass of limbs and nude, coppery bodies. The white metal sphere, the hideous *Thúnru'u*, Helé'a's weazened features merging with the skull-visage of Prince Dhich'uné – and – and – then – nothing…

Blank.

Vridékka bowed toward the dais. "He will cooperate with us now. I can get no further details – the shield remains intact – yet his willingness to save the girl is clear. I know this priest's life as though I had spent all my years within his skin."

"Remove the Worm of Death before it enters her," the Prince commanded. "We shall require her again later when this lesson grows dim in the young man's memory." Helé'a hastened to recapture the tiny creature.

"There is one matter, mighty Lord." The mind-seer approached the dais and muttered.

Prince Dhich'uné's head snapped back as though he had been struck.

"Return the priest to his senses. Quickly!"

Hársan floated muzzily up into consciousness. He found himself looking towards Eyíl. She seemed dazed but unharmed. The Worm of Death was gone, and her face told him that it had not been allowed to bore within. Her limbs were glazed with perspiration, and she trembled yet with remembered terror, tears of mingled fear and relief staining her cheeks. Hársan became aware of Prince Dhich'uné leaning over him, a white-faced phantom in the dancing torchlight and shadow.

"I will serve you, mighty Prince…" He could say no more.

"Indeed, you shall serve me," the Prince responded in a strangely altered tone, "but I now must know one thing more."

He bent very close and whispered, "Tell me, priest, when did you ever see the great black citadel of Ke'ér?"

"What?" This made no sense whatever.

"Come, boy, the keep of Baron Áld's fortress is famed throughout all the northlands. How is it that you know that place?"

"My Lord, I know not what you mean! I have never been north of our monastery –" Suddenly he saw again that vision of the grim citadel clinging to the crags above the gloomy sea. He was too amazed to continue.

"Mighty Prince," Vridékka interjected softly, "my probe was strong – so strong that it may have picked up images from the minds of others than this priest. The ritual he saw – and I saw with him – was almost certainly from the girl: it is the initiation into the Third Circle of the Temple of Hriháyal."

"But Ke'ér, man! Has she ever seen Ke'ér?"

"I think not, my Lord. I shall try to discover who amongst us here has so clear a picture of the Baron's capital."

The old mind-seer pivoted to face the chamber. Sensing something amiss, all stood transfixed, an orange and brown tableau.

The scribes glanced at one another with faces of fear; those guards who bore swords loosened them in their belt-clips, and those with halberds gripped them the tighter. Hársan raised his head and saw that Eyíl, too, was watching.

Vridékka pulled at his long chin. His scuffed leather sandals made soft hushing noises upon the flagstones of the floor. He went to a scribe, looked him up and down; then to a guard, hooked a finger against the man's cheek and drew his head around to face him; then to the dais, and then back again to the table upon which Hársan lay.

At last he approached Prince Dhich'uné and whispered, "Mighty Master, there is now no sign of Ke'ér in anyone's mind. Someone knows well how to block his thoughts."

He turned to Eyíl – and as quickly whirled back again; he shouted, "Yán Kór! Victory to the Baron of Yán Kór!"

Scribes scattered, pencases clattering. Swords flew out, and halberds leaped up to menace him.

Prince Dhich'uné smiled.

"What did you see?"

"A hint, master. A flash as of green-lacquered armour in someone's memory." Without warning, he cried again, "Yilrána! Avenge my Yilrána!"

There was tumult. A glimpse of a strangely beautiful, sloe-eyed woman with tresses piled in curls and ringlets flickered through Hársan's mind, but he could not tell whether this came from within himself or from without. Soldiers stared this way and that. The scribes below the dais huddled amidst their clutter of papers and pigments, terrified. A servant dropped an ewer with a mighty clang –

And that seemed to do it.

Vridékka's bony finger swung round as surely as the needle of a compass, pointing, pointing –

To Helé'a of Ghatón!

There was a blur of motion. The tiny silver casket flew from the Ghatóni's hand to clatter open upon the floor; five wriggling brown worms spilled out. His other hand dipped into his robe and came forth again as swiftly as an *Alásh*-snake's striking. He held a nut-sized, grey object in his fingers.

"An 'Eye!'" someone yelled. There was bedlam.

A sword grated awkwardly upon the wall by Helé'a's head. Two halberds clashed and tangled as their wielders both attempted to engage the Ghatóni at once. Scribes bleated and scrambled for nonexistent cover. Prince Dhich'uné shouted something, but none heard him over the uproar. The dishes and goblets went ringing and bouncing in all directions. Someone hurled himself against the table upon which Hársan lay, overturned it, and sent him toppling helplessly to the floor beneath it.

It was this that saved his life.

A faint, sweet, musical note sang through the chamber, a vibration almost too high for hearing, and Hársan felt the passage of a cascade of cold above him, so bitter that it burned. Crystals of ice showered down, and the planks of the table became agony, so frigid that he wrenched himself wildly away from contact with them.

Vridékka was scrambling up beside him – it had been he who had tipped over the table – fumbling for something within his tattered robe.

There was light.

Not the ruddy, orange-red warmth of the torches, but a flaring, bloody, crimson glare that burned itself into Hársan's retinas even though he lay behind the fallen table.

All was silence.

Then he heard Prince Dhich'uné's voice calling something, and a babble of voices poured forth in reply. Vridékka clambered to his feet, one bony knee in Hársan's ribs. There were footsteps, shouts, and the rattle of armour and weapons, excited yelling... Hands tugged at the table, and someone cursed at its unexpected cold. It was dragged upright, Hársan perforce along with it. He writhed against the icy surface, yelped involuntarily in pain. The table was still almost too frigid to touch!

Hársan would have cried a further warning, for Helé'a of Ghatón still stood, the dull-gleaming "Eye" in his fingers, mouth open, poised to fire. Then he saw that Helé'a did not move, did not seem to breathe. The man's posture was curiously stiff, as though he were a waxen doll.

Prince Dhich'uné now stepped around a soldier who was gingerly flicking the Worms of Death back into their casket. The Prince carried another "Eye," one with an iris that glinted darkly red.

"Mighty Prince," Vridékka wheezed, "you are safe?"

"Had I to depend upon my favoured Legion of Kétl, I might have been as empty of life as the Desert of Sighs! Fortunately I am not one to go without a second shaft for my bow. The 'Excellent Ruby Eye' has drawn his fangs —"

"'Excellent Ruby Eye?'" Hársan hardly knew that he had spoken.

"Yes, priest. But for it – and me – you would now be frozen meat to baffle the embalmers in the City of the Dead! For it was at you that Helé'a aimed his own 'Eye of Frigid Breath,' not at me, not at Vridékka. It seems that the Baron of Yán Kór prefers the Man of Gold to remain lost for all time to come, rather than see it in our hands."

"But Helé'a, mighty Prince?" That was Vridékka. "An agent of such loyalty – he could have slain you at any moment..."

"Baron Áld doubtless schooled him well." The bone-painted lips curved up in a wry grimace. "The best dagger is the one your foe cannot see. Helé'a served me faithfully for many years, and I was remiss to trust so many of my purposes to him. But... thus it is. We have been lucky to unveil him this night; else he might have done us greater harm in the days to come. You, Vridékka, were clever to try him with the name of the Baron's dead mistress."

"Mention of Yilrána carries much emotion for all who dwell near to the Baron of Yán Kór, my Lord. This I knew."

"We are grateful." Prince Dhich'uné moved to stand before the motionless figure of Helé'a. "He is trapped now, as a fish in the ice of his own northern seas, frozen forever in one long, eternal moment out of time. He knows nothing, senses nothing until he is released again by the 'Eye.' Were I to use it to free him, he would return to that precise instant in which he was caught: take another breath, depress the stud of his weapon, and think those same thoughts he held at the moment of his capture."

"None can touch him now, mighty Prince." The old mind-seer, too, went to gaze into Helé'a's open, staring eyes. "Will you not let me have him, My Lord? His mind-screens may be of the strongest, but I have many strings to pluck as well."

The Prince chuckled. "I am tempted to immure him in the pits beneath this prison, Vridékka, even in the Ultimate Labyrinth from which no one has ever come forth again. – Or leave him in his present plight and sink him in the bottomless swamps off Thayúri Isle where he would lie until Lord Vimúhla's conflagration burns all life from Tékumel at the very terminus of time." He seemed to shake himself. "No, he may serve us better in still another role. What is the hour?"

One of the soldiers replied, "The *Túnkul*-gong of the temple of Ksárul across the river has struck the half-night, my Lord."

"Four *Kirén* – two hours – still remain, then…" Dhich'uné mused. "Vridékka, I entrust Helé'a to you, but your questioning must needs be brief. The High Adept of our Temple of Sárku has appointed me officiant at this night's Giving of Praise unto the One of Mouths. Would it not be salutary for Helé'a of Ghatón to be guested at that feast? There will be many present – and some who will doubtless report our hospitality back to the Baron of Yán Kór. He shall thus gain fresh insight into our alertness and our unwillingness to be spied upon."

The blank, black marble eyes turned to Hársan and thence to Eyíl. "These two shall join our celebrations as well – another lesson in obedience may not be superfluous. And there will be one there whom I wish them to meet. Do you unbind them, Vridékka, place them in a cell, and then escort them to the great hall of our Temple of Rising from the Tomb when the time draws nigh."

Chapter Nineteen

Eyíl collapsed upon the stone floor of the little cell, rubbing her wrists and ankles. One of the guards tossed her soiled street-cloak into the chamber after them, and this Hársan wrapped about her shoulders. He reached for her hand, and silently she drew it to her cheek. He felt hot tears upon his fingers.

"He will slay us, Hársan," she said, "just as soon as he has the Man of Gold." She rocked her body back and forth so that her long tresses cascaded down over his wrists.

"Prince Dhich'uné shall not have it, Eyíl. I know now. The Globe will not let me speak. I – tried – when he would have hurt you."

"I know. I saw. Yet he does not need your telling, my love. He can make you guide him, and at each turning of the path that hateful old man will be there to try you, to test you, and to trick you. Whenever the seal drops across your mind, Vridékka will know that he stands all the closer to the truth."

"There will be a way –"

"He will use me against you!" she burst out. She realised, as though struck by a summer lightning bolt, that this man – this Hársan, this priest of a God opposed to hers – meant much indeed. His wide, high-boned, serious, rustic-silly-scholarly face was more dear than ever she had thought her emerald and purple Goddess to be. Prince Dhich'uné had inadvertently opened one door too many within her mind.

How could she right this wrong?

"Oh, Hársan, the Skull-Prince made me agree to aid him – to plead with you, to let you play the romantic hero of the epics –" Her fingers tightened about his wrists, nails digging into his flesh. "Listen well, Hársan! If ever you felt – affection – for me, you must cease to feel it now! You must hate me, care nothing for me. If you do not, he will herd you before him as a peasant goads his *Chlén*-beast, and the Man of Gold will be his."

"How can I hate you, Eyíl?"

"You – you will." She drew a deep and ragged breath. He saw that she was trembling, near to breaking, still so shaken by the events of this awful night that she could hardly collect her thoughts.

"I shall tell you what I am, and then you will despise me. The Eyíl you know is head to foot a scroll of lies, Hársan! I am no worshipper of your motherly, cherubic Avánthe! I am a priestess of Lady Hrihával, the Whore of the Five Worlds and Mistress of the Thirty-Two Unspeakable Acts! There is no Lord Retlán, no clan-elders sending a naïve little girl to be wed in Béy Sü! I am *Aridáni*, Hársan, *Aridáni* – one who has renounced your domestic, bucolic life – and obedience to her clan, and all else that you seem to hold dear!"

It had all poured out in a rush. She paused for breath, then hurried on. It was important to say it before the Worm Prince – or her own devious subconscious mind – made her stop, dissemble, and try to befool him again.

"For twenty generations we of the Green Kirtle Clan have sent our most beautiful and talented daughters to serve either mighty Dlamélish or else her Cohort, Lady Hriháyal. Five of those women became High Priestesses, three achieved the final and greatest of all devotions, the Thirty-Second Act! I am one of Hriháyal's handmaidens, Hársan, a member of the Fourth Circle. The things I have done – and have gladly had done to me – the rituals – your sexless, high-minded grey-robes could never imagine –!"

He stood blinking at her. "Eyíl – it does not matter now."

"You ask why I drew you into my net? Because our temple desires your treasure too, as badly as does the Skull-Prince – or your pious Lord Dúrugen hiNáshomai, or a half dozen other temples. What we would do with the Man of Gold I know not – I was not told. But we sought it so mightily that the Lady Misénla, our High Priestess, sent to the Lady Elulén hiQolyélmu, the Commandant of the Rituals in our temple in Tumíssa, and bid her choose just such a girl who could appeal to you, a young scholar of Thúmis, untried in the world outside of his monastery, filled with zeal and – and –" She strove to gain control of her voice. "Yes, I was to prevent you from reaching the Man of Gold, steal its secrets if possible, and above all to make certain that it fell into no hands but ours."

"Why, then, did you not slay me and take the relics?" he asked gently. "You had every opportunity."

She waved him to silence. "My Lady Elulén is not of the Clan of the Emerald and Silver Crown, the inner society within our hierarchy which Lady Misénla leads. The Clan favours violent action. But Lady Elulén is not eager to break the Concordat – there are political reasons, as well as theological ones. She thus chose me – she knows I am no murderer – and she was sure that Misénla did not know me. I was to do with my body – and my arts – what Misénla would have accomplished with a dagger or with poison or with sorcery. Our teachings say that the flame of sex will always triumph; little need for swords or arrows or spells!"

"In this your teachings speak truth," Hársan muttered ruefully.

"Yes, and soon I would have had it all, too. Then that stupid girl Sríya tried to drug you – Misénla's doing, for she is impatient and would not wait for my slower methods to work. Sríya's blunder did open a path into the heart of your temple for me. Oh, Hársan, I could have made you betray your God and your duty and your soul itself with no more than these poor, small breasts and these thighs! Do you not hate me for this?"

"No. I guessed long ago that you were not what you seemed."

"I did make mistakes. But –"

"There were many little things. Even on the road I think I had doubts, though I explained them all away to myself. You knew too little of the doctrines of Lady Avánthe, yet you argued so cleverly about theology. Had you really been just a naïve little clan-girl, you could hardly have disputed with me so. And then there was the amulet of Tahelé, the Maiden of Beauty, that I bought you. You did not wear it. At first I thought that you did not care for me, or that it was too poor a gift. But it is the custom of the worshippers of Lady Avánthe to wear a symbol of Tahelé, especially when it is given by a lover, a suitor... I felt that no true devotee of the Blue Goddess would refuse Her protection thus. Tahelé shields a young girl's beauty from harm and keeps old age at bay."

"I see." Her hands brought his up to cup tear-wet cheeks.

'Then there was the Legion of Káikama. I could not have known at the time, but when I met a soldier of that Legion in the governor's garden, I realised that he served Hriháyal – the purple and green uniform..."

"'I had a lie ready for you. That Legion is generalled by Lord Káikama hiMrachiyáku, a brilliant young man who prefers men. I would have told you that Rétlan's 'son' was of that predilection, and that he had abandoned the faith of Avánthe to follow a lover of our sect."

"I might have believed it," he replied, "though by then I was adding up all too many of these little wrongnesses. Still – I managed to conceal all of this from myself. My capacity for self-deception is well-nigh as great as that of others for duping me – alas, greater!" He sighed.

"As we say, 'self-deception is one of the Greater Aspects of love.'" She pushed him away, then drew him back again with a convulsive shudder. "Hate me, Hársan, hate me! Make me useless to the accursed Skull Prince! He may kill me, but he may also cast me aside as a pawn who has been captured! In any case I shall not then be a halter for your neck, and they will have to use Vridékka to play at guess-me-not with you! You may find some way to win! Perhaps you can mislead them, delay them, and halloo them hither and thither until there is a chance for escape – or rescue – or for others to find the Man of Gold first! Or at least you can die your own death and cheat them of their goal!"

The cell was cold. He warmed her body with his.

"I cannot, Eyíl. I care nothing for who you are, or who you were. Now I cannot do your bidding, for you have wrought only too well with your arts."

Above them, in the darkness, a tiny aperture closed. Vridékka smiled to himself and rubbed skeletal fingers together. How very wise of his master to place these two together thus. The youthful, gallant bonds Hársan had forged with his lady-love were now reinforced a thousand times over by this exchange of confidences! A city defended by such strength would be impregnable! He chuckled and crept away down the winding passage to report to Prince Dhich'uné.

Chapter Twenty

Time flowed silently by in the darkness of the cell, its eddies and currents uncharted, its depths unplumbed.

Four *Kirén* had Prince Dhich'uné said?

One twelfth of a day: time enough to rise, to eat, to work, to sleep, to plough a field, to recite a cycle from the epics, to enjoy a repast with friends, to win a battle, to make love and then lie all warm and drowsy against one's mate…

Yes, time enough, too, to prepare oneself to die, to confront the demons of fear and pain, to contemplate the mournful barque of Lord Belkhánu, the Final Arbiter of the Excellent Dead.

Hársan lay wrapped together with Eyíl in her cloak upon the hard flagstones. She dozed fitfully, for she was exhausted. He could not sleep. Instead, his thoughts wandered whimsically of themselves. A remembered story came to him: of the aristocrats of the high clans who affected to make only subjective distinctions between the measurements of time and space. Four *Kirén*? When one was in the company of one's beloved, then a year could be counted as a single *Kirén*, while one moment of boredom might be counted as more *Kirén* than a tree had leaves! The distance from Tumíssa to Béy Sü was only one *Tsán* if one were happy, but that from one's couch to the wardrobe might be a thousand *Tsán* if one were weary of life…

He smiled wryly to himself, recalling chubby, argumentative Waréka hiSanusái and his lessons in philosophy at the Monastery of the Sapient Eye. Waréka affected the Doctrine of the Effulgence of the Now. Rejoice, Hársan, he would say. Enjoy! Do you not lie presently limb to limb with your beloved? The now is the all, the totality of being. As each second passes it becomes only a memory, whilst the future is naught but shadows and vague pathways yet unknown. Let the Weaver of Skeins anguish over the knots of your destiny!

Damn Waréka! Would that he were here now to take their place in this dungeon...

Then there were the dogmas of Pamaviráz the Livyáni, named the Canon of the Establishment of Blessed Memory, popular with the adherents of the war-gods of the Tsolyáni pantheon. Ohé, there was a brave song for you! Let both your life and your death form a pattern of beauty, they preached; make your deeds a rich skein worthy of heroes; live well and die gloriously, for your total worth consists only of the "noble actions" inscribed upon your epitaph. The most praiseworthy being is that one whose name is sung the longest by the bards of generations yet to come...

All of the God-accursed philosophers were welcome to Hársan's present predicament!

The hinges of the heavy door screamed, and torches thrust in to dazzle their eyes. Rough hands pulled them apart, put manacles of cold bronze upon their wrists, and sent them staggering out into the corridor where Vridékka waited, accompanied by a squad of soldiers of the Legion of Kétl. These were zealots of the Inner Temple of Sárku, he saw, for beneath their copper helmets their eye-sockets were blackened with *Tsúnu*-paste, and their cheekbones had been daubed with white.

"Put cloaks upon their shoulders, Jésekh," the mind-seer ordered. "The way is long, and the catacombs are chilly."

The old man led off at a rapid pace through the passages beneath the prison. Rows of cells, tunnels, dim chambers in which enigmatic engines of torment loomed upon pedestals, dark and dripping caverns full of movements and secret scuttlings, all were traversed without comment. At length they stood before a round grating constructed of many little metal bars. A soldier produced a long, lever-like key, and five men thrust the gate open to reveal a dank, black-mouthed corridor beyond.

Once again Hársan entered the alien world of the labyrinths. Halls, porticoes, arcades, rooms, twisting stairs, narrow and rubble-filled tunnels, mighty chambers embellished with the ornate inscriptions of the Bednálljan kings of the First Imperium; then starkly bare crypts, improvised ladders; an oval court set about with slender columns and decorated with squarish, formalised motifs in a style Hársan did not recognise; the precise, geometrically perfect vaultings of the Engsvanyáli Priestkings of the Golden Age... Stone demons leaned down to watch them pass, nightmares from the legends of the darkness, eyes that might have been carven – or filled with malevolent life – and mould-splotched, eroded bas-reliefs that kept them company as they marched.

All at once they emerged into an open gallery. High balconies cut from the living rock hung over their heads on every side, and thick pillars of a circumference greater than twenty men together could encircle by extending their arms and joining hands held up the ceiling. Rows of webbed, knife-edged glyphs along the walls bespoke the immortal, ever-living majesty of Káà Drángash the Third, ruler of the Bednálljan Empire, dead now these many long, dusty millennia.

At the end of this chamber Hársan caught the glimmer of torchlight.

"Are they Ssú, Master Vridékka?" the soldier named Jésekh hissed.

"Not likely so close beneath the surface. Moreover, those monsters prefer bluish light. They do not see well otherwise." The mind-seer stepped forward and called out, "Ohé! Who is there?"

"Who, indeed?" A high, mocking voice rang back from the shadows ahead.

"Servants of Lord Sárku. He Who Coils."

A black-clad figure glided out from behind one of the monolithic pillars. The mask of a priest of Ksárul gazed upon them with its blank-eyed, meaningless smile, all silver stained with blood-scarlet in the flickering glow.

"You go to your temple for the Giving of Praise?"

"We do. We require only passage from you."

"Take it, then." The figure stood aside, waved a graceful hand.

Vridékka's party started forward, halberds held high, watching all around. The mind-seer reached out and jerked the cloak-cowls down over his captives' faces. Hársan had only a momentary glimpse of many men: some in black, and some in the sable and purple of Lord Ksárul's feared Cohort, Lord Grugánu, the Knower of Spells. There were others as well: naked slaves with torches, and still more who were chained together and who bore picks and mallets. A heap of rubble told where they had been digging.

"So," Vridékka said conversationally, "you Black-robes would drive a tunnel from the Hall of Méttukeng into the Maze of Unreturning? I wonder what you seek there?"

"On your way to your temple, servant of the Worm," the pleasantly sardonic voice replied. "The Concordat does not hold down here."

Vridékka cackled. "Yet we are allies, eh? Slay us, and more than one pot will be shattered! We follow the same road this night, though your Doomed Prince loves not our Lord of Worms overmuch."

The other gave a derisive, rippling laugh but said no more. Could this be Keréktu hiKhánmu? It sounded like him, though the timbre of this man's voice seemed higher. Harsan took a chance and suddenly shook his head as hard as he could. The cowl slipped down upon his shoulders, and he turned his face toward the Black-robe, opening his mouth to cry out. The Temple of Ksárul was no friend to Lord Thúmis, but if there were two rival players in this game, might there not be three – or more?

A hard blow took him in the back of the head, and he would have fallen except for the rough hands of his captors. The cowl was jerked back down over his face. A fist caught him in the ribs so that the words he planned became only a grunt and a gasp for air.

"Lá, it seems that one of your guests would not mind missing your feast!" Was the man coming toward them?

"Perhaps because he may sleep tonight with the One of Mouths." Vridékka sounded matter of fact, almost bored. Iron-hard hands continued to propel Hársan on toward the far end of the chamber.

"On your way, then, and may your great Worm crawl forth and kiss the backsides of the lot of you!" Again came the high, pleasant laughter. Someone barked a command, feet shuffled, tools clanged, and the echo of picks upon stone dwindled away behind them as the mind-seer led on into the darkness.

At length the hands upon his arms pulled Hársan to a halt, and the cowl was thrown back from his face. He blinked confusedly, at first unable to comprehend the kaleidoscope within the chamber at whose entrance they stood: swirls of brown and gold and black and russet and ochre, a thousand colours, a myriad shapes, seemingly boundless distances.

Hársan had never before been inside a temple to Lord Sárku, Master of Worms. The Temple of Rising From the Tomb was one of the mightiest of these, renowned throughout the Five Empires.

A tessellated pavement of smoky amber quartz and white marble swept away between legions of ponderous, demon-carved pillars to a broad staircase at the end of the nave. This led up to a colonnade on a higher level, the upper shrines of the temple. The in-curving, barrel-vaulted walls of the great hall displayed tier upon tier of sculptured figures: priests and kings and nobles and soldiers and slaves – and creatures who could only have been conceived in the dark, fearful race-memories of mankind. All were done in mosaics of red carnelian, brown jasper, glittering tourmaline, and a host of other stones, with eyes of black onyx and secretive yellow topaz. Each figure brought offerings to the frieze of coiling worm-lords depicted in the upper registers.

Still higher, under the painted vaulting of the roof, a narrow gallery ran along each side of the chamber in the grandiose, monumental style beloved of the architects of the Bednálljan kings. Chains of bronze, half again as thick as a man's wrist, swung down from the ceiling to support massive chandeliers of branching oil lamps. All along the lower walls of this nave were niches containing images of the one hundred and eight Aspects of Lord Sárku: the fearsome monsters of the Undead, Ku'ún the Corpse-Lord, Siyenágga the Wanderer of Tombs, Chmúr of the Hands of Grey, and a score of others. He did not wish to look upon them.

The nave teemed now with worshippers: men in brown vestments, faces painted with the skull-white of the Lord of Worms, others in ritual masks fashioned in the likenesses of beasts and demons, women in robes of dull russet and sombre earth hues, aristocrats in rich blues and reds and yellows, but always with the copper worm of Lord Sárku upon their breasts. Lesser folk, servants, and slaves circled about the outskirts of the throng or squatted patiently at the bases of the columns.

Over all hung a sickly sweet fragrance: resinous, smoky incense compounded with the sad, funereal perfume of flowers, the oily stench of the lamps, and a submerged, subtle flavour of decay.

Vridékka did not enter but instead presented himself to an officer in the brown livery and skull-helmet of Lord Sárku's temple-guard. This man pointed them to a tiny door hidden behind the nearest pillar. A cramped, winding stair led upward from this to the balconies. Here Vridékka's soldiers took careful hold upon their captives, for the balustrade was only of knee-height. One of the guards gripped Hársan's wrist chains tightly, and another walked behind him with halberd butt poised to strike, should he display any urgent yearning for self-sacrifice. The groining of the ceiling leaned out into space at a frightening angle just above their heads, and the swarming worshippers below were like begemmed insects. Old Vridékka stepped out upon the narrow balcony with surefooted confidence, but the others hugged the wall. Once Eyíl stumbled and gave a muffled cry, but one of her captors muttered a nervous oath, leaned into the wall, and dragged her back.

At the far end, the balcony gave onto one corner of the upper colonnade. This level, too, teemed with devotees. Twinkling lamps provided unnatural life to the rows of images crouching along the carven walls; stony eyes shifted and stared; bronze lips writhed; and misshapen arms and tails and tentacles wriggled In the glimmering, smoky murk. Urns of incense and tall cult-standards of ebon and ochre plumes stood here and there amidst the crowds of devotees. On each side of a single central aisle sat groups of ritual priests, their faces ruddy in the glow of little braziers of coals, to chant the litanies of the Lord of Worms, Master of the Everlasting Life Beyond the Tomb.

The odour of things dead was stronger here.

A black-silhouetted Lector Priest pointed on across the front of the colonnade to where several senior hierophants stood with Prince Dhich'uné upon the brink of the staircase that led back down to the nave.

The Prince had exchanged his brown robe for the vestments of ceremonial office: a surplice of silky *Güdru*-cloth the colour of dark humus; a collar of copper, engraved with runes; a golden pectoral set with topaz and chrysoberyl, from which two lappets of jewelled plaques hung down to his knees; a pleated kilt of rust-red brocade worked with iridescent threads of shiny black; and heavy armlets of massy copper, Lord Sárku's favoured metal. Upon his head he wore an intricate headdress of little golden skulls intertwined with ebony serpents. Feathery *Khéshchal*-plumes towered above this and swept down behind him almost to his heels. His hands and feet were bare, painted with the bone-white of the Worm Lord.

The Prince had seen them. He motioned Vridékka to have them wait beside one of the squat columns.

"There are preliminaries," the old man muttered to Hársan. "First must we satisfy those who have paid for the performance."

A distant, moaning thunder filled the cavernous hall, and in its centre Hársan glimpsed a figure upon a pedestal who blew into a mighty horn, some two man-heights long and hung by chains from a high tripod. He had heard of that horn, "The One Who Is Mournful of Life." The echoing boom of the *Túnkul*-gong of the temple added its voice to the dirge.

Prince Dhich'uné went to stand at the head of the stair, and those below became silent. One earthen hand went up, and the *Túnkul*-gong roared again. He pointed, and a phalanx of copper-helmeted temple-guards advanced to clear the throngs from the centre of the nave. He made another sign, and now a rectangular area of the pavement there slid soundlessly down. A sloping rampway appeared, from which arose the dank smell of a sepulchre long sealed from the sun.

Things milled and swarmed in the shadows of that pit: pale creatures who held up gaunt arms to shield themselves from the amber lamplight. Presently one ventured up, then another, and another. Hársan knew not whether he looked upon reality or upon an illusion like those cast by the adepts of his own temple. For the beings that emerged were the Undead: liches and corpses and cadavers, the withered husks of departed life, the dwellers in Lord Sárku's myriad heavens – the hells of other Gods. Warriors clambered up the ramp, accoutred in armour of antique fashion, green with verdigris and corruption. Then came spectral beings wrapped in tattered cerements and graveclothes, clay-hued apparitions whose skeletal limbs yet glittered with funerary armlets and finery, all that forlorn wrack that men and women leave behind when they pass forth from this life.

Others were there as well: creatures muffled in robes of charcoal black with the flat faces of serpents, towering monsters of pallid yellowish fungus, flying things with the heads of dead men and creaking leathery wings, bulbous *Thúnru'u*, deformed and twisted crypt-dwellers with rodent snouts and razor claws – a thousand horrors of nightmare and beyond.

The priests ranked along the aisles of the upper colonnade shouted out a litany. Drums thuttered, flutes shrieked, and horns brayed. The living flowed forward to greet the grey tide of the Undead. A woman rushed to clutch at a lurching corpse, to press her lips to its fleshless face, to cry endearments against its rotted winding sheet. A lover who had died? A husband who now spent eternity in this travesty of life? Another, a stout nobleman, embraced the grinning remains of a child and held it, weeping, to his breast. A young man threw off his mantle and took the greyed cadaver of a woman into his arms, to fall in tangled embrace to the floor where they were lost to view.

Some knelt and stretched out their hands to Prince Dhich'uné above them on the stair. Some cried, "Life forever in the tomb, Oh Master!" and danced and jigged in a frenzied parody of joy. Some chanted and sang and dragged the relics of the catacombs into their midst to be caressed and fondled. "Life forever!" they shrilled, "Life! To die and yet to live!"

The vast hall was a spinning turmoil, a maelstrom of noise and light and music and shadow, a streaming glare of lamps and torches, a choking stench of oil and flowers and sweat and drugged incense… Above all hung the overweening redolence of death.

The *Túnkul*-gong clamoured again. Prince Dhich'uné turned and strode back into the darkness of the upper colonnade. Five senior hierophants and five Lector Priests bearing lanterns of brown glass fell in behind him. Vridékka motioned for his captives and their guards to bring up the rear.

In the far wall, a high-arched corridor led off away from the nave. They traversed this for some distance and halted before a great bronze valve of a door, guarded on either side by stone gargoyles who bore unintelligible symbols of gold. This gate opened upon a round tunnel that led down at a steep slant.

The passage was rough and unornamented. Curious gobbets of frozen stone hung from its roof – a natural cavern created by the fires of Tékumel's creation. They ended in an oval room, egg-shaped, entirely empty, stained with the white hoar of age. The Prince crossed this chamber to stand before the entrance to a still smaller tunnel that plunged almost vertically down into blackness. The five hierophants knelt behind him, and the Lector Priests arrayed themselves along one curving wall. Vridékka stationed his party at the rear of the room where they could see, signalling two of the men of the Legion of Kétl to stand by the entrance. The rest he dismissed to return to the great hall. Silence seeped into the chamber; not even the cacophony of the nave above reached them here.

Then another figure appeared in the tunnel through which they had come. It was Helé'a of Ghatón. He was alone.

Helé'a stood for a moment in the entrance, blinking almost apologetically and looking from the two groups of priests to Prince Dhich'uné. He seemed not to see Hársan or Eyíl, but moved slowly forward past them all to face the mouth of the smaller tunnel in the opposite wall.

"He knows and accepts his fate," Vridékka murmured. "He cannot escape, and suicide or cowardice would give him no dignity in the afterlife. He has chosen the 'Way of *Nchél*,' the Yán Koryáni path of resignation to an inexorable doom. He will let us do with him as we will."

Helé'a now removed his simple tunic, folded it beside him on the floor. Then he knelt and unlaced his high boots, undid the waistband of his kilt, and finally stood naked before them, a stooped, ugly, bandy-legged, ordinary little man of middle years.

Hársan wondered how he could ever have feared him.

Two of the priests arose and laid the Ghatóni down upon his back, spread his limbs, and bound them apart to copper stanchions on the threshold before the farther tunnel. Helé'a's eyes never left Prince Dhich'uné's face, and when the hierophants had finished their task, he spoke:

"Though I served Yán Kór – for reasons that you may not comprehend – yet never did I any harm to your purposes, mighty Prince."

"In my game there are no counters which are both white and black."

"When the unreality of games is laid aside, it can be seen that loyalty, like life and death themselves, is no one simple thing. Our Skeins are complex, of more than just one hue. What you do will have repercussions – a blow begets a blow in return…"

Prince Dhich'uné said no more but stooped and rearranged certain ceremonial objects before him upon the floor. The priests along the wall saw to their lanterns. Those who knelt swayed uneasily, shapeless shadows in their heavy robes. Hársan glanced at Eyíl and saw that her lips were compressed as though with pain. He contrived to reach out and take her hand in his, for which she threw him a look that was half of gratitude and half of terror.

The distant note of the *Túnkul*-gong trembled through the chamber, the last sobbing breath of a dying man.

Prince Dhich'uné stirred now. He raised his hands and cried words in a language that Hársan did not know: great, rolling, hollow syllables that reverberated like the strokes of a drum. The kneeling priests took up the litany in a lower key, almost a whisper, and the air thickened with a susurrus of sound, a rising, falling, gently undulating ripple of eerie voices.

The amber lanternlight seemed to dim, the air to flow and pulse. Hovering shadows crept down from the walls and twined before them upon the floor. The Prince's figure grew indistinct, veiled in a sepia haze, and the skull faces of the priests, too, were lost in the gloom, save for a line of bone-white jaw here, a staring black eye-socket there. Hársan felt a pressure upon his eardrums, a soundless presence, a ponderous, purposeful coming forth…

To his horror he realised that his own heart now pounded in time to the rhythmic cadence of the chant! Worse, he understood the words, though he knew that he had never heard that archaic, alien tongue before!

"Worm Lord, Nighted One, Eater at the Tomb's Repast,
Come forth, Lord, rejoice! Take sustenance from us who live!
Bright wings on high, pearl-dark sea; these are not Thine;
Mountain peak, forest vale; these are not Thy dwelling;
All return, all descend; each comes to heed Thy call!
What has lived must die; what has died is Thine,
Crypt-Lord of the encompassing, all-enfolding dark…"

Something moved there, within the farther tunnel. The room reeked with the suffocating odour of moist earth, the cloying fragrances of dissolution. It was round and hollow, a black circle the thickness of a man's waist. It grew, and a faint, oily slithering came to Hársan's ears. The front edges of the thing were soft and pulpy, a mottled, ichor-gleaming brown-grey; they trembled in the tenebrous ochre light. It quested forward, feeling its way along the mucid walls of the passage.

Hársan looked upon the mouth of a great, blind worm.

Something else came squeezing up out of the shaft: another black oval, another eager mouth. And then another. More of the worm-demon emerged into the chamber, streaked ashen and black and pallid white, delicately bristling cilia behind the shapeless lips wriggling in a dance of their own. The second head curved up and swung toward the priests along the wall. Prince Dhich'uné raised a globe of chiselled copper before it, and it withdrew, the soft mouth making tremulous sucking, gulping motions in the air.

The first head arced down to hover over Helé'a. Wetness dribbled from the worm-mouth to splatter upon the stones by the Ghatóni's shoulder. There this spittle hissed and smoked and fumed like the deadly fluids of the alchemists. A drop of the liquid clung to Helé'a's cheek, and Hársan saw the flesh there turn grey, then black, then begin to deliquesce and slough away.

Helé'a shrieked.

More of the slime drooled from the other heads — there were six of them now — viscous gobbets splashing upon the floor. An acrid stench arose, as of burning corpses, but when the liquid had boiled away no trace was left.

A thick drop fell full upon Helé'a's breast and clung there, sizzling. He yelled another wordless cry, his body bucking and writhing against its bonds. Black liquefaction spread over his skin. His feet hammered the rough stone again and again and again, making the strangely gelid air shiver with the agony of his sacrifice.

One of the worm-heads bowed in horrid imitation of courtly grace. It touched the prisoner's outstretched arm. There it fastened, pulsated, humped, and disgorged seething, turbid fluid upon the floor. Another mouth found Helé'a's face, and the bulging, terror-glazed eyes disappeared forever beneath it. The third head sank down upon the Ghatóni's abdomen. His body jerked, kicked, and then lay still. A stink of burst entrails filled the room, but then this too was gone, replaced by a mingled stench of burning and corruption.

Now Hársan observed another terrible thing. Prince Dhich'uné stood rigid before the worm-demon, arms outspread and head thrown back as if to receive the benediction of a master. As he watched, the Prince seemed to flicker, to flow, to shift from white-daubed skull-face to a softer form: a saturninely handsome youth of delicately epicene features, a straight and well-modelled nose, a proud jaw, sallow cheeks, lips which were both full and sensual, a high rounded forehead. Then the image altered again; it became a looming, mighty worm, its gaping mouth swaying out from human shoulders to join in sucking sustenance from the wretched victim on the floor. All three of these seemings mingled and blurred and ran together, as a painter mixes pigments upon a palette, until at last Hársan's eyes and brain could bear no more, and he wrenched his gaze away.

If the reality of Prince Dhich'uné were that slender, studious-appearing youth, then the dry, brown stick-figure he and Eyíl knew and this ghastly worm-thing were both aspects, signs of servitude, laid upon the Prince by his god.

Dhich'uné had paid most dearly, it would seem, for the immortality he sought.

The taste of vomit and of blood from bitten lips brought Hársan back to himself. Eyíl slumped against him, her face buried in his shoulder. He did not know whether she was conscious or not – he hoped not. Vridékka's teeth were clenched, and the ritual priests held their lanterns with trembling fingers.

Prince Dhich'uné alone appeared unmoved. His chanting rose to a final high note and then ceased. He raised the coppery globe again before the twining heads, then a staff of black wood, making convoluted gestures in the air. Reluctantly, affectionately, as a lover leaves his beloved, the worm-thing drew in upon itself, coiled, retreated. There was an ugly, glutinous, sucking sound as it sank back down into its lair.

Two hands and two feet still lay in the shackles upon the threshold, but these ended in blackened, grisly stumps. There was no body between them.

Eyíl's knees gave way, and she would have crumpled to the floor had it not been for Hársan's supporting arms.

Prince Dhich'uné motioned for one of the ritual priests to aid Hársan in carrying Eyíl back up the passageway. He turned to depart, and the hierophants and the others followed.

Chapter Twenty-One

The upper nave was chaos. So thick was the press that the troops of the Legion of Kétl used their halberds to clear a way for the Prince and his entourage. They reached the brink of the broad staircase and looked down through swirling incense smoke into the packed mass of celebrants below. Prince Dhich'uné stood for a moment to peer out into the shouting, chanting maelstrom, apparently seeking someone. Vridékka took up a position beside him.

Hársan looked around. The priest who had helped him carry Eyíl up from the worm-demon's shrine was gone, perhaps to join in the revelry. The Lector Priests and the other officiants had broken up into small groups and were scattered about behind them, talking. The guardsmen focussed their attention upon their master. No one was now nearby!

It was perhaps thirty or forty paces across the width of the upper colonnade to the entrance of the balcony by which they had come. If he could reach that, then navigate the dizzy gallery – then leave the temple, traverse the labyrinth, get out into the world above...

What was he thinking of? Improbable, to say the least! Yet there was no other way to cheat the Prince of the Man of Gold. If death came, at least it would be as a consequence of "noble action."

He glanced down at Eyíl. She seemed dazed and only half conscious, staring with tear-smudged eyes into the lamplit uproar below. What to do with her? She would hinder any escape. If he did the logical thing and abandoned her, the Prince might well let her go; why harm her once Hársan had flown from his net? On the other hand, he might well slay her, for now she knew too much of his scheming.

Hársan made up his mind. He shrugged out of the heavy cloak Vridékka had laid over his shoulders, pulled Eyíl's away as well. Such garments would only be in the way. With Eyíl nude and himself attired only in his stained and crumpled kilt, they might pass as somebody's slaves. He took Eyíl's arm in his manacled hands and half-dragged, half-guided her toward the inviting balcony entrance.

Thirty nervous paces later he looked back. The Prince and the mind-seer were hidden now by a score of beast-masked worshippers bearing black and copper symbols upon tall poles. A few steps more. Now he was there ... within...and out upon the narrow walkway!

Shadows clawed up from below. Plumes of oily yellow smoke enveloped him. He ducked involuntarily to avoid the ponderous ribbing of the ceiling arches. The reeling dance of lamplight and corpse-candles, the racking, rhythmic thunder of drums and chanting, the sick-sweet stench, all turned the long gallery before him into a swooping, undulating tightrope, hard enough to cross alone, much less burdened as he was with Eyíl. He steeled himself and took a cautious look at the footing. He had often carried game along the lofty avenues of the trees of the Pé Chói forests, and now he could only pray that his childhood reflexes would not desert him. He set off as fast as he dared.

Someone approached from the other end: a temple guard by the gleam of his burnished copper cuirass! There was no retreat. He let Eyíl go and saw that she had become fully aware of her surroundings. He motioned her to lean against the wall beside him.

The man came up, a broad-shouldered, thickset soldier with features that appeared carven of brown lava. He stopped a pace away and looked them up and down.

"Slaves? What do you here?"

"I – I return to my master, – with his bond maiden," Hársan improvised. "She ran away – afraid of those below. She is young and untrained." He hoped he sounded credible.

The soldier peered. "You both wear manacles. How is this? To whom do you belong?"

"My master punishes me for –" Hársan began.

Eyíl smiled then. Smoothly she broke in, "Sir, I – we – are taught to accept, nay, to prefer – punishment. And I admit to an enjoyment of the embraces of the living over those of the dead." She ran her hands up from the velvety shadows between her thighs over her belly to cup her breasts.

The soldier stared. He reached past Hársan to touched a fingertip to one dark nipple. "Ohé, your owner must be more a lover of Lady Dlamélish than of the Worm Lord!" He grinned at Hársan. "Go back to your master, slave. I shall send this bit of property along to you presently. He – or she – will not miss her for a few minutes more."

There was nothing to be said. Hársan could not return to the upper colonnade – nor did he really want to leave Eyíl to the mercies of this stone-faced guardsman. (She might not mind all that much, a little thought whispered, since priestesses of Hrihával were supposed to exercise good taste in such matters but little reticence otherwise…)

Hársan decided. His hand shot out to seize the soldier's outstretched arm, to topple him over into the abyss below. Astounded, the man teetered, yelled, flailed with his other hand. They grappled for a long moment, swaying this way and that, struggling as much for balance as for victory. Then the guardsman heaved himself backward to fall with an audible crack of muscles upon the balcony floor. Hársan sprawled on top of him, rolled, tumbled, flung up a hand to clutch only empty space – and fell head downward over the railing toward the nave far beneath!

Calloused fingers grasped at his calf, slid down to clamp upon his ankle. Hársan swung down to smash with blinding force against the frieze of worm lords carved on the outside of the balcony railing. The soldier shouted hoarsely, and his hand slipped but caught again. Hársan dangled by one leg, scrabbling with his hands at the stony eyes and pitted teeth of the bas-reliefs. He did not know whether he wanted the man to save his life or to let him fall to a quick and final death. The chandeliers whirled before his vision; the crowds of devotees were black and ochre beetles below. His shins scraped stone as the guardsman – and possibly Eyíl – hauled his legs back up over the balustrade to safety.

A crunching crack sounded above him. Pebbles, crumbling mortar, and a fist-sized chunk of rock struck his shoulders and went plummeting on past him into the nave. The balustrade! He heard a curse, a panting cry, Eyíl's voice screaming. The hand on his ankle slipped away entirely, and he knew that he must fall.

A strange and easy peace overcame him. This was the last knot of his Skein. No more decisions, no more pain. No more desiring. Nothing was left but that last burst of agony before he joined the concourse of the Dead on their way to Belkhánu's Isles.

He fell free.

There was a clattering in the air all around, wind beat at his face, and he thrashed out wildly with his arms. Claws dug into the flesh of his back, raked along his ribs, his thighs, encircled his waist. Something chittered in his ear, smelling of mouldy leather and death and carrion. He was lifted horizontally out over nothingness, drawn entirely away from the balcony to kick his heels above that fearsome drop! He must have screamed, but he could not hear his own voice. Blood pounded in his ears. A great bronze chandelier hurtled toward him. He snatched at it instinctively, only to have the claws drag him away again and carry him on upward, so close under the roof that he could see the peeling paint and the webbing of cracks in the murals there.

Behind him he heard a shriek. He caught a glimpse of a figure, arms windmilling, tumbling over and over to disappear amongst the little insects below. Was it Eyíl? He could see no more. Blood rushed to his head. Wings of clammy leather flapped in his face. The stairs and columns of the colonnade swooped up at him. Tiny dolls there pointed and gesticulated as he was brought down to a jouncing, painful landing.

Prince Dhich'uné waited upon the steps, once again skull-faced and rigid as Hársan had first seen him. The pupilless eyes glowed yellow in the fires of the lamps.

"So, little priestling, you have learned to fly? Were it not for our *Vorodlá* here you might have joined the Worm Lord all too soon."

Hársan rolled over and saw for the first time the things that had rescued him: three tall, dingy-black, bat-winged beings with powerfully muscled torsos, elongated limbs, and narrow, triangular faces. They had never been spawned of living flesh, however; their eyes were the pallid white of the Undead. Somehow he knew that they — or parts of them — had been human once; now they were numbered among Lord Sárku's legions. The *Vorodlá* were mentioned in the Epic of Hrúgga, but he had never dreamed that they existed in fact!

The Prince addressed the creatures. "Go," he said, "and harry the girl to one end of the gallery or the other. I do not think she will find the courage to hurl herself down as this priest almost did." He turned back to Hársan. "As it is, you have cost the Temple of Sárku a soldier this night. Perhaps I shall let you live long enough to pay *Shámtla* in kind for that offence! I grow impatient with you, priest, and I freely confess that you try my skills as a teacher. The lessons I can yet impart are severe ones indeed!"

"Mighty Prince," he panted, "if you would let the Lady Eyíl go free —"

"No. No more of your logicking and bargaining! I should make your Eyíl our guest at the next Giving of Praise to the One of Mouths!" He leaned down over Hársan. "Note well, priest: not only will your priestess suffer if you again seek to escape or to betray me, but you have witnessed my power over the Undead. Even were you to succeed in suicide, I can resurrect your body and enough of your mind to make you guide me to the Man of Gold. You are not needed alive, only in somewhat undamaged form! Slower and less responsive would you be, but far more pliable if your soul were gone..."

One of the Legion of Kétl approached and murmured something.

Prince Dhich'uné nodded and spoke again:

"My original purpose in bringing you here still holds. Since you shall soon journey to Púrdimal in my service, I would have you meet your escort." An officer in blue and brown livery was making his way through the crowd. At first Hársan thought him one of the Undead as well, for he was thin and gaunt, shaven-headed, his face wrinkled as a corpse dried in the sun. The man halted and saluted, fist to breast.

"This is Lord Qurrúmu hiKhánuma, Commander of the Battalions of the Seal of the Worm, my father's Ninth Legion of Medium Infantry, a unit devoted to the Empire — and also to our Temple of Sárku." He turned to the officer. "You have a Cohort marching to Khirgár within a six-day?"

"It is so, my Lord. The First Cohort."

"You shall prepare space within your baggage wagons for two guests. Neither shall come to any harm, but let no one speak to them. I shall send attendants to care for their needs. When you reach Púrdimal you will hand them over to a priest of our sect, one Jayárgo."

"I know the man, mighty Prince. Was he not at Tumíssa a year back?"

"The same. I have had him reassigned. He will be waiting in Púrdimal for these whom you bring."

"Shall I take custody of your guests now, Lord?"

The still features gazed down upon Hársan once more. "I think not. I would teach one further lesson to this obstreperous little priest." He cast about for Vridékka. "Is the girl retaken, old man?"

"She is, mighty Prince. As she fled down the spiral stair."

"Then do you transport these two back to the Tólek Kána Pits and find accommodation for them in one of the Chalices of Silence. When Lord

Qurrúmu sends to say that his troops are ready, you will accompany them to Púrdimal. You alone can be counted upon to squeeze the truth out of this grey-robe."

"My Lord, I am too old! My place is here, with Lord Arkháne – my own work –"

"A baggage cart will be splendidly appointed for you, old one. Your scrawny feet need not touch the earth all the way, and you shall be wined and coddled until you are as fat as a *Hmélu*-calf. The weather grows cooler, and you may enjoy the change." The mouth did not smile.

"I must obey…"

"Indeed. To do otherwise would be disappointing."

Prince Dhich'uné turned his back and departed. The worshippers were leaving as well, the service over. The Undead were no longer to be seen. Had they descended again into their catacombs, or had they ever really existed at all? The *Vorodlá* were assuredly real enough!

The soldiers of the Legion of Kétl escorted Hársan down across the emptying nave to where Eyíl hung limply between two temple-guards. Vridékka did not allow them to speak to one another but formed up his party, gestured sharply to its subaltern, and led the way back through the subterranean labyrinth.

The journey was uneventful.

The captives were led through the silent corridors of the Pits. At length they stopped before a row of little ladders of four steps apiece. Each of these led up to a square metal door, much like the mouth of a potter's kiln. One of these hung ajar, and Hársan saw a black shaft slanting down into the rock. He and Eyíl were unbound, and a soldier took away the remains of his stained and tattered kilt. Two guardsmen then wrestled him up the ladder and thrust his legs into the shaft.

"I would not have ordered this for you, boy," Vridékka said, not unkindly, "but my master has commanded it. The Chalice of Silence is a cell barely large enough to lie at full length, no room to rise or to sit up, and barely enough to turn over. Food and water are poured down to you through this hole in the door, and your wastes pass out through a grating at your feet, for the cell slopes somewhat." He twisted a finger in his straggling beard. "Sometimes the keepers of this place pour down filth or boiling water in lieu of sustenance, but I shall see that this is not done to you. At least you may be consoled that this condition will last only for a day or two – some there are who have lived in these holes for as long as a year. Most are insane within a month."

"And the girl, master Vridékka?" one of the soldiers asked.

The mind-seer sighed. "She will probably fare better with her priest here than alone without him. More, I see no other Chalice vacant at present. Put her in with him."

Arms wrestled Hársan into the narrow aperture. He fought, scrabbled at the smooth sides of the shaft, found no purchase, and slipped down within. His feet jarred against bars of slime-encrusted metal, and he came to a stop in blackness. He tried to flex his knees but only bruised them against the low roof. There was a little room at the sides to extend his arms, but as he did so Eyíl's legs struck his shoulder, and he had to press himself against the slimy wall to let her slip down into the cell beside him. His arms went around her automatically, and she came to a halt panting against his breast.

The cell door clanged shut above.

Smothering darkness closed in upon him. All was silent.

Slowly, insidiously, the terror of being buried alive seeped in to fill him with icy fear. The nightmare of being wedged into a black box to suffocate – the terror of a small boy left alone in the dark, the memory of a near-fatality during a boisterous cave exploration in his childhood – arose to overwhelm him. He gasped, struggled, and fought to gain control of himself. His temple training helped.

Then Eyíl stirred, thrust her hands against the stone walls of their coffin, kicked out, and screamed.

It was a long time before they were calm again.

Chapter Twenty-Two

Hársan awoke to an urgent sense of wrongness.

Interminable hours had passed. His logic-schooled mind had finally mastered his own fear of the in-pressing walls, the blackness, the silence, and the numbing terror of being buried alive. Somehow he had also soothed Eyíl. It was as Vridékka had said: what saved their sanity was the knowledge that this imprisonment would last no more than a few days at most. That – and being together – helped to bolster up their mutual courage. Alone, he might have given in to madness, clawed and scratched at the stone walls, and died howling in this smothering coffin.

He and Eyíl gave one another strength. They made what adjustments they could against the narrowness and their cramped limbs, recovered from their hurts, slept, and rested. Three times – once a day, judging from the sharp remonstrances of Hársan's stomach – a mixture of *Dná*-porridge and water was poured through the hole at the top of the shaft. They caught as much of this as they could with their bare hands and licked more from the slimy stones as it trickled down past their bodies and out through the grating at their feet.

The grating?

That was what was wrong! His exploring toes encountered only empty space there. The grating was gone. That was what had awakened him!

Amazement, fear – a dozen thoughts – fled through Hársan's mind.

"Hársan –! Something – my ankle!" Eyíl gasped.

Even as she spoke her body slipped down against his, her face pressed against his chest. He fumbled for her but only barked his knuckles against the low ceiling. Eyíl kicked out and screamed, and Hársan shouted as well. If these were the Prince's soldiers come to get them, why did they not take them out of the upper door? Why did they not at least reply?

Something pulled Eyíl inexorably downward. Visions of the nightmare denizens of Lord Sárku's catacombs rose before his eyes. He got an arm around her shoulders but could not gain a solid purchase. No one answered their cries.

Eyíl slipped down even farther, her nails raking the flesh of his hips.

"Oh –! Help me, Hársan!"

Her body threshed and bucked, and he could hear her nails rasping at the slime-slick walls. Her tangled hair whipped and coiled at his thighs as she flung her head to and fro. Hársan groped for her wrists, touched her head and shoulders but could not hold her. Now Eyíl's nails drew blood from his calves. Then her hands were pulled away entirely, and her screams dwindled into the blind darkness below.

Then they stopped.

Hard, clawlike fingers seized his own ankle. Hársan bellowed, humped up against the ceiling to keep from sliding, elbows and knees splayed out against the walls. Nothing availed. Slowly he slithered down along the mucky floor of their cell. Spikes of pain drove into his fingers, and he knew that his own nails were broken and bloody. The taste of fear gagged in his throat, and he threw back his head to yell again.

A voice from below hissed, "If you would only quit howling, priest, I could tell you that we are friends. Can you not hear me?"

Amazement choked him. Before he could collect his wits, the hands upon his ankles dragged him tumbling down through the opening at the foot of the cell to sprawl in slimy, stinking water.

More hands gripped him, pulled him to his feet. Bodies bumped against his. Someone swore fervently in the rude language of the gutters.

"Chá! How these two smell!"

"As you will for a month, after we're all free of this!" another, higher voice answered. "No lights yet, not till we're out of these sewers."

"Eyíl?" Hársan rasped. He heard ragged weeping near him and reached out. Her body came trembling into his arms, and relief swept over him.

"She's all right, priest; just frightened," a third, hoarse voice said. "If you'd heard us calling when we opened the grate, you'd have known we were no corpses from the pits!"

"We must have been asleep –"

"No matter now. Come, watch your head. This place is just high enough to stand. It's used to carry off the sewage and remove the dead from the Chalices. Say no more as we pass below the other cells, or we'll have all the other customers belling in chorus as well."

Someone said something reassuring to Eyíl, a smaller, lighter man by his tone. Guiding hands pulled Hársan around and led him splashing and stumbling along the narrow tunnel. Life returned to his legs in a numbing tingle.

Metal clanked against stone as somebody replaced the grating at the foot of their cell.

They proceeded a hundred paces or so along a black passageway. Then his unseen pilot helped him find the entrance to a winding stair that spiralled up to emerge into a larger tunnel.

"A light, let's have a light," a voice complained.

They halted, and a luminous blue sphere appeared from a pouch or sack. In its nacreous azure glow Hársan had his first look at their liberators.

There were three men. One wore the leather harness and brown livery of the Legion of Kétl, a grizzled older man, as thick as a *Chlén*-beast through the shoulders. The second was smaller, with a lined, bitter, big-nosed face. He was attired only in a frayed breechclout like that of a labourer or dockworker. The third man was young and whip-thin, with the indefinable air of a marketplace dandy about him. He had a sword slung in a leather baldric at his waist and a pleated kilt that might have started the day clean.

Yet it was not upon these that Hársan's gaze lingered but upon the fourth member of the party, he who held the blue-glowing sphere. It was a Pé Chói – a male, all gleaming black chitin!

"Chtík p'Qwé –" Hársan cried. But it was not his friend.

Eyes that glinted with their own inner scarlet fires looked back at him in puzzlement. "No – you are not he. I – I took you for another..."

"Through here – to the river gate," the soldier said gruffly.

"As riddled with tunnels as a tree full of *Osó*-beetles!" the small man growled. He must be from somewhere in the north; the beetle he named did not favour these hot southern climes.

170

"Come," the soldier replied, "we must be out of here before I am missed. The watch changes at dawn, and some poke-nosed guard may wander in here to piss before breakfast."

"You are of the temple of Thúmis?" Eyíl addressed the younger man, he with the sword.

He looked her raffishly up and down, let his gaze linger upon her nudity. "Not so, my Lady. Let us say only that we dance to the same measure in this endeavour."

Hársan drew abreast of the Pé Chói. "Do you know one Chtík p'Qwé," he asked, "a Scholar Priest in the temple of Keténgku? I seek news of him."

The other shrugged, his small upper limbs pressed tight against his gleaming black thorax. "I have only heard his name." The accent was oddly foreign and bore an uncharacteristic lilt. This Pé Chói was not from Dó Cháka then – perhaps some place beyond the Mu'ugalavyáni frontier to the west?

Hársan tried again. "We would know who you are. And whom you serve."

"My identity is of no import. What matters is that you and the girl be delivered safely to Púrdimal – to friends there." The creature put out one of his middle pair of limbs to steady himself. "You must leave the city tonight."

Something pricked at Hársan's mind, but he could not think what it was. Could this be some charade of Prince Dhich'uné's, meant to coax him into easy collaboration? He had to know. He spoke again, this time in the Pé Chói tongue:

"Some currents lead not to the shore but out into the whirlpool. Tell me at least the name of him who sent you."

The Pé Chói did not reply but only opened its long, lipless mouth in an imitation of a human smile.

The young swordsman came forward and hissed, "No more talk! Time for that later."

The tunnel ended at a corroded metal door. This stood ajar, and Hársan smelled the cold, yet gloriously free, odour of the river. Beyond, a flight of steps led down to a ledge. A boat was made fast there to a green-crusted bronze ring, rocking and chuckling gently upon black water. The burly guard went down first, followed by the Pé Chói, then Hársan and Eyíl. The hard-faced little man and the swordsman brought up the rear.

"Hand down the girl first," the soldier called up. "Better for balance. Past this cavern is the river gate; then we're out. The watchman there is my man."

Eyíl pressed close to him upon the stair. "Know you these people?" she whispered. "They are none of ours."

There was time only to shake his head. The Pé Chói stood aside to let her by, then shifted the blue sphere from one of his central pair of hands to the other in order to help Hársan. There was something strange about this gesture. Hársan stopped, and the bitter-faced man behind bumped into him.

"Why," Hársan asked in the Pé Chói tongue, "do you never use your uppermost limbs? Do you suffer a paralysis? Never was it the custom of your people to assist a friend only with your *T'qé*-hands – your middle limbs!"

The creature hesitated, then turned away muttering something.

"Your nest contains despicable chewers of *K'nékw*-bark," Hársan added conversationally in the same language. He switched to Tsolyáni: "Do you not agree?"

"He knows, master!" the man behind him cried. And flung himself down upon Hársan striving to pinion his arms. The attack was not unexpected.

Hársan stooped and let the fellow lunge right over his back to tumble into the Pé Chói. The blue orb spun free and bounced out onto the ledge. The creature scrambled after it shouting words in a harsh, breathy tongue Hársan did not recognise. A slithering noise on the stair behind warned him that the swordsman had drawn his weapon. He yelled and heard Eyíl's answering cry in return. A string of oaths, a splash, and a barking scream told him that she must have got in a surprise blow against the prison guard.

He had no clear idea what to do; only a determination not to be taken alive for more of Prince Dhich'uné's subtle games! The sword whickered past him. Its owner was more practiced at slashing than at thrusting, and the blade scraped sparks from the rough stones of the wall. Hársan plunged back up the stairs to grapple with the man, but his prison-weakened legs betrayed him. He succeeded only in blocking the sword and gaining a handful of his opponent's kilt. Fabric tore. He heard a crunch and a grunt of pain: the fellow had aimed a blow left-handed at Hársan's head, missed, and likely cracked his knuckles upon the wall! Hársan made a stiff wedge of his fingers, jabbed hard somewhere below his fistful of kilt, and was rewarded with a satisfactory whoof of expelled breath. The sword clattered down the steps past him. Did he dare let go of the man to pick it up? He thought not. Another successful push and he might break past this fellow into the larger tunnel above – but where after that he did not know.

Hands clawed at his naked back, wrapped around his waist. The ugly little man had untangled himself from the Pé Chói. Hársan let go of the swordsman, kicked out, twisted around, splayed fingers stabbing for his foe's eyes. The man ducked his head, and Hársan's hand thudded against his forehead – apparently hard enough to unbalance him, for he pitched backward down the stairs.

Brilliant blue light burst in upon his senses. Eyíl's voice cut off in mid-cry.

In the eldritch afterglow Hársan saw another thing: no Pé Chói now stood below upon the ledge but rather some creature out of an ancient bestiary, furred all over, a snarling animal muzzle rimmed with up-curving fangs, pointed ears like those of a *Rényu*, two arms that were over-long, jointed in places where no human – or Pé Chói – had joints. It was nude save for a harness of belts and straps and pouches; he could see six black breast nipples on its sleek belly but no visible sex organs.

Then the edges of the beast's image sparkled, faded, and solidified into other features: a stout, fussy, middle-aged man in a pleated saffron kilt: Lord Arkháne hiPurúshqe!

So this was how these people had gained access to the Pits: a creature who could take on the semblance of any he – she – it willed! At some point this strange shape-shifter must have impersonated the prison governor to get in here!

Then Lord Arkháne blurred, too, and Hársan looked upon the Pé Chói once more.

The blue orb lifted toward him.

He never saw the second flare of azure light. He floated in a sea of warm honey, sweet and somnolent, serene as a ship upon a summer lake. He still saw and heard, but he could not move. He felt nothing of his own body, nor did he seem to care.

The figure before him swam at the bottom of a grotto of sapphire. It wavered, and Lord Arkháne's face hung superimposed upon a Pé Chói torso. The lilting voice said, "I have taken care of the girl, Zhu'ón. Do you go down and fish clumsy Quró out of the water."

The big-nosed man arose, rubbing his bruises. He staggered down the stairs, and his voice floated up from below. "I see him not, master. Only foam and a bubbling…"

"The fool has drowned then. Or else the tales of the pits beneath this dungeon are true. Return and aid me with the priest!" The beast-muzzle approached Hársan. Glinting red eyes looked up past him. "Étqole, do you live?"

The younger man limped down the stairs to pick up his sword. His left hand was bloody and had begun to swell.

"Help Zhu'ón bear the priest down to the boat."

"I cannot," the man gritted. "He has broken my hand." He swung his sword-hilt suddenly in a vicious blow at Hársan's naked groin. The shape-changer reached out and knocked the weapon aside.

"No foolish revenge! He is not to be maimed. We deliver him to Púrdimal – or slay him if we must."

"I'll have him then, when you're all done with him. And his naked wench there as well to pay me for my pains. Once she is bathed, of course!" He sniffed in disgust.

The man named Zhu'ón reappeared, and he and the shape-changer wrestled Hársan's rigid body down into the skiff and flung him upon the damp decking beside Eyíl. Hársan felt only a profound tranquillity. Face down, he could see nothing, but his hearing was as sharp as that of any Zrné-beast.

"Can these be transported to Púrdimal in this condition, master?" Zhu'ón asked.

"No. They will die as their bodily processes slow and grow cold. We can get them out of Béy Sü thus, but thereafter we must use other means."

"Alas that he discovered our masquerade before we had him safe at Púrdimal," the little man growled. He sniggered. "Never will he believe that we're his precious grey-robes now!"

"I should not have taken on the seeming of a Pé Chói. Étqole, it was you who counselled that this would reassure the priest."

"Who was to know that he spoke the stinking insects' language?" the other replied peevishly. "Only so much could be learned in such a short time!"

"We still take the girl?" Zhu'ón interrupted.

"It is so. Prince Dhich'uné showed wisdom in this – but in little else, I think. His slaughter of our good Helé'a, his eagerness to abandon his allies… This is only the first page of the accounting; there will be more later when our master has the whole tale."

There was silence for a time, save for Zhu'ón's wheezing as he rowed. The plash of oars echoed back from the roof of the cavern.

"Master," the little man said at length, "if your orb can keep these two cosy for a time until they're out of Béy Sü, our network can supply the rest: a cubby-hole in a merchant's cart, a leisurely route along the back paths away from the Sákbe-roads, mayhap a party of harlots to take the girl?"

"Chá!" the swordsman called Étqole put in sarcastically. "Both the Prince of Worms and the grey-robes will have watchers out. And likely the girl's people as well. You'll be Küni-birds chirping in the net before a six-day is done!"

"No. We need fear only Prince Dhich'uné," the shape-changer murmured. "None other has reason to seek these two along the way to Púrdimal-unless they, too, have spies within the Legion of Kétl."

"Then?"

"The best hiding place is in plain view. My orb has other uses than those you saw. Once we Mihálli were a mighty race, as skilled as your human ancestors before the Time of Darkness — and more. A touch within the priest's brain, and he shambles along as a poor victim of the shaking sickness, unable to speak, to write, or even to feed himself. When we are amongst friends in Púrdimal he can be restored and made to do our bidding."

"The same for the girl?"

The shape-changer seemed to consider. "An addict to *Zu'úr*. Not in reality for she will also be needed. But my orb will give her the semblance of one: a pallid, frozen cataleptic. All within your human realms know that such a one can be roused to further frenzies of sexual ecstasy by another grain or two of the drug. There are those who buy such hapless slaves."

"And the sending of them, master?"

"Openly. With Chnesúru the Salarvyáni. Soon he takes a cargo of slaves to Khirgár, and he can carry these two as far as Púrdimal. We know him: he loves gold more than any god."

"A slaver's caravan!" Étqole's voice was full of scorn. "The first place I'd look, were I Prince Dhich'uné!"

"The priest shall be disguised. His head is shaved, his face painted blue with Livyáni tattooes. The shaking sickness hides his walk and his posture. None will heed him amidst a herd of field slaves. The girl, too, will be altered; she'll travel in a sealed litter, the purchase of some lordling known for his curious tastes. Zhu'ón, can you name such a one?"

"There is a certain Lord Keléno, master, a High Priest of Ksárul lately posted to Mrelú. Men say that he favours eccentric delights: the waxen pallor of a *Zu'úr* addict would send him into spasms of lust. No ordinary watcher would question a slaver bringing such a present to him."

"This is madness," the swordsman snarled. "We do not deal with ordinary watchers! Great master — lord — we humans may be innocents in your ancient and all-knowing eyes, but —!" He broke off and began again in a more conciliatory tone. "We shall certainly be caught out, Lord! The Tsolyáni are not fools. Even if the grey-robes think that the priest is being sent to Ch'óchi, there are only two routes west: the direct one across to Tumíssa, and the northern road through Púrdimal, Khirgár, and Chéne Hó. They'll be sitting on both, as a bird squats on her eggs! We must plan, master, devise a means, make arrangements…"

"And find the Worm Prince's huntsmen sniffing upon every path? We dare not give him time to organise a pursuit." The creature added slyly, "There is, of course, a third way to Púrdimal: the tunnel-cars built by your ancestors before the Time of Darkness. We could be in Púrdimal — or even in Ke'ér — in a trice. I know where they lie in the Underworlds beneath the city for I travelled hither by that means. Those who guided me would demand further payment, of course, which I cannot now provide. The labyrinths are risky — and the favoured province of the Worm Lord. Would you dare that route, Étqole?"

"You do not hoodwink a child, Mihálli — master! I have heard tales of those places — and of what guards them! You paid me money for my services, and you shall see me earn it. But I'll not offer my tasty flesh to the *Dlaqó*-beetles or to any others of the horrors of the pits! Still, your slave caravan is no better — nay, worse! Try it, and the last journey we take is the 'high ride' on the impaler's stake!"

"Ah, brave Étqole! No one asks you to go. Indeed, Zhu'ón and I can travel in a separate party — charcoal merchants, tanners of *Chlén*-hide, coppersmiths — and thus keep an eye clapped to old Chnesúru."

"Shall I then be cheated of the bigger share of my pay?" the swordsman cried, "and of my revenge upon the priest — and a little time with the girl? You would cast me aside so soon?"

The creature made an odd, non-human growling sound. "Then join us. Or shut your shop and go your way!"

For a time there was only the soft wash of the oars. Finally the swordsman grumbled: "Chá, I'll not be left behind! Yet let us risk no more than is needful. We make no visible connection with the slaver but remain apart — as you say. I shall travel as a noble, with sufficient coin for good food, wine —"

"Ohé, and a golden palanquin, and a cortege of little girls to sing as you journey, and a pisspot all set with emeralds, and —"

"Shut up, Zhu'ón. Else you'll wear a second gullet!"

"Be silent, both of you! We approach the river gate. Tell me, Zhu'ón, when does Chnesúru depart?"

"Tomorrow is the twelfth of Pardán. He leaves the day after, master."

"Find him. Give him several golden reasons to advance his calendar a day. We must make haste."

"Ohé, there's one more crack in the pot," Étqole interrupted in still-sulky tones. "What of the white globe and the silver rod? Quró said the Worm Prince got the first, but the second…"

"The globe has no value now. As for the rod, who knows where it is? Still in the temple of Thúmis, mayhap? And perhaps our employer has no need of the rod but seeks only to find the Man of Gold and destroy it…This is no affair of ours."

Fingers of mist and a dappled greyish light curled along the deck before Hársan's staring eyes. They were out upon the river, then, and it was dawn.

Zhu'ón's voice came once more: "Master, what of the real Lord Arkháne?"

The Mihálli gave a low chuckle, almost human. "Why, let him wake where I put him, in the Chalice of Silence. His Legion of Kétl may believe his pleas and pull him forth – or they may serve him boiling water for his breakfast…"

Chapter Twenty-Three

This was the task Tlayésha hated most: ministering to the field-slaves. The women she did not mind; the children she treated with affectionate patience; and Chnesúru's "special wares." Were interesting, if sometimes sad or strange. But the field-hands –! A blister here, a stomach pain there, a suppurating sore, a fever, a flux, a nose mashed in one of the interminable fights in the pens! Often they teased her, pinched her, laid hands upon her, or even tried to pull aside the thin veil she wore to conceal the deformity of her face.

That thought she pushed firmly from her mind.

Far back down the *Sákbe*-road, Béy Sü lay to the southeast beneath the blanket of pre-dawn mist. Somewhere there the sun would shortly stride up into the sky to begin another weary day. Tlayésha sighed and set down her bucket of water and bag of medicaments. They were ten days out of the capital now, and pompous old Chnesúru was in the worst mood she could remember: a trustee slave had decamped, taking a woman and two sacks of *Dná*-flour with him, and the pair had not yet been recaptured – and already Tlayésha had more than she could handle to keep her charges healthy!

Was this the slave Múru the cook had sent her to cure? Yes, he lay with a cheap clay amulet of Balmé, the healing Aspect of Mother Avánthe, pressed to a red and infected cheek, and he moaned softly in his sleep. He must be treated. Chnesúru kept his merchandise in the best possible health. Soon the month of Halír would come, when the crops were cut and the demand for field-hands would be at its peak. At every village and *Sákbe*-road tower the overseers of the manors of the nobility, the stewards of the temple farms, the officers of the Emperor's state lands, and the elders of the agricultural clans awaited Chnesúru's coming with impatience. Slaves might not do all the work, but if the *Chlén*-cart of the Empire had four wheels, then the slave population certainly made up two of them.

She squatted down on her heels beside the man and took out a clay pot of salve, a relatively clean rag, and her most treasured instrument, a needle of rare iron fixed in a wooden handle.

"You're not asleep," she said. "Get up, and let me look at that cheek."

A sullen eye opened, and the fellow made a great pretence of waking up, a big muscular man burned almost black by the sun. Tlayésha was used to such responses; she brought her needle up to point directly into the open eye. The slave sat up.

"In the name of Qón, girl, it's only a boil." He was probably trying to ingratiate himself. Many thought she worshipped Qón, Lord Belkhánu's canine-headed Cohort. The clergy of the Temple of Qón wore veils to conceal their faces – some odd tenet of their sect – but theirs were invariably yellow while Tlayésha made do with any bit of fabric she could find.

"It must be seen to, man. No pretty *Aridáni* lady will buy you for her harem until that carbuncle is gone."

"Chá! Go tickle the boy with the shaking sickness there! He needs healing more than I!" He reached out a hand to caress her thigh, but she set the needle's point firmly against the skin of his wrist.

"Be patient. Bountiful Chnesúru arranges harlots for all of you tonight when we reach Tkomán Village."

"The decrepit hags he provides are only useful to frighten demons!" He gave a coarse laugh. "Why not minister to me yourself? Are you not a physician? Some say that you are ugly, but others claim you are so lovely that you hide your face to keep us all from going mad. For my needs, my lady, you can keep your head-scarf; the parts I want are lower down."

"I am no slave to lie upon the open road with field-hands. Master Chnesúru employs me – for what his coppers are worth. Come – let me lance your cheek, else I must advise him that he would profit by having you altered for service as a eunuch. Mayhap you would enjoy the soft life of a servant in some clanmaster's harem!"

The slave grunted and spat, but he held up his face and made a show of feeling no pain. Tlayésha salved the boil and rose, dodging a final pat on the backside. She walked on down the line.

There sat the boy with the shaking sickness. They had picked him up outside of Béy Sü, the Gods knew why! Some demon must have muddied Chnesúru's wits that day! They'd be lucky to get twenty *Káitar*s for him. A hereditary disease, people said, and reason enough for his clan to sell him off for a pittance. No room for such in a peasant's household! At first they had had to feed him, and he had not even been able to hold his bowels. He bore bruises and manacle-scars on his wrists as well. Fright and nervousness at being sold into strange hands had doubtless added, too, to his condition. Now he was steadier, and she had only to see that others did not steal his food or kick him too severely when he stumbled and drooled.

She stopped beside the boy. Actually he was a youth as old or older than Tlayésha herself. She had got into the habit of thinking of him as a boy, a child almost, because of his malady. He had no name, or if he did he could not control his tongue to tell it. She did not even know if he understood Tsolyáni. He was almost certainly from some low clan of Livyánu, for his face and torso were covered with *Aomüz*, the arabesques of red, blue, and black tattoos every Livyáni received in childhood. They indicated the wearer's clan, city, and religious affiliation. Yet when two of Chnesúru's Livyáni slaves had tried to question him, they had got no farther than had Tlayésha. There was a riddle indeed.

Like most of Master Chnesúru's slaves, the boy wore no shackles. The lot of a slave was no worse than that of many peasants, and at least a slave's belly usually stayed full. A squad of overseers, a few guards, and the ever-present row of impaling stakes that graced the gates and plazas of the cities of the Five Empires were enough to vouch for good behaviour under most circumstances. When they had first left Béy Sü the boy had hung back or stumbled away from the column two or three times; Chnesúru had put this down to his illness rather than to any wish to escape and had not even scolded him, much less had him beaten. Now *there* was a second puzzle!

"Here," she said, and held out a sponge of water and a blob of greasy *Vé*-root paste for him to soap himself. He looked up at her with some odd emotion showing in his eyes, and for a moment it seemed as though he would speak. But then his tongue lolled out, his eyes unfocussed, and he fumbled for the sponge with shaking fingers. Tlayésha poured water over his back and noted idly that the skin there was still sunburned and peeling. His previous owners must have kept him indoors. She wondered again what his history might have been.

"Hói! – Ohé!" Someone called from the front of the column, and the slaves groaned and stumbled to their feet. The day's march was about to begin.

Behind her the horizon showed as angry-red as that slave's boil, but to the north the Kraá Hills still bulked black beneath diadems of cloud. Only the sword-bright pinnacle of Akonár Peak thrust above the foothills there, blood-splashed by the dawning sun. Tlayésha looked to the northwest, but Thénu Thendráya Peak was not yet visible. Once the road turned after the town of Tsurú, they would journey under the shadow of that granite monolith – "The Sentinel of Hrúgga" people named it – for many more days before reaching the swamps surrounding old Púrdimal. Thénu Thendráya Peak guarded the jumbled mountains and deserts of the impoverished and fragmented nation of Milumanayá, it was said, although there was nothing there to see but wild nomads and sand and barren stones. Beyond, however, lay Yán Kór.

Tlayésha picked up her bucket and medicines and walked along beside the coffle, ignoring the calls and obscene pleasantries of the slaves. She had heard all of that since she was twelve years old and had fled her clan in Butrús in Pán Cháka. Her deformity had stirred up the superstitious fears of her clanspeople. But the fault lay more with a certain facile rogue who had called himself noble and called her by many more honeyed names! Chá, he had sold her soon enough into the brothels of Jakálla! There she had spent five miserable years earning her freedom again by "the tasks of the bed," as fat Taneré the brothel-keeper charitably named them.

Remembered hurt and insult arose to plague her memory. She was not unbeautiful. Were it not for her birth-curse, she might have attained the higher status of courtesan. As it was, she was forced to cater to those who were too low, too uncaring, too strange in their desires, or too drunk to notice. As Taneré said, "Darkness makes everyone beautiful." She had taught Tlayésha to keep her room shuttered, the candle low, and to dance nude save for a veil upon her face. "Mystery adds attraction – and coins upon the brass plate."

After Jakálla there had been a dozen cities. Freedom does not fill the belly, and those days were not easy ones. At least she had learned about medicines, drugs, and treatments – among other things – and when Master Chnesúru offered to hire her as physician for his merchandise, she had accepted gratefully. For two – no, almost three – years now she had accompanied the slaver's caravan from Thráya in the southeast to Khirgár in the far northwest of the Empire. Twice she had gone beyond: once to Khéiris in Mu'ugalavyá, and once to Pijnár on the shores of the foggy northern sea. Now she counted herself experienced, travelled, and able to look upon her Skein of Destiny without fear – though with no particular joy.

Qoyqunél, the chief of the caravan guards, was coming back along the column to pick litter bearers for the morning shift. The pretty girls, the trained courtesans, the dancers, the children, the old, and the sick were not required to walk but rode instead in palanquins or in the trundling *Chlén*-carts.

There were a few closed litters as well, tended by selected female slaves or by some of the slaver's nonhuman henchmen: Shén, Ahoggyá, a Pé Chói or two, and others. On this trip Tlayésha had been called to minister to the occupants of two of these. One was a beautiful little girl of ten or twelve, to whom she had given dream-potions to help her forget her lost home in Háida Pakála, a land so far away across the southern ocean that Tlayésha had heard no more than its name. The other was a delicate-looking, long-limbed girl, a victim of the dreaded *Zu'úr*, who lay like a corpse behind the heavy curtains of her litter. The Gods take pity upon that one! But then the poor wretch would never know what was done to her, and that, at least, was a mercy. Her mind was gone, and within a few months she would surely die. Such was the way of *Zu'úr*. Those who supplied it risked their lives, but there were those, even in the highest places, who made use of its addicts for their own morbid pleasures. This, to Tlayésha, was the worst part of slavery, and she realised only too well why the profession of slaver was held to be the lowest of the low in all the Five Empires. Master Chnesúru might become as rich as a God, but never would he be received within the gates of any clanhouse save those that followed the same greedy occupation.

Qoyqunél waved his scalloped sword of hardened *Chlén*-hide and shouted. The fool had never used the weapon and wore it only to impress the village trollops. He chose a score of slaves from among the plodding field-hands and sent them trotting forward to help with the litters; Tlayésha saw that the boy with the shaking sickness was in the group. Well, he seemed fit enough to hold up a litter pole.

Tlayésha let herself fall into the mindless rhythm of walking, her thoughts far away from the dusty vistas of yellowing grain and baked-brick hamlets. The morning passed.

She was awakened from her reverie by shouting and the sound of blows ahead. Someone was being flogged. She hitched her bag of medicines higher on her hip and went forward to see what was amiss.

As she drew nearer she saw that Old White-Side, the Ahoggyá overseer, had somebody down upon the roadway, belabouring him with its knurled cudgel and hooting obscenities in a mixture of human languages and its own gurgling, gobbling tongue. The victim was the boy with the shaking sickness! Tlayésha broke into a run.

She had always disliked this particular Ahoggyá for its needless cruelty. Now she ran up to it and snatched the staff from its four-fingered hand.

"What do you, woman?" Old White-Side cried, and reached for its cudgel with another of its four arms. Everything about the Ahoggyá came in fours: a knobbly grey carapace of horny material sheltered a brown-furred, barrel-shaped body. Just below this carapace, four arms were set equidistantly around its circumference, and below these, at the base of the barrel, four gnarled legs bent outward in a permanent crouch. Between each pair of arms, high up under the carapace rim, it had two wicked little eyes on each side. Below one of these pairs of optics was its fanged, crude-looking mouth, and in similar positions on the other three sides were its organs of hearing, smell, and reproduction. No human could pronounce an Ahoggyá name, and hence Chnesúru's people called this one "Old White-Side" because of a patch of bristly silver fur on one of its "shoulders." The creature smelled rank, like a barnyard in a swamp, reminiscent of its homeland in the sea-marshes along the southern Salarvyáni coast.

Tlayésha held the cudgel out of reach. "Why do you beat this slave? Master Chnesúru has forbidden the flogging of slaves save for serious offences! You'll spoil his value!"

"What value?" Old White-Side wheezed. "No money in one who slobbers and soils his breechclout! And just now he would have pulled open the litter curtain and looked within."

This was more serious. None was allowed to see into the Zu'úr-victim's litter. Chnesúru might indeed order a whipping for such a transgression.

"You are mistaken. The boy is witless."

"Even witless humans make sex," the Ahoggyá retorted in its rumbling bass voice. It made obscene gestures with three of its four hands. "See!" It pointed with its remaining hand. The boy was sitting up now, looking at Tlayésha, but with one shaking arm extended towards the litter. He looked more appealing than lustful, and she could not imagine him opening the curtain for any purpose other than half-witted curiosity.

"He has had enough," she snapped at Old White-Side. "You know not your own strength. You may have marred him."

"No loss," the Ahoggyá grunted morosely; but it desisted. Then it added, "I say he be sold, woman. Tonight at Tkomán Village. Lord Fyérik comes to buy field-hands, and we can put this idiot into the midst of a lot where no one will notice. At least Master Chnesúru gets a *Káitar* or two for him."

Tlayésha knew that the creature said this only to vex her. She tossed her head contemptuously and held out a hand to help the boy to his feet. She found him surprisingly strong and lithe for one with the shaking sickness. Other cases she had seen were always softer, flabbier, less muscular. The look he gave her as he returned to the coffle surprised her too: his eyes seemed to contain a spark of real intelligence. And something else: anger, perhaps, or was it determination?

She motioned another man forward from the ranks and got the litter picked up and moving again. Then she went back to join Qoyqunél, leaving Old White-Side to stare maliciously after her from its back pair of eyes.

They marched, then rested during the afternoon in the scanty shade of a *Sákbe*-road tower, then marched again. By the time the sun sank down into the dust-haze on the western horizon Village Tkomán lay before them, a huddle of mean little buildings overtopped by a row of temple spires and the jutting stump of an ancient, ruined citadel.

Master Chnesúru ordered his tent set up on the *Sákbe*-road platform nearest the ramp down to the village gates. The litters were ranged in a circle, and some of the older women were sent to fetch cool water for their occupants. The others had to make do with the muddy tank at the base of the road platform wall. Múru the cook got the commissary going, and soon the amber-gold twilight was filled with the pat-pat of dough being shaped into bread-cakes, the sweet-harsh smoke of charcoal fires, and the clatter of knives upon wood as the pulpy *Shiryá*-tubers and fat *Káo*-squash were chopped up for stew. Tlayésha helped with the buying of a great heap of black *Hréqa*-fruit, now at the best of its short season. Canny Chnesúru was a good provider; his slaves were sleek and healthy, and he had few problems with escapes. The Salarvyáni were sound businessmen.

The slaver himself disappeared into the village to look for buyers, and it was not long before a troupe of harlots arrived, true to Tlayésha's prediction. The sounds of cooking became submerged beneath the clash of silver bangles, the thready notes of a *Sra'úr*, and the laughter of men and women. Tlayésha had never quite sunk to the level of a *Sákbe*-road trollop!

She strolled along the platform. This was a frequent stopping place for travellers, and there were peasants with fruits and meat to sell, peddlers bearing hampers piled high with cheap cloth and jewellery, itinerant priests, hawkers of amulets and potions, and what seemed like a legion of children selling wine, bitter beer, and *Chumétl*, the salted *Hmélu*-buttermilk that everybody preferred to the dubious-tasting water. There were other wayfarers too: a family of villagers in ragged breechclouts who ogled the harlots with interest, a party of sturdy merchants, some men from one of the *Chlén*-hide tanners' clans, two or three litters belonging to the Temple of Avánthe by their blue curtains and insignia, several soldiers of at least three different legions – probably going north to join their units at Púrdimal or Khirgár – and even a lesser nobleman, judging by the gaudy clan-symbols that swung from the pole before his tent.

All of this was as familiar to Tlayésha as a well-worn sandal, and she went to stand in the charcoal-and-spice-smelling dusk to look down over the jumbled shadows of the little town. Soon she saw Master Chnesúru returning in the company of a slender, ageing man in the pleated kilt of a minor aristocrat: probably Lord Fyérik, whose fief lay about ten *Tsán* to the south of Village Tkomán. Two brawny overseers trailed along behind. Her employer appeared a little tipsy, but she knew this to be part of his cleverness. When it came to selling his wares Master Chnesúru was a consummate actor.

"Here," the slaver cried, "you have strong hands for your crops, my Lord!" He called for torches, and Qoyqunél herded the slaves up into the light so that they could be inspected.

Lord Fyérik made a sarcastic face, walked up and down in front of the group, and then snapped his fingers. "Fifty men – a score of *Káitar*s for each!"

Chnesúru made the expected gestures of astonishment and pain. "My Lord, you do not buy old women! These slaves are sound, perfect, industrious, experienced, willing…" He seemed to run out of qualities and shifted to his hurt but honest expression – a good actor, Chnesúru. "You have dealt with me before. You have seen that I never wrong you!"

They chaffered awhile, at first amiably, then with pretended acrimony. At last Chnesúru was satisfied with ninety *Káitar*s apiece for his brood. Not a bad sum, more than Tlayésha had thought he would get – but then demand was high during the month before harvest time.

Suddenly she felt anger rising within her. There, in the midst of the group, stood the slave with the shaking sickness! Old White-Side had been as good as his – its – word!

It was too late to do anything now, and Tlayésha could only stand and watch as the overseers herded him and the others down from the *Sákbe*-road platform. Lord Fyérik took his leave, and then they were gone. She could not repress a pang of – something. She had no idea why she cared. Was it only because the Ahoggyá had flouted her, or was she going all soft and motherly at the age of barely twenty summers? By all the Gods…!

The following morning she sought out the Ahoggyá.

"You did it, didn't you?" she accused. "You sold off the sick boy."

"What would you have done? Kept him to tickle you, as the priestesses of Dlamélish keep little boys and *Rényu?*"

"Of course not," she bridled, "but you did not have Master Chnesúru's permission!"

"He will be pleased. Ninety *Káitar*s for one worth less than ten."

"When Lord Fyérik finds out he has been sold a sick slave –!"

"We shall be long gone." The creature turned around so that she faced another pair of slyly wicked eyes. "Why did you not order the slave to lie with you? Master Chnesúru would not have minded. The boy might have enjoyed it – little enough pleasure for his kind in this world. And maybe later another infant to sell for a few coins!"

"Tlá! Chá! You talk foolishness!"

"Or you might find a normal man to jolly you?" Old White-Side gurgled a chuckle. "Some say that your body is appealing in spite of your veil. Now if it's pleasure you seek, then know that we Ahoggyá have eight sexes and –"

"Wretched pisspot with legs! Shall I give you a drug that will loosen your sagging bowels all over the road?"

The Ahoggyá turned, flipped his dangling reproductive organs at her, winked broadly with one of the eyes on that side of its body, and lumbered away.

They camped that night at a place called Ha'akél's Wall, some twenty *Tsán* before the market town of Tsurú. Tlayésha busied herself with a pregnant woman slave and had almost succeeded in putting the matter of the sick boy out of her mind when she saw Master Chnesúru waddling toward the sick-cart. His expression told her that something was seriously wrong.

"Where is the man with the shaking sickness?" the slaver asked abruptly in his accented, mushy-sounding Tsolyáni. "Qoyqunél said you were treating him yesterday." He laid a stubby hand on the lashing of the cart and peered within. "He is not here with the sick?"

She knew better than to compromise Old White-Side; the creature was capable of a hundred devious little vengeances. Yet the situation seemed to call for at least part of the truth. "Why – I believe that he was among those sold to Lord Fyérik –" She got no further.

"WHAT?" Chnesúru actually shook her, something he had never done in the years Tlayésha had known him. "The slave is sold? Somebody sold him? Who –? How –?" She had never seen him so furious. His features went to dirty grey, then to apoplectic red. Terror filled her for Chnesúru could be cruel.

The slaver whirled and bawled for lanterns. The camp was swiftly searched from end to end. The boy could not be found. Nor could anyone recall who had made up the lot offered to Lord Fyérik – Naturally.

Chnesúru stamped and swore and fumed, calling upon his unpronounceable Salarvyáni gods. At last he ordered Qoyqunél to take two men and return to Lord Fyérik's estate. Now. Tonight. Not tomorrow morning! The slave boy must be brought back – at any price! This last was easily the most amazing thing Tlayésha had heard her employer say yet. He vouchsafed no reasons for his concern but strode into his tent with all of the dignity a small, fat man can muster. He pulled the flap shut.

Qoyqunél had wit enough to make no protests. Somebody would surely pay for his long run back down the *Sákbe-* road and his return the next day under a scorching sun. If he ever found out that his discomfort was to be laid at the Ahoggyá's door, then the smelly old beast would need all of its eight eyes to keep watch over its skin!

To Tlayésha's even greater wonderment, Chnesúru did not march on at dawn. Instead, he had the caravan tarry at the road tower (and what Ha'akél's Wall was – or had been – she never found out) until Qoyqunél returned in the late afternoon, panting and perspiring, with the boy in tow. He glared at his comrades, screwed up his mouth, and pushed the slave into Chnesúru's tent. Presently he emerged and bellowed for Tlayésha.

"He calls you, woman! The idiotic slave has been beaten, and you are summoned to coddle him."

The nameless boy squatted on Chnesúru's elegant carpet, as filthy and sweaty as ever she had seen a slave. Old White-Side's weals were livid upon his shoulders, and he had a new abrasion upon his belly as well, probably a kick from one of Lord Fyérik's overseers when they discovered the nature of his malady. She bit her lip and began to wash his wounds. They were angry-looking but superficial. Chnesúru must be badly shaken to show such interest. There was more to this than met the eye.

On impulse she said, "Master, this slave may have internal damage. Someone has kicked him. May I keep him with me to observe for a time?"

The slaver raised a thick eyebrow. He seemed to ponder. "Why not? Why not? He'll likely come to less trouble. Yes, girl, take him with you." He smoothed his thick-woven *Hmélu*-wool tunic down over an expanse of hairy belly. The Salarvyáni were always cold away from their hothouse southern lands.

Tlayésha finished, bowed, and urged the slave out of the tent before Chnesúru could think of anything else. There were times when he conveniently forgot that she no longer had to cater to men's needs for money.

The more she thought the stranger the affair became. A Salarvyáni might weep bitter tears over the loss of a copper *Qirgál* but never over the hurts of an idiot field-slave. Was the boy a "special," then, to be sold to some customer with tastes odder than most? She did not think so. The slaver's mood seemed more that of a man who has safely managed to skirt a deadly peril.

Tlayésha could not resist a further chance to interrogate the boy. As soon as the evening meal was done and her sleeping mat was spread beside one of the ponderous wooden wheels of the sick-cart, she sat him down and began to question him as gently as she could.

His responses were as she expected: trembling, infantile sounds, and meaningless gestures. She speedily verified the existence of some affinity between the boy and the *Zu'úr* victim, nevertheless. As far as she could recall, he had not been bought from the same person as that unfortunate girl. Or had he? Chnesúru had acquired both of them on the last morning before they broke camp outside of Béy Sü. But from whom? She wracked her brain to remember and came up with nothing.

Then there was some enigmatic business about gold and Múru the cook. The slave took Tlayésha's arm in his quivering fingers, and clutched at her one gold bangle while waving at old Múru, whose sleeping mat was nearby. Did he mean Múru specifically, some other man, or just people in general? Perhaps he was trying to tell her how he had been bought with gold?

One thing puzzled her: unlike others with the shaking sickness – this victim appeared almost normal until he tried to communicate. In repose he hardly trembled, his face and body were still, and his long-fingered, sensitive-appearing hands lay quiescent in his lap. But when he had to respond to her queries his eyes twitched, his jaw convulsed, ridges of strain stood out upon his neck, his tongue refused to obey, and he made childish gagging noises.

Tlayésha sighed and gave up for the night. Later, when she awoke in the pre-dawn chill, she found the boy sitting much as she had left him, staring down at her. He saw her looking at him and smiled back, as easily and normally as though there were nothing wrong with him at all.

What would it be like, she wondered sleepily, to lie with him? Would it help to have a woman? The sleep-demons came and took her again.

Chapter Twenty-four

Chnesúru made up for the delay by marching throughout the next day. They halted at Tsurú the following night, quite exhausted, with the massif of Thénu Thendráya Peak a ponderous boulder hanging in the northwestern sky. The *Sákbe*-road branched here: one route led directly north through craggy foothills and ever-narrowing canyons to the ancient and demon-haunted City of Sárku, the major pilgrimage centre for those who served the Lord of Worms. Another, broader thoroughfare continued on in a north-westerly direction amidst stands of black-leaved *Tíu*-trees to the swampy basin surrounding Púrdimal. Still further branches then took travellers west to Mrelú, or northwest again to Khirgár and the Milumanayáni frontier where the armies of the Imperium and of Yán Kór faced one another over an uneasy truce.

The sick boy soon became Tlayésha's apprentice. He followed her on her rounds, carried her bucket of water, and squatted patiently nearby while she diagnosed and prescribed and treated her charges. The slaves teased her, as was to be expected, calling the boy her *Rényu*, or her belly-warmer, or her long-lost child. She did not really care: to be truthful, she was unsure in her own mind as to her feelings for the slave. Qoyqunél was prevailed upon to give the boy a coarse kilt, just as though he were one of Chnesúru's trustee slaves, and

Tlayésha saw to it that he received all of his food instead of having half of it stolen by others. He was useful, she told herself, and she took pleasure in his silent companionship.

She was certain, too, that the boy had more intelligence than was normally left to sufferers of the shaking sickness. He examined her instruments and medicines with what appeared to be reverent interest, and it was as though he understood something of the healing arts himself, for he quickly learned to hand her the correct tool or jar of ointment from her bag.

Once she let him watch while she ministered to the Zu'úr-victim, taking great pains not to let Chnesúru or Old White-Side see him there. His reaction surprised her: rather than curiosity or sexual desire, his eyes filled with tears. He wrestled with his tongue to speak, but then his seizures took him again, and he crouched and beat his fists upon the stones.

She did not try that experiment again.

It was clear that some connection existed between the girl and this slaveboy, something deeper than the accident of being bought together from the same previous owner. Had they been lovers perhaps, before the girl was given the deadly drug? They could not be relatives: the youth was a Livyáni, while the Zu'úr-victim's high cheekbones and slender build hinted at Chákan or possibly Mu'ugalavyáni origins – Western, anyway.

Presently the caravan began to see the swampy patches that heralded the Huqúndàli, "the Great Morass," the many Tsán of treacherous marshes just to the west of Thénu Thendráya Peak. A natural basin caught the run-off from the western slopes of the mountain range that formed the northern border of Tsolyánu, and the water lay upon the land here like curdled milk in a saucer. The Sákbe-road was now carried for short distances upon stone arches, long bridges really, allowing the water free passage to the west and south where it overflowed and fed the crops of the central plains of the Empire. As one travelled up from the southeast, however, it was as if the world suffered from some daily-increasing blight. The fields became poor and shabby and gave way to clumps of Tíu-trees; these in turn were replaced by reedy thickets and underbrush; and finally by stretches of algae-blotched, squelching swamps over which Hú-bats hovered on rattling wings to seize the fen-worms wriggling just beneath the surface.

There were also patches of the poisonous purple vegetation called the "Food of the Ssú." Tlayésha did not recall seeing so much of the stuff when she had passed this way the previous year. Now whole areas, mostly the inaccessible islets in the midst of the swamps, were covered with pulpy vines and clusters of leaves like slashed liver, fleshy blooms of reddish violet hue, and sticky pods, veined and ichorous, resembling nothing so much as a naked human lung. In the Time of the Gods, it was said, the world was covered with the "Food of the Ssú." The Ssú, hideous monsters that they were, ate it, cultivated it, and dwelt with their cousins, the Hlüss, alone upon Tékumel. Then the Gods came and tried in vain to destroy the Ssú and their habitat. None succeeded until Lord Vimúhla, the Master of Flame, blew His fiery breath upon the world and made it a fit place for humankind to dwell, together with certain nonhuman species. Now there was an Imperial decree ordering the eradication of these plants, but who was going to enforce it in such a dismal place? Once Tlayésha had thought to pick some of the ugly flowers for examination, and her fingers still smarted from the remembered pain of the burns! No useful medicines were to be had there!

The landscape became more and more a gloomy land of dark waters and hidden, secretive undergrowth. The *Sákbe*-road was reduced to only one level, and this was frequently replaced by a wooden causeway carried on black-tarred pilings and balks of timber. The Gods knew how the old Emperors had constructed this highway! During its repair a generation ago so many workers had died that the Imperium had decreed the building of a new route along Thénu Thendráya's mighty flank where the cliffs plunged down from the heights into the bogs to the west. But "the Sentinel of Hrúgga" had shaken himself and thrown down their bridges and tunnels, and at last the priesthoods had persuaded the Emperor to desist.

Twelve days after leaving Tsurú the slaver's caravan sighted the first of the villages of the Hehecháru, the "First Dwellers" of the Great Morass. Rickety hovels of grey sticks and reeds rose from the swamp upon stilts and were connected by bridges of woven grass. Sections of the wooden causeway had been widened at regular intervals and made into wharf-like platforms. Travellers along the *Sákbe*-road used these as halting places, and the First Dwellers came there, too, to sell their swamp-fruits, eels, reptile skins, bird plumage, and fangs of ivory-white *Ssár*-wood from which all manner of batons and staffs were carved. No tax-gatherer ever visited the villages of the Hehecháru, and as long as their inhabitants left the *Sákbe*-road in peace and surrendered a few copper *Qirgáls* a year, no administrator bothered them.

Even so, everyone distrusted the First Dwellers. They were indisputably human, but they were squat, wide-mouthed, and of a mottled greyish tinge, like meat left too long in the sun. They were clearly related to the Old Ones of Púrdimal, the Hehegánu, who were similar, if still uglier. But one rarely saw those latter creatures any more, except deep in Old Town in Púrdimal. One of Chnesúru's Mu'ugalavyáni overseers held the theory that both of these odd races were related to – or intermarried with – the nonhuman Swamp Folk who lived along the Putuhénu River in his own land. The slaver himself heaped scorn upon this idea: was it not well known that the slave-breeding clans had tried all of the possible combinations of races in the past and had ended with nothing save frustration?

Whatever the truth might be, the Hehecháru behaved meekly enough, spoke little, and never stayed the night on the platforms along the *Sákbe*-road.

Chnesúru followed his usual custom and did not halt at the first of the wayside platforms. He decided instead to go on to the second one some ten *Tsán* farther into the swamplands. The quicker one marched, the quicker out of these fens – though Púrdimal itself was but little more appealing.

Like the other platforms, the one the slaver chose extended out some ten man-heights to the side of the roadway. It was perhaps twenty man-heights long, and at its southern end stood a handful of rude pavilions used by the Hehecháru peddlers during the day. To the north, the platform ended in a crumbling guard tower, its stones hauled from great distances and sunk who knew how far down into the ooze to provide a firm foundation.

There were few other wayfarers: two or three parties of merchants, soldiers from several legions, a courtesan and her retinue, and the litter belonging to the nobleman whom Tlayésha had seen at Village Tkomán. Just after dark, however, a company of about forty Shén mercenaries arrived, members of one of the Imperium's nonhuman auxiliary legions, possibly 'The Splendour of Shényu' itself, to judge by their crested helmets and the tall-plumed *Káing*-standard that two of the huge reptiles set up before their officer's tent.

These new arrivals crowded the sleeping accommodations beyond reasonable capacity. The Shén arrogantly took over the best places near the tower, and Tlayésha observed their commander and two of his hulking black troopers go in to pay their respects to the captain of the road-guard garrison. (In Avánthe's name, what had the man done to deserve posting to a place like this?)

Some of the merchants joined with Chnesúru in occupying the peddlers' hovels – in spite of the fact that Chnesúru was a slaver, a Salarvyáni, and of low clan-status. At this point no one cared. The courtesan and her servants were allowed to sleep there as well, but the rest were left to put up their tents beside the roadway wherever they could.

No one wanted to sleep near the platform's outer railing, and Qoyqunél had to use both words and blows to persuade some of the older male slaves of the wisdom of this. The supply wagons and the sick-cart were stationed in front of the row of huts, and Old White-Side presently emerged from one of these buildings to order the cookfires lit, the armoured *Chlén*-beasts fed and watered, and the women and children to begin the evening meal.

The insects were unbearable. Even now, during the month of Halír, there were so many pests that cooking was slowed by half! Slaves slapped and scratched and grumbled until they were issued sleeping-shawls in which to swaddle themselves, and some of the men were set to flapping cloths at the bumbling *Aqpú*-beetles lest these fly into the cookpots and become unwelcome additions to the stew. The *Hú*-bats and the black and purple *Qásu*-birds were even greater nuisances, for they dived to snatch morsels not only from the pots but from peoples' bowls and fingers as well. Qoyqunél was forced to remind Múru the cook with the flat of his sword that the *Qásu*-birds were sacred to Lord Wurú, the Cohort of mighty Hrü'ü, and hence not to be swatted with a spatula.

Tlayésha was happy to share space in a tent with one of Chnesúru's nonhuman overseers, a beautiful bone-white female Pé Chói named Ítk t'Sá. These creatures were so graceful, the males a gleaming ebony and the females just the opposite: the hue of summer clouds, with shadings of pearl-grey along their ear-ridges. Female Pé Chói were uncommon outside of their homeland in the Chákan forests, but Ítk t'Sá had joined the caravan in Mrelú a year or so before. She gave no reasons for leaving her people but quietly took charge of Chnesúru's occasional nonhuman slaves and aided Tlayésha with the human women and children. She was marvellously deft. Tlayésha had attempted to befriend her but had met with a wall of placid, amicable – and unbreachable – aloofness.

Ítk t'Sá gave her human companion a polite nod and went on preparing herself for sleep. She used the chitinous ridges on the outside of her upper pair of hands to scrape and brush her face and limbs, refused the water Tlayésha offered her (did the Pé Chói ever bathe, or did they only rub themselves clean in this fashion?), squatted down, folded her six limbs tightly, and curled her segmented tail around her body.

Tlayésha undid the laces of her high leather walking boots, removed her sleeveless over-tunic, and loosened the drawstring of her skirt. Her veil, too, she laid aside. Automatically she glanced over at the Pé Chói, but Ítk t'Sá had her long head down between her two upper limbs, asleep. What would a Pé

Chói know or care about human uglinesses anyway? From her medicine bag Tlayésha brought forth a piece of *Balür*-bark to burn in their clay lamp; its pungent smoke would make their tent uninviting to any insect guests.

She had just begun to wash herself as best she could in the narrow confines of the tent when she heard a scratching sound at the tent-flap. She fumbled her veil back over her face and peered out.

The sick boy stood in the doorway. She had forgotten about him! His face was spotted with scarlet insect bites. Although she had given him a sleeping-shawl, it was obvious that it had provided little protection. She made an impatient sign for him to enter and close the flap. There was room for him to sleep at her feet.

She turned away to find the Pé Chói staring at the boy. The intensity of the lambent green gaze surprised her.

"Do you know this slave?" she asked.

Ítk t'Sá did not reply at once. The slave boy returned her look with the same fierce concentration. He was not trembling now.

"No," the Pé Chói replied at last, "I think not. Yet he is familiar ..." Abruptly, surprisingly, she said something guttural and clicking in her own harsh language.

The boy strained forward, seemed to listen, and then made a monumental effort to reply. Once this would have been enough to convince Tlayésha that he was witless indeed; no human had ever mastered a nonhuman tongue! Yet he was so determined, so serious! He opened his lips with such care that lines of muscle stood out upon his jaw. Then his malady overwhelmed him. His whole body shook, and he strove to keep his clenched teeth from chattering.

The Pé Chói looked at Tlayésha. "He is — how do you call it? — mind-harmed?"

"Yes. The shaking sickness. Some intelligence is left to him, more than most cases, I think. With training he may make a useful household slave. Certainly any master will be able to discuss his secrets in this man's presence without fear of disclosure." Tlayésha found herself speaking rapidly, as though to hide something. She discovered, to her own bewilderment, that she harboured certain further, unformed suspicions. She did not know how to put these into words.

"You have examined him well? It is really the shaking sickness?"

"I — I believe so. I am no skilled physician, of course, like those in the temples of Thúmis or Keténgku ..."

The Pé Chói looked from Tlayésha back to the boy. Then she put her head back down between her forearms. Her attitude suggested that human affairs were no concern of hers. Tlayésha could not see the boy's expression; he had turned his head so that his face was in shadow.

Later, Tlayésha awoke to total darkness, jolted from sleep by a stab of pain in her wrist. She slapped with her other hand and felt a fuzzy something wriggle weakly and squish under her fingers. The clay lamp had gone out. Where one insect could find a way a thousand others would follow! The bowl of the lamp was dry .There was nothing for it but to get up and beg more oil from whichever of the overseers had been given the miserable duty of guarding the supply cart this night. She prayed it would not be Old White-Side.

She retied her skirt, settled her veil over her head, and arose. The slave boy was instantly on his feet as well.

"It is all right," she gentled him. "Come, we go to get more oil."

Both of the moons were up. Káshi's dim ochre light mingled with Gayél's paler green radiance to splash weird double shadows over the sheds and crumbling pilings. Water gurgled and bubbled beneath the platform, and she felt a momentary twinge of fear of falling through some rotted board into the slime below. Slaves huddled under sleeping-shawls around the black bulk of the supply cart, and she saw that Chnesúru had loaned some of his elegant Khirgári carpets to provide cover for the women and children. Not out of any altruistic motive, she thought wryly, but because there was no profit in merchandise all red and puffy with insect bites.

Cawing, alien laughter eddied to her from the Shén tents across the platform. The reptiles would not be bothered with insects – they were probably snatching them from the air and eating them! Tlayésha was a little afraid of Shén. She almost stumbled over a pair of slaves rhythmically copulating under a coarse sleeping-shawl. At least that never stopped, no matter what else! Chnesúru must have given permission tonight for the male slaves to sleep with those women who were willing. Not only did it keep his wares occupied and uncaring of their insect tormentors, but there would also be more babies to add to his sales. A woman with a child drew a better price, and such a one could expect less arduous duties than a female who had none.

Something was happening there by one of the tents. She paused to squint, and the slave boy stepped on her heel from behind.

A struggle was going on. Two men – they looked like soldiers, though they wore mantles with cowls – were wrestling with somebody. Whose tent was it? One of the merchants? No, the pavilion belonging to the noblemen. Clan tabards dangled limply from the pole before the entrance.

Looters? Bandits? Drunk, perhaps? She started forward with the vague intention of calling to the road guards in the tower.

A flapping black shape loomed before her, and she gave an involuntary squeal of fright. It was another soldier, an officer in dully gleaming armour, a thick cloak about his shoulders. He held a naked sword.

"Be still and return whence you came, my Lady." His voice was calm, almost detached. "What is not perceived makes no tangled knots in one's Skein."

As her eyes adjusted, Tlayésha had a better look at him: a tall, gaunt man, his face shadowed by the helmet visor. His armour glinted with the red-gold of copper: an officer of one of the Legions devoted to Lord Sárku or his ugly Cohort, Durritlámish, probably. A man of status anyway. His cheeks bore the triple cicatrices of one of the mountain clans of the Kraá Hills. She started to obey him, motioning blindly behind her for the slave boy to move back as well.

The struggle before the tent was apparently over. The two soldiers had subdued a third man – the nobleman or one of his servants (did he have any – she had not noticed?). He hung between his captors as though unconscious. Light flared up within the tent. Someone had uncovered a lantern, and dancing shadows upon the tent walls told her that the nobleman's possessions were being ransacked, the Gods alone knew why.

Three more men appeared in the doorway of the tent. Two were soldiers, and the third was a bent, sharp-featured old man attired in a voluminous robe that showed black-brown in the light. They seemed to have found what they sought, for the elderly man pushed past his two comrades and made an imperious gesture to the officer who still barred Tlayésha's way.

The captive was almost halfway across the open space in the middle of the platform. As the soldiers brought him nearer Tlayésha recognised the young nobleman, a thin, raffish-looking fellow, now wearing only a breechcloth of some fine material. He had obviously been surprised as he slept.

Without warning the prisoner jerked one arm loose from one soldier and dealt the other man an open-handed blow in the face. The trooper's head rocked back, and his helmet went rolling and clattering upon the planks. Then the young nobleman was free of both of them and racing on bare feet towards the guard tower.

He could have reached it easily. But he seemed to falter and change his mind. Then he sprinted off in a tangent toward the Shén commander's pavilion. The soldier he had struck still stood spraddle-legged, hands to his face; the other ran out to intercept him.

Tlayésha knew better than to interfere. There were sounds behind her now, and heads appeared from under sleeping-shawls. A Shén guard arose to bark a question at the soldiers but went unheeded. On her own side of the platform she heard Old White-Side's bass voice rumble a challenge as well.

The officer in front of her shouted to the soldiers still before the tent, and these sprang off to block the nobleman's access to the roadway. Only the elderly man stood motionless, staring, seeming to concentrate without actually looking at the scene before him. He raised one hand toward the fleeing prisoner. The half-naked young man was apparently confused – or bewitched? He had almost reached the Shén guardsman when suddenly he threw up his hands as though confronted by some terrible apparition. He gave a hoarse yell, veered away, and stumbled over a just-awakening slave. He ended with his back against the western parapet, that which overhung the blackness of the swamp below.

The first soldier came up to cut his quarry off from any further flight, feinting with his sword but not actually striking a blow. The nobleman must be wanted alive! The second trooper was almost there too, running hard, and the remaining pair were not far behind. The officer cursed and left Tlayésha to join his men.

The nobleman dodged his opponent's clumsy swing, reached nimbly past the man's guard, and caught his wrist. A deft twist, and the sword went skittering away along the planks, its owner after it to sprawl headlong. Before the second soldier could interfere, the thin-faced dandy had scooped up the weapon and swung to face this new foeman.

The second soldier saw his doom, but his momentum was too great to stop. Horrified, Tlayésha watched the sword point skid against the lacquered cuirass and slip smoothly up to lodge in the man's throat. He jacknifed, coughing blood. The noble youth retreated gracefully to the parapet again, like a trained duellist after a match. Somewhere in the darkness a slave snapped his fingers in applause, the way the crowds praised a winning gladiator at the *Hirilákte* Arenas.

The first soldier was on his feet, dark blood oozing from an abrasion on his cheek. The remaining two men joined him and circled in from opposite sides, their officer just behind them. The latter bawled a command to surrender.

Their quarry swung his weapon from side to side, assessing the situation. He was outnumbered. There was only one avenue of escape, perilous though it was. Before anyone could stop him he whirled, took one quick stride up onto the wooden railing, and teetered there undecided for a long moment. He seemed to be looking for help – did he have accomplices amongst the slaves? His servants? No one moved.

He shouted something then. Tlayésha thought he cried, "I told you mother-suckling clanless dung-eaters that it would never work –!"

He turned and jumped outward, into the swamp. A splash and an oily squelching sound came up from below. Then silence.

Without knowing how she got there, Tlayésha found herself at the parapet, jostled by merchants, slaves, overseers, soldiers, and some of the Shén. People seemed to crowd in from everywhere now that danger was past. A trooper called for torches, and a youth in the shabby livery of the *Sákbe*-road guards (and how cleverly *they* had stayed out of the fray!) shouted for a rope. A crag-faced older man, a tanner by his leather tunic and the checkerboard design on his headband, snatched a spare tentpole from a cart and pushed it down to probe the dark bog beneath. A little fellow with a huge hooked nose – the tanner's apprentice, probably – came up beside him and took the pole from his master's hands.

There was a form down there, spreadeagled upon the quivering surface of the marsh. The young nobleman lay in no more than a finger's breadth of water. Under any other circumstances he should not even have been stunned by the fall – and ought to have been away, free, into the darkness by now. But all around the bases of the gnarled pilings Tlayésha saw the bloated pods and stunted fronds of the "Food of the Ssú!" The young man struggled, face down, in the midst of the stuff! Even as she watched, his body thrashed weakly, he made gagging sounds, and his fingers tore at the dark-veined tendrils upon his face.

Then Tlayésha witnessed a thing that capped all of the other horrors of this frightful night. The tanner's apprentice shoved the tentpole down to touch the nobleman's bare back. Yet instead of using it to roll the victim out of the deadly foliage, or give him its end to pull himself free, the ugly little man set the tip of the pole against the base of the nobleman's skull and carefully, deliberately, pushed his head further down into the black-violet, pulpy vegetation! The body twisted spasmodically, and the hands came back to paw futilely at the pole. The young man made a last spluttering sound and lay still.

"He perished, masters, before I could aid him!" the apprentice cried. The tanner hastened to agree. None of the others were close enough to have seen this act of murder, and Tlayésha's involuntary protest was lost in the babble of voices. The tanner might have heard, however, for he glanced in her direction.

A soldier panted up with a rope, and soon the body was hauled feet first from the swamp, dripping wet, yet wealed and puffed all over as though burned by fire.

The officer in copper armour now approached the captain of the road guards and produced a document. The latter scanned it briefly, shrugged, and handed it on to the commander of the Shén contingent. The first man signalled to his remaining three troopers.

A billet of wood was found and lashed to the tentpole to serve as a crosspiece. The soldiers stripped the body of its kilt, methodically inserted the point of the tentpole between the legs, and pushed until nearly three handspans had entered the abdomen. They then lifted the limp form upon this improvised impaling stake and lashed it to the parapet railing.

Tlayésha turned away, nauseated in spite of herself. She had once seen an impalement – a living victim who shrieked and beat at his belly as the terrible stake pushed up through his entrails – but this senseless degradation of a man already dead was somehow worse. It seemed to deprive him of any last shred of dignity. How would he appear before the Ferryman to Lord Belkhánu's Isles of the Excellent Dead? To humiliate a noble corpse in this fashion meant a great crime against the Imperium – or against someone of awesome power!

She stumbled back into the slave boy. Without any conscious volition, her arms went out to embrace him, and his came up to encircle her waist. She had no idea whether she needed to console him, or whether she herself wanted comforting. They stood together for what felt like aeons while people around them chattered and pointed and stared and finally began to drift away.

The boy's fingers cradled her cheek. They did not tremble at all. Before she could react he lifted up her face to look directly into her eyes. She wondered, confused and astonished, if he was about to kiss her! But then he pressed her head firmly on around so that she looked into the throng still gathered beneath the limp body upon its stake.

The boy's mouth was open, his jaw muscles working with the strain. Then he spoke. In clear, perfect Tsolyáni, he said: "The tanner – is – a Mihálli. Of – Yán Kór...Soldiers —— from Prince Dhich'uné – Sárku. They seek me – and Eyíl, the girl, the one given *Zu'úr*."

He could say no more. His eyes closed, and two tears squeezed out upon his cheeks. His shoulders began to shake in the spasms of the shaking sickness, and he let Tlayésha go to stumble back into the darkness.

She was left to stand, openmouthed, gazing first after the slave boy and then into the crowd where the tanner and his apprentice had been.

Now they were gone.

Chapter Twenty-Five

Nothing more could be learned from the nameless slave boy during the night. In the grey drizzle that accompanied the dawn Tlayésha picked through her meagre array of drugs and medicines, but nothing suggested itself. The flawed yellow crystal she had purchased in Jakálla did not capture his soul, as its seller had sworn it would. She then had hopes of an infusion of pounded *Ngáru*-bark; sometimes that kept a person on the borderland of sleeping and waking, leaving the mind free to speak what was sealed within the heart. But the slave only went to sleep, exhausted.

The rest of her pharmacopoeia – soporifics, anaesthetics, simple stomach remedies, bandages and potions that could clean a wound or slow menstrual bleeding – were of no use at all. As soon as they got to Púrdimal she could go to the drug-sellers who sat in the Court of Cries below the black pyramid of Lord Ksárul's temple. Chnesúru's fellow-countryman, evil-visaged Gdéshmaru, had his apothecary's shop there. He would know how to restore the boy's wits if anybody could. Gdéshmaru was unlikely to betray her. She knew of a score of instances in which he had aided Chnesúru, and the plump slaver still lived. Moreover, Tlayésha had had dealings of her own with him: was there not the affair of Chnesúru's slave girl and the governor's clan-niece, a matter in which Gdéshmaru had provided a handful of bitter little seeds to break the latter's infatuation? The niece was happily married now into the Clan of the Golden Sunburst, and her new kinfolk would not take kindly to revelations of behaviour more suited to a devotee of Dlamélish – or virginal Dilinála, who loved other women – than to Lord Hnálla.

Something very wrong had happened last night, a thing far too momentous for Tlayésha. It might be a matter too high even for Gdéshmaru, who handled the peccadilloes of the aristocracy as smoothly as a ship sails downriver. She could of course remain silent, pretend ignorance and hope to keep the impaler's stake out of her belly. Perhaps she had already seen too much.

Fear struck her like a wave. In the name of all of the Indigo Aspects of Lady Avánthe, what was she about?

She tried to put the events of the night aside, but her mind kept nibbling at them as a *Hmélu*-calf chews its mother's udder. She cursed herself for a fool. One of her earliest memories was of her clan-mother laughingly accusing her of being a living incarnation of Shaka'án, the Little Girl Who is Curious, one of Lady Avánthe's Lesser Aspects. Lá, what had been meant as a loving gibe might well have been a forecast of her death!

There was more to it, of course: more than stupid inquisitiveness! What were her feelings for the wretched slave boy? Did she want to lie with him, tie herself to him? No calm, brave, noble provider he! Not the sort of husband about whom a girl weaves her dreams! Nor did she want to be a mother to him, nurse him, and clutch him to her as a clan-wife dandles her babes! Lady Avánthe's maternal instincts could be allowed to go only so far!

She threw her jars back into her bag, angry at herself for even thinking such confused thoughts. Whatever the boy knew was fraught with danger. He had mentioned the dread name of Prince Dhich'uné, and she herself had seen the copper-trimmed armour and the blazon of the Worm upon the soldiers' breastplates. She shivered. Stories of the secret societies within the temples trickled like underground streamlets along the trade routes of the Empire. Rumour had it that one of these, the Society of the Copper Tomb of the Temple of Lord Sárku, was headed by the Emperor's youngest son himself. Beyond this the wagging tongues babbled a myriad tales, but who knew what was true and what was no more than the embroidery of imagination?

To add spice to the sauce, there had also been mention of Yán Kór, though she could not remember the boy's exact words.

What was the other thing he had said? That the tanner was a Mihálli? She had heard the legends: once the alien Mihálli had shared Tékumel with mankind and the other nonhuman species. They had lived someplace – she racked her brain to recall – far away to the northeast, beyond the Empire, beyond Saá Allaqí which was the homeland of the Baron Áld, the man who was now overlord of Yán Kór, beyond Jánnu and wild Kilalámmu, somewhere in the unknown lands where nobody went. The Mihálli were famous as shape-changers. The market storytellers used them in their plots: almost every tale-cycle had a Mihálli villain in it. What they looked like Tlayésha was not sure. The puppeteers in Béy Sü had a beast-like creature with many heads painted in gaudy colours, and in the Story of Gáru, which she had once seen acted in Jakálla, the costume had been that of a serpent-like creature with the face of a man. Most of the tales agreed that a Mihálli could always be found out by its eyes, however; these never changed no matter what form it put on: they invariably glowed red and were hollow, with no pupils.

The slave boy had been certain that there was a Mihálli among the crowd on the parapet. Whatever other symptoms the shaking sickness had, it did not bring on hallucinations. The boy really believed that there was a Mihálli here somewhere. Superstition? An ignorant Livyáni peasant-lad, who saw monsters in every tree? He did not impress her as such. Not at all.

This morning Tlayésha wandered the length of the platform, peering into tents, talking to everyone, and listening to a hundred different accounts of the incident of the previous night. Of the tanner and his apprentice there was no sign. Travellers came and went, of course, and they might have departed before Gayél set. But then why would a tanner wish to journey by night along this dismal, dangerous road?

Ítk t'Sá added to her apprehensions when they met over breakfast by the sick-cart. The Pé Chói looked at Tlayésha and whispered, "What did the slave see?"

Not "What happened?" or any of the more likely questions she might have asked.

Tlayésha dared not confide in the creature – not yet. She only shrugged and grunted a noncommittal reply. The Pé Chói touched the sleeping slave boy's face gently with her chitinous fingers and went away.

Chnesúru soon appeared to give the command to march. He kept a stolid, impassive face and said nothing of the night's events. The overseers caught their master's mood and lashed the caravan into almost a trotting pace. They made excellent time. On this morning, however, the skies chose to grieve: slow, warm rain fell, and tatters of cloud clung to Thénu Thendráya's skirts, sometimes drifting aside to reveal seamed black cliffs like the cheeks of an old woman. Around noon the sun appeared and turned the air into gasping, dripping steam. One day went by, and then another. The mornings continued to weep grey rain-tears, while the afternoons were humid and sticky beyond endurance. They marched through a silent landscape upon bridges of wet, black timbers, over waters that were sheets of muddy agate. All around were thickets of impenetrable marsh-reeds: ominous, full of eyes, and creatures, and the promise of secret death. It was enough to make one believe in the legends of the *Tsóggu*, the drowned corpses who wandered the wastes all covered with slime and burning green liche-fire ...

Tlayésha could stand it no longer. When they camped on the last night before reaching Púrdimal she brought the slave boy into the tent and confronted Ítk t'Sá directly. She sat the Pé Chói down and made the slave squat before them both. Then she told Ítk t'Sá some of what had occurred since he was brought to the caravan outside Béy Sü. She omitted mention of the *Zu'úr*-victim, and of the terrible things the youth had told her there upon the road platform. Those matters – and certain of her gloomier suspicions – were too dangerous to reveal to anyone as yet.

Ítk t'Sá heard her out, then said only, "It is as I had seen it."

"You knew something all along? Why –?"

"I want no involvement in the plottings of men. Some of my race take part in your doings. Others do not." The Pé Chói hesitated. "Why I am here is intelligible only to one of my people and concerns no one else. My life is one of silence. Were I to speak, it would be otherwise. 'A stone thrown into a stream cannot help but make a splash.'"

"But –"

"There is a reason, however, for me to speak now." Ítk t'Sá raised a porcelain-white, many-jointed finger. "You must have heard that we Pé Chói suffer from a sense of empathy: the ability to feel – and endure – the emotions of those we meet. In some cases this amounts almost to telepathy, particularly amongst our females."

"You can see minds, then? Like a sorcerer?"

"Not the same. Not as some humans do, who pierce through the many skins of reality to draw force from the Planes Beyond. What I experience is different. When you first brought the slave into our tent – do you recall it? – you asked him to come inside, and I awakened from sleep to look upon him."

"Yes?"

"For a moment, when he stood before me, I thought to see a Pé Chói, one of my own race."

"A Pé Chói? A shape-changer? A Mihálli –!"

Ítk t'Sá shook her long head, a very human gesture. "Not so. It was as though there were two beings there: a young male of my race and this youth of your species. When my eyes focused the illusion was gone."

"You spoke to him in your own tongue."

"Yes, I was off guard. It was the *Ch'kétk N'tú*, the feeling, the empathy – there is no word…I felt that this slave was one of my own people, even though I knew this could not be so."

Tlayésha turned to look at the slave. He sat by the tent-flap, attentive, without trembling. His eyes were fixed upon Ítk t'Sá.

"I cannot enter his mind. Yet I know – I feel – that he is the victim not of a disease but of sorcery."

"Sorcery! Oh, if only he could speak! I have tried everything, even simple gestures of yes and no, but each time he tries to communicate in any way he suffers a seizure."

"More proof. Not damage to the brain, but a spell that binds him. Yet I think he has improved since he came to us?"

"Yes, much. When I first saw him he shook almost constantly, and he could neither eat nor hold his bowels. Now he is almost normal – until he is addressed…"

The Pé Chói rose and took up the lamp. She held it close to the slave's eyes and moved it from side to side. Then she spoke again in her own harsh language. The slave's pupils dilated, wavered. He tried to speak, but Ítk t'Sá laid bony fingers upon his lips. "Whatever the spell is, it wears off. Slowly, slowly. In time…I can help him."

Tlayésha took a deep breath, made up her mind, and launched into the rest of the story. This time she omitted nothing.

No one moved when she had done. The Pé Chói was a graceful statue of buttery-gold lamplight, the boy kneeling before her a mural from some temple wall.

"There are those in Púrdimal who might aid you – him," Ítk t'Sá said carefully. "I cannot read your heart, yet I think that your motives are plain – to me, even if not to you."

"My motives? Concern for a patient – fear for this poor boy –"

"Chá! What is he to you? Go to the Palace of the Realm in Púrdimal, girl, to any officer of the Omnipotent Azure Legion. Let them have this slave and do as they will! Or leave the matter to the soldiers of the Worm Prince – or to the Mihálli, or to the Yán Koryáni, or to the *Hú*-bats! Is your Skein of Destiny so wretched that you would see it so soon torn asunder?"

"I cannot! Never —!" Tlayésha felt hot anger rushing into her cheeks. She knew not what more to say.

"You see," Ítk t'Sá said dryly, "your motives are unclear to you — or were until now. My words were but a test." She curled her tail around herself, as if to prepare for sleep.

The slave moved, then, and came forward to sit close before Tlayésha upon the sleeping mat, his eyes pools of shadow. She could not read his expression. He raised an arm and pointed to the Pé Chói.

"I do not think she will — can — aid you, at least not now," Tlayésha said, "nor am I sure that I should. Whatever is woven for you lies in the hand of the Weaver. I am not able to do much myself, alone, one poor woman, not very brave — no mighty Hrúgga to rescue you from whatever has been done to you."

The boy cast about, then took one corner of her blue veil into his hands. Again he gestured, this time beyond the tent, toward the sleeping encampment. His lips moved, but no words came.

She did not know what he wanted. To see the deformity of her face —? That was the thing that always leaped first into her mind! She pulled the veil from his fingers. Or did he mean the colour! The blue of the Imperium, of the Omnipotent Azure Legion? His eyes held a hurt look, and she softened toward him.

"I did not mean it like that," she exclaimed. "You — you know that I do not show my face? You have heard?"

He shook his head, but she could not tell what he meant. Then he reached out once more, very gently this time, and touched the edge of her veil. She did not snatch it away.

"I do not know what you want!" she cried almost despairingly. But she knew what *she* wanted, what Ítk t'Sá had hinted. She glanced over at the Pé Chói to see that the creature had turned away, head down upon her little upper arms, apparently asleep. Slowly, trembling herself, Tlayésha undid the clasp that held the veil to her hair. She drew it away from her face.

For a moment she saw admiration in his eyes, the look of any man who sees a lovely woman before him. Then, as always before, his eyes widened, and he made a gesture toward the lamp. Despair, self-loathing, hatred, all blew up before her as do leaves in a wind. Abruptly she raised the light and held it close before her face.

"You see!" she hissed. "You see!"

Her eyes were not brown, or black, or hazel, or amber, or even green, like the eyes of all the rest of humankind. They were a light sky-blue!

She expected the boy to recoil, as so many others had done. She found herself waiting, almost hoping, for him to shudder and turn away. Blue eyes, they said! Blue eyes! The sign of an impure child, the curse of Lady Avánthe! A witch, a loathsome and evil thing! The stylised villains of all of the rustic puppet shows had blue eyes! The legends abounded with monsters and sorcerers whose eyes were always blue!

But the boy did not retreat. He stared. Then he touched her hand. Suddenly he was the physician and she the patient. Two tears found their way down her cheeks, but his fingers came up to catch them there and wipe them away.

Slowly, as though she dreamed, Tlayésha let her veil fall away completely. She undid her tunic and helped the boy out of his clothing.

Ítk t'Sá arose in the night to find the slave boy curled next to the human girl upon her mat. Feeling carefully with her mind, the Pé Chói sensed the passion, the release, and the calm that now covered them both as a blanket enfolds a child. She squatted down again upon her own mat and slept.

Still later, Ítk t'Sá woke again at the whisper of the tent-flap being drawn aside. It might have been the force and power of her Pé Chói mind that made the copper-armoured soldier see only a Livyáni slave and a small, pretty, high-breasted Chákan girl sprawled in sleep there together. In any case the man pursed his lips in admiration – and envy – and went off to report to his superiors that no youth of the desired description was to be found in Chnesúru's caravan.

Ítk t'Sá began collecting her few possessions. Some she bound up in her leather travelling pack, others she placed in Tlayésha's scuffed medical bag. It was as though there were an hourglass within her brain, and something told her that the last few grains of sand were running out.

Chapter Twenty-Six

Sweat dripped from the fat Salarvyáni like wax from a burning candle. Qútmu hiTsizéna pushed his baton of office forward upon his knee so that the torchlight played full upon the golden medallion of the Imperium – And, more usefully here, upon the gleaming copper worm of Lord Sárku that wound around the staff beneath it. Even a foreign slaver would know – and fear – a *Kási*, a Captain, of a Cohort of Four Hundred in a Tsolyáni Legion. This should be especially true when that Legion was the one called the Battalions of the Seal of the Worm.

"I am a *Chrí*-fly," Qútmu remarked to no one in particular. "I buzz here, I buzz there. I light upon meat, and upon bread, and upon the cookpots, and upon the fruits, and upon the blossom of the *Másh*-tree. At length I come to the heart of that sweetest and stickiest of all flowers."

"Lord –"

"The girl is indeed she whom I seek. Eyíl hiVriyén, priestess of the Temple of Hriháyal. It seems I have alighted full in the midst of the honey. It is not tasty to mix sugar with fat-drippings, slaver, but it now behooves me to light upon you."

The officer's gaze flickered up to the four skull-helmeted troopers behind the Salarvyáni. One of these tapped the slaver upon his balding pate with the flat of his sword. The blow was not hard, but the effect was enlightening: Chnesúru fell as though struck with a mattock to lie grovelling upon his rich Khirgári carpet.

"A victim of *Zu'úr*, poor girl! Ohé, you carry strange and illegal cargoes! I do not think your license to deal in slaves in our Empire covers such merchandise."

"Master, I did not know…I was given the girl for sale…"

"All shall be clarified in time. If you are blameless, you shall not suffer. We Tsolyáni are just, pleasant to guests, and noble in our actions."

"Lord, you and your men – I have money." Chnesúru cast an anguished eye toward the bronze-bound black chest that stood beside the pile of sleeping mats upon which the officer sat. "I have a copper amulet of your Worm Lord, high master – magical and holy – a gift for you…"

"My writ is broad," Qútmu broke in pleasantly, "and aside from this specific maiden and her male companion, it empowers me to correct such irregularities as may be discovered within our land. Shall we speak of unpaid taxes, customs dues still owed upon slaves – possibly small packets of items that go unnoticed and forgotten in your eagerness to cross our borders?"

The Salarvyáni actually wriggled.

Qútmu stood up and reached out a broad, scarred hand to lift the lid of the box. "Documents, bills of sale, ladings, accounts – all boring and correct, no doubt. Much money. Perhaps enough to buy a palace? A high officer's post in the Legion? A farm in the Kraá Hills where I can raise *Dlél*-fruit and become as wealthy as Súbadim the Sorcerer when he sold the shell of the Egg of the World to the demon Tkél?"

Chnesúru peered up through clenched fingers, a glint of hope in his eyes. "Yes, yes, Lord. Take what you will…"

"The Imperium must not be cheated, of course. And there are other matters, other pots of sugar for this poor *Chrí*-fly to dine upon. My Lord Vridékka?"

The weazened oldster who had followed the officer into Chnesúru's tent gathered his robes and cleared his throat. "He has what we seek, good *Kási*. His mind tells me that the young priest is also within our grasp: in the sick-cart, or in the tent of the harlot this *Shqá*-beetle uses as a physician. He knows nothing more, though we must speak privately later of a certain tanner – from Yán Kór."

Qútmu raised a thick eyebrow and turned to one of the soldiers. "Chónumel, send men! I had thought that this damned coffle had been searched from end to end!"

"Those who were inattentive might find it beneficial to do duty in the labyrinth below the Lair of the Undying in the City of Sárku," Vridékka muttered.

They waited.

A soldier thrust the tent-flap aside, saluted, and sketched the writhing worm of Lord Sárku in the air. "Sire, the girl's quarters are empty. There are no such persons in the encampment."

Qútmu stared. His heavy features worked, but words did not come. Then he was on his feet, leather creaking. A booted foot caught Chnesúru's shoulder and spun the slaver over to lie gaping up at the lurching torches.

"The Salarvyáni knows nothing of this," Vridékka said. "Leave him, *Kási*. We may still take the priest. Did anyone see him?"

"The slaves say that the youth, a girl, and a white Pé Chói were seen descending the ramp toward the city, Sire. The gates have opened for the day, and they must have entered by now. We have sent troops after them."

Qútmu was already out of the tent, men, torchbearers, overseers, slaves, and onlookers scattering before him. "Take the priestess Eyíl hiVriyén to our barracks within the city and hold her upon this writ." He threw the document back at one of the subalterns. "She will be returned to her temple as soon as the Imperium is done with her. – Oh, and confiscate this wretched caravan in the name of the Emperor! We can get a decree from the Imperial courts later – the judges here in Púrdimal are friends of ours. Sell the slaves, dismiss the overseers, convert the goods into money, and send whatever is fitting to the Governor of the city. Keep a tithe of the wealth for our temple, of course – and none will look too closely if you retain a few *Káitar*s for us, eh?"

"The Salarvyáni, Sire?"

Qútmu looked back for a final glance. "Why, summon the priests of Lady Hriháyal. They will reward him well for what he has done to their little priestess – perhaps peel all that hairy hide off of him and serve him up to their Demon Prince Rü'ütlánesh! He will make a pretty centrepiece at one of their feastings!"

He did not stop to hear Chnesúru's last despairing cries.

Chapter Twenty-Seven

H ot in the summertime, windy in the spring and the autumn, blustery and sometimes chill in the winter, that was Khirgár.

Upon its steep hill, the old town hoarded its memories to itself. The lowest concentric ring of walls was of red sandstone and black basalt, and their gates bore the sigil of Emperor Metlunél II "the Builder," who had ruled Tsolyánu eleven hundred years ago. Within these ramparts, the second ring skirted the lower slopes of the hill; this was made of Engsvanyáli grey granite brought from the mountains to the east where Thénu Thendráya lowered upon the horizon. The third and highest battlements, those surrounding the edifices of the dim age of the Bednálljans, the First Imperium, were of marble and black diorite, stones that were not found in these parts and came from no one knew whence – perhaps from beyond the Plain of the Risen Sea, where the cities of southern Yán Kór stood today? Bands of sand-scoured glyphs marched around these innermost and highest towers, proclaiming the majesty of Queen Nayári of the Silken Thighs, she who had founded the First Imperium by efficiently mixing just two ingredients, the histories said: sex and poison. Other, slenderer spires were crowded within this innermost enclosure, and their inscriptions spoke of the Priestkings of Éngsvan hla Gánga, the Golden Age of the Priest Pavár. The truncated pyramids and monumental walls of the present Second Imperium jostled for room amongst these older, more graceful structures. A hundred years, a millennium, were as days in the life of Khirgár, the Heartbeat of the North.

Táluvaz Arrío climbed up to High God Hill for the third time in this six-day. Once more, he thought, and the dry desert air would burn holes in his lungs and he would be too weak to tramp the many hundreds of *Tsán* back to Livyánu. The warmth of his beautiful city of Tsámra, the moist sea breezes, the graceful colonnades set like crystal playthings amidst the feathered *Já'atheb*-trees, the sipping of essences in the slumberous afternoons when the sun made amber and russet tableaux of the halls of his temple of mighty Qame'él, the Lord of the Livyáni Shadow-Gods...How he longed for them! – And how had he wandered so far from home, to this dusty relic of a city?

The streets of Lower Town were full of striding soldiers, babbling Tsolyáni merchants, Milumanayáni tribesmen in their dun-hued desert cloaks, Yán Koryáni traders here in spite of the war (no one harmed merchants, unless it was proved that they were spies – not like Livyánu, where all foreigners were suspected, watched, and delicately shunted off to harmless pursuits), stern and hatchet-faced Mu'ugalavyáni, sly Pijenáni and cloaked Ghatóni, nonhuman Pé Chói from the Chákas and shaggy-furred Pygmy Folk from somewhere off to the northeast, a few Shén and Ahoggyá and Swamp Folk and Páchi Léi, and a hundred others he could barely recognise. Khirgár was usually crowded, but the war with Yán Kór had made everything worse; and what with an Imperial Prince in residence, it was well-nigh impossible to find accommodations that left a man any shred of dignity. The place was crammed with all sorts of odd persons who would never have been let out of their temple districts at home!

Táluvaz checked his purse, saw that the bodyguards loaned him by the Livyáni Legate in Khirgár and his own personal guard, a N'lüss warrior-woman who stood a head taller than most Tsolyáni – or Livyáni, for that matter – were all within reach. It would be unthinkably degrading to be touched by one of these rustics. He also swept a glance back at the slaves who bore the gifts he had selected for Prince Eselné. This time, he thought morosely, he would finish his business and be off home!

The guards at the gates of Upper Town admitted his entourage with no objections (but no proper deference to speak of). Here it was quieter, the narrow, wind-worn, many-storeyed clanhouses leaning against one another like old ladies exhausted from a day's excursion. A matron in yellow and black appeared from one of the winding alleyways that passed for streets, and Táluvaz moved aside to let her and her following of clansmen by; throughout northern Tsolyánu – indeed, all of Yán Kór and Saá Allaqí – the women ruled the clans, made the marriages, and dictated policies to their menfolk. It would not do to offend such a matriarch. The north seemed to breed extremes: the Yán Koryáni were dominated by women, while the wretched Ghatóni kept their girls penned up like *Hmélu*-beasts and allowed no female of any species to walk the streets!

"Each *Tetél*-blossom upon its own stem," Táluvaz thought tiredly. He had been selected for his willingness to endure the irrationalities of other nations. At home it was one's clan status and one's rank within one's temple that started a person out upon the road to power; these things showed upon one's face – the *Aomúz* tattooes – and what one became afterward depended upon one's ability to play at the subtle games of priestly politics and doctrinal rivalries that balanced one another so prettily. A man, a woman – what did gender matter? Or species either? Even the nonhuman Shén and the little Tinalíya, some of whom dwelt within Livyánu's borders, were welcome to join in the dance – as long as they were obedient to the dictates of the Shadow Gods.

Another steep climb to the Gates of the Blue Fish, named, the guides had told Táluvaz, for some hoary local deity. The archway still bore a crumbling marble mosaic depicting the creature, scales, tail, pop-eyes and all. Some wag had climbed all the way up to paint a huge red phallus on the fish's underbelly.

The edifices on High God Hill had once been arranged in a neat square around a central plaza: the armoury and barracks of whatever Legion was in residence to the left of the gatehouse at the southeast corner; the colonnades of the administrative offices opposite in the southwest; the temples of the Tsolyáni gods crowded together along the crest of the hill in the northwest; and the Citadel of the Victories of the Emperor on the summit to the northeast, facing the windy deserts beyond which lay Milumanayá and Yán Kór. The fortress probably dated from the First Imperium, Táluvaz supposed, rebuilt by the Engsvanyáli, occupied by some local dynasty of warlords during the Time of No Kings, and refurbished a dozen times more by the Tlakotáni Emperors since the Second Imperium had come to power 2,358 years ago – if the chronology were in any way accurate. Táluvaz prided himself on being somewhat of a scholar; he enjoyed picking out the architectural and artistic details that identified each epoch.

The pattern of the place was spoiled now, alas, by accretions of buildings thrown up helter-skelter during the past millennium. The plaza existed only as an irregular patch of rutted stone around the stump of an Engsvanyáli obelisk, and the clanhouses of the newly rich jostled each other for a place in its shadow. The army had built more barracks here, the priests an annex to this temple or that over there, the Imperium another hall of scribes and records in this corner – the place was an architectural *Mnór*'s nest: a jumble of glittering trash mixed in with real treasures! Such a hodgepodge would never be permitted at home in Tsámra.

The soldiers at the bronze-banded gates of the citadel were smart troops indeed: members of the Tsolyáni First Legion of Ever-Present Glory. Here was something Táluvaz could secretly envy. The armies of Livyánu were far less imposing for all their rich armour and pretty *Khéshchal* plumes. This related to the matters Táluvaz had come to negotiate.

A soft-eyed, sandal-shod chamberlain took them on through halls of decaying and dusty Engsvanyáli grandeur, past fountains that no longer played, into a vestibule of rose-tinted porphyry, and on to the Governor's suite, now vacated for Prince Eselné, the Emperor's second son. (And how did the Governor like that arrangement? Táluvaz wondered. The quarters the Governor now occupied were probably once a scriptorium or a library: vast, empty, and full of desert dust. The prerogatives of power...)

The outer audience hall was filled with people. Children ran amongst the carven columns and shrieked. Three soldiers had occupied the only available daises, documents scattered upon the floor between them, held down by a wine-ewer of scarlet Mu'ugalavyáni glass and a brass tray filled with empty goblets. Five or six women sat crosslegged upon a figured Khirgári carpet in one corner, pausing in their chatter only to bawl unheeded commands at this child or that. These were probably the wives or concubines of the officers of the Prince's court – or even of mighty Eselné himself.

A ghastly, squealing roar from the latticed windows along the side of the chamber made Táluvaz jump. Somebody must be peeling the hide from a *Chlén*-beast down there! This operation had to be performed every six months or so to keep the animals' skin from growing ragged. The tanners then took the plates of raw hide, applied their smelly liquids and their secret skills, and produced the light, flexible, and immensely strong sheets from which armour, weapons, and a thousand other things were made.

The bellowing was followed by the heady scent of *Chlén*-dung: fright often caused the beasts to void their bowels. Táluvaz surreptitiously extracted his pomander of *Kílueb*-essence from his robe and pressed it to his nose. In the name of the Lords of Shadow, why so close to an Imperial residence? Prince Eselné was indeed supposed to be an informal, blunt, military sort of man, but this was carrying that image too far!

The chamberlain beckoned them on. The ornate doors at the far end of the hall gave upon a pleasant, polygonal room – probably in one of the corner towers – that overlooked the grey-brown deserts beyond. Graceful Engsvanyáli pillars held up the painted vaulting of the ceiling, and marble lattices opened out onto a narrow balcony, its tiled floor shimmering with hot sunlight.

Within the chamber, two slavegirls pulled on the cords of the dusty sweep-fan that hung from the ceiling. A third ground spices in a mortar for *Chumétl*, the ghastly buttermilk concoction the Tsolyáni favoured. Táluvaz wished fervently for a cup of wine, a tiny goblet of scented *Tsuhóridu*-liqueur, or even a draught of cold water. He knew that he would be unlikely to get any of these; the Prince had his "common-soldier" military façade to maintain, after all.

There were two others in the room: a short, middle-aged military officer, and the Prince himself, now rising from his dais to greet his guest.

Prince Eselné hiTlakotáni was impressive, a soldier from head to foot. He towered over his companion, brawny, bronzed by the sun, and as thick through the shoulders as any *Chlén*-beast. His sharply hooked nose and broad forehead bespoke the heritage of the most ancient and aristocratic clan of Tsolyánu, and his fierce, proud gaze was of the sort that would someday look most noble indeed upon a golden *Káitar*. The women of the court, Táluvaz knew, called him "the Hrúgga of the Age."

Yet there was something lacking in this man; when one summed him all up, he seemed a bit bland and not quite fulfilled. The eyes were too far apart, the brow too unlined, the craggy jaw not as strong and determined as first impressions indicated. There were other names for Eselné in Avanthár: "the *Chlén*-beast in Azure Robes" and "the Two-legged Ahoggyá" were two that Táluvaz had heard. This Prince would be as soft as warm wax in the hands of his advisors, the generals of his Military Party, and the Omnipotent Azure Legion. Once within the Golden Tower, he would make a splendid and heroic-appearing Emperor. But it would be others who would rule.

Prince Eselné would require much assistance to overcome his brothers and his sister in the *Kólumejàlim*, the Rite of the Choosing of Emperors, Táluvaz thought. He might win over Hrúgga himself in the trials of physical endurance and soldierly prowess, but he would have to choose his allotted three champions carefully from amongst the best of his followers to defeat Mridóbu or Dhich'uné – both shrewd and devious men – in the contests of cleverness, knowledge, statecraft, and sorcery that must follow. No, this man might be what the Tsolyáni Imperium needed – a glorious soldier-emperor figurehead – but the priests who oversaw the *Kólumejàlim* would be hard put to make him win it!

Táluvaz' superiors in Tsámra wanted Prince Eselné to gain the Petal Throne. He was precisely what was needed for Livyánu's broader goals.

Prince Eselné wore only a breechclout and a light shirt of *Thésun*-gauze. A heap of *Chlén*-hide swords – and two that glittered with the silvery grey of rare iron – lay upon the carpet before the two Tsolyáni, attesting to the topic of their conversation.

This was good; the audience would be informal, just what was needed. It would have been impossible to speak freely in some stilted court ceremonial. Táluvaz' agents in Khirgár had given excellent counsel: this Prince was best approached as one soldier speaking to another. Táluvaz took only a moment to push his own more delicate tastes to the back of his mind and take on the outward attitudes of a tough man of affairs. This was another reason why the High Council in Tsámra had chosen him for this mission.

"Most gracious Prince –" Táluvaz bowed and launched into the required roster of honorifics. Even this was too much; he was cut short.

"Ohé, Lord Táluvaz! I see you have ascended to our eyrie once again." Prince Eselné omitted the "you of wide journeying," appropriate to a high-ranking foreigner, and used the simple "noble you" instead. His voice was light and smooth, a trifle too gentle for the gruff soldierly picture he wanted to project.

"Most mighty Prince, accept the gifts of Tsámra!" That ought to be short enough! Táluvaz' slaves obediently began opening chests and parcels wrapped in brocaded *Güdru*-cloth.

Eselné waved them aside. "Accepted, with thanks. Give them to Shirétla – the chamberlain who brought you."

This Prince moved faster than common etiquette allowed! Táluvaz struggled to keep in character. A glance sent the slaves scurrying from the room, packages and all.

"Know you my Senior General, Lord Kéttukal hiMráktine?"

The fame of this man – and the intrigues that had for a time cost him his generalship of the First Legion – were indeed part of Táluvaz' briefing. It had taken the war with Yán Kór to persuade the Imperium to bring General Kéttukal out of semi-exile in Chéne Hó and put him back in command of his troops! Táluvaz kept this from his face and made polite responses.

"Get the money for the steel weapons from Shirétla," the Prince gestured to the General. "The *Chlén*-hide swords are too poor to be worth buying. I'd have the smith-tanners impaled were they not clan-cousins of the dung-smeared pederast who passes for a governor here. Send them back and demand better."

General Kéttukal grinned, reminding Táluvaz of the stone *Sró*-Dragon on the cornice of Lord Qame'él's temple in Tsámra. If his information was correct, this stocky, leather-faced soldier was the best tactician the Tsolyáni had. He would be useful in today's discussion, though possibly dangerous. The General snapped his fingers, and a servant appeared from a concealed doorway to gather up the offending weapons and carry them away.

"Now. Sing your song, noble Táluvaz. Two days back you offered us a pretty melody or two. I want my Lord Kéttukal to hear it."

So the Prince needed advice from his backers in the Military Party? The General's presence today was certainly no casual accident. Táluvaz swung smoothly into his argument, omitting the usual preamble of eulogies.

"Mighty Prince, as I humbly urged two days back, we in Livyánu have for centuries endured the wicked attacks of the pirates of the Tsoléi Archipelago. Each year, when the sea winds are right, they come forth to raid our provinces of Kakársh and Nuférsh. As you and noble General Kéttukal are no doubt aware —"

"Yes, yes," the Prince interrupted, "your High Council of the Priesthoods now proposes to take several legions away from your northern frontier with Mu'ugalavyá and sail off westward to gobble up Tsoléi."

General Kéttukal's grimace became wider.

Prince Eselné raised a fingertip to his cheek to express a clever discovery. "A neat and timely move! A handful of miserable white counters captured with a very few black ones. But nice because you then control the Sea of Aishúl and the Gulf of Teriyál and block the Red-Hats of Mu'ugalavyá from expansion farther west. Nice, if done smoothly."

"Also an end to Shényu's hegemony over the southern ocean there, and a bridge to the unexplored and uninhabited lands of the southern continent, eh?" General Kéttukal remarked in a rumbling bass voice. The slavegirl proffered brass cups of *Chumétl* to the three men. Kéttukal drank his off at one gulp. "I assume there's a turd in the stew somewhere?"

Eselné smiled broadly. "Lá, my Lord, no turd at all — only a lack of meat! Our noble Livyáni friends have not the troops to hold their enclave north of the Tláshte Heights against the Mu'ugalavyáni *and* swat the pirates of Tsoléi both at once! Hence our distinguished Lord Táluvaz, come all this way to push us to push my father to push the Mu'ugalavyáni, who can then not afford to push down into Livyánu and seize Ncihái or Hemćktu." He made little brushing motions with his fingers, as an apothecary sweeps powders into a prescription-paper.

General Kéttukal had the look of a stone idol receiving sacrifice. "Ohé, but what would Tsolyánu gain from joining in this feast? A chance, perhaps, to go to war with the Red-Hats of Ssa'átis? As though we have not enough to do with the Yán Koryáni invasion! Three months, and we have yet to regain the Atkolél Heights – and the Baron's armies threaten both Chéne Hó and Khirgár here!"

Táluvaz made no reply. These devotees of the war-gods had a disconcerting habit of dumping all their counters out openly upon the board. It was like talking to an Ahoggyá-or, worse, to a literal-minded Tinalíya! He sipped at the *Chumétl* the girl had brought him – and nearly spat it out upon the delicate wine-coloured carpet; the wench had laced it with too much hot *Hlíng*-seed! The Prince and the General seemed oblivious to his distress.

Prince Eselné rubbed his cleft chin. "If only that idiotic worm-kissing officer had not started the war with Yán Kór before we were ready to strike!" He made an obscene gesture. "All over a fine sense of noble dignity! If the fellow had been in one of my Legions instead of Dhich'uné's Battalions of the Seal of the Worm, his heart would have been steaming upon Lord Karakán's altars long ago!"

No reply seemed to be expected. All three were silent for a time. The Prince mused. General Kéttukal peered into his cup.

Eselné spoke again. "The Baron sits upon the Atkolél Heights. His troops occupy Pijéna. His 'Weapon Without Answer' pushes south towards Khirgár – or possibly southwest to Chéne Hó, whichever he sees the weaker. The Salarvyáni on our eastern frontiers nibble at Chaigári and Kerunán. My God-Emperor father grows old, and my brothers oppose me – Mridóbu and Dhich'uné – Rereshqála is too busy with his scholars and his concubines to compete for the Gold. My sister Ma'ín Krüthái might well marry me, as is our custom, and exchange Imperial rule for a quiet life in the Golden Tower. But she might also draw enough support from the temples of the two Goddesses and their Cohorts to stand by herself in the *Kólumejàlim*..."

He took a turn about the room, strong splayed toes digging into the fragile arabesques of the carpet. "Now too, of all times, the priesthood of Thúmis chooses to bring forth one of my father's brood of secret heirs, the whimpering little temple clerk Surundáno. Damn their High Adept Gámulu and his old toady, Lord Dúrugen hiNáshomai! Half of my support amongst the temples of the Lords of Stability either disappears or wavers like smoke in the wind!"

Táluvaz had heard about these manoeuvrings of Imperial politics. They complicated the lives of diplomats, he thought, but that was the nature of the task.

The Prince rounded to face Táluvaz. "It might be well for us to aid you Livyáni in your little excursion. If we cannot keep the Mu'ugalavyáni off our western flank – and out of an alliance with the Baron – the Empire will be as luckless as a *Chlén*-beast beset from all sides by *Zrné*!"

As though hearing its name mentioned, the *Chlén* outside bellowed, shaking the marble window-lattices. Táluvaz and the three slavegirls were the only ones who appeared to notice.

"I cannot send troops on my own authority, you know, nor do I dare do anything to bring the Mu'ugalavyáni in openly on the Baron's side. Arms, a few mercenaries, and some ships to you people. A little rumbling along the Chákan frontier and a medley of negotiations and threats to worry the Red-Hats: these are the only strings I can fit to my bow for now."

"This will not discourage the Baron, Lord." The General actually laid a hand upon the Prince's brawny wrist. These Tsolyáni had so little sense of Imperial dignity! "Yán Kór does not need Mu'ugalavyá. To Baron Áld the Mu'ugalavyáni are *Qásu*-birds awaiting their chance to scavenge. They yearn to snatch the Chákas if we lose the north, but they won't risk a fight by themselves – another defeat like the War of 2,020 would ruin them – and the Baron abhors them and gives them no encouragement. Beg your father for permission to attack around the north-eastern flank, through the Pass of Skulls! Take Milumanayá – Lord Firáz Zhavéndu there is a strutting popinjay – he cannot resist us – and on into Saá Allaqí or up to Tléku Miriyá to knock upon the Baron's back gate!"

"I have already been on my knees before my glorious father at Avanthár a dozen times. I'd kiss the backside of a Ssú to do as you suggest, my Lord, but brother Mridóbu only smiles and counsels sweet patience."

"Foolish," Kéttukal growled, "if I were the Baron – or the High Prince of the Red-Hats – I would do my best to hammer out an alliance and invade Tsolyánu from two sides at once. Áld must be mad to refuse the opportunity! Mu'ugalavyá is strong now, and the Baron has unified Yán Kór into a real nation – not the gaggle of miserable city-states it was before he took power.

If the Baron and the Red-Hats were to combine, we'd have a war that would make that of 2,020 look like a skirmish! My Lord Prince, it is best that we strike first, now, before either the blockheaded Mu'ugalavyáni or the Baron decides to make common cause and serve us defeat for our supper."

"Lord Táluvaz asks little enough. I need no permission from my glorious father to send a few ships and light a few fires along the borders."

"Forget not the colonies on the southern continent, mighty Prince," Táluvaz injected gracefully. "If we take Tsoléi, we counter the power of the reptiles of Shényu in the southern seas. Even now they dicker with Mu'ugalavyá for concessions and alliances there. Accompany us, and Tsolyánu plays a role in settling the unknown lands beyond."

"And how had you Livyáni planned to deal with Shényu? The reptiles' ships and warriors may be fewer than yours and they cannot match you in sorcery, but any Shén can slay two humans with a blow!" The Prince refilled his cup and offered more *Chumétl* to the others with his own hands. Táluvaz thought it prudent to accept. A burning bowel movement in the morning was a very good price to pay for success this afternoon.

"The Shén are divided into egg-groups, mighty Prince, as you know. Each is hostile to the others. We have made alliance with the Shén of Mmatuguál and the other little states of their species to our south. They hate Shényu more than any human can imagine: insensate, instinctive…They will fight for – with – us."

General Kéttukal spat out a *Hlíng*-seed and fixed a jaundiced eye upon the girl who had ground the spices for his *Chumétl*. "Aside from a few ships, a handful of troops, and whatever else we can manage, how can we really help you? Tsoléi is too distant, and we can send too little."

"Busy the Red-Hats and it is sufficient. They then cannot seize our northern provinces. But there is more." Táluvaz made himself draw a careful breath. "We know that our armies are not, ah, well seasoned and strong, mighty Prince. We depend overmuch upon sorcery: magically, Livyánu is a 'fertile' area, where the many skins of reality are thin and easily pierced. The Red-Hats and the Shén do not invade Livyánu for fear of our sorceries. On the other hand, the islands of Tsoléi are a 'barren' region; it is impossible to draw power from beyond this Plane in such a place. Spells and those devices of the ancients that depend upon such forces do not work there. We must thus rely upon our military prowess, which is, ah, not so great as to make our landing a speedy success. We can therefore make good use of a few Tsolyáni officers, some troops from whatever Legion you can spare, some ships from your coastal fleets – unneeded in any war here in the north or the west – and permission to raise mercenaries in your Empire. Military expertise, mighty Prince, and experience – these things we require. The rest we can do ourselves."

"So, we firm up your *Chlén*-hide with our iron," the General said.

Prince Eselné frowned. "I know that the Temple of Thúmis has already sent some sort of secret mission to your colonies in the southern continent. My dear Táluvaz, you play not only with me but with the grey-robes – and their new Prince Surundáno."

This was all too true, but it seemed more politic not to own up to it – not unless it became an issue here.

The new Prince might indeed become a problem. He did seem to worry Prince Eselné; unduly, Táluvaz thought. The Temples of the war-gods ought not to be alarmed by this new counter on the board. Some support would vanish, of course, and some new alignments might result, but Eselné's backers and those of the Flame-Lord, Vimúhla, should still be able to come to an understanding. Prince Surundáno might be an unexpected impediment, but he was too weak, both personally and in his backing, to be more than a minor annoyance.

What an insane system of government this land had! The Seal Emperors of Tsolyánu proclaimed only some of their offspring to be Princes and Princesses as soon as they ascended the Petal Throne; others were given as infants into the keeping of the great temples, the clans, and the highest noble houses to be brought up in secrecy and declared later – like white counters suddenly turning black upon a *Dén-den* board! The Tsolyáni said that this guaranteed the throne to the cleverest, strongest, and most resourceful contender. It was better to keep all of the heirs awake and prepared, the theory ran, rather than let the succession pass to a child already spoiled by a surfeit of luxury and power. The Gods alone knew whether the idea had merit or not. Táluvaz doubted it; had not Livyánu existed far longer than the Tsolyáni Imperium, and was it not more efficacious to select one's rulers through the recondite deliberations of the High Council of the Priesthoods of the omniscient Shadow-Gods?

Carefully, Táluvaz said nothing.

"No, Lord Táluvaz, you must know that Tsoléi is the smallest thorn upon my *Tsúral*-blossom," the Prince said. "Even if we aid you, I fear it is too late to halt the Baron's 'Weapon.' By the time you take Tsoléi – or Thúmis' all-too-blatant secret mission reaches its destination – our Skeins will have been unravelled for us by the Yán Koryáni. We stand; we fight; we live or we die here at Khirgár or at Chéne Hó, as Lord Karakán decrees. What more can we say?"

A noble but perfectly *Chlén*-brained attitude! Failure – or less than wondrous success – loomed as a distinct possibility. Tsámra would not be pleased.

General Kéttukal sat down crosslegged upon the figured carpet. "The Baron's turd-shooting weapon! We had hoped to find –" He stopped.

Prince Eselné grunted and tossed his cup to the slavegirl to be refilled. "Oh, finish it," he said irritably. "The Livyáni have their *Vrú'uneb* everywhere, just as we have the Omnipotent Azure Legion. If Lord Táluvaz does not know the tale, he is as useless to his masters as a clay sword to great Hrúgga! He uses us, and we may be able to use him. 'One *Aqpú*-beetle dies alone, but six build a nest...'"

"When I was at Páya Gúpa, my Lord," the General continued reluctantly in his deep, hard voice, "I had heard that there might be a counter to the Baron's toy..."

"Chá, everyone in the Five Empires has heard the story! At Avanthár or Béy Sü secrets are like water in a cracked jug! There was supposed to be some priest of Keténgku – or was it Thúmis? – who knew of a device that would halt the Baron's 'Weapon Without Answer.' It was a great bone of contention between the priesthoods half a year back – do you recall? – before the war with Yán Kór. Then the fellow disappeared. Magically: a veritable Súbadim the Sorcerer! Your people knew all this of course, Táluvaz."

Taken aback, Táluvaz started to shake his head in negation. He changed his mind and nodded instead.

"– Out of the Temple of Eternal Knowing in Béy Sü, as neatly as a virgin spits out a *Dlél*-fruit pit!" This from the General. The Tsolyáni idiom was unknown to Táluvaz, but the sense of it was clear.

There was no reason now to pretend ignorance. Táluvaz said, "My, ah, friends here told me...Was there not something about the city of Púrdimal?"

"As if your people did not join the dance!" Eselné snorted. "Yes, we followed certain of my beloved brother Dhich'uné's ugly henchmen for a time, but the priest vanished into the stews of Púrdimal! The Temple of Sárku dangled a pretty little captive priestess over the water, but the fish never rose to the bait. We finally rescued her with an Imperial writ from Avanthár – brother Dhich'uné is not the only one with access to my godlike father!"

Táluvaz had heard of this also. There had been pressure upon Prince Eselné from the Temple of Hriháyal to free the girl. He imagined he knew what form this pressure had taken. Eselné's dalliance with Misénla, the High Priestess of Hriháyal in the Empire, was common table-gossip.

"My agents fought Dhich'uné's men – or what he uses for men – and Mridóbu's, and those of at least three temples, and even my father's people. Did you know that the Yán Koryáni were there was well? Half of the Five Empires chasing each other like Hriháyal's greasy priests plucking at little boys, and not a hair of the thrice-damned catamite ever seen again!"

Táluvaz debated how much to say, but the Prince was still speaking:

"And while this was happening, the Temple of Thúmis found it opportune to pull poor Surundáno out of their temple at Haumá and declare him a Prince! One day a clerk in a copying-hall, the next a Prince of the Empire!"

General Kéttukal guffawed, an unseemly and ignoble sound.

"And then – of all the stupid times to act – the Temple of Vimúhla began to worry – as fearful as an old lady goosed by an Ahoggyá! Two weeks ago they trotted forth a Princeling of their own: somebody named Mirusíya, raised in secret by the arrogant Vimúhla-loving Vríddi clan of Fasíltum! Did you hear of this, Lord Táluvaz? The fellow was trained as a warrior, an officer in a good Legion – that of the Lord of Red Devastation, as devoted to the Flame-God as a babe to its mother's teat – and all too appealing to the army and the temples of our war-gods."

Táluvaz had *NOT* heard. It overturned the entire *Dén-den* board!

He struggled to look knowledgeable, thinking furiously all the while. What the Prince had left unspoken was that such an heir would be almost an exact copy – on the side of the Lords of Change – of Eselné himself! Dangerous! The war-gods' temples, Lord Karakán of Stability and Lord Vimúhla of Change, had been close to a rapprochement of sorts; now there would be no reason for it, and the intrigue for alliances and power must begin all over again. The Temple of Vimúhla deserved to rot in Sárku's wormy hells for causing this turn of events!

This new Prince – and the shattering of what had until now been a secure power base – cut right under the foundations of Prince Eselné and his Military Party! Dismay ran through Táluvaz' limbs like a fever: everything was changed. All the effort spent cultivating Eselné and his brash, loutish generals would be for nothing! There was no time to start afresh with this wretched flame-worshipping newcomer – though Tsámra would certainly send someone as soon as the Livyáni Legate in Béy Sü heard of it. An immediate stroke was needed. Prince Eselné must have a victory: some resounding deed that would echo through the palaces and temples of Tsolyánu like a *Túnkul*-gong. The defeat of the Baron's armies here in the west suddenly became urgent and imperative, whatever the cost.

"– Frightened that Prince Eselné would make too much capital out of the war with Yán Kór," General Kéttukal was saying, "or perhaps that Ma'ín Krüthái would betroth herself to Eselné and thus bring about an unbreakable alliance between her Goddesses and our Military Party! At any rate –"

"Yes, at any rate there are times when I wish I could candle my ever-victorious father's head! We not only have a major war upon our borders, we also have a well-fuelled fire in the heart of our Empire! How many puling brats has my father spawned anyway – and hidden here and there about the country as a *Shqá*-beetle hides its eggs in a ball of dung? Now Karakán knows how many more little Princes and Princesses lurk behind the altars of this temple or that! How many noble clans have little boys and girls with the Omnipotent Azure Legion's golden Seal upon their plump arses? One more such revelation and I renounce the Gold and retire to Salarvyá to breed virgins for Lady Dilinála!"

The three girls in the corner giggled.

Táluvaz strove to think the matter through. He felt like a swimmer in a rushing mountain river. An idea surfaced, and he snatched at it. He almost pushed it away: it was too perilous, a jag-edged Ssú sword that would cut many ways! Secrets would have to be disclosed – he ought to check with Tsámra and his colleagues in the *Vrú'uneb* first. The Tsolyáni might gain too much. Yet it was almost certainly the key to more Tsolyáni cooperation than Tsámra could have hoped! There was no time. What should he do? Táluvaz again wished the Temple of Vimúhla and its flame-loving Prince into Lord Qame'él's darkest and coldest hells.

Still, the more Táluvaz thought about it, the better his key seemed. But to use it could mean his death. The secrets of the Shadow Gods and the *Vrú'uneb* and the High Council were not for one man to babble freely. Yet…

Prince Eselné and the stern-faced General were looking at him.

Slowly, carefully now. Táluvaz fumbled for his cup of *Chumétl*, something to delay with, to hold back his words until he had had time to weigh each one. The stuff burned his throat like Vimúhla's raging flames. He could not help making a face. He gasped and spoke:

"Mighty Prince, I have made our needs plain to you, plainer than I would have spoken them to my own brother-priests." The language was coming easier, the musical Tsolyáni syllables following one upon the other of their own accord. "I am honoured by your, ah, confidence." He paused. Now he must plunge into the maelstrom. "Know that we – were indeed aware of the Man of Gold, the weapon to defeat the horrible device brought forth by the Baron Áld."

General Kéttukal made an impatient sound in his throat, but the Prince gestured him to silence.

"My Lord, we were indeed aware of the priest of Thúmis, and of something of what he might have discovered. But it was not – useful – that he be found – by any of you – ah, at that time." Táluvaz' spread his hands palms downward in a gesture of apology. "Too much power – either to Tsolyánu or to Yán Kór – you must understand..."

Prince Eselné gave no sign. Politics were politics. Thus far, Táluvaz had said nothing that Tsámra would find objectionable. If his guess were wrong, what he was about to add now would seal his death warrant at the hands of the ever-efficient *Vrú'uneb*.

"We did not seek very diligently, nor did we use all of our resources, mighty Prince. Had we done so, we would have found the priest as assuredly as the journeying of the sun through the sky. For – for we can command the aid of –" he filled his lungs with the dry air, "– the Hehegánu, the Old Ones of Púrdimal."

"What –?" The Prince looked puzzled; then his gaze hardened.

"We are old, my Lord, older than Engsvanyálu, older then the First Imperium of the Bednálljans, or any of the empires that have come and gone upon Tékumel. We do not say it, but our Shadow-Gods are not distorted forms of the Gods of the Priest Pavár, as those outside of our sanctuaries are led to think. Within, we carry on the traditions of Llyán, of the First Kingdom after the Latter Times – of Llyán of Tsámra, my Lord. We have wisdom lost since the days of man's first creation, from the ages before the Time of Darkness, before the lights in the sky were extinguished, and the lamps of the Old Gods went out, and the earth shook, and the waters walked, and the fires rose from the hells below..."

"What has all this mythology –?" General Kéttukal began.

"Hear me. There are peoples and things – from the First Times – allegiances and liaisons made then, before the world was as it is. One of these, ah, relationships is with the Hehegánu, the Old Ones of Púrdimal, who are now debased, a race so circumscribed and so poor and so disillusioned – and so disinherited – that they dwell in the places below and no longer walk abroad in the light of day. They know where your priest is, mighty Prince. They have given him refuge. They want no resurgence of the great conflict that he – the Man of Gold – would revive from the dust of the ancient past, no battle between that thing and the 'Weapon Without Answer' that the Baron drags down toward your frontiers.

"Yet we – who are allied by certain bonds to them – can cause them to bring forth the priest and aid in finding his device. We can winkle him out for you. If the Man of Gold is as it is supposed to be, if it still operates after all these millennia, if –"

"In return for which, we aid you with Tsoléi and Mu'ugalavyá – and the southern continent," Prince Eselné drew a long breath.

"Yes, those – and perhaps certain other mutual favours to be discussed – I must speak with my superiors in the High Temple of Qame'él at Tsámra. But I have opened the kernel of it for you. Yes, we will help you stop the Baron of Yán Kór. And you shall give us what I have asked today."

Prince Eselné stood up. He clapped his hands twice. A panel opened in the wall, revealing darkness within. "You are there, Chiyúrga? Take these three girls and apply your magic to their minds; let them recall nothing of what was said here. Harm them not."

The slavegirls squealed, terrified in spite of the Prince's soothing and the fat purse of gold he tossed to them. The three men remained talking until late in the night. Táluvaz eventually received not only an ewer of excellent, cool wine but a fine dinner as well.

Chapter Twenty-Eight

They often came here, up where the wind off Thénu Thendráya's mighty flanks drove the dank mists away in grey rags and tatters. It was cool, less muggy, and – what they needed most of all – less crowded and odoriferous than the labyrinths of the Splendid Paradise of the Crystal River, as the denizens of Púrdimal ironically named the oldest and most dilapidated section of their city.

If ever there had been a paradise here, it lay buried beneath millennia of rotting bricks and slums and offal, and the Crystal River was no more than a brownish slough that wound through slimed, turgid canals out to the Water Gate and thence into the swamps to the west of the town.

Hársan lay back upon the narrow ledge to look up at the curve of the roof-comb that bellied out above his head, a huge cylinder of mortared masonry some four man-heights in diametre set horizontally along the highest summit of Lord Hrü'ü's Shrine of Evanescent Change as a thick log might be laid upon a stool. The stained and dingy stone was deeply pockmarked with hollow bubbles, some tiny and others the size of a man's fist. Tlayésha said that it reminded her of a loaf of black bread, baked by some legendary baker for a feast of the Gods. The ornate sculptures of the comb were chipped and wind-worn, and one of the five tall spires that rose from its summit had fallen

– five hundred, a thousand years before? No one remembered. The masonry itself was webbed with cracks, each lush with its own miniature garden of scabrous moss and russet fungi.

One day it would collapse. Then perhaps a score or more of the priests and the wretched poor of Púrdimal's Splendid Paradise would perish beneath the cyclopean blocks. No matter! The Imperium would take the calamity in stride. Taxes would be raised in this province or that; carts laden with materials would arrive; engineers would scribble upon parchments and dangle their plumb-bobs; and legions of priests, scribes, and toiling slaves would come to build it all back up again. A new temple of Lord Hrü'ü, the mightiest of the Lords of Change, would rise upon this spot, and all would be as it had ever been.

Across the way, beyond the plaza named the Court of Cries, the cupolas of Lord Ksárul's pyramidal temple rose like some leviathan of the sea from amongst the wrack of tenements and steep-pitched tile roofs. The wind brought them the distant thunder of drums and the shriek of trumpets from the esplanade behind it. Today the red-robes of the Temple of Vimúhla rejoiced and paraded there in New Town: their favoured Legion, that of the Lord of Red Devastation, had led General Kéttukal's armies to victory in the deserts north of Khirgár. News had also come from General Korikáda hiKurúshma of the Legion of the Givers of Sorrow, fanatics devoted to Lord Vimúhla's Cohort, fierce Chiténg. His forces had sent the Yán Koryáni back north in headlong flight from before the gates of Chéne Hó in the far northwest. It was indeed a day of heady glory for the followers of the Flame. Prince Mirusíya, the latest of the Emperor's heirs to be declared, would be pleased.

Already the smoke of burning arose from the truncated cone of the Flame Lord's shrine in the distance. Yán Koryáni captives would go chanting – or screaming, or pleading, as their Skeins allowed – into the fire-pits there, and the city would stink of roasted meat and entrails for a time. The Gods would rejoice, the priests said, although one might well wonder just how many times in history the victory pyres had been lit and how many men and women had died to please these, the grimmest of the Lords of Change. – And all for different and probably contradictory causes!

The wind was in their direction. Hársan had no desire to await the smoke and the stench. He stretched, wrapped his kilt about his waist, and began rolling up the reed sleeping mat upon which he had been sitting. Tlayésha still slept, nude and ruddy-bronze in the shadow of the roof-comb, upon her mat beside him. His loins stirred, and he thought of making love one more time before going down. The clash of cymbals and a sustained, wordless, lusting roar from the crowds in New Town drifted up to him, and he decided against it. He ran a finger along the curve of her calf instead.

"Come, it is time."

She woke, then, and reached up to him. Even now he found himself surprised and a little unsettled by her sky-hued eyes, paler still in the westering sunlight. He changed his mind again and sank down beside her. After all, what was the hurry? The breeze would not bring unpleasant smells for at least a few moments yet.

She was not Eyíl – how long had it been since that one had walked in his dreams? Tlayésha was not as deft and skilful in her love-making. She did not play upon each nerve and each touch in turn, as Eyíl had drawn forth melodies from the *Sra'úr* of his body. Sometimes Tlayésha was inept; sometimes she hurried on before him; and at other times she could not keep up with his own eager impatience.

Yet she was Tlayésha. It was enough.

He helped her gather up her clothing, her mat, and her little urn of soothing oil. Together they descended the bronze-runged ladder that led down through the thick walls of Lord Hrü'ü's ancient temple, along the galleries of carven friezes that hung high over the apse below, and on into the maze of ventilation shafts that would take them home.

The purple-robed priests of the Master of the Lords of Change never looked up. They would have been most upset if they had known what had just transpired upon the roof of their temple. But they were mostly old, fusty, and as devoted to their rituals as a *Chlén*-beast who plods round and round upon the threshing floor. This temple was not like the splendid new shrine to Lord Hrü'ü over in New Town. None but the aged, the unambitious, the seekers of solitude, and those who had been passed over for lack of talent ever served here. Worshippers in this section of Púrdimal were the ragged poor, the halfbreed mixtures of human and Hehegánu, and the flotsam of the slums. Those who sought power and riches – the young, hard-eyed clergymen, the great scholars and sorcerers, the high pontiffs with their retinues of guards and scribes – rarely came to this place.

Hársan was not sure just where the ventilation shafts of the pyramid left off and the warrens of the Undercity began. There were no streets in the Splendid Paradise, just intricately confused layers of little passages, rooms, and scruffy halls of pockmarked stone or rotting brick. It had taken him all of the many months since his recovery to learn his way about the maze. Families, some human, some Hehegánu, some mixtures, and some – other – hung up mats and curtains and made their homes wherever they chose. No one cared. No Imperial bureaucrat came to ask questions or demand proof of ownership. This was the Splendid Paradise, after all.

Down, left, right, down again, through the hall where the legs of colossal statues rose like columns to the ceiling, their bodies and heads gone or entombed forever in the masonry of later structures above. The occasional shafts of bloodied sunlight gave way to the orange-red twinkle of rush-candles. The ramshackle curtains of the human poor were replaced by the loose-woven reed mats of the Hehegánu. No search party could ever find its way down here, the Old Ones said: the mats and curtains were made to be shifted and rehung in a matter of moments, altering the plan of these warrens beyond recognition. What were rooms could become passages; what were twisting subterranean alleyways turned into interlocking warrens of hovels and cubicles; and all was changed. In the whispering darkness the children of the Old Ones squatted on their haunches to stare solemnly at passersby as they had done for more centuries than were recorded in any book of histories.

The sweet, rotting, sickly stench of dead flowers struck Hársan like a wall. Here the many varieties of *Tsuhóridu* were made, the most precious liqueurs of Púrdimal and of all Tsolyánu. He helped Tlayésha down into the corridor beside the rows of stone vats. Gangs of human slaves and some of the Old Ones stirred a cauldron of *Alúja* as big as a room: the most strongly perfumed of all of the *Tsuhóridu* vintages, it was rumoured to deprive a man of his virility if more than a thimbleful were drunk each day. There bubbled the vats of *Nezu'ún*, a grass-smelling essence that gave dreams of unendurable ecstasy; farther were the pots of *Siyanúkka*, sweet-breathed as a child but bringing about the decay of the mind as surely as the clouds brought rain; beyond stood the green-corroded copper stills of the vendors of *Diqonái*, swamp-smelling and acerbic, providing an illusion of physical strength that the nobles of the Five Empires vied to obtain. A bottle of undiluted *Diqonái* no bigger than one's palm sold for a thousand *Káitars* in the marketplaces above.

Torchlight glistened upon sweating shoulders, furnaces flared in the glassblowers' shops down the way where the bottles and vials for the liqueurs were made. Over all hung the distant, rhythmic thump-sigh-thump of the great bellows, worked continually by gangs of chanting slaves, that brought in fresh air and kept this metropolis of no night and no day alive.

Hársan stepped carefully over the bodies of the *Mératorayal,* the Woeful
Seekers: men, and women, and others who lay beside the vats to lick up the
spilled drops of the precious essences. These were the true derelicts, tolerated
by the vintners, chained here by the bonds of their addiction more tightly than
any prisoner in the Tólek Kána Pits. Some, he knew, had once been noble,
clansmen and women of status; now they lay like beasts beside the dribbling
cauldrons, certain to die of starvation or of their wretched habit within a few
months at most. There were always others ready to fight, to kill, to take their
places.

The Old Ones had given them a dwelling place just behind the workshops
of the bottlers. It was cramped, no more than a triangular alcove between the
soot-encrusted foundations of two ancient Engsvanyáli mansions, the upper
storeys of which had later been levelled, razed, and roofed over during one of
the *Ditlána* ceremonies of the Second Imperium. Empty save for dust and the
stench of the distilleries, it had become their home – and their hiding place –
during the long period of Hársan's recovery.

Someone stood now by the torn matting that served as their door. Hársan
stopped, thrust Tlayésha behind him, and stood poised for flight. Then he
recognised the satiny gleam of white chitin: a Pé Chói. Ítk t'Sá! After their first
six-day in Púrdimal she had gone her way with no explanation; now she had
returned. Tlayésha gave a glad cry and ran past him to greet her.

Another waited with Ítk t'Sá, one of the grey-skinned Hehegánu,
pockmarked and ugly as the stones of the crumbling city itself.

"You are well now," Ítk t'Sá said in the Pé Chói tongue. It was not a
question. She touched Tlayésha's hand and then Hársan's cheek with her stick-
dry fingers.

"I am. It was your kindness. And Tlayésha's." He motioned them inside,
spread mats, and brought out the cracked pottery flagon that held wine
whenever they had the money. It was half full of the cheapest of the vintages
of the Kraá Hills. There were no coins to spare even for the poorest *Tsuhóridu,*
not even for a goblet of the dregs. Tlayésha set four of their misshapen clay
cups upon the flagstones before them, but Ítk t'Sá made a gesture of refusal.
The Hehegánu accepted a mug in silence.

"You live in ease? You are not *nto'óltk?*" The Pé Chói term covered all
combinations of unhappiness, hunger, pain, illness, and distress.

"It is well with us." Hársan knew she would sense the lie: he longed for the
forest, for the Monastery of the Sapient Eye – even for the bustling, scholarly
life of the Temple of Eternal Knowing. Anything but this: a few copper *Qirgál*

for copying petitions and letters for the lowest classes of Púrdimal, the hiding, the distrust, the fears that came to wake him in the night.

The worst dreams were those of opening his lips and finding that once again be could not speak.

They had not dared to make friends, human or otherwise. The Hehegánu remained courteously aloof, and all others might be spies. Life in the Splendid Paradise was lonely, dark, and hopeless. This Skein led nowhere.

Ítk t'Sá gave a whistling sigh. "And she?"

"As I." Another lie. If anything, Tlayésha's suffering had been the greater – and yet he had dared tell her only a part of the story. There was always the chance that she would be caught, too, as poor Eyíl had been. Tlayésha earned a pittance with her potions and salves. Hársan had not asked whether she had gone to New Town to use those other arts she had learned long ago in Jakálla. She did always seem to have a coin or two when they needed it most.

"I bear news. Hársan, know that Chtík p'Qwé lives – our people in Béy Sü have sent word. He lay wounded and broken under the earth in the Temple of Eternal Knowing. He was pulled free, and now he is healed – partially, at least. He greets you."

A wash of love, relief, longing, sadness for the world left behind – emotions too many to name – swept over Hársan. He leaned back against the rough stones of the wall.

The clicking Pé Chói language was lost upon Tlayésha, but she caught the name of Chtík p'Qwé, of whom Hársan had spoken. He smiled at her reassuringly, and she touched his arm in sympathy. The Hehegánu waited.

Ítk t'Sá nodded to change the subject. "You went to the temple of your God, Lord Thúmis?"

"No. The Old Ones – the Hehegánu – told me that watchers were posted at all of the entrances of the Splendid Paradise. They said that magic – spells – were being used, and that I would be known. Their skills keep us safe here."

"The Omnipotent Azure Legion…? Friends could be summoned hither to take you from this place. Or the tunnels beneath the city…?"

Hársan stared moodily into his cup. "Even if I eluded the spies and reached my superiors – even if my people returned me to Béy Sü escorted by an Imperial Legion – did not the Worm Prince once pluck me from the heart of our greatest temple? He could do the same again."

The matter was more complex by far; Hársan searched for words. "More… more – I sense that the priests of my own temple would use me little better than did Prince Dhich'uné. I tire of being a piece in some high, invisible game of *Dén-den*. I may have begun as a pitiful little white pawn; now, for the moment, I am a blue – or even a black. But I am still no more than a counter – a counter who likes the game not at all! I will either become a player or else hop off the board to be lost under the mat!"

"'Better the house of poor friends than alone in the forest.'"

"I know, I know. My superiors must think I am either dead or a traitor to Lord Thúmis – or both." He put his palms over his eyes and pressed until colours writhed behind the lids. "How long can we go on hiding here?"

"You know that others seek you besides the Worm Prince? The Yán Koryáni – the followers of your war-god, Lord Karakán, the Omnipotent Azure Legion, the –"

A vision of Eyíl, smiling, arm in arm with a tall, jowly man whom the Hehegánu said was one Jayárgo, a priest of the Worm Lord, arose before Hársan's eyes: how had they got her to do that? Perhaps Vridékka had ensorcelled her with his arts. Hársan and Tlayésha had hidden – remembered guilt arose to accuse him – and Eyíl and the priest of Sárku had eventually gone away. She had not returned.

Hársan cried, "Yes, the whole thrice-cuckolded Empire – As if there was naught more important than this – this one artifact, whose location I know – and then know only vaguely! I cannot believe –"

"You alone can assess its value. But you have asked the one question that must eventually be answered. You cannot go on hiding here forever. What is to be your move now, Oh newest player in the game?"

Hársan could not reply.

"They still search for us above?" Tlayésha spoke in Tsolyáni.

Ítk t'Sá glanced at the silent Hehegánu. Then she said, "It is so. More than ever now. Every path is watched, every exit to New Town is guarded. You cannot leave without falling into one net or another."

"The Hehegánu protected us when we came." Hársan could not keep dejection out of his voice. "It was long before I recovered, thanks to you and to Tlayésha here. When I could speak again, I found things as they are now. I know of no sure way to reach safety, and even if we did, I am not sure that it would be safety after all..."

"This situation must change," Ítk t'Sá replied. "Ormudzó, here, met me when I returned to Púrdimal. He will speak of it." She settled back upon her gleaming chitinous haunches and nodded to the Hehegánu.

The Hehegánu was old, puffed and wrinkled, bald and grey like all of his race, mottled as a serpent of the swamps. He blew out his cheeks. "Man

Hársan, you came to us upon the words of the apothecary Gdéshmaru, who deals with us. You aid us and make no trouble, and the woman Tlayésha heals us and gives us consolation –"

The careful, stilted words bore menace. Hársan looked a question at Ítk t'Sá, but she only made a gesture of patience.

"The Gods do not like those who betray a hosting. Not our Gods. We are thus bound to you, as you have bound yourselves to us."

"What does he mean?" Tlayésha murmured.

The creature would not be hurried. The tiny flame of the rush-candle limned the grey-stippled cheeks with orange shadows, painted fire upon the hairless skull, turned the round eyes to staring rubies. "Many sought you, and you were not found. It is so?"

Hársan nodded. Tlayésha's fingers closed hard upon his wrist.

"There were others, persons whom we saw and whom you did not see. Men of different professions, soldiers, questioners, even some of my own species. There were a few whom even we did not recognise – creatures better left unnamed." The Hehegánu made a jerky, punctilious little half-bow. "In any case, none came upon you. When we guest someone, we perform all things well. You honour 'noble action'; to us, this is noble."

"High One, why –?"

The wide mouth seemed to stretch halfway around the noseless head. Hársan could not tell whether the Hehegánu was amused or angry at the interruption.

"Now I obey the mightiest of our commands of hospitality. When the host is required to break the guesting – to cease the protection it gives – it is a duty first to inform the guest. I bring you a warning, and a choice. Know that – one – has come who can compel us to deliver you into his hands. We cannot refuse him."

"One of the minions of the Worm Prince –?"

"Not so. Another. We must acquiesce to him – or circumvent his commands."

It seemed that the most important of all of Hársan's questions must now be resolved.

"Who –?" Hársan began, but he was forestalled by Tlayésha's angry cry of "*Why?*" The Hehegánu turned his lumpy body to face her.

"You are not affected, woman. No one seeks you. It is the man Hársan who is wanted. You may remain."

"I – I cannot. We are –"

Emotions coiled within Hársan's stomach: anger, despair, cold, fear. "You must listen to him," he said harshly to Tlayésha, "for I am the one they pursue. Why involve yourself further? You rescued me, and that in itself is more than I can repay. There are many caravans, many who would employ a physician…" He could say no more but gestured wordlessly at the squalor around them.

Her oddly coloured blue eyes told him that all his reasonings would be in vain. Tlayésha would not leave him.

Hársan let out his breath slowly. He had not realised that he had been holding it. "You mentioned a choice, High One."

"It is a tree of three branches," the creature replied. "The first branch takes you – and the woman, if she desires – to the one who seeks. The second branch leads to a gate known to us, there beyond the quarter of the mat-weavers, on through a tunnel, and so to the outside, where a skiff can be given you to cross the Great Morass…"

Tlayésha interrupted him, "Hársan, we could reach Mrelú – go to Dó Cháka – Ítk t'Sá's people could hide us, take us through the forests – to Mu'ugalavyá – or north to Pijéna…" Her eyes sparkled red in the rushlight, and he could see how much she yearned to be free of this dreadful place.

"Fugitives forever?" He sighed and considered. "No, love, I have already thought upon this. They could catch us with their sorceries, take us as we fled – and those who have aided us would be imperilled, a fine reward for their guesting! And even if we were successful, the Mu'ugalavyáni or the Yán Koryáni would use me as I have told you the Worm Prince would do."

"Yet you – we – cannot go on living here forever!" She clenched her fists and glared at him, angry for the moment. "Hársan, would you spend the rest of your life in a hole? Oh, I know that you await an opportunity, for time to pass and all to be forgotten. But – but now…"

She was more right than she could guess. He *had* delayed, postponed the decision, been content to dwell in this lair, like a *Mnór* lurking in its den to let the hunting party pass it by. Nothing had been resolved. Now, however, he must make his move, willy-nilly. He turned back to the Hehegánu.

"And the third branch, High One?"

Ormudzó held out a tiny vial of dull red glass in his rough, grey fingers. "This is *Onka'óm*, the *Tsuhóridu* of Ultimate Destinations. What you would leave behind upon this Plane could not be revivified by sorcery, nor could your souls be made to speak from beyond the tomb."

Tlayésha drew back, eyes wide. Hársan waved the thing away. "It is not to be considered, High One. I – we –"

The Hehegánu rocked back and forth upon the mat. "It is sad, man Hársan, for this is perchance the noblest of all the branches. A joyous feast which we would provide; a pleasant evening; a few farewells; a quiet toast and a drinking. All would be tasteful. Noble. The drawing-together of an exquisite Skein. It is an ending that appeals to us – that keeps certain secrets hidden, that raises no spectres from the lost graves of the past."

"You would not force us – me –?"

"Who could compel a guest and yet remain noble? No, this branch must be of your own choosing."

"They are too strongly bound to this life for any such honourable termination," Ítk t'Sá said. "Break this last branch from your tree, High One, and cast it aside. What of the first of your branches: the one who seeks? You said that this is no servitor of Lord Sárku? Who, then?"

"The laws of our guesting permit no more. I have uttered too much."

"Tsolyáni, Yán Koryáni – or other?"

"I must not say."

Ítk t'Sá spread her upper pair of hands. She drew in a hissing breath, and Hársan could hear the spiracles in her thorax taking air into her abdominal lung-sacs as well. "Old One, Ormudzó of the Hehegánu, look upon me. Say what you know of me."

The knobbly round head turned toward her. "It is your desire. You are Ítk t'Sá, of the Pé Chói, sent by your people, we are told, to confer with all those races of sentient beings who dwell under the hand of humankind. With us you hold the status of an envoy."

Tlayésha frowned in puzzlement, but Hársan realised that he knew. Ítk t'Sá was no exile or common criminal; she was a *Tú Pétk*, a speaker for her people. He opened his mouth, but she forestalled him.

"Yes, Hársan, I am entrusted with a charge," she said in the Pé Chói tongue. "I am not of the 'tame' Pé Chói of your Empire, nor do I serve the Four Palaces of the Square of Mu'ugalavyá. Your government would say that I am a 'wild' Pé Chói, one of those from the inner depths of the forests, who give no allegiance to any of the nations of humankind."

"But –"

"I am here to test the wind, to speak to all of those races who have intelligence and yet who languish under the rule of humankind. The Hehegánu are but one such."

"What do you – the Pé Chói of the forests –?"

"Plan? A revolt? A war against your kind? Hardly! We would lose – be defeated, brutalised, exterminated, as the Mu'ugalavyáni dealt with the Páchi Léi at Butrús some eight hundred years ago. Two things you humans have that no other race can match: the first is your numbers, and the second is your callousness. You breed like *Drí*-ants, and you destroy whatever is alien to you, even when it does you no harm."

"There are some…" Hársan began. Ítk t'Sá and her people knew all that. He, too, had heard these arguments during his childhood in the Chákas. Instead he said, "Then? What do you seek?"

"Perhaps no more than a network of friends – nonhumans who can aid one another, pressure human officials for concessions and mutual cooperation… Thus far I admit that I have found no easy path. There are too many varied species, too many conflicting ideas and goals. The least we can do is to speak, to let others know that we are there. At most we can hope to exploit human weaknesses and attain autonomy within our own regions – places of our own, an end to our dependence upon human goods and resources, our own pride – no more foppish, twittering Pé Chói imitating human dress and customs."

Hársan had a brief vision of Chtík p'Qwé as he had first seen him. He replied, "Some races have these things now – the Shén, certain of the Ahoggyá enclaves, the little flying creatures – the Hláka – and others. They dwell apart in their own regions, of course, while some – the Páchi Léi, the Swamp Folk of Mu'ugalavyá, the little pygmy creatures of Yán Kór, the Tinalíya of Livyánu – seem to live well enough in companionship with humans in our societies. I cannot see where your mission leads you – the Pé Chói. Do you not stir up mud from the bottom of what is best left as a quiet pool?"

"I – we – stir up nothing. We only wish to talk, to see what can be done, perhaps to help those species who now suffer." She shot a swift glance at the Hehegánu.

"You are sent by the 'wild' Pé Chói of the forests. To whom else, then, do you speak?"

Ítk t'Sá looked down at the tattered reed matting. "There is not much to say to the mighty races, those who occupy lands and places of their own: the Shén, the Hláka, the Ahoggyá, and others you mention. They do as they wish to do. We cannot deal with the Ssú, the Hlüss, or with certain other species, for they hate us almost as much as they do you. There are many more, however: the Underpeople, the lesser species who live here and there upon Tékumel. You know of the Hehegánu and their cousins of the swamps, the Hehecháru. Many more exist. Some dwell with you in your cities and yet you see them not, while others hide in the mountains, the jungles, the wastelands, even in the seas. Several there are who prefer the dark places beneath the most ancient of your cities. There are some who have only a flicker of intelligence, yet they would also weave their own skeins under the sun. The *Rényu*, for instance, who are treated as clever pets in your land; the *Dzór*, who are thought to be half-witted giants of the woodlands; the *Sérudla* and the *Sró*, whom you consider dragon-like monsters..."

Hársan shook his head. "I see no purpose in this. You cannot expect humankind to grant lands and provinces and cities to – to every species that lives beneath the bowl of the sky! And where would it end? A *Hmélu* has some intelligence – shall we invite it to share our dinner instead of roasting it as the chief course? Must I seek *Shámtla*-money in compensation from a *Chrí*-fly when it steals a crumb from my plate?"

"As you say," Ítk t'Sá replied stonily. "Few things are sharply divided; there are always vaguenesses between. The brown waters of the river mingle imperceptibly with the green of the ocean. Almost any theorem can be voided by calling forth examples from the extremes. While this may destroy a hypothesis for a mathematician, there are no such demands upon the complexities of human – and nonhuman – relationships." She turned back to the Hehegánu and spoke in Tsolyáni:

"Old One, I would now return to my meaning. As 'one sent,' an envoy, I can call upon my hosts for things that are beyond the customs of guesting. Is it not so? Your laws allow this to a speaker from outside, as ours do?"

The Hehegánu spread his pudgy grey fingers in agreement.

"Thus do I ask that you take this Hársan and show him the one who compels you to break the protection of guesting. *Before* he chooses a branch from your tree of decisions. You need speak no words – that would violate your laws too greatly. What he sees is his alone to understand."

The Hehegánu shook himself all over, a strangely alien movement. He rubbed his bald skull. At length he replied, "So it shall be. You are allowed this favour, Pé Chói. You are more than a guest." He paused, then added in a harsher tone. "But tell me this: why do you do so much for a human, one of those who oppress you, one who is as alien to your race as clouds to a fish?"

Ítk t'Sá raised her two upper arms in a shrug. Her segmented tail switched slowly from side to side. "This human was raised amongst us. He speaks our tongue. He knows us as no other of his kind can know us. I – sense – that he feels for us. He may even share something of the *Ntk-dqékt*, 'the Sorrow of Remembering,' an emotion which only we Pé Chói know – and suffer – from the moment of our birth." She folded her four hands in front of her. "This man Hársan may be the best salve for our ills: one who at least reaches out to know the heart of another. Some of the distance he has travelled, but much remains. We would preserve him to complete his journeying."

The Hehegánu turned his cup over and rose. "Then I shall come again for you four *Kirén* from now. The man shall see from hiding. He shall look upon the one who seeks him. Then he may choose a branch from the tree of the future."

He drew dignity around his lumpy shoulders as though it were a cloak of cloth-of-gold and *Khéshchal*-plumes. Hársan had not imagined that one of this race could appear so noble.

Chapter Twenty-Nine

The shop of Simanúya the Glassblower, of the Clan of the Black Hand, lay just within the precincts of the Splendid Paradise. A ragged hole in the flank of what had once been part of the city wall in times long past, it now sported a striped awning, a raised floor of oiled and sanded wood, shelves, and mats of woven *Firyá*-cloth for Simanúya's clientele. Those who came here were quite respectable: travellers from other parts of Tsolyánu, sightseers and connoisseurs, nobles and clansfolk from New Town, and others who required the most elegant bottles and ewers and goblets for their *Tsuhóridu*. Simanúya had no real need to dwell here upon the outskirts of squalor, but the slight thrill of possible peril – really no danger at all – in the age-worn alleyways sent delightful shivers down the spines of many a jaded noble lady and gave an opportunity to their brave escorts to lay hand upon sword hilt and pretend to vigilance and knowledgeable courage.

Simanúya was human. He held clan membership to prove it. Too strong a light would reveal a greyish cast of skin, however, and there were rugose patches upon his body that he took pains to conceal beneath a sleeveless vest of *Vringálu*-leather. A kilt of thick fabric, dyed with the black and yellow colours of his clan, and long strips of *Chlén*-hide wrapped around his arms from elbow to wrist protected him from broken glass, the chief hazard of his trade. He enjoyed the atmosphere of danger that prevailed within the Splendid Paradise, however, and this he enhanced by affecting a curious skullcap of leather that covered his missing eye, lost years ago to a sliver of molten glass. The hideous sight he presented probably added at least a silver *Hlásh* or two to each sale.

A tiny, winding stair led up within the wall at the rear of the shop and debouched into a storeroom. Hársan, Tlayésha, and Ítk t'Sá negotiated their way past racks of ruby, emerald, and amber glassware, straw-smelling baskets, mounds of *Hmá*-wool batting for packing, and bundles of dusty parchment – Simanúya's correspondence and records, a deliberate nightmare for any tax gatherer, no doubt. Ormudzó clambered up after them and signed to two younger Hehegánu who awaited them there.

"Spells?" Ítk t'Sá murmured.

"None from without that we can detect," Ormudzó wheezed. "Morkúdz here has laid a damper spell upon all sorcery within this area. This will be detected, of course, but it is commonly done by merchants who would avoid eavesdroppers, and we should be long gone before anyone investigates."

Hársan held up his rush-candle. In the centre of the floor a pit half a man-length square opened into blackness below. He skirted the rim of this warily, Tlayésha clinging to his arm.

"An easy way to dispose of broken merchandise," Ormudzó whispered. "It goes all the way down to the waters of our Crystal River. What cannot be used – or hidden – goes there."

A battered wooden door opened from the shop, and Ítk t'Sá drew back before Simanúya's fearsome visage. Ruddy light, an odour of incense, the sweet-sour fragrance of *Tsuhóridu*, and the chatter of voices poured in after him.

Over his shoulder, the glassblower grumbled, "A moment, noble sirs, and I shall find the very decanter you seek." He made a complicated sign with his fingers to Ormudzó and pointed to the front wall of the chamber.

The Hehegánu drew Hársan up behind him and pushed aside a flap of thick, brown matting. Hársan found himself looking out into the shop through a smoke-yellow, distorted peephole, probably a nicely inconspicuous glass platter displayed upon a rack on the other side.

What he saw told him nothing at all.

There were three separate parties in the shop. Two plump clanswomen in longish northern cloaks and coifs of blue and green examined bowls of many-faceted cut glass, while an escort, a lumpish youth in the livery of the same unknown clan looked on. Farther away, a balding, dignified gentleman in a squarish mantle and a flat hat that instantly identified him as a senior

Mu'ugalavyáni merchant chatted amiably with Simanúya's shop-boy. Jingling golden flame symbols at his throat indicated one of the Vimúhla-worshipping clans of the far west, possibly that of the Red Sun or of the Red Sword.

The third party was a middle-aged, genteel-appearing Livyáni nobleman. Black and red tattooes covered his pointed features from his artfully curled and pomaded hair down to his collar of enamelled plaques. His arms and legs, what Hársan could see of them beneath the dags and twists of his fashionably elaborate tunic and kilt, were similarly covered with tattooed scrolls, glyphs, and arabesques. With him stood a tall, broad-shouldered, young woman who wore the brief over-tunic, short skirt, and leather leggings of a N'lüss mercenary. The hilt of a sword protruded from beneath her arm. A traveller from abroad, it seemed, seeking curios and a whiff of adventure, accompanied by a hired bodyguard. A bureaucrat attached to the suits of some Livyáni embassy or mission?

Puzzled, Hársan pulled back so that Tlayésha and the Pé Chói could see as well. The Hehegánu held up three stubby fingers and touched the third with his other hand: the group farthest to the right. The Livyáni, then.

What could this mean? The fellow could be an agent of almost anybody, Hársan knew, but somehow he sensed that the man was no emissary of Prince Dhich'uné. If the Worm Prince had sent him, then why had he not used his power to compel the Hehegánu before, when Jayárgo had come here with Eyíl?

Could the man be from the Temple of Thúmis? The Omnipotent Azure Legion? The Yán Koryáni? Why use a Livyáni anyway – a foreigner from a nation that was not involved in the matter at all, as far as he was aware? And what could possibly bring the Hehegánu to surrender him to this stranger when they had not done so previously to anyone else?

Hársan looked a question at Tlayésha and Ítk t'Sá, but both made silent gestures of negation and perplexity. Ormudzó stood motionless, as did his two comrades.

A decision had to be made.

He made it. A nod of the head, and it was done. Whatever his Skein of Destiny was to be, the thread was now in the hand of the Weaver.

Ormudzó signalled again to the glassblower, who took down a fat, saffron-hued decanter from a rack and departed. His voice came to them plainly through the half-open door. "Sire, I have others of this same type in various patterns and colours. Should you wish to step within…?"

The Livyáni entered. Sharp, black eyes danced over Hársan and the others from above a complex, bird-like glyph that stretched from the man's right ear over his nose to dangle red and black plumage down his left cheek to his chin and beyond into the creases of his throat. His left eye was encircled by red curlicues, while tiny black symbols swept away from the other in wave-like undulations back to the line of his black and silver-shot hair. These were the *Aomüz* of a highborn noble.

"This one will do," the Livyáni said in the sibilant, blurred accents of Tsámra. At random he picked a ewer from a rack. His gaze never left Hársan's.

One of the Hehegánu signed toward the shadowed entrance to the staircase at the back of the room. Ormudzó nodded, and Hársan and the others began to move back toward it.

They never arrived.

Glass chimed and shattered out in the shop. Hársan heard a gasp and a muffled feminine cry; then the little storeroom erupted into light and motion. One of the lamps from without came crashing into the chamber to spurt burning oil over Simanúya's racks.

A figure followed: one of the middle-aged clanswomen, but now transformed. The clan robes were cast aside to reveal a muscled torso, undeniably male, and a short-muzzled object that Hársan could not for a moment identify. The thing twanged, and a slender white splinter stood out suddenly from the Livyáni's breast. The nobleman fell back and plucked the dart out of what Hársan now saw to be a thickish pectoral — a small but efficient breastplate.

Tlayésha was at the stair. She whirled and shouted, "Betrayed, Hársan! The Hehegánu are gone, and the way is closed!"

Ítk t'Sá was somewhere behind one of the racks where Hársan could not see her. More glass shattered.

The heavy-set escort, plump and foppish no longer, appeared now at the door. Hársan found himself holding a long, blue bottle carved in the shape of a leaping fish. The neck of this vessel disappeared in a shower of splinters against the wall, and then the escort took the rest of the jagged cylinder directly across the eyes. Red exploded to drench the sapphire glass.

The N'lüss warrior woman, weaponless now, almost received the next stroke, but the Livyáni cried something in his own tongue, and her arm came up in time to knock Hársan's impromptu sword aside. Her rough blue over-tunic was slashed, and her left shoulder was drenched in blood. Hársan had no time to inquire whose it was.

"More come," she gasped.

Where was the false clanswoman, the one with the little crossbow? A glance told him that she – he – now faced Tlayésha. Some other weapon was in his hand, a claw-like dagger with three curved blades. For a moment the fellow feinted and then made to strike. Hársan saw the blow coming and knew that Tlayésha had no skill to dodge it. He shouted, but his words were drowned out by a clashing, shattering roar. The foeman disappeared under a glittering cascade of fine glass bottles. Ítk t'Sá's bone-white face, jaws agape in a ferocious grimace, appeared behind the fallen rack.

Tlayésha stooped, and when she rose Hársan saw that her iron physician's needle dripped red in her hand.

The room was chaos: noise, shouting, the crackle of flames, moans from the man buried under the terrible shards and slivers of broken glass. Feet pounded toward the shop from without, followed by yells, the clatter of *Chlén*-hide armour, a glint of red copper and the swirl of brown military tunics. No city guards these, but troops of one of the Worm Prince's legions!

They were trapped.

Simanúya appeared at the door, leaped nimbly over the prostrate escort, who lay clutching his face, and jerked a thumb at Hársan, the nearest. Together with the N'lüss warrior woman, they wrestled the body of the blinded bodyguard aside and forced the door shut. The glassblower dropped a thick bar of black *Tíu*-wood into its slot and leaned against the door panting. Bodies thumped against it from without.

Simanúya pointed. "Down!" he cried, "Down into the pit! The river is deep enough – torches, there, on a ledge beside the water!"

The Livyáni was the first to react. He made no protest but took one quick, appraising look, then leaped feet first into the hole. Hársan seized Tlayésha's arm, yelled encouragement, and half pushed her after the man. The big N'lüss girl, teeth bared in a grimace and clutching her wounded shoulder, went next. From somewhere under the wreckage of broken glass one of the younger Hehegánu appeared and scuttled over to jump as well. Hársan had not known the creature was still in the room. Hársan motioned to Ítk t'Sá and then stopped, appalled. The Pé Chói stood with all four arms limp at her sides, a stance he instantly recognised as utter defeat. Of course! She could not swim! Her chitinous exoskeleton contained little room for extra air, and the lung spiracles in her lower abdomen would fill and drown her in no more than hip-high water!

"Go on, Hársan," she hissed. "This is my death-place. I shall defy them as long as I can!" She snapped the end off a glass rod, making it into a lethal javelin, the favoured weapon of her people.

"Jump! Jump!" The glassblower howled in his ear. Thunderous banging at the door gave urgency to his words.

"Better drown than guest with worms!" Hársan muttered. He reached out a hand to Ítk t'Sá as though to touch hers in farewell. Instead, he seized her small upper limb and jerked her off balance! She teetered, eyes wide with terror, all four arms flailing, and then plunged over the edge into the pit. A wailing hiss came up, followed by a splash. Shouts echoed below.

If only the promised ledge were handy! If only Tlayésha were safe and had the presence of mind to fish the Pé Chói out before she sank...!

"Who will pay me for this ruin?" Simanúya moaned.

"Ask it from Ormudzó!" Hársan grated. "Either jump with us or explain your folly to Lord Sárku's soldiers!" He did not wait to see whether the glassblower took his advice; a final look around, and then he drew breath and plunged into the black abyss.

Chapter Thirty

Hársan spewed water upon cold, wet stones in total darkness. His feet had not touched bottom when he struck the river, but they had indeed passed through layers of soft, pulpy substances, and he felt nausea rising in his throat. At least the stream was deep enough to prevent him from striking any loads of broken bottles Simanúya might have previously dumped down the hole!

A hand touched his thigh. Hoping that it was Tlayésha, he reached down to grasp it. The fingers were long and slender but heavily calloused. He sensed that the hand was that of a woman: the N'lüss.

"It is I, Hársan," he managed. "The man your master came to meet. Can you make a light?"

There was no answer, but a whisper of movement and the scratch of steel against flint told him that she had understood. Tiny sparks danced against the impenetrable mantle of darkness.

Farther away, a ball of luminescence grew. It limned a squat, crouching figure. The Hehegánu! The creature had enough sorcery, then, to be able to create light.

From the corner of his eye he caught the gleam of a blade emerging from a sheath in the thigh-high leather legging the N'lüss woman wore. "Don't kill him!" Hársan exclaimed. "At least not until we have learned all we can!"

"Hársan?" That was Tlayésha, her voice echoing with distance. It came from beyond the lip of the ledge above the black waters to his right. "Where are you? We – the Livyáni and I – have Ítk t'Sá here. She lives –"

They must be on a ledge similar to their own but on the other side of the river. Hársan took a breath and glanced around. The Hehegánu's light revealed a long tunnel, the roof low and arched, through which the Crystal River flowed silently out to the swamps beyond Púrdimal. There was a crumbling ledge no wider than a man-height on Hársan's side, and pools of stagnant water filled gaps and fissures in the ancient stones. He could not see Tlayésha in the spell's glow, but she could assuredly see him.

The N'lüss girl was on her feet, stooping beneath the rough blocks of the ceiling. A long, dark slash ran down her back from her left shoulder to the broad *Chlén*-hide cincture that wound about her waist below her heavy breasts. She had cast aside her bloodied tunic and sopping skirt and now stood mostly nude, feet wide apart before him, her knife menacing the Hehegánu.

Motion behind them brought the girl around, weapon ready in fighting stance. The colourless radiance turned Simanúya's leather skullcap into a ghastly mask. So, the glassblower had taken his counsel and jumped after all!

"Ohé, hold your dagger, woman!" The merchant spat out something unpleasant and edged forward, hands open and empty.

"The torches?" The Livyáni's lighter, foreign voice came from across the Crystal River.

"There, on your side, by the buttress," Simanúya called back. To Hársan he said, "We must swim to them – or they to us. Better the first, since we – ah, certain comrades and I – have explored that side for some way. A few hundred paces and we come to a stair that leads back up to the dwellings of the Hehegánu"

"I will not use it," Hársan retorted. "One betrayal is enough."

The Hehegánu spoke for the first time. "No betrayal at all, human. Ormudzó led only the foreigner – the Livyáni – to you. The assassins were Yán Koryáni, I think, and the soldiers, too, were not our doing. What transpired was not our affair."

"Let me peel the face from his ugly skull," the N'lüss girl suggested pleasantly. Her voice was rough and deep, the accent harsh and yet purring.

"Do as you would with me. Yet know that only I can bring you forth from this place. The glassblower there has only knowledge sufficient to lead you back into Old Town. If your foes have raised a hue and cry, our people will take no action. They will rearrange the mat walls and let you wander until you are taken by your enemies. The Hehegánu will want no part of this."

"We must decide, then, and act together." The thought of diving once again into the mute, secretive waters of the Crystal River nauseated him. Yet Ítk t'Sá might not survive a second wetting.

"This bank of the tunnel —" the Hehegánu was saying. "I have not seen them, but my elders have told me of other exits — some beyond the city walls —"

Simanúya interrupted. "I have heard the tales. Mayhap we can get out into New Town, or outside Púrdimal entirely. Then you can go your way, and I can return to see what remains of my shop! Oh, I shall demand *Shámtla* indeed! Come, young man, tell your comrades to come over to us. The torches are tied in a bundle with a length of cord. If your woman cannot swim she can hang onto them and kick with her feet."

"It is the Pé Chói who cannot live in water. She will prefer the mercies of the Hehegánu — and all of Sárku's legions — to another soaking."

The Hehegánu arose, his dripping robe clinging to the unfamiliar joints and curves of his body. "Since I am with you — for now — let me go to her. I can cast a dazzle upon her mind so that she will not know that she is in the water. Your comrades there can then float her across upon the glass-merchant's bundle of torches."

"Do not trust! Let him not —" the N'lüss woman began. She retrieved her garments, wrung them out again awkwardly, favouring her left arm.

The creature shrugged. "I wish to live upon this Plane of Being as much as you. More, I honour the law of noble comradeship until such time as we may mutually and favourably end the matter." He clenched his fist, and the light he bore went out as suddenly as though a door had closed upon it. A splash told them that he was gone.

Minutes passed, uncountable in the folds of darkness. Then the Hehegánu's cold light flared again on the other side of the river. Hársan could see only a huddle of figures there. The light went out, then appeared once more some distance downstream but on their side. Tlayésha knelt on the ledge above a bone-white huddle that must be Ítk t'Sá.

The Livyáni, nude now save for a loincloth, a belt of many pouches, and his gleaming pectoral breastplate, splashed his way toward them. "Come," he called, "Morkúdz, the Hehegánu, asks that we follow him."

Hársan hesitated. The N'lüss girl pointed, however, and he saw that a long rectangle of dancing, ruddy light fell upon the surface of the river from above:

torches held over the pit! Something – a rope ladder, probably – splashed down into the current. Prince Dhich'uné's soldiers would not so easily be denied their quarry!

Water still trickled from the spiracles in Ítk t'Sá's abdomen when Hársan reached her. She was trembling, and Hársan realised that he had never before seen a Pé Chói so miserable. He joined Tlayésha, and the two of them raised her, supported her, and half-carried her along the tunnel after the others. Ítk t'Sá was not heavy, and a momentary vision of the Chákan forests blotted out the dank stones: so had he borne Nékw p'Kí, one of the Pé Chói friends of his childhood, when he had broken a leg in a fall. Hársan would have given almost anything for a breath of fresh air, the scent of green trees, the warm dappling of sunlight upon the leaves.

"Here," Morkúdz broke into his reverie. "The branch that leads down to the Mouth of the World."

This was no time for questions. A sloping oval passage opened into the wall to their left. A gentle breeze, cool and yet faintly alien, came up through it. The Hehegánu set foot upon the slippery stone floor and gingerly began to descend. The others followed.

Chapter Thirty-One

They rested in a great-columned chamber where shapeless mounds of fallen masonry warned of danger from the unseen roof above. The current of cold air was greater here, whispering around the jagged blocks to give a semblance of life and movement to a place that seemed not to have known living things for aeons. Shattered effigies of unknown kings lined the walls, and panels of stucco glyphs, blighted and crumbling, climbed into the gloom above them as high as the Hehegánu's light could reach.

"We can speak here, if not too loudly," the Livyáni breathed. He cast a cautious eye over the stones. "There, by that entrance in the far wall."

The tunnel he chose was the one from which the breeze came, however, and they settled instead for a sloping, rubble-filled space between two of the colossal statues nearest to it. Tlayésha wrung out her skirt and used a piece of the N'lüss woman's torn tunic to sponge and bind her wound. The girl refused to don the garment again but indicated that it should be given to her master. He waved it back to her, however, and sat down crosslegged upon a patch of dry earth. Simanúya the glassblower would have squatted near enough to the Hehegánu to whisper privately with him, but Hársan foiled this by placing himself between them. There were enough secrets here already! Ítk t'Sá crouched in front of them all, tail wrapped around her feet, her eyes still glazed with shock.

The Livyáni nobleman was shivering. Hársan could not repress a glimmer of amusement at the dance the red and black tattoos performed upon his narrow shoulders. The man was not young, and they must soon find warmth if he – no, if they all – were to survive.

Hársan settled himself upon a carven block, the eroded, unreadable symbols upon its sides making comfortable places for his heels. "Your presence here indicates that you do not serve Prince Dhich'uné," he began wryly. "You may as well tell me who you are and which of the mighty, unseen players of this game pushes you about the board."

The Livyáni affected to consider. "I am Táluvaz Arrío, of Tsámra, of the High Temple of Qame'él, and presently in Tsolyánu upon a political mission. Its essence concerns you not at all. A certain circumstance has arisen, however, that made my finding you imperative. Understand that you are only indirectly important to us, the Livyáni, but you are a bridge upon which we would cross to other destinations."

"Lá," Tlayésha pushed her damp tresses back from her face. "I have called Hársan many things myself, but never a bridge! Speak more plainly."

The Livyáni ignored her. "At this moment, young man, I serve a power that is friendly to you: one of the servitors of the Lords of Stability and a mighty person in your land."

"Who?" Hársan snapped. "I tire of invisible and unthinkably puissant masters who prod me hither and thither!"

Táluvaz pondered again. "I see no harm in stating the case as bluntly as the girl demands. It is your Prince Eselné who seeks you through me. I was able to – to cause – the Hehegánu to bring you forth where others could not." Morkúdz raised his bald, mottled head to stare expressionlessly. "Your Prince requires the thing you know of, Hársan, priest of Thúmis. He must have it to defend against the Yán Koryáni who invade your land. Without it, you Tsolyáni may win, but it is unlikely. Baron Áld has summoned forth certain forces which only your treasure can combat. As for me, I aid Prince Eselné – and your Empire – in return for favours that concern you not. And, believe me, I am not here in this dungeon with you through any choice of my own!" He spread his hands so that the red and black patterns on his fingers stretched and twisted. "Is that plain enough for you?"

"The soldiers in the shop –" Ítk t'Sá put in. Hársan threw her a sympathetic glance. She seemed to be regaining some of her composure.

"Not my doing – nor that of the Hehegánu. The assassins, too, were, ah, unexpected."

"It is so," Morkúdz said. "We took precautions. A guest is, after all, a guest. And I sensed no sorcery. How did they come upon us?"

"Probably by the oldest method known: the Temple of Sárku has spies in every place in your realm. They must have observed my audience with your Prince; they followed me from Khirgár to Púrdimal, right to the shop of the glassblower here. My bodyguard, Miruré," he gestured to the N'lüss woman, who gave him an enigmatic look, "is not inconspicuous, nor, for that matter, am I."

"As you say. And now? What if I cannot – or do not – choose to deliver my – my treasure – into your hands?" Hársan found that his fists were clenched, from the cold or from anger he was not certain.

"Look you, priest. Do not imagine that you are yourself powerful enough to resist the demands of such as Prince Eselné and Prince Dhich'uné! There are others as well: rulers of empires, great lords and pontiffs who can turn the fates of nations upside down with a word. They will use you, whatever you might wish. Such powers care nothing if a few Drí-ants are crushed beneath their feet!"

"I am sick unto vomiting with these things!" Hársan snarled. "Chá! I desired no more than my quiet studies in the Monastery of the Sapient Eye. Now I have been the cause of the deaths of men, the injuring of a Pé Chói friend who was dear to me, the suffering of those I – I love –" he could not look at Tlayésha, but he felt her eyes upon him. From somewhere inside a vision of poor Eyíl also arose, quite unbidden. "– I would see all of your glorious potentates buried head-first in the wormy mud of Sárku's lowest hell –!"

"'A bird who nests upon a volcano's skirts cannot blame it for her fate,'" Táluvaz responded reasonably. "Now the lava rushes directly at you. Why not give over this thing you possess? Let those more skilled than yourself deal with the destinies of Gods and men. Prince Eselné is no foe to you. Of all of those who seek, he has the power – and the nobility, the generosity, and the highness of purpose – to give you what you seek; peace, riches, a place within the Temple of Thúmis, or whatever your heart desires."

"The aristocrats he serves, the ancient clans, the clique of army generals – are they any better than the hierophants of Lord Thúmis? The servants of Baron Áld of Yán Kór? Or even the minions of the Skull Prince?"

"The Omnipotent Azure Legion?" Tlayésha added from where she sat with the N'lüss girl.

"The purposes of Prince Dhich'uné you may know better than I. No one can fathom his objectives in this," the Livyáni insisted imperturbably. "What you possess appears – to me, at least – to have importance mainly to military matters. As you have seen, the Yán Koryáni might once have taken you to Baron Áld and made you give over your treasures, perhaps to aid their armies. Now it is clear that they mean to slay you instead – for what reason I am not certain.

"The Temple of Thúmis? Your grey-robes lack the nerve to use your device to save your land. They are no soldiers, no clever diplomats or shrewd politicians. The Yán Koryáni would seize your northlands, ruin your cities, rape and pillage your people, and give your nation over to the Baron's vengeful gods. That is what follows from *that* Skein! How many would perish because of you then?"

He eyed Tlayésha. "The Omnipotent Azure Legion serves your Emperor in Avanthár, to be sure, woman, but its masters are only human; they dance for gold and for power and for the favours of princes just as smartly as any grubby merchant in the marketplace." He leaned toward her. "And who is there in Avanthár who operates the puppets of the Imperium? Who appoints the chiefs of your Omnipotent Azure Legion? Who is as nice at the intricacies of your bureaucracies as a *Zrné*-beast is at its hunting – and just as rapacious? Prince Mridóbu, of course: an ally if not himself a servant of the Temple of Lord Ksárul, the Doomed Prince of the Blue Room! For your priest here to give over the Man of Gold to him would empower the cleverest and most selfish of all of the Temples of the Lords of Change to win the Petal Throne when your Emperor dies, to seize and hold the reins of the Imperium possibly for centuries to come!"

"What, then, if I were to keep the secret? Disappear? Find an exit from this awful place and vanish into the swamps? Travel to some distant city where none would know?" This was the path Tlayésha urged, he knew, and he felt her love reach out to him.

"Possible, possible. Assuming that you could avoid those who followed – and those who might learn of your unique possession later."

"Or I could take the way the Hehegánu offered me: a gentle death. I could even cast myself into the waters of the Crystal River – some bottomless hole here in this labyrinth – a place where none could retrieve my body and call back my soul from the Paradises of Teretané to speak for them!"

"Also a chance, priest. And not an action that is noble, nor one that fits with your Skein of Destiny as I see it in your face." Táluvaz mused and then continued, not unkindly. "No, I see only one course that offers you peace – and life – and some of the good rewards of this world. Prince Eselné can take this thing from you; he serves objectives that are not too far from your own; he can return you to the cloisters of your monastery; he alone can provide the threads for the Weaver to fashion a Skein of Destiny that will be pleasing to you, and to your clan, and to your quiet, scholarly, grey-robed God."

"My clan –?" Hársan began.

Táluvaz caught the question, saw the expression that crossed Hársan's face. "Yes, of course. And should your clan be not – grandiose enough to suit you, he alone, an Imperial Prince, can speak for you in Avanthár. He alone can cause your acceptance into another clan of whatever manner and station you desire. Lá, did not his sister, Princess Ma'ín, recently compel the haughty and ancient Clan of the Golden Sunburst to accept two foreigners into its ranks? Two common soldiers, not even the dust of her sandals, were exalted thus because of an afternoon's whim! Now they are officers of a good Legion, men of station and power."

He stopped, sensing that his point was made.

Hársan rose, stretched, rubbed his icy hands together, wrung out the folds of his still-damp kilt one more time.

It was well that he did so. There was a glint of movement amongst the columns on the other side of the hall, there by the door through which they had entered.

The N'lüss woman, Miruré, saw him stiffen and was on her feet beside him. The others stood as well.

"Who are they?" the girl whispered in her thick, purring accent.

Their pursuers had no torches, no lanterns. Hársan peered, then Tlayésha, sharper eyed than himself, exclaimed, "They are skull-faced – the soldiers of Sárku!"

Stones and pebbles clattered, and a head rose over one of the mounds of fallen masonry no more than twenty paces away. Skull-faced, indeed! The eyes beneath the dull-gleaming coppery helmet glinted with Other-Planar fires. The mouth showed teeth but no lips.

"The Undead!" Morkúdz the Hehegánu cried despairingly. "*Mrúr* or *Jájgi*, those who retain all of the intelligence they possessed in life!"

Hársan seized Ítk t'Sá's slender arm, pushed Simanúya ahead of him, pointed into the mouth of the tunnel from whence the breeze blew. Tlayésha brushed past him, then the warrior girl and the rest.

He paused only for a moment there in the soughing wind. It was time to repay the servitors of Sárku for Chtík p'Qwé, for the guards in the Temple of Eternal Knowing, for the pain and shame he and Eyíl had suffered, for the poverty Tlayésha had endured here in Púrdimal because of him.

He threw back his head and shouted.

Dust fell. Then a block of stone, then another and another. Something groaned and cracked in the darkness above them. Masonry rained down.

The roof collapsed in a thundering, blinding torrent. He waited no more but dived headlong into the open mouth of the wind tunnel.

Chapter Thirty-Two

They ran, pursued by clouds of dust and the sustained clamour of collapsing stones behind them. Eventually there was silence, whether from cessation or from distance they did not know.

The passage branched, and branched again. Each time the Hehegánu chose that tunnel from which the wind blew forth to buffet them. Heads down and clutching what remained of their garments, they advanced into a continuous, whining, sighing blast. The air held a faint tang of something coppery, acrid, and alien.

Hársan drew up short within the opening of yet another side corridor, one that opened off to the left of the windy main gallery. All were out of breath, the Livyáni more than any of them. The man sank gratefully to the floor, and Tlayésha knelt beside him. (Ever the physician, Hársan thought to himself.) Miruré, red staining the dirty bandage upon her shoulder, stood apart to watch, one of their unlit torches held ready to use as a weapon. Ítk t'Sá, Simanúya, and the Hehegánu squatted on their heels within the branch gallery and leaned against the seamed blocks of the wall.

"How much longer can you sustain that light?" Hársan asked the Hehegánu.

"A few more hours. It draws only a little power from the Planes Beyond." The creature held out the dancing globe of colourless radiance upon his palm.

The greyish, almost noseless face already showed lines of strain, belying his words. "Then I must rest for a time."

"An exit?" Táluvaz Arrío panted. "You spoke of an exit."

"My elders told me of a passage near the Mouth of the World, one that leads beyond the city walls. We should reach it soon."

Ítk t'Sá turned her long, bone-white snout to look at Morkúdz. "This Mouth of the World: what is it?"

"A place from whence all of these subterranean chambers receive air." The Hehegánu pointed vaguely down the tunnel with his free hand.

"An opening into the swamps, perhaps?" Táluvaz muttered to Hársan. The glassblower nodded hopefully.

Tlayésha came to lean herself into the crook of Hársan's arm for warmth. "You say you have never come here before," she said to the Hehegánu. "Can we not miss the exit and wander these catacombs forever? The lessons of one's elders are not always well remembered." She tore yet another strip from the tatters of her kilt to tie back her long hair.

Morkúdz did not deign to reply.

Táluvaz Arrío fingered the cyclopean stones of the wall, great rough-hewn boul-ders fitted so closely together that even a *Drí*-ant would find it hard to squeeze between them. "I wonder who built this place," he murmured to no one in particular. "The masons of the First Imperium were capable of such work, but this is different from their style. The Dragon Warriors? Even the Llyáni?" He seemed genuinely interested.

"We had best move on," Hársan rubbed his own and Tlayésha's limbs for warmth. "There may be other entrances into this place. Such tunnels are the favoured dwellings of Lord Sárku's servants."

Táluvaz raised his head sharply, struck by an idea. "Tell me, priest, do you recognise where you are? Have you any sense of the nearness of your artifact – the Man of Gold? Can you find it from here?"

Hársan had not even thought of this. Now he felt about carefully within his mind, looked up and down the tunnel. "No. There is nothing. I am as lost as you. Perhaps as I become more familiar –"

"Possibly. But perhaps this area was built after the concealing of the Man of Gold and the placing of instructions into the teaching device you found. You would not recognise any passages added later."

It crossed Hársan's mind to ask how the Livyáni knew of the Globe of Instruction, but that could wait. As an experiment he opened his mouth to tell the man something of what the thing had taught him, but he found his lips still sealed by the ancients' spell. He shut his eyes and struggled in silence for a moment. Apparently the inner core of his being did not entirely trust this urbane, tattooed stranger. Not yet. Perhaps not ever.

Did the Livyáni truly serve Prince Eselné and the Military Party? And if so, did he, Hársan, really want to give the Man of Gold over to that Prince's faction: the generals, the lords of the high clans, and the hawk-eyed soldiers who preached war and expansion and the glory of the Imperium? He had heard talk of Prince Eselné in the monastery – who had not? The reports were good, as far as they went: a brave warrior, a ruler who admired noble action, if not always brilliant. But there were others with – or behind – the Prince who did not fit so well with Lord Thúmis' more peaceable philosophy. Still, better Eselné than Dhich'uné – or Mridóbu, or any of the rest ...

The suggestion of a clan was something else. Táluvaz could not guess how deeply he had struck when he had mentioned that.

A clan! To be something more than "Hársan of Slave Lineage," as the Master of the Tólek Kána Pits had named him!

He could never gain a lineage – to be "*hi*-Somebody"– since his ancestry was not known. But if only he could look to one of the great clans of the Imperium and say, "These are my people!" To him, as to most citizens of the Five Empires, this was more precious than gold and gems and slaves and palaces...But would Eselné do this thing? The promises of princes were notorious: "written upon the surface of the stream," people said.

Yet...Hársan had yearned for this ever since he had been brought to the Monastery of the Sapient Eye. If only it were possible...!

His head was beginning to ache, either with the cold or with all of this thinking. He wished, deeply and urgently, that these dangers and political manoeuvrings could be further postponed, pushed away, avoided yet for a time. Or ignored entirely! Forever!

No, that was wishful fancy.

Something told him, too, that further hesitation was no longer a useful option. Whether he liked it or not, he must take action. "Only a fool sits to admire the beauty of the forest fire," as his Pé Chói foster-parents used to say.

He suddenly felt a strange sensation of freedom, a realisation of something that had lain unrecognised behind the gates of his consciousness all along. It was as though he stood in a prison and turned to see the cell door standing open!

He was free – really free – to choose for himself whether he wanted to lead Táluvaz Arrío to the treasure or not!

To be sure, he could not speak of the Man of Gold to those who were his foes, or to those whom he instinctively mistrusted; but a conviction grew in him that he could seek the thing for himself! And if he found it, he could dispose of it as he alone saw fit: he, Hársan – not as certain mighty Princes decreed, not as he was bid by any temple hierarchy, not according to the dictates of some vast and cryptic game of power played for distant – and debatable – goals! His Skein of Destiny belonged solely to him. "Back away from any problem and prune off all that is not essential," Zarén had told him in the Monastery of the Sapient Eye. "Then trust yourself first and the Gods second."

Now he had the chance to find the Man of Gold. Once it was in his grasp, then all of the rest of the players of this game would have to wait for him to make his move! Táluvaz Arrío was wrong: if the thing were this valuable to the game, then he, Hársan, had a black counter to move, and he was only one step from the Sun Circle in the centre of the *Dén-den* board! He might die for his decision; one of the great players might surround him with blacks and blues and contemptuously toss him off into the counter-box; but for a moment, at least, he, Hársan *hi*-Nobody, would be a power unto himself, a player with his own Skein to display to the Gods!

This newfound sense of independence was a heady one indeed!

He embraced Tlayésha quickly and got to his feet. "Come," he said, "we have farther to go." If he could get her out to safety, he would chance re-entering the labyrinth to search for the Man of Gold. He thought that he could convince Ítk t'Sá and quite probably Simanúya to take Tlayésha – by force, if need be – on to some secure hiding place to await him. Should Táluvaz and his woman – or even the Hehegánu – decide to join him in the search, then their fates were their own to endure.

They turned back into the larger passage to face the wind. Another few dozen paces and the tunnel slanted off to the left; fifty steps farther and it turned in the opposite direction; then it doubled back again and yet again in a series of zig-zags. A door-sized aperture appeared in the wall to their right, opening into a narrow gallery that ran parallel to the main tunnel, out of the moaning blast. This they entered. At intervals there were smaller embrasures in the left wall of this smaller passageway, like windows, oval and waist-high; these looked into the circular wind tunnel beyond. Hársan muttered a question to Táluvaz, but the other returned only a grimace of puzzlement. The purpose of this arrangement was a mystery.

They came at last to the Mouth of the World.

Their little side gallery ended in a circular chamber, no more than a man-height in diametre, and barely high enough to stand erect. A loophole, angled to shield it from the blast, opened out into the wind tunnel. Across this latter, perhaps five long paces away, an identical aperture was visible in the opposite wall. The Hehegánu gingerly extended his hand into the wind, a roaring hurricane here, and with the aid of his ball of light Hársan glimpsed the dull shine of a metal ladder through the corresponding narrow window facing them.

The promised way up! Yet it might as well be as far away as one of the moons; no one could squeeze out into the main tunnel, cross against the buffeting tempest, and enter the hole in the other wall!

There must be a matching gallery on the opposite side that led to the room visible there. The last left-hand corridor they had seen was the one in which they had paused to rest. They would have to retrace their steps.

Simanúya was examining the far front wall of the room. Now he summoned Hársan. "Look, priest," he shouted into Hársan's ear, "another window here, but filled with glass." His tone held a tinge of professional jealousy. "It is excellent work, flat, without bubbles or waves, undistorted."

Hársan looked. The neatly glazed little window gave a view of a tumbled landscape of high mountain crags and streaming dun-hued clouds. The sky was an ominous reddish orange, brighter below and darkening almost to black above. What time of day was it then? – More, how could there be peaks and jagged ranges of hills out there at all? Púrdimal sat in the midst of a swamp, too far for Thénu Thendráya Peak to be seen – and too low, certainly, for it to be visible as they were seeing it now!

Above, in the strangely ebon sky, myriads of tiny points of light glittered. Tékumel had none such; aside from the two moons and four sister planets, the skies Hársan knew were empty.

He went to the other aperture, humped his body up into the embrasure, shielded his face with one arm, and thrust his head out into the screaming torrent of air. Through slitted eyes he looked to the right, toward the source of the gale. The corridor ended there. The strange landscape was visible beyond. All around the opening he saw a faint, greyish muzziness, a shifting, sparkling boundary line of something that was not something. It was no substance at all. His eyes hurt to gaze upon it.

The bitter stench of an alien atmosphere was overpowering.

He pulled back, gestured to the others, and began moving back up the side passage, the way they had come. Only when they had passed the last of the baffle-walls and were again within the left-hand side corridor did he stop and seek out Táluvaz Arrío.

"In the epics heroes sometimes discover doors to other worlds. Is it not so? Have you seen or heard of such in reality?"

The Livyáni eyed him warily, not sure how much to reveal. "I have. Sorcerers call them 'nexus points,' places where the lines of force converge from one bubble of reality into the next. Some can find them, even summon or create them, open them, pass through into other Planes …"

"A – a friend told me that one can put objects 'around the corner,' into other-space. But a door –!" Briefly Hársan related what he had seen.

Táluvaz nodded. "A door. A permanent source of air for these catacombs, a door that must have been opened and set here long ago – not by any civilisation now surviving but by the wise ones of the Latter Times, the sages of old who still understood the mysteries of the Many Planes. After the Time of Darkness, when the metal cities of the ancients were laid waste and brought down to ruin, there were still a few who could create such sorceries. Not even the mightiest of the scholars of my land could do as much today."

"The Time of Darkness? The Latter Times?" These were high matters. Hársan had only heard mention of them in the epics. This Livyáni seemed to know more than did his teachers in the Monastery.

"Once only the Foes of Man dwelt upon Tékumel: the Ssú, the Hlüss, and a few others. The epics tell us that men – such as ourselves – and certain other races came then from afar. They took aid from the Gods and made this world over into a home for themselves. Later there occurred a cataclysm, a sundering from all of the rest of their own Planes – for what reasons no one knows – and then there were great tempests, and movements in the earth and the seas, and the skies went dark – the little lights you saw were extinguished. Afterward when all was at rest again, there came a time when some of humankind still remembered: the Latter Times –"

"And those who remembered slowly perished," Ítk t'Sá interrupted, her voice solemn, as though she chanted a litany. "The ages closed in, the metal things died and could not live again, their food and the substance of their bodies were exhausted – the metal iron, for one – and all became as we know it now. The world transformed, the skies no longer full of lights, the comings and goings of the Great Races ended, the doors of the cosmos shut upon Tékumel, all the glory gone."

"And after the long, slow afternoon of the Latter Times came the endless dark, the debasement of wisdom," Táluvaz intoned. "Men and woman,

Shén and Pé Chói, Ahoggyá and Hláka – all of those species who came with humankind – all turned to this world, the only one they now could know. Even the First Races, the Ssú and the Hlüss, became as they are, settling down as embers sink into ashes in a dying fire. Only after aeons did new peoples arise. Such was the ancestor of my nation. Llyán of Tsámra…"

"And in the Latter Times the Gods bestrode the lands. And fought amongst themselves for the power over all creatures. The Battle of Dórmoron Plain, at which great Lord Ksárul stood against the Nine Gods –"

"And the One Other," Táluvaz whispered.

"Yes. He too. And Lord Ksárul was defeated, and the Nine Gods and the One Other erected the Ten Walls around the Blue Room in which He is held asleep, forever, and the Ten Gates were made, and the Ten Keys and the Twenty Wards were scattered about the world for seekers to find…" She stood silent, eyes closed.

"And 'She Who Must Not Be Named' entered into this Plane, the Dread One; she who would end all things: all 'being,' even this veritable bubble of existence itself. 'She Who Is the Enemy of All,' the Goddess of the Pale Bone, mocked the Gods, weaker because of their war with Lord Ksárul and weaker still because of His absence, imprisoned for all eternity in the Blue Room. She and her *He'ésa*, who served her from another of the Planes and who are called 'The Seen Yet Unseen' by the scholars of my temple, did battle with all of the Gods, and with humankind, and with those races who sided with the Gods. She was driven hence, indeed, but only for a time. Now it is said that she seeks to return…" The Livyáni's sibilant, accented voice died down to a whisper.

Hársan shivered, and Tlayésha pressed close against his side. Ítk t'Sá looked away. Simanúya made the complex, curling sign of Lord Ksárul's beetle and crescent moon in the air. Hársan had little sympathy for the Doomed Prince of the Blue Room, but he felt sorry for the poor glassblower now.

The woman, Miruré, listened, mouth agape. If she understood their High Tsolyáni at all, these were things that could only awe her; the N'lüss might be powerful warriors – and two handspans taller than the peoples of the south – but their abilities as sorcerers were the butt of jokes throughout the Five Empires.

The Hehegánu looked on, too, his lumpy grey features expressionless, his eyes like chips of black glass.

At last Hársan said shakily, "If ever I would escape beyond the grasp of the Worm Prince I have only to hurl myself through that portal."

"And fall from the Gods know what height down into the chasms of an alien world," Táluvaz breathed. "Yes, priest, that would indeed end it all for you."

"No!" Tlayésha cried. "We have not come to the ending of the Skein yet! I saw the metal ladder. We have only to follow this passage until we come to the one that leads thither." She pulled away from Hársan, her face filled with exasperation, and began to feel her way into the blackness of the side gallery.

At times his hesitations and ponderings must frustrate her, Hársan thought, but then somebody had to think before leaping! "The chick who flies before its wings are strong does not live to feel the sky," he quoted to himself, one of the maxims he had copied out endlessly in the schoolrooms of the Monastery.

Tlayésha did not stop but continued down the corridor. Hársan would have reached for the Hehegánu's ball of glimmering light but remembered in time that it could not exist apart from the creature's hand.

"Wait – we are coming!" he called. "I do not speak yet of ripping the fabric of my Skein from the loom!" He urged the others to their feet and followed.

The passage slanted downward, then became a series of long, shallow steps. Water dripped from overhead. They must be under the swamps – possibly under the Crystal River itself. Masonry gave way to solid rock, the mighty island of basalt upon which Púrdimal stood amidst its dismal bogs. Yet this was no cavern formed by nature. The marks of adzes were as fresh upon the walls as they had been when their wielders toiled to dig this place long ago in some forgotten age.

They entered an irregular, oval, steeply sloping chamber. At the lower end the floor was submerged beneath a creased, undulating surface. Miruré poked at this cautiously with the butt of her torch, but it was solid: stone.

"Liquid rock," Táluvaz said, "turned hard and cold now, the leavings of some erup-tion from Lord Vimúhla's flaming hells from under-earth. We have such fiery mountains in my land, and one can walk upon ashes and cinders for hundreds of *Tsán* around them."

"Three exits hence," the Hehegánu panted. The effort of maintaining his light showed ever more clearly upon his face. "One left, one right, one there in front."

They could see that the tunnel directly ahead of them sloped down into the frozen ripples of Lord Vimúhla's blackened, stony sea. After a few paces the ceiling was too low to continue. Whatever lay below was sealed, now, forever.

"The left-hand passage takes us back toward the cavern where we collapsed the roof," Hársan said. "The right, then. That should lead toward the Mouth of the World."

There were steps here, too, however. They wound down, turned, twisted, went this way and then that, until all sense of direction was lost. The ancient adze-marks kept pace with them. The tunnel was barely wide enough to walk, not high enough for tall Miruré to stand erect.

Táluvaz kept glancing at the walls. He came up behind Hársan and pointed. "There is mould here – damn. We must once again be below the marshes."

"There is no other way to go. Not unless you would return to the hall where our Undead pursuers lie beneath the roof stones. Or unless you have some magic to pass through Lord Vimúhla's river of rock."

"I speak only as a warning. Get your woman back here and give over the lead to my Miruré. She has experience. Many species of creatures live where mould dwells, some not very pleasant. And certain moulds are themselves deadly."

"Chá! I know of this," Hársan retorted a bit testily. "My tutors did indeed tell me that mould does more than ruin one's bread!" Nevertheless, he called to Tlayésha, who returned reluctantly to join him. The N'lüss girl and the Hehegánu now led their party.

The walls took on a splotchy appearance, particoloured and almost gay beneath tapestries of yellow, pallid white, and dusty blue. They passed a niche to their left, a dead end, constructed perhaps to permit parties of labourers to bypass one another in the narrow tunnel. Morkúdz said something to Miruré, and she sent word back to touch nothing and to move carefully without disturbing more than was necessary. The air grew close, and there was a smell as of a root-cellar long shut away from the light.

Miruré stopped. Hársan heard the whisper of her knife emerging from her thigh-sheath.

"What –?" Simanúya exclaimed, but the Hehegánu reached back with surprising adroitness to clap a pudgy hand over his mouth.

Hársan inched past the glassblower in time to hear the warrior girl hiss, "A man! A soldier awaits below!"

Before them, ghostly faint in the waning light of Morkúdz' globe, the corridor descended a little further, then levelled out, heaps of shapeless mould almost choking it from side to side. More festooned the walls and hung in rags and tattered banners from the ceiling.

A man did indeed stand there. He gazed toward them from under the visor of a heavy helmet, one that had cheek-pieces with lappets of mail that draped down upon his breast. Armour gleamed dully beneath a cloak of scarlet material. He held a weapon, a sword, its point buried in the mould at his feet.

"Back –!" Hársan murmured.

"No," Miruré answered curtly without turning her head. She had her back to him, only the sheen of her bare shoulders and plaited black tresses visible in Morkúdz' dim radiance. "He has seen our light and now sees us as well." In a louder voice she cried, "Lord Táluvaz? What would you have me do?"

Hársan did not wait for the Livyáni's reply. No other course seemed sensible. "Ohé!" he called to the warrior. "We would pass! We mean you no harm." He could hear rustling as Táluvaz moved up behind him.

The stranger stood immobile, silent.

He tried again. "Name yourself. If you stand aside, we will leave you in peace." What was the fellow doing down here? He was apparently alone, who knew how far beneath the warrens of the Splendid Paradise, armed only with a simple shortsword.

There was no response. Miruré edged forward, torch held out like a duelling weapon, dagger ready in her other hand.

"Come now," Hársan almost pleaded. "Let us by. We wish no altercation, nor should you."

The armour was like none that he had seen before. Was the fellow a foreigner? Did he understand their language? It made no sense for such a person to be in this place.

The N'lüss woman advanced another pace, lips drawn back, tension rippling over the muscles of her long limbs.

Another step. Then another, until she stood only a pace or two from the man facing her. She peered.

And struck.

Hársan had his mouth open to prevent her, but the blow surprised him, and he got out only one syllable of her name before it connected.

The results were even more astounding. The torch, a stout stick ending in a lump of coarse fabric smeared with pitch, smashed into the side of the warrior's head at ear level. The head turned, stared regretfully – and almost comically – sidewise at them for a long instant, and then bounced free to roll in the spongy white mould at its owner's feet!

Both Miruré and Hársan yelled. The girl plunged backward into Hársan's unready arms, and both lurched still farther back to stumble into Táluvaz and the Hehegánu.

It was this that saved them. The scarlet cloak seemed to unfold, jerking and emitting tiny, horrid plopping noises. The warrior's skeleton appeared beneath, filled now with patchy, coloured fungi as it must once have been with flesh and organs in life. A fine, pinkish haze surrounded the figure.

"Spores!" Táluvaz screamed.

Hársan found himself shouting too, and the others joined in, unable to help themselves. They all struggled back, helter-skelter, in a tangle of limbs and bodies.

They fled, retreating back to the alcove they had passed, some distance up the shallow staircase. From there they watched as the red cloak slumped and writhed amidst the ghastly mess. Rotting bones crackled, the ancient breastplate heaved and vomited puffs of bluish dust, and the sword and helmet disappeared into folds of sickly, doughy white on the floor.

Tlayésha wept and shuddered, and Ítk t'Sá went to comfort her. The glassblower begged loudly and devoutly for aid from his God, mighty Ksárul. None came. Miruré's harshly pretty, aquiline features were ashen pale, and even Táluvaz appeared shaken. Morkúdz curled himself into the farthest reaches of their niche, dimmed his light to a shadowy glow, and turned his face to the wall.

Amidst all of these horrors Hársan alone found himself unmoved. There was a limit to what one soul could bear; beyond this one could only become numb, immune, almost uncaring.

The soft popping of spore pods continued for a time and then died away. They were too far, and too high, here, to be much endangered.

What they needed now was rest. And food — and water — neither of which they had.

But after resting, what then? They could not pass through the moulds. The terrible fate of the ancient warrior loomed as a signpost of almost certain death. Should they return to the chamber filled with solidified flowing rock and try the only passage left, that which would take them back toward the great hall and lord Sárku's Undead minions?

Hársan stood up. It was their only remaining course. He gentled Tlayésha with words of encouragement, laid a comforting hand upon Simanúya's thick shoulder, and helped Táluvaz to his feet. Whatever the Gods willed; whatever the Weaver of All chose to weave...

He went to the mouth of their alcove. Faint bluish phosphorescence shone from the heaps of mould down the stair to his left.

He heard something! Sounds of movement, he thought, a slow and prolonged grating, dragging noise.

It did not come from the moulds. It approached from his right, back up the tunnel!

Chapter Thirty-Three

Whatever it was, it took its time coming. They crouched at the rear of their alcove and armed themselves as best they could with chunks of jagged stone from the floor. Hársan wished for the sword the ancient warrior had carried, but it was lost beneath the deadly moulds in the corridor below. He thought of having Morkúdz extinguish his little ball of radiance, but then he realised how stupid it would be to fight any foe in almost total darkness! And some of these creatures of the Underworlds could see without light!

There was a ponderous crunching on the stair above them. Then a panting, whistling sound, as of an old crone negotiating a steep hill. Pebbles bounced and rattled down past them.

Better dead than unready. Hársan put his head around the corner.

At first he could make out nothing but velvety blackness. Then something glinted iridescent greenish-purple; more glimmers appeared: reflections from polished surfaces. Armour? Those surfaces moved and rotated in a curiously mechanical way, almost like the paddles of a millwheel...

They were mandibles. Behind them was a forest of legs, claws, and what might be feelers! Above these, three circles of round, faceted, amber light must be eyes.

The thing was as big as Lord Thúmis' sacred altar! It filled the narrow tunnel from side to side and almost from top to bottom. There was no room for it to turn, no way that they could rush up past it.

"A *Dlaqó*!" Morkúdz gasped. Hársan had not felt the Hehegánu come up beside him. "A carrion-beetle, like those that emerge in the corpse-pits outside the city where the dead – slaves and paupers – are thrown!"

"How do we fight it?"

"Are you mad? We cannot. Its carapace is as sound as a targe of steel, and its mandibles are like scissors! They will snip you in two!"

"Then we die here. Make noise!" he cried to the others. "Scream, bang on something – yell! It may retreat – or go on past."

It did not. Three pairs of bottle-green legs pushed the beetle down the tunnel toward them as inexorably as any conquering army. A saw-toothed proboscis twisted to probe into the niche, the blade-edged mandibles just behind.

They huddled against the rear wall of the alcove. The proboscis scraped and clattered against the stone, and the *Dlaqó* slowly twisted its bulky body over until it lay almost on its side, one set of legs twisted underneath it, the others scrabbling against the rocky ceiling. Another pace or two and it would be in upon them.

It struggled, then stopped.

The *Dlaqó* could not turn far enough to get into their refuge! They were safe for the moment.

The monstrous carapace, as big as a small boat, rolled this way and that, the plates on the creature's belly visible, stretching and sliding over one another. Its smaller front claws struggled for purchase. The proboscis attempted to withdraw. As it did so, Miruré whacked it with her torch-club; one might as well beat Thénu Thendráya Peak with a twig!

The monster squirmed and emitted hissing, chirruping noises. The stench of rotted meat nauseated them. It halted. An impasse.

The three eyes glared at them balefully. The limbs ceased to churn.

"We could always wait until it starves to death," Simanúya suggested in a tremulous voice.

"We would be skeletons before that happened," Morkúdz retorted scornfully.

"What else? We cannot go either way." That was Tlayésha.

"Lá," Táluvaz panted, "Miruré, light your torch!"

Wondering, the girl knelt and did so. Ruddy light filled their niche, and the smoke made them cough.

"Now reach around the corner and throw it there, underneath the thing's hindquarters!"

The wisdom of this immediately became clear. The powerful rear legs kicked and jerked as the torch blazed up beneath the *Dlaqő's* abdomen. It whistled, then screeched in an eerie, almost human voice. Then it pulled itself over and blundered forward, down the stair.

Miruré shouted something in her throaty N'lüss tongue. She waited only until the beetle was past and then ran out to retrieve her torch. Before anyone could stop her, she danced up behind the creature and applied the flame again from behind to its blunted, atrophied wing-casings. These did not burn, but they did smoulder, and a cloud of greasy smoke arose from the *Dlaqő's* offended posterior. The N'lüss girl yelled something that sounded like a joyous war-whoop and pursued the behemoth down the stairs, torch waving. It ploughed into the piles of mould, carried all before it like the prow of some mighty ship, and plunged on out into the dank corridor beyond.

Miruré stopped, retreated precipitously to avoid the cloud of angry spores that poured up after her. Her eyes sparkled, and Hársan saw that she was laughing. Truly, the N'lüss might be barbarians, but they did have a certain style!

They stood together, arms about one another's shoulders, and rested. Hársan found that his legs were shaking; he sat down. The others joined him. Táluvaz said something in sibilant Livyáni to the warrior girl, and she replied in kind, still repressing giggles that were probably more of relief than of amusement.

At length Hársan managed to soothe his shuddering limbs back into obedience. "What now?" he asked. "The path back up is open."

"About that I have doubts," Morkúdz said slowly. "If you are indeed pursued by Lord Sárku's minions, I question whether the crushing of a few of his Undead soldiers will deter them. There will be many more – and other beings as well." He did something, and his little globe of radiance rekindled upon his palm, a trifle stronger than before. Miruré put out her torch; it served better as a weapon than as a source of light.

"Then?"

"The *Dlaqó* will have cleared the corridor yonder of much of the mould. When the spores become quiet we can still travel that way."

"And when the beast finds room to turn about and come back?" Simanúya sneered. "Its outrage will know no bounds!"

"I hear nothing now. My hearing is better than that of any human. The moulds will do their work upon it as well as upon us. It lives and hence must breathe."

"How can you urge that we go on down — into that place?" Tlayésha seemed close to tears, and Hársan moved to comfort her. She let him embrace her, but she would not be still. "No. No, let us go up! If we must fight, die, then let it be where there is a sky — air —" Behind her, the glassblower and Ítk t'Sá murmured agreement.

"I know more of this place than you," the Hehegánu continued in his soft, patient voice. "The regions near the great hall that you collapsed are familiar to us. I do not think that the path that leads to the exit by the Mouth of the World is there — or if it is, then it can be reached only by one who knows its secret. Instead, near the Crystal River one soon comes to the precincts of the buried shrines of Lord Sárku, Lord Hrü'ü, and Lord Ksárul, maintained by those hierarchies after the levelling of Púrdimal during the last rite of *Ditlána* a thousand years ago. There will be priests, warriors, temple servitors…"

"You did not speak of this before," Hársan accused.

Morkúdz raised sloping shoulders in a shrug. "None inquired," he said simply. "And there was then a chance for us to pass them all by before any serious pursuit could be organised. Now I believe it is too late. If we are to live, then our choice is apparent." He said no more but arose and began to descend the shallow steps outside of their alcove.

They followed him, watching both for spore clouds and for the return of the *Dlaqó*-beetle. The corridor was empty and silent, a swathe of pallid mould ripped from the floor, the walls, and the ceiling, as though *Chlén*-beasts had been harnessed to a plank to clear a roadbed through mud.

The flagging was still ankle deep in mould, cold, viscous, as slippery as the organs of a corpse. It was quiescent now, its spores spent. All but Tlayésha and Ítk t'Sá wore closed footgear of some sort. The mould would not affect the Pé Chói, but an act of iron will was needed for the girl to plunge her open-sandalled feet into the stuff. Hársan offered to carry her, but she waved him away. He promised himself that once this was over — if it ever was — he would praise her, make love to her, kiss her for her courage, tell her how much strength he had drawn — and continued to draw — from her. He would have spoken now, but that in itself might undo her precariously balanced calm, he thought. Tlayésha was delicate, slender, and nowhere as strong as the tall N'lüss woman, but she possessed the stamina of mighty Hrúgga of the Epics himself! Still, even she could bear only so much.

Another thought came to him: would Tlayésha have surrendered to the blandishments of Prince Dhich'uné in the Tólek Kána Pits as easily as Eyíl had done? He much doubted it.

Táluvaz removed his loincloth entirely to tie it over his nose. The rest copied him as best they could, although he himself made no claims for this precaution. Simanúya stumbled upon something hard, perhaps the weapon of the long-dead warrior, but no one wanted to reach into the mould to retrieve it. Holding hands and balancing like gymnasts to avoid the splotched walls, they picked their way along the passage in the wake of the monstrous *Dlaqó*.

The corridor of the moulds was not long. A sullen reddish glow lit the ceiling ahead. The moulds were thinner here, patchy, brownish, and stunted. The walls gradually became bare again: sombre basaltic rock and no more. They took counsel, then approached with all the caution they could muster.

The light streamed up out of a jagged fissure in the floor. Rags and shreds of mould caught upon the stones announced the passage of the *Dlaqó*, but there was no sign of the creature. If the Gods willed, the monster had fallen blindly over into the pit!

Hársan went to peer down but could not see the *Dlaqó*. Shattered fingers of stone reached up along a precipice coated with sooty grey ash. Far below, scarlet mingled with black, the embers of Tékumel's deep-buried inner hearth-fires. A whiff of something sulphurous came to his nostrils; were Lord Vimúhla's blazing hells this close to the surface, then?

The right wall of the tunnel gaped open: the fiery chasm ran off there, roughly at right angles to their passage, to become no more than a tortuous slit a hundred paces away. That direction was impassable. The other wall promised more: part of the original flooring extended along the brink of the abyss. The corridor continued beyond, a black mouth in the far gloom.

They scouted the edge of the chasm. Miruré murmured something about being hampered by Tlayésha's makeshift bandage; this she pulled off, lower lip clenched between strong white teeth, and advanced to reconnoitre.

When she returned she said, "We can cross, I think, there on the left. Face the wall, cling with your fingertips, feel with your feet, and watch for sliding stones."

Hársan was glad to have her take charge. If anyone could negotiate cliffs and mountains, she could. The home of the N'lüss tribes lay amongst steep gorges to the northwest of Mu'ugalavyá.

She removed her leather leggings and boots, as well as the slashed remains of her brief tunic, slung them all upon the empty weapon-belt at her waist, and went first. She extended a long leg, dug bare toes into cracks and rough places in the rock, and brought her other foot over to find purchase beside the first. She repeated this, smoothly and efficiently, until she stood in the opening of the passage on the far side.

Ítk t'Sá followed. The Pé Chói had the advantage of four hands, and her segmented tail added balance. She apparently found little challenge in the feat and returned to guide Tlayésha, Simanúya, Morkúdz, and Táluvaz over the abyss. Hársan brought up the rear.

Was that a sound? Was he too excited by the dangers of this place, or did he hear something behind him, back there in the corridor of the moulds? He could not turn to look back.

It was fortunate that he did not pause. As he stepped upon the last cracked and sundered flagstone extending out from the wall, the one just before it gave way and went sliding and rolling down the slope into the fiery pit. He heard Tlayésha gasp; then strong feminine fingers seized his, and a skeletal chitinous hand took hold of his wrist.

One last teetering step, and Simanúya's thick arms were around his waist. He fell in a heap on top of the glassblower.

He rolled over and stood up to look back. A figure appeared on the far side of the chasm, then another, and still others. Something big and dark loomed there amongst them; smaller, scuttling forms approached the brink to peer over. He saw the gleam of red copper.

Someone moved forward to the lip of the fissure: a graceful, pleasantly portly man, a head taller than any of the rest with him. It was Jayárgo, the priest of Lord Sárku who had brought Eyíl into the Splendid Paradise in search of Hársan! The man's bald, egg-shaped skull showed brick red in the glow of the fire-pit. Hársan looked for Eyíl, but she was not with him.

"Ohé, priest Hársan!" Jayárgo called affably. "We greet you!"

The man was either fearless or mad. If Hársan had possessed a bow – or if someone in his party had had a missile weapon, an 'Eye,' or some other magical device – this priest of the Worm Lord would have required immediate resurrection as one of the Undead!

"Come to us if you can!" Hársan replied. The gap in the ledge precluded that. He saw no winged things in Jayárgo's party, no flying undead *Vorodlá*.

"For the moment we shall not. But there are other entrances to this maze, other doors to your bedchamber! And we know this place better than any of you." Jayárgo's deep, pleasant, baritone voice took on an organ note of sorrow. "You also go the wrong way to reach your treasure – and unless you accept my aid, you will likely meet strange sleepers in the beds you now go to occupy."

Something with long, spindling limbs crawled out upon the ledge. It came to the breach, extended a pale prehensile foot, turned a tiny knobbed head to look down. Fingers clawed for a handhold. Then the creature leaped. It missed its footing, and went tumbling down the steep to plummet into the depths. It uttered not a sound.

Jayárgo sat down crosslegged upon the brink of the chasm. "Reason it out, priest of Thúmis. Let your temple's famed logic guide you for once! You cannot leave this place alive; there are dwellers here whom even *we* fear. You cannot find the path to the regions built during the Latter Times, those in which your Man of Gold lies hidden. You – and your woman, and your Pé Chói, and even the wretched glass merchant – can only keep your hides intact by joining with us. Once we have the Man of Gold, we shall all take a beaker of *Tsuhóridu* together in the Splendid Paradise, and then we shall say farewell and go to weave our Skeins separately."

The priest of Sárku had not named the others in their party. Hársan spared a glance behind him. Tlayésha crouched there in the mouth of the passage, Simanúya beside her. Miruré lay prone, face down upon the uneven floor, the line of her blood-crusted wound black upon her shoulder. She would be invisible to those on the opposite side of the abyss. Táluvaz, Morkúdz, and Ítk t'Sá were not to be seen. They must have gone further into the new tunnel beyond.

Their pursuers assuredly knew of Táluvaz Arrío; they had followed him into Simanúya's shop easily enough, had they not? Did they believe him to be dead – or, worse, did they consider him powerless? Perhaps the Livyáni had nothing to offer: he might well be no more than a courier, a messenger, a finely mannered, aristocratic, foreign diplomat enmeshed in a task that suited him not at all. They probably were aware of Miruré, too, but they might not have seen the Hehegánu: "A friend in ambush is better than two comrades at one's side," as Zarén used to say. There might be a chance yet. The Livyáni had knowledge of these ancient places. With that, and with Miruré's skills and the Hehegánu's spells (whatever they might be!), it might still be possible to win past this skull-faced priest. Anything was better than the dubious mercies he offered them.

"I have no great liking for *Tsuhóridu*, priest Jayárgo." Hársan began to crawl backward toward the others, Miruré following. "I admit that I am also tired and would seek those beds you mentioned. Their occupants will simply have to move over and make room for me!"

"You do me and my hospitality an injustice. We may have to rescue you before you can lead us to your relic. Lá, we may even have to summon you back from the Isles of the Excellent Dead in order to chat with you further!"

Hársan made no further answer. Jayárgo sighed, stood up, dusted his pleated kilt, and signalled to his followers. Whatever they were, they began to scramble back into the corridor of the moulds.

Chapter Thirty-four

The place that was not a place smouldered with scintillations like many torches seen from atop a tower. What might have been draperies shifted and wavered, although there were neither walls nor any breeze to move them. Sparks of cold light swam through the thick, hot air. This was no habitat for humankind, and only sorcery could make it so, even temporarily.

Those same four who had met here before were gathered again: the Baron of Yán Kór, Lord Fú Shi'í, who was the Baron's confidant, Prince Dhich'uné of Tsolyánu, and the silent Mihálli whose globe of power enabled them to come together. They sat crosslegged upon a surface that was not earth or stone, but which served admirably as such.

"You summoned this meeting, Baron." The white skull-face showed no emotion. A subtle hint of carefully leashed hatred showed in Prince Dhich'uné's posture, nevertheless.

"Not I. You."

"Not either of you," Lord Fú Shi'í said. "It was I."

"You take much upon yourself!"

A long-fingered hand slid out to lie palm up upon Lord Fú Shi'í's russet-garbed lap. "Your quarrel threatens both your interests, masters. Allow me to mediate, for I serve issues rather than men."

"Speak." Velvet rustled. This time Baron Áld wore no armour but a cowled, soft robe of dark forest green. He looked as though he had been called forth from his bed.

"Lord Baron, were we not the ones who sent Helé'a of Ghatón upon his journey?" Fú Shi'í inquired blandly.

Áld of Yán Kór scratched his stubbled cheeks, then grunted, "Who can dispute such a small matter?"

"And, great Prince, did you not reward Helé'a for his perfidy – as you saw it?"

The colourless lips moved, but no reply came.

"Both the sending of spies and the elimination of spies are the proper behaviour of rulers, as Amiggá Mriddáshte says in his treatise, 'A Sceptre for Princes.' Is it so?"

He waved down the words of protest that would have erupted from both sides and continued.

"Spies are thus a matter of statecraft, not an affair of honour upon which *Shámtla*-money is demanded and given. You are not merchants to wrangle over a false bargain in the marketplace. No, if both of you acted nobly, as princes should, then what blame can either attach to the other? Who censures whom?"

The Baron was the first to respond. He chuckled. Then he glanced about as though seeking a goblet of something with which to toast Lord Fú Shi'í. There was nothing; perhaps there was no wine or anything else potable upon this strange, darkling Plane.

"But should I not ask *Shámtla* for those of mine who perished at the hands of the soldiers of noble Prince Dhich'uné?" he asked. "Besides Helé'a – those who died in the Tólek Kána Pits, on the road to Púrdimal, later in the stews beneath that city –?"

"You lost only fools," the Prince said. "One might argue that your network of agents, your *Surgéth*, is better off without them."

"Perhaps. Or I might admit that one cannot win at *Dén-den* without surrendering counters. Helé'a was at best a green. The others were no more than whites. And you may be a man or two – or a creature or two, at least – short as well."

"My Lords," Fú Shi'í interrupted, "this contact cannot last. Our meeting must be short. I pray you both to make peace – lay aside your grievances. Be reconciled – for now, if not forever."

"Yes, enough," Baron Áld grumbled. "Let us roll up this scroll – for the present anyway. You did not summon me from my mistresses in order to have me clap the shoulder of sweet Prince Dhich'uné and give him the kiss of peace! At least not without something drinkable to seal our troth! Lá, Lord Fú Shi'í, what is the urgency?"

"My sources –" A nod towards the Mihálli, who paid no heed whatsoever. "My sources tell me that the bird has flown from its tree. Even as we speak, mighty Prince, your servants pursue the priest-boy and his paramour through the Undercity below Púrdimal."

"They will soon take him." The brown, fleshless hands clenched upon dun-robed knees. "This time I sent no white counters but rather blues and blacks. The task will be done, and the Man of Gold will be mine. Then I shall be in a position to honour our bargain – if you would still have it, Baron."

"You need my favours now as never before, Prince. The weather has changed in your land, has it not? There are clouds of grey on one horizon and fiery orange-red on the other. Once you were four half-brothers and a half-sister who vied for the throne of your father. Now there are two more."

"Let the temples and the clans bring forth half a hundred! Weak schoolboys like Surundáno are an embarrassment to the Temple of Thúmis – and to my divine father! He should have himself made a eunuch for spawning such an insipidity!"

"But the other, Prince Mirusíya, is no milksop, eh? A warrior of Lord Vimúhla's Flame, raised by the quarrelsome Vríddi clan of Fasíltum! Not a pot easily piddled in."

The skull-face turned from side to side. "Chá! Vimúhla's flame-orange balances Karakán's scarlet: Mirusíya against Eselné! Let them lose sleep over one another – and the favours of sister Ma'ín Krüthái! Our other brother, Mridóbu, will dandle first Eselné and then this new Mirusíya: half an army to each with which to fight your northerners, Baron – but not on the same front! Is this not good news for you? One force in the west under brave Eselné, and a second to Mirusíya in order that he may try the impossible in the east: march up through the Pass of Skulls, take Milumanayá, and come around to your back gate! You can defeat two halves of an army easier than one whole one."

White teeth glittered in the black beard. "We are ready. Our troops hold the Atkolél Heights and welcome Prince Eselné's coming. My generals hold counsel with the lords of Saá Allaqí at Tléku Miriyá. Let your father give this Prince Mirusíya even two whole armies and offer him Milumanayá as the prize of his inheritance. He may take the dry wastelands there, and he may even reduce the city of Sunráya – a long and costly siege. But then I shall snap at him from the northwest, and the Saá Allaqiyáni will pounce upon him from the east. He cannot maintain his lines of supply for long. The distance, the weather, and the size of his force preclude it. The tribes of the Desert of Sighs sing to my music too, not Tsolyánu's. Eventually Mirusíya and his army will perish, and the sand-worms shall set a crown of brambles upon his skull!"

"Do not offer up paeans of victory to your gods too soon –!"

"My Lords, my Lords," Fú Shi'í interposed, "no need of battle chants and heroic speeches here in this place! We are not gathered to bandy tactics and the strategies of armies. We must come to a greater understanding."

"The priest and the Man of Gold?" Prince Dhich'uné moved restlessly beneath his stiff, brocaded robes.

"Yes, Lord. Consider. There are others who would aid him."

"The Omnipotent Azure Legion?" the Prince raised two fingers in dismissal. "My people have led them a weary round. They are convinced that the priest-boy is dead – or fled out of the Empire. In any case Mridóbu sets little store by this Man of Gold. His agents poked about beneath Púrdimal, but now they seem to have given up the chase."

"And I am told that the Livyáni have taken up the game."

"WHAT? Father of dungbeetles, WHY?" the Baron exploded. "Does every fish and fowl in the Five Empires covet my – the wretched thing?"

"Their actions – and their goals – are unclear. Yet it was because of them that the Hehegánu prodded the priest-boy out of his sanctuary."

"They may know more of it than we," the Prince mused. "Some use of it, some way to profit from it themselves –"

"To accomplish what?" Baron Áld clawed at his beard. "Victory over Mu'ugalavyá? The conquest of the Isles of the Hlüss? The defeat of the Gods and the freeing of Lord Ksárul from his nap? The drying up of the sea and the extinguishing of the sun? Tsámra cannot possibly need such a device to conquer the Isles of Tsoléi – those savages are chaff in the wind against any good military force!" He leaped up to pace to and fro.

The Mihálli lifted scarlet-glowing eyes from the globe in silent appeal. Lord Fú Shi'í arose to calm his master and sit him down again before the balance of that place that was not a place was overturned.

"Of course, Tsámra may not *have* a good military force," Lord Fú Shi'í murmured. The others did not hear him.

"Baron, we are aware of the efficacy of the Man of Gold against your 'Weapon Without Answer' – if either of them still operates after all these millennia." The Prince ignored the black look he got. "This is why I would obtain it – both to keep my divine father's legions from defeating you too handily before I can ascend the Petal Throne, and also to hold as a counter against you should you yearn to let your 'Weapon' carry you all the way to the walls of Avanthár!"

"I keep my oaths. Your northern cities – and General Kéttukal hiMráktine – in return for my aid in seating you upon the Petal Throne!"

"As you say. But if the Livyáni aid the priest to find the Man of Gold, and if they then use it – or bargain it off to the highest bidder amongst my fellow heirs –?"

"– The reason I summoned you together," Lord Fú Shi'í said.

"– Then we must lay aside our differences," the Prince continued. "We must hold true to our original covenant and join in finding the Man of Gold before the Livyáni do. If my sages speak aright, the thing can do more than drop dung in the road before your 'Weapon Without Answer,' Baron! Ohé, you may yet see it fry the walls of Ke'ér as Lord Vimúhla might cook a sausage! We have both seen the powers of the devices of the Ancients: The 'Eyes' that were once their smallest tools, the hammers of their smiths, the chisels of their masons; the vehicles that travel through tunnels below the earth; the cars that fly; the Lightning Bringers that deliver bolts of energy farther than any sorcerer can toss his spells –." The Prince made a circular gesture in the air with one corpse-hued finger. "This Man of Gold may do real mischief to our mutual causes: there are hints, stories –"

"Legends –!" the Baron began, but Prince Dhich'uné would not be silenced.

"Yes, legends. Ancient threats to your – allies: tales not only of harm to your 'Weapon Without Answer,' but also to the *He'ésa*, whom you have so carefully established in positions useful to us both, and even to the power of the Goddess Herself to enter into this Plane! The priest-boy cannot know the capacity of this Man of Gold. But the Livyáni may. And their game is unknown. All their counters lie concealed within the temples of their Shadow Gods! Will you not now call upon the *He'ésa*? We must rectify matters before it is too late."

"I agree that we must act – both of us. Unfortunately none of the *He'ésa* is close enough to be of use at this time. Your agents combined with mine should be sufficient, nevertheless. After all, neither this Thúmis priest nor his Livyáni friend is Súbadim the Sorcerer! My Lord Fú Shi'í, can you contact our folk in Púrdimal? The hour is late, but…"

"It will be done, master. The Mihálli here knows paths that traverse Planes through which none other travels. And you, Prince? Your agents?"

"Already in action. But I have telepaths who will speak with others in Púrdimal. Our pursuit will increase by five-fold within this night."

"Our matters are complete, then?"

"For now. Success, Prince!"

"To you as well, Baron Áld."

The Mihálli moved supple, many-jointed fingers above the globe. The scene flickered and flowed away into darkness. The sparks of light flipped their tails lazily and swam to and fro in a sea that might have been air, or water, or something entirely different.

Chapter Thirty-Five

The tunnel ascended, which cheered them. Then it descended again, which did not. Táluvaz paused to pronounce the walls similar to those made during the latter Llyáni dynasties. To Hársan the passage was no different than before: a squarish tunnel hacked out of the living rock. For all he cared at the moment, it might have been built by *Shqá*-beetles! Its eventual destination was what worried him now. Why a tunnel so deep – and so long? This question he put to Táluvaz.

"Cities shift over the centuries," the Livyáni replied. "Today's palaces and mansions are tomorrow's slums, then naught but ruins on the morning thereafter. When one has ancient and venerable shrines, treasuries, and the tombs of one's fathers below one's dwellings, it is noble to maintain them even after the folk above have gone elsewhere. Thus it is with *Ditlána*: surface structures are razed, the cellars filled in, and new buildings rise up to please the Gods. Yet the priests keep some of the subterranean shrines open, and rulers do the same – for reasons less pious."

"I have heard of this." Hársan thought of Helé'a.

"And when one's new city has wandered far from the old, those with secrets to keep dig passages to connect them. So we do in Livyánu, and so your Tsolyáni – and so the many empires that have gone before: the Engsvanyáli on top of the First Imperium of the Bednálljan kings; they upon the ruins of the Dragon Warriors, the ancestors of my Miruré here; they in turn upon the Three States of the Triangle; they upon the Llyáni; and Llyán's buildings over the wrack left from the Latter Times. Aí, there are deeper ruins still: the fragments of the metropolises that existed before the Time of Darkness, all metal and glass. And underneath everything else lie the crypts of the First Races: the Foes of Man, the Ssú and the Hlüss."

"Yet this is solid rock, not stonework. This is no crawl-hole from one warren to the next."

"So it is." Táluvaz wriggled his shoulders, making his *Aomüz* tattooes dance. "As I said, certain places were built as catacombs for the dead, others for the storing of valuables, and some for reasons now known only to the Gods."

They came to another large cavern, a natural bubble which the ancient miners had exploited to advantage. Here they halted. A broken bronze adze lay on the floor, mute evidence of one who had laboured here long ago. Miruré hefted the blade but opined that it was too corroded to serve. There was no sign of the handle; if Táluvaz were correct, anything made of wood must now be dust.

The lowest section of the cave held a pool of water. From this they gratefully drank and washed themselves. Once they sat down, however, the need for rest swept over them like a wave. Tlayésha and Miruré were used to walking, but there was no telling how long Táluvaz and Simanúya could keep up. Ítk t'Sá might be tired too. The Pé Chói could go without rest for days, but their rhythms were different from those of humankind, and when fatigue finally struck, it felled them as surely as any spear-blade. Hársan massaged his own limbs and decided that neither Jayárgo nor all the monsters of Sárku's hells would get him up until he had slept for a time.

They busied themselves with prosaic little tasks. This took away from the mute and malignant darkness, the terror that hovered just beyond their circle of light, and the uncertainties of the future. Tlayésha saw to Miruré's wound again, for it was growing painful. Morkúdz then let his spell of radiance expire, and blackness swept in to press upon their eyes like the silver coins that Lord Belkhánu's priests lay upon the eyes of the dead. Hársan could not begrudge the Hehegánu his sleep; his sorcery had exhausted him more than any of them. There was only one other entrance to the cave: the continuation of their tunnel. It seemed best to post someone to watch while the rest warmed themselves against one another and dozed. He asked Ítk t'Sá and she did not demur, saying that she could remain alert a while longer.

They woke hungry, but there was no food. They drank again, and took counsel. Their only course was to continue. Jayárgo might have lied about another entrance through which he could come at them, but even this would be more cheering than to discover that this corridor ended in nothing, a dead-end, a blank wall from which they would have to retrace their weary steps – and find some way to recross the fiery chasm!

The passage turned, wound up and down, and finally began to rise in earnest: slanting corridors interspersed with flights of long and shallow steps. Simanúya exclaimed that he felt a breath of air coming from up ahead, and their pace became quicker, their spirits higher.

Even if their pursuers did know the labyrinth, was it not possible that they might await them at some other entrance and hence miss them? Or that Hársan and his party might emerge before Jayárgo could reach the place?

"If we come forth from here alive, you must hide us in the city," Hársan said to Táluvaz. "Later I shall return with you to seek the Man of Gold. I have made up my mind to take you at your word – for now. I shall give it over to Prince Eselné. Let him worry about the future!"

"You shall not regret this, priest Hársan."

"I regret every moment since leaving the Monastery of the Sapient Eye." He knew that this was not true even as he said it. Had he remained there, he would never have experienced life at all! Whether he lived or died now, at least he was a player, a swatch of gold thread amidst the dull warp and woof of the Weaver's tapestry. More, he never would have met Tlayésha. (– And Eyíl, a voice within him added primly.)

"Prince Eselné will arrange protection for you – and these others as well. Be assured that he will employ your Man of Gold wisely, for the good of your nation." Táluvaz extracted a pomander from a pouch at his belt and sniffed at it. The sweet, heady, resinous fragrance of *Kílueb*-essence trailed after him in the dank air.

"I hope so." Hársan forbore any mention of his own private reservations. Only after he had examined the situation as carefully as an old woman inspecting vegetables in the market would he really consider handing the Man of Gold on to Prince Eselné.

He might find a way to benefit from it himself – or pass it on to others with whom he had more in common.

They plodded on. Then Hársan said, "I do not suppose that you are willing to tell me more of your own part in this, Lord Táluvaz?"

The other stopped and turned about to face him. "I cannot, priest Hársan – I cannot. But I swear – by all my Shadow Gods and by my Arrío ancestors and by anything else you name – that my arrows are not aimed at you, nor at any target dear to you! This I say to you as a friend."

"I accept your word. And Prince Eselné? He will help? He must have someone in his service who knows this maze well enough to lead me to the area in which the Man of Gold is likely hidden? Some priest of Karakán? Some scholar of my own temple?"

"I do not doubt it. The high Prince's priests and soldiers will be ours to command." Lord Táluvaz waved his pomander again under his black-tattooed nostrils. He seemed almost buoyant. "More, I have other contacts if we need them – among the Hehegánu. Their leaders can be made to aid us further…"

Hársan pulled at his chin sceptically. He said only, "You say that I shall not regret this decision. I hope indeed that you speak the truth."

Lord Táluvaz gave him a courteous smile.

The passage in which they walked was now intersected by another: a narrow tunnel that entered almost at right angles on their left and departed at a steeper bend from the right. The walls here were once more of masonry; they had left the depths. Hársan looked back to Morkúdz for guidance but got only a dubious shrug in return.

They stopped to test the air. Simanúya again felt a breeze from in front of them; Tlayésha said that it came from the right-hand corridor. Ítk t'Sá took the glassblower's side, and Hársan was disposed to agree. The Pé Chói possessed a canny wisdom when it came to matters of location and direction.

They hesitated, debated, and stood irresolute while Táluvaz once more inspected the crumbling blocks of the wall. These were small, neatly laid, well mortared, and undamaged by water or time.

"Engsvanyáli? Was not this city a provincial capital during the time of the Priest-kings?" He dug a fingernail into the mortar. "If so, we are well above the Llyáni regions."

Morkúdz whispered, "Something approaches from the left!"

There was no place to hide except in the farther reaches of the darkness, no time to make a plan. Hársan, Tlayésha, Ítk t'Sá, and Morkúdz fled back down the corridor by which they had just come. Táluvaz, Miruré, and the glassblower scattered into the right-hand tunnel.

The Hehegánu extinguished his light. They waited.

The darkness did not last long. Orange and amber lamplight sent shadows rocking out of the left-hand passage toward them. Voices sounded, the clatter of sandals, the sibilance of fabric, the squeak of leather.

Hársan tensed himself for one last confrontation with the minions of Lord Sárku. He would prefer to fight here. Should the foe win, they could only race blindly back down into the long tunnel to Vimúhla's flaming crevasse. If he could not cross that, he would let it claim him as a sacrifice!

Somebody sang, "Ohé, maid of Jakálla, the garnet ring-stone cries envy of your lips, the onyx its jealousy of your eyes…!"

The melody was a popular air, the voice deep and rich but terribly off-key.

A small being raced out of the left-hand passage in a whirl of arms and legs. As Lord Thúmis loved the *Tetél*-flower! It was a child!

Four people followed. They were labourers, lower-class, nondescript, ordinary human beings. Three wore cloaks, the fourth a mantle cut in distinctly feminine style.

Tlayésha gasped and would have rushed forward. She ran full tilt into Morkúdz, who blocked her way. The Hehegánu was a good handspan shorter than she, and both went down. For one wonderstruck second Hársan stood, too bemused to intervene. Ítk t'Sá made as if to go around the two on the floor, but Morkúdz shot out a hand to seize her plated tail. His expression warned Hársan that something was terribly amiss. Instead of helping Tlayésha up, Hársan crouched and put one hand over her mouth. He used the other to motion her to silence and then to clutch the Hehegánu's oddly doughy shoulder.

"What is it?"

"Look you," Morkúdz gasped. "Look at their legs – so thick, like columns. Look at their bodies: heavy and round. See how they all move in unison."

Tlayésha struggled in his arms, but he kept his palm over her lips until she quieted.

"They are not what they seem. We call them *Srámuthu* – in my tongue it means 'those who dwell together.' They – they put on the seeming of those they meet, pretend to be friends or harmless persons, seduce them, lure them –"

"Why?"

"So that they may consume them. The beings of the underworlds require sustenance as you do. Their ways are not yours."

"They have intelligence?" Ítk t'Sá gently freed her tail from the Hehegánu's grasp.

"Yes. They are symbiotes, creatures who dwell amongst you, imitate you, use your habitations so that they themselves do not have to build. They live from your larder – and take some of you as food. My elders say that they dwelt in the cities of humankind since before your ancestors came to Tékumel, and they accompanied you all undetected when you came. They prefer the dark places of your great cities, where their disguises will not be questioned, where no one will ask..."

The four who might have been human were moving away from them. The child pranced on before; they could hear its high, happy prattle. The singer broke off to whistle the song's refrain.

Ítk t'Sá stood up. "If they have wisdom enough to speak, then they are part of my seeking, my mission. Stay here. I will go and talk with them." Her eyes glittered opalescent green.

"No!" Tlayésha pulled Hársan's hand away.

"What else? We are already seen. Even now one has turned to look. I shall take care. But I must try; such is my undertaking as Speaker for my people. You know it, Hársan. If they are of the 'Underpeople,' if they have the intelligence to think, to converse, then they are not insensate monsters."

"I – we – cannot let you – you must not!" Tlayésha pleaded.

Ítk t'Sá touched Hársan's hand with one of her upper, smaller ones. He stood back. To her this was noble action; to stop her would be ignoble. He pressed her hard chitinous fingers in return.

One of the labourers raised his lamp high, the child clutching his stumpy legs. "Ohé, there," the full, deep voice called, "who are you?"

The Pé Chói glided forward, four hands empty and open at her sides. "We offer no harm. We seek an exit from this place."

"Lá, it's a Pé Chói!" the female cried with all of the pleasure of a woman just introduced to a new baby granddaughter.

There was a babble of genial voices. The child, a girl, came running back to stare up at Ítk t'Sá's bone-white features.

Hársan pulled Tlayésha up, stole forward with her until they reached the cross-tunnel on the right. Morkúdz skulked behind.

Ítk t'Sá drew abreast of the eldest male. The others surrounded her, their lamp held high. Someone said, "Exit? Aí, we can take you there – we go now to work in the distilleries. Easy to go out of the Splendid Paradise from there."

"Your comrades, then," one of the younger males questioned. "They would come too?"

"Yes, when they are satisfied that no harm will befall them." Ítk t'Sá paused. "Who are you people? How is it that you are here, below even the warrens of the Hehegánu?"

The three males eyed one another uneasily. Their movements were stiff, like the actions of puppets, Hársan thought. He never would have noticed if it had not been for Morkúdz' warning. The female grinned vacuously at Ítk t'Sá. The little girl went around behind the Pé Chói to gaze raptly at her segmented tail.

"I am told – I have heard –" Ítk t'Sá obviously did not know where to begin. How does one accuse a party of simple tenement dwellers of being nonhumans?

"Yes? How can we help you?" The speaker addressed her as *Tùsmikrú*, "the You of Courteous Alienness," as was polite and proper. This was difficult.

"Oh, look at her dear companions, Kórush," the female cried. "All bruised and dirty – lost down here, no doubt of it! Come, girl, and let me see," she made a motherly gesture toward Tlayésha. "I have a spare shawl in my bag here. You'll be needing it."

The one called Kórush raised his lantern. "Ah, gentlepersons, as my wife says! Come you here and let us tend to you."

Hársan sidled a pace or two into the cross-tunnel, Tlayésha's hand gripped so hard in his that her fingers must surely be crushed.

"Go on ahead," Morkúdz answered them. "We need nothing. We will follow."

"Not so, now…" The female made as though to advance upon Tlayésha, arms out to embrace her.

Ítk t'Sá said, "I am told…I have heard…Are you *Srámuthu*?"

Everything stopped. Prince Dhich'uné's 'Excellent Ruby Eye' could not have frozen the scene any more completely.

"*Srámuthu*?" one of the younger males asked slowly. "What be that?"

"Never heard of that clan – such folk –" the female muttered.

The little girl said, "They know us."

Her voice was no longer childlike and trilling but soft, muffled, and susurrant, like the rasping of an insect.

"Arúja, Mrelúr, Síggu, do you go and aid the boy and girl," the one named Kórush said in his pleasant, bass voice. "Tísa and I will wait here with this Pé Chói."

"Hold!" Ítk t'Sá hissed. "Truly, we mean you no harm. I am a *Tü Pétk*, a Speaker sent by my people. Let us talk. I would speak to all of the Underpeople, to all of those who dwell with humankind upon Tékumel."

"Lá, that's very nice," the female replied. "I do so enjoy a good chat, dears." She began to edge around to Ítk t'Sá's left. "And I have a loaf of bread here in my bag, fresh-baked, and a little jug of beer. Just let me get them out for you…"

The child stood up on her thick, short legs. "They have no weapons, nothing." She spread her arms.

Her features cracked, split down the middle. Her left eye and her cheek peeled away to slide down upon her shoulder; her right eye hung oddly suspended in her hair. She wriggled. Her small chest opened, tunic and all, to reveal a tangle of dark, damp limbs within.

"You're too quick about it, love!" the female scolded, still in her jolly, maternal voice. Then she, too, began to change.

"Will you not hear me?" Ítk t'Sá screamed. "Listen!"

Kórush's cloak parted in two at the back with a delicate tearing sound. Wing-casings, black and damp-glistening, showed beneath. His voice dropped an octave or two and took on the same dark, burring note.

"Aí, we'll be happy to heed what you have to say, Mistress Speaker, or whatever you be. Aí, we'll give full attention to your words…" He said something else, but his speech had become no more than an unintelligible buzzing mumble.

"Run!" Morkúdz shrieked. "Run, Pé Chói!"

They fled into the cross-tunnel. Tlayésha was the fleetest of foot, but the pudgy little Hehegánu almost overtook her. Hársan lagged behind, wondering as he ran if he could not somehow aid Ítk t'Sá. Weaponless, what could he do? The Pé Chói were a trifle faster than humans; he only prayed that she could take advantage of that!

They panted to a ragged standstill in near-darkness. With horror Hársan saw that a figure stood before them with a lighted torch, no more than thirty paces away. He shouted and almost turned to fling himself back in the other direction. Just in time he recognised Miruré. Táluvaz and Simanúya crouched farther down the corridor behind her.

There was no sound from the direction they had come.

The Hehegánu gabbled out his story of the *Srámuthu* in one long breath. Hársan shushed him to listen. Still he heard nothing.

Something moved up the passageway. They poised themselves. The ruddy torchlight danced upon white chitin.

"Ítk t'Sá!" Hársan cried in utter relief.

The Pé Chói stumped forward upon thick, cylindrical legs. "My friends," her voice warbled between a high soprano and a deep bass. "I managed to get free —"

They fled again. And this time they did not stop until the darkness and several intersections had swallowed up the *Srámuthu* behind them as surely as a tomb.

Chapter Thirty-Six

"Will they follow?" Táluvaz Arrío panted.

"Who knows?" Morkúdz answered, then shook his head. "No, I think not. They are not swift, nor are they fond of armed prey who know their tricks. No, Lord, we should be secure here for the moment."

"Where are we?" Táluvaz guided the Hehegánu over to examine the walls of the new cavern into which the tunnel had debouched.

"A section of catacombs, I think. These domes conceal tomb-shafts…"

"The nobles of the First Imperium, the Age of Queen Nayári of the Silken Thighs, built such. Yes, these appear to be of that period…"

Morkúdz showed no interest in ancient history but went off to make a circuit of the chamber.

The Livyáni cast a worried glance back at Miruré. She sat near the entrance consoling the physician girl. The priest of Thúmis squatted there also, his face blank and numb. Shock did that, the sudden loss of a friend. The Weaver of Skeins would have to add many threads before these memories could be folded away and lost within the fabric of the tapestry.

The glassblower came up beside Táluvaz to squint at the rows of masonry domes lining the uneven floor of the chamber. These resembled nothing so much as the kilns of a potters' clanhouse, being perhaps a man-height tall and two or three man-heights in diametre. In front of each stood a pentagonal stone stela proclaiming the quality and deeds of the sleeper within.

"I have heard tell of this place," Simanúya said. "Acquaintances of mine in the Splendid Paradise have returned with tales —"

"Tomb-robbers!" Táluvaz sneered. "The mighty heroes of the Age of the First Imperium now lie helpless prey to petty thieves, burrowers in the earth, looters, eaters of carrion...!"

"As may be, Lord," the glassblower displayed offended innocence. "Yet what use fine grave-goods to these folk? Who's to eat from their golden plates or drink from their crystal goblets?"

Táluvaz turned away impatiently. Those who pillaged tombs in Livyánu were handed over to the cold mercies of the *Vrú'uneb*, the intelligence arm of the Temples of the Shadow Gods. He himself had participated in the judgments meted out to such culprits, for Lord Qame'él honoured those who honoured their ancestors.

He walked over for a closer look. Several of the domes showed openings in their smooth casings; someone – likely Simanúya's friends – had indeed visited here. They had been most assiduous in their willingness to share the wealth of the dead.

Morkúdz returned. "No other exits," he reported. "Either go back to those last intersections or find some hidden way out of here. Or join these notables in their final rest."

"Do the tombs connect to one another – or to further passages below?"

"Aí, some do, Lord," Simanúya said. "Some go down to a single guesting chamber where food and drink were left. Beneath the floor – ofttimes a single stone slab a handspan thick – are the crypts proper. Other shafts open out below into several rooms and storage places for the goods of the noble person – ah – honourably reposing there. A few are still larger and join to other sepulchres."

"An expert upon the burial customs of the ancients!" Morkúdz commented acidly.

"We all must live, masters. Never have I duped a rich traveller with a maze of mat walls and lost him beneath Old Town so that he could be caught and ransomed – or killed and plundered – as some I know have done." He returned the Hehegánu look for look.

"Peace, the two of you." Táluvaz wandered back towards Miruré. He saw that she had risen to her feet and was watching the entrance.

"You hear something?" he asked her softly in Livyáni.

"I do," she replied in the same tongue. Her slim sheath-knife hung ready in her hand. "Not the shape-changers, I think. Echoes: armour, clanking, quicker footsteps. Soldiers? They are distant yet, but they come."

"Yes, love," Táluvaz sighed. "We must move quickly." He stood close to brush a hand against one rounded breast just visible beneath the ruins of her torn and stained tunic. She gave him a hidden look of adoration, her face averted so that the others might not see.

Miruré had been gifted to Táluvaz by his clan-fathers when the Hierophant of Tsámra had first pricked the glyph of the Tenth Circle of the Temple of Qame'él upon his right cheek. He had then been forty, she perhaps no more than fifteen summers. What lay between the towering N'lüss girl and the diminutive, urbane, middle-aged Livyáni was theirs alone to share.

"Ohé, glassblower!" he called. "Naturally your bazaar story-tellers will have men-tioned which crypts are dead-end shafts and which lead to further labyrinths below?"

"Great lord —"

"Oh, spew it forth! Else we shall all be a repast for Sárku's worms! Someone approaches."

Simanúya glanced anxiously around, counted domes. "That one, I have — ah — heard, master. The one with the triangular hole in it…"

Together they got the priest and his woman on their feet, she still weeping, he with a face as waxen as an incense-candle.

Hársan turned to Táluvaz. "We — I — must try to carry on Ítk t'Sá's mission. In her memory, as a *Tíi Pétk* — speak to the Underpeople —"

"That water has not flowed down the river yet. Come, pursuit is near." Táluvaz took Hársan by the hand. He noted with distaste that the young man's fingers were cold and clammy. It felt odd to touch anyone but one's beloved, one's children, or the others of one's sodality in the Mysteries of the Temple of Qame'él. To lay a hand upon another person was a ritual act of personal identification in Livyánu.

Something would have to be done to bring this Hársan back to the reality of their predicament. Táluvaz paused to consider the alternatives: curse him, slap him, remonstrate with him — what else? He decided to continue kindness for the moment. "On, priest Hársan, this dome over here. There will be opportunities later. All things in their times."

The others had already crawled through the narrow aperture into the dome. The floor within was covered with shattered pottery, stone tablets engraved with the powerful, virile script of the First Imperium, heaps of fallen plaster and rubble, and a heavy, circular slab of stone that had once hidden the opening of a shaft in the centre of the floor.

Morkúdz stooped nervously to hold his ball of radiance over this pit. "Those crevices – handholds?"

Simanúya growled, "Hold the light. I'll show you how to get down."

They descended, the glassblower first, then the Hehegánu, Hársan, Tlayésha, and Táluvaz. Miruré came last, dagger clenched between her teeth.

"No haste," Táluvaz whispered. "Our light will not be visible to any outside this dome, and they'll look for other exits before starting to search each tomb – if they believe us to be here at all."

The shaft was perhaps six or seven man-heights deep. At one point a tiny crawl-way led off to the side, but Simanúya forbade them to enter this, saying that it only became smaller and smaller until one could go no farther. Sharp ridges and projections of rock had been constructed around the circumference of this side-tunnel along its length at an inward-pointing angle, making it easy to move forward but difficult to go back. The bones of many previous violators of this place were heaped there, he added. Even Táluvaz forbore from inquiring how he knew.

The bottom of the pit was littered with shards of stone, the remains of a plug that had once sealed a low, horizontal passage. Two or three paces along this, and they entered another chamber. This was filled with crumbled pottery, the desiccated remains of wooden chests and boxes, standard-poles from which wisps of dim red and gold banners still hung, cult symbols of beaten gold, tables that had collapsed beneath the weight of their marble and onyx inlaid tops, and a myriad other things too numerous to see all at once in Morkúdz' flickering illumination.

Miruré gave a soft cry and bent to pick up a gold-hilted sword from the ruin. The blade showed black and pitted, but it was steel. In this dry, musty place it had corroded but little. Who knew how strong the metal was after the passage of so many centuries? Still, a sword was a sword.

"Your acquaintances did not exhaust this place completely," Táluvaz observed coldly.

"Only the best jewellery and the finest artifacts are worth bearing forth," said the glassblower. "That sword your warrior-girl found would have brought much money, had – ah, someone seen it." He poked ruefully in a mouldering mass that might once have been a delicate casket of carven *Ssár*-wood and extracted a ring of massy gold and dark, somnolent peridots. This he pocketed with an apologetic smile. "It is a long and dangerous path back from here."

"It would seem that you may know that path."

"He is a veritable guidebook, Lord," Morkúdz put in.

"And, like any book long unread, he would benefit from a little dusting and a shaking out of his pages," Táluvaz looked over at Miruré.

Simanúya quailed. "Well, it is true that I have been an industrious student of the past, Lord – of a practical nature, one must admit. Ah…"

"Then you could lead us out of this catacomb if we can evade our foes long enough to send them haring off in some other direction?"

"I – I think so, master. Not easily, of course, but…"

Morkúdz made as though to spit. "My people know this Simanúya, Lord Táluvaz. He could lead us a dance around the innermost shrines of the ancient gods below Púrdimal, and never a priest would see us! He is almost more native to this place than we, as were his vile fathers before him!"

It was Táluvaz' turn to screw up his lips, but his mouth was dry and no spittle came. He addressed Simanúya. "And I suppose that you could lead us hence for some small but suitable recompense?" A thought struck him. "Lá, when we met the *Srámuthu*, were we not close upon the exit? Was that route not as familiar to you as your own greasy palm? How else do you – your 'acquaintances' – find their way hither to relieve these poor corpses of their unused wealth?"

The glassblower dug a sandalled toe into the rubbish, bent to retrieve a small coin and rubbed it on the stained front of his leather vest; he tossed it back when it showed only the green verdigris of copper. "As you say, Lord. I am somewhat travelled in this part of the labyrinth. We would have soon come to the exit, had it not been that the fool Pé Chói chose to dispute passage with the *Srámuthu*!" He let out a windy sigh. "Let those who follow us go by, and then I'll take us out of here – into the very cellars of the Livyáni Legate's house or into the palace of the High Governor, as you please."

"So you shall." Táluvaz turned around. "What else is here, good Simanúya?"

"Three exits, Lord. That one leads to another storage chamber, now pillaged, alas, by disrespectful persons. The second – the one behind that clan-banner – goes to a similar room, and from thence a crawl-hole has been dug into a neighbouring tomb chamber. The sarcophagus there is overturned and sadly despoiled, and there is no way up into the guesting room and its shaft above. The third is promising, as I – ah – recall hearing. It opens into another sepulchre: several rooms like these. One can easily clamber up the exit shaft there."

"We can stand in the passage between these two places?" Miruré asked. "My Lord, if our foes come down this shaft, we go up the second, and if instead they choose that one, we retreat up this one, the way we came."

The plan of their refuge proved to be as Simanúya had described, and Miruré's idea was adopted for lack of any better. Táluvaz strove to bring Hársan and Tlayésha back into the discussion and was relieved to find both of them responding. The resiliency of the young! There were compartments in the mind, he knew, and the death of Ítk t'Sá must be shut into one of these in order for life to go on. Grief, mourning, vengeance – and final acceptance – could come later.

They explored the tombs quickly. All of the storage cubicles had been roughly looted; all were rubbish-filled, musty, and dry. In the floor of the guesting room of the adjacent tomb they discovered a hole. Of this, the glassblower disclaimed knowledge, saying that it was new to him, and that it must lead down into the sarcophagus chamber. He stood to admire the work; after all, as he remarked, it took real enterprise to hack a man-sized hole through a basalt slab a handspan and a half thick!

Morkúdz again allowed his light to fade, and they sat together in darkness so total that their eyes themselves created colours and phantasms, and the spirits of the ancient dead awoke to dance before them against the ebon curtain. The air grew close and bad, smelling of dryness and sweat and fear. Hársan allowed Ítk t'Sá one last sad, mental farewell and found that his mind was already nibbling at the problem of breathable air here in this sepulchre. There ought to be cross-currents down the two open shafts from the great cavern above, should there not?

Tlayésha dozed in his arms; from close by, on his other side, he heard the cadence of the Hehegánu's heartbeat, its rhythm strangely different from his own. Rustling noises announced that Simanúya was still grubbing about in the rubbish for coins, stones, and whatever else the Gods might disclose. No sound emanated from where the Livyáni and his warrior woman leaned together against the wall.

Only a *Kirén* or two could have passed; then something grated and slithered above. Colourless light, brighter than that of Morkúdz' spell, trickled down their original shaft to raise gleams and shadows amongst the wreckage of the funeral furniture.

Hársan was on his feet, through the storage room and the narrow passage beyond, and into the neighbouring guesting chamber almost before he knew it. Táluvaz and the Hehegánu still arrived before him, however, and a large but feminine hand upon his shoulder told him that Miruré followed.

He guessed from the chaotic shadows that someone ahead had started to climb up into the second shaft: probably Táluvaz Arrío.

Noise exploded there: rattling, scratching, banging, and then a sound like a sack of grain striking the planks of a wooden floor. A voice gave a choking cry – Táluvaz? – and Hársan fell jarringly against the wall as Morkúdz tumbled back upon him.

Something wet and unpleasantly familiar splashed Hársan's legs. He struggled beneath the Hehegánu's weight and felt the nonhuman muscles stretch as the creature strove to rise. A foot, probably Tlayésha's, stepped hard upon his thigh. He grunted involuntarily and rolled aside. Morkúdz' radiance, flaring and dimming like a lamp in the wind, brought the chamber to view as a painter unrolls a picture before an audience.

The Livyáni lay half-stunned beneath a short, robust-looking man in a leather tunic and grey *Firyá*-cloth kilt. The fellow lay face down, long braided hair hiding his features.

Miruré pushed past to deal with the intruder, but there was no need. At first Hársan thought that the man had been struck unconscious in his fall, but when the N'lüss girl pulled him over, they saw that he lay in a spattered pool of scarlet. Whoever he was, he was dead, his tunic slashed across the breast by what must have been a terrible blow from a heavy weapon: a halberd or a two-handed axe. He was no one Hársan knew: thin-featured, wisp-bearded, perhaps ten years older than Hársan himself. He had the look of a hired mercenary.

Tlayésha tended to Táluvaz while Miruré and Hársan examined the body. The man now bore no weapons. He wore a helmet, shoulder pauldrons, and arm-wrappings of scuffed, common *Chlén*-hide; his clothing told them nothing. From a pouch at his waist, however, the N'lüss girl extracted a handful of copper and silver coins. Most of these she threw down, but one she handed to Hársan. It bore an inscription in square, jagged symbols and, on the other side, a portrait of a thick-set, balding man with a square-cut beard.

The Baron Áld. Hársan had often seen Yán Koryáni coins at the Monastery of the Sapient Eye.

Táluvaz Arrío was sufficiently recovered to reach out for the coin. He had suffered no more than scrapes and bruises, but, as Hársan noted wryly, he would have to pay a call upon his tattooer for repairs! The man's boot had caught Táluvaz just at his receding hairline, and a longish flap of torn skin there dribbled blood down over one ear.

"Others have brought their own wine to the feast," Hársan said fiercely. "The Yán Koryáni appear to be quarrelling with Lord Sárku's folk. Did your sources tell you that it was the Baron's servants who spirited me out of the Tólek Kána Pits – made me into a mind-sick idiot for a time?"

"I – ah – have heard the tale. It seems to be so." The Livyáni brightened. "If one feaster arrives, then may there not be more?"

"Who?"

"The Gods know," the older man probed his scalp, wincing as his fingers brought away redness. "Many sought you: your own people, the Omnipotent Azure Legion, Prince Eselné's agents, the Yán Koryáni. All have watchers, telepaths, sorcery....We can hope that there are more guests at the banquet!"

Miruré returned from the base of the tomb-shaft. "Fighting above, Lord," she said. "An explosion sound, a red light –" She looked as though she yearned to go and join in, but Táluvaz laid a restraining hand upon her wrist.

"We have no choice but to wait and see whether the *Zrné* eats the *Mnór*, or the other way round."

They returned to the connecting passage. Miruré stood watch by the body near the second shaft, while Morkúdz crouched at the base of their original entrance. Simanúya tried on the dead man's helmet but found it too small. He proffered it first to Tlayésha, then to Hársan, but neither wanted to anger the spirit of one so recently deceased by wearing it.

They waited.

Chapter Thirty-Seven

"They come!" Hársan heard Miruré shout from the first tomb.

Simultaneously cold, pale luminescence poured down the second shaft, the one nearest him. He took a chance, put his head in, glanced up, and narrowly missed being struck by something metallic: a dagger, perhaps, or a throwing axe that clanged and went spinning off into the rubbish. Whoever they were, there was no question of their hostility – and of their disinclination to parley!

He backed out and looked around for the others. Miruré was visible at the door leading to the tomb through which they had first entered. Táluvaz, Tlayésha, and Simanúya were close by, just on the other side of the tomb robbers' hole in the floor. Of the Hehegánu there was no sign.

"Down – into the sarcophagus chamber!" the glassblower bleated. "There may be further tunnels there." He suited action to words and thrust his not inconsiderable bulk into the hole. What he would use for light did not seem to occur to him.

The N'lüss girl retreated further into the chamber, still fighting, the ancient sword (shorter by a handspan broken from its tip, Hársan saw) in her right hand, and her dagger in her left. Her opponents were more of the Undead: black and withered things animated by other-planar power and the fearful sorceries of Lord Sárku. Two were skull-faced: *Mrúr* or *Jájgi*, as Morkúdz had named them. Another just behind appeared mummified, greyish, wrinkled, and shrunken. The holes where the embalmers had inserted thongs into the lips to close the liche's mouth still showed, and copper corpse-amulets swung like bridal necklaces from its raddled neck and arms. This must be one of the *Shédra* of legend: the Gods knew whether the tales of its hunger for living flesh were true! Hársan had no wish to find out.

All of the foe bore thick, bronze-bladed halberds – axes, poleaxes – Hársan did not know the proper term. These they swung skilfully in the cramped space, and Miruré was hard put to get within a range where her shorter weapon could do its work. The Temple of Sárku had the permanent pick of the best of its warrior devotees, after all; dead, they were only somewhat slower and less clever than they had been in life, and quantity made up for quality ...

A different being glided in behind the Undead: a stooping, slender, dark-robed thing. Its face was a whitish blur, and Hársan first mistook it for another of the *Mrúr*. It whirled to avoid one of Miruré's blows, however, and he saw that the head curved out from the sloping shoulders upon a long columnar neck. Scales glittered at its throat. The face was flat, ophidian, the eyes wide apart and slit-pupilled. It opened a fanged mouth and hissed something to those behind it. Another creature out of children's nightmares: a *Qól*, "They of the Serpent Faces!" Some of the epics listed the *Qól* among the creations of the Temple of Lord Ksárul, while a few spoke of them as a race artificially manufactured during the Latter Times and employed by all three of the Temples of the Dark Trinity, those of Ksárul, Sárku, and Lord Hrü'ü. He could now declare the latter theory to be empirically proved, although whether he lived to report it or not was as yet undecided by the Weaver of Skeins.

There were more foemen, human and nonhuman, in the passage behind the *Qól*.

Had the Temple of Sárku mobilised all of its legions against them?

Hársan thought so. From far in the rear he heard a cracked, ancient voice shrilling commands: it could only be Vridékka. If these people knew their business, Jayárgo would be in command of those descending the second shaft into the chamber in which they now fought.

Ruddy light glimmered up from the tomb robbers' hole. The glassblower had found something inflammable in the sarcophagus chamber. Táluvaz Arrío lifted Tlayésha by the waist, dropped her into the opening, and followed himself, crying out to Miruré in Livyáni. The warrior girl parried a halberd thrust by one of the *Mrúr*, aimed judiciously, and stabbed; the wielder lurched backwards and fell.

"You, too!" Miruré shouted at Hársan. She followed this with a string of rasping syllables in her own tongue, cut and parried again, and was rewarded by a shrieking hiss from the serpent-headed thing.

He had no reason to stay, lacking any weapon with which to aid her. A moment to assess the drop, and then he jumped. Paper-dry corpse windings crunched beneath him, and he lost his footing to sprawl amongst crumbled bones and rotted wood.

There was no time to see what the room contained. He had only an impression of stacked coffins, open and tumbled helter-skelter upon the ruins of what had once been drapery-shrouded biers. The glassblower crouched by an impromptu bonfire made from these.

Tlayésha helped Hársan to his feet. A crash behind them told him that Miruré had arrived. Something else came with her, a threshing, hissing whirlwind of black cloth and sinuous limbs. The arms terminated in bluish-white tentacles rather than hands. The fire scattered in an explosion of embers as the N'lüss girl battled to keep the snapping jaws of the *Qól* from her face, and its saw-toothed short sword from her belly. Hársan seized the limb nearest him and was whipped to and fro like a kite at the end of a string. The creature was strong! He glimpsed Táluvaz Arrío moving in behind the *Qól*; heard a thumping, hollow sound; and felt the sucker-covered tentacle go limp in his grasp. The Livyáni stepped back, a small, gleaming brass tube in his fist, a canister from which a triangular blade protruded: a spring-loaded dagger, a weapon beloved of the assassin clans – and apparently by Livyáni noblemen on foreign missions! Táluvaz carried more than a golden pomander in his waist-pouch, then!

There was a pause. Rustling and scraping sounds filtered down to them.

Vridékka's familiar voice called, "Come up, priest Hársan. Your comrades may depart unhindered. It is only you we want."

"They are short of fighters," Miruré gasped. She was out of breath, and her breasts and flanks shone with the gleam of perspiration. She did not appear to have been injured, however. "The Yán Koryáni must have killed many; otherwise they would risk an assault at once." She wiped ichor from her hands, cleaned her blade upon her leggings, and methodically began to braid her hair. It had come undone and would have been a hindrance in further fighting.

"Say nothing, priest Hársan," Táluvaz said. "Our foes prefer you alive, although they can still use you dead. We have a little respite, it seems. Let them wonder where you are and what you think. – All of you look about for any exit!"

"Where is Morkúdz?" Hársan asked. Only now did he have time to inquire.

"Dead, I think," Miruré said. "Or surrendered. This was never his cause." She seemed indifferent, but Hársan felt a twinge of regret for the sly Hehegánu.

Whatever Morkúdz' fate, that was the end of their light, except for Simanúya's fire.

Indeed, the glassblower's bonfire was spreading amongst the dry corpse-wrappings and shattered coffins. Smoke arose to choke them. Simanúya had not used all of the fuel available, but what he had would at least delay the Undead for a while; they, too, would burn.

"Here!" Tlayésha exclaimed. "Behind these caskets…. An opening!"

Simanúya seized a brand, a painted coffin-board. The flames ate away the glyphs of its owner's rank and titles as he waved it. He plunged into the doorway. – And stopped so suddenly that Hársan and Tlayésha both stepped hard upon his heels.

"What –?"

"Hold, priest! Look there – upon the sill!"

Hársan let his eyes adjust. He saw only a scrawled, wavy mark in blue chalk upon the threshold just inside the door.

"The argot of the tomb-robber clans! This place contains a trap. The ancients had as much love for underground visitors as your Lord Táluvaz!"

Hársan backed out, then stood in the opening while Simanúya inspected the place. The man was thorough: he held his torch high to peer at the ceiling, at the walls, at the floor beyond the sill. He prodded and poked with all the care of a hunter who wakes a sleeping *Zrné*. At length he twisted about.

"Ohé, Livyáni!" he called. "We have a nice choice. These grooves in the doorway: a falling block, a portcullis. That sill-stone: a balance, a trigger. Whoever enters steps upon the trap; he is sealed into this chamber forever, while those in the entrance are crushed, and those outside cannot break through. Do you prefer to die of smoke, to surrender to the Worm-priests, or hop over the sill and bring it down behind us once we are all inside? We can then suffocate in peace – a splendid tomb for our corpses until Lord Ksárul returns to illumine the world!"

"Another exit – from within?" Miruré's voice sounded muffled in the narrow space.

"Possible. Not likely. The ancients provided tranquillity for their dead, not a game of 'your room or mine,' like noble ladies in a palace!"

"Well, priest Hársan?" Táluvaz asked.

"Inside. Better unlikely than no chance at all. Show us what to do, glassblower!"

Simanúya said no more but leaped clumsily across the threshold, avoiding all contact with the sill-stone. Hársan handed Tlayésha across; then he jumped, followed by Táluvaz and the N'lüss girl. They gathered themselves, hesitated.

Hársan himself placed a foot upon the trigger-stone. He pressed down firmly.

For a moment nothing happened. Slowly at first, then with gathering speed, the ceiling above the doorway slid groaning and rumbling down in its grooves to crash into place. The block was perhaps two handspans thick.

There was no return; the play was made.

The light of Simanúya's brand brought forth glittering eyes, winking moons and planets, streaks of ruddy gold and scarlet-drenched silver. No robber had looted this place, afraid of the trap, perhaps, or pressed for time.

This was the sepulchre of a great noble, one of the mighty of the First Imperium.

All was crushed and ruined, nevertheless. Images of Queen Nayári's dread gods leaned against one another in tumbled disarray; the shards of a delicate crystal pedestal reposed beneath the weight of an embossed casket from which gems spilled forth like fruit from a basket; fragile tapestries and draperies lay crumpled and tattered in the dust, torn by the currents of air and the weight of their own gold and silver thread. Beyond, in an alcove as large as the antechamber from which they had come, the sarcophagus itself loomed upon its bier, its corners guarded by time-blackened demon figures, its fallen canopy now no more than a gossamer coverlet for the carven face of the sleeper within.

"As I am but a slave to the Lord of the Blue Room... !" Simanúya breathed. "Oh, for the chance –" He glowered, brought back to the present by the urgency of their problem.

"An exit – Search!" Táluvaz commanded.

"There is air aplenty for now." Miruré put up her sword and looked about for something to use as a light. She had lost the torch she had brought from the glassblower's cache above. A dainty table caught her eye, and in a moment she was igniting one leg of this from Simanúya's flame.

They found nothing. The sepulchre had been cut into solid rock.

"One last possibility, priest," the glassblower wheezed. "I have – ah – heard of tombs in which there was a secret stair beneath the coffin itself, a way out for one who might have been drugged and entombed while he – or she – yet lived." His expression held more cupidity, Hársan thought, than any interest in escape. The fellow might still survive, even if Vridékka's minions managed to break through. Wealth beyond dreaming lay here; the Temple of Sárku would profit mightily; and what, really, did one wretched merchant of Púrdimal mean to the Worm Prince?

It was a chance. No other course seemed open to them.

The remains of the canopy were swiftly brushed away as easily as swamp-spider webs to reveal the enamelled and gilded sarcophagus lid beneath. This, too, the glassblower inspected for snares. Then he gestured Hársan to the foot of the coffin and himself took its head within the narrow end of the alcove.

"The lid is made to be lifted a finger's breadth," he grunted. "Then it slides." He lifted two of the demon figures down from their pedestals, then began to strain at the frieze of golden figures that ran around the rim.

"No!" Táluvaz cried. "There may be further deadly devices within –!"

"Not so. This is not Engsvanyáli. Those of the First Imperium put their trust in deep-buried catacombs, gates and portcullises, roofs that collapse, pits and stakes. No prettily poisoned spines or other frills here!" He gasped and sucked in air, the muscles under his leather vest cracking and bulging with exertion. "Now, boy!"

"Desecration!" the Livyáni shouted again. He made as if to rush upon Simanúya. "Leave the dead be, tomb-robber! Here sleeps a prince of the First Age, a devotee of Enomé, the forbearer of your own Lord Ksárul – likely no more than another name for your same God!"

"At this moment I am unconcerned by gods." The glassblower's fingers slid beneath his vest; probably he carried some small weapon there. Táluvaz hesitated. Simanúya continued to eye him shrewdly but positioned himself to heave again at the lid.

Hársan glanced apologetically at the Livyáni. "He may be right. I have myself read of such exits from tombs. And it is only a matter of a *Kirén* or two before Vridékka's creatures smash through the stone block. We must do what we can." He lifted hard, and was gratified to feel the massive lid rise a trifle.

"Miruré, stop them!" Táluvaz broke off into slurred, rapid Livyáni.

The warrior girl stood undecided. Then she answered not in Livyáni but in her throaty, accented Tsolyáni:

"Lord, I have always done your will. I am yours, as you are mine. Yet now I must disobey. You may slay me for it, but if this thief speaks truly, then we are out of here. If he is wrong, then naught but a handful of bones is disturbed. In my land we love life more than bones. – And I – I care too much for your life to think of bones."

She turned away, squatted down, let her hands fall to her sides, and bowed her head. Her braided hair tumbled down to shadow her face.

The spring-dagger was in Táluvaz' hand. For a moment he stood thus, his features convulsed and furious. Then he flung down the weapon, went to Miruré, and raised her. Before their astonished gaze he embraced her, kissed her, and brushed her hair back from her eyes. He turned to the others.

"We are one," he said. "She and I. A master enslaved by his slave – Look not so hard upon us, girl – priest – tomb-robber! As is my right, by the canon of our Shadow Gods, I shall free her and make her the mistress of my clan-house." He shifted into Livyáni, and only Miruré knew what he said after that.

Tlayésha was the nearest. She went to them, but she had no idea what to advise. The matter was simpler in Tsolyánu than in theocratic Livyánu, where all social relationships were dictated from birth by the rigid strictures of the Shadow Gods' temples. Here, such a slave as Miruré could be freed, declare herself *Aridáni,* and wed her master all on the same day – and marry as many other men thereafter as she pleased. It was not frequent, but it happened.

"Lift! Nay – hold fast! Halt it, you puling priest!" Simanúya yelped suddenly. "The whole weight comes upon me!"

The ponderous lid rested upon an inclined rim and must have been mounted on rollers; once raised, it was designed to slide. As Hársan watched with horror, it rumbled majestically towards the glassblower, who vanished behind it. The lid finished with a thunderous boom against the rear wall of the alcove. There it balanced, tilted down, scraped along the wall, and came to a stop with Hársan's end angled high above the head of the sarcophagus.

They looked to see Simanúya mashed like a *Chrí*-fly against the wall behind the thing. Then his voice arose, cursing and praying and wheedling, from the gap underneath the lid. He crawled, little the worse for wear, out of the dark triangular opening underneath, between the lid and the sarcophagus itself.

"Kill me outright, you milk-sucking fool! Never would I have you upon any venture of mine!" Simanúya exploded into curses.

Hársan heard but paid no heed. He stood gazing into the coffin.

The face of the occupant had been covered with a mosaic mask. The wooden backing of this had crumbled away long ago, and the stones, red garnets and yellow zircons and brooding fire-opals, were scattered dewdrops upon the gold-laced cerements beneath. The arms and hands, sheathed in gauntleted vambraces of precious metals, lay folded upon the breast amidst collars, necklaces, and gorgets of enamel and filigree, all blackened by time and inevitable corruption. He could see nothing of the torso or the legs, so thick were the wrappings of what had once been lacy *Thésun*-gauze and age-dimmed brocades.

He saw all of this, yet he saw none of it. Instead, he stared at the three objects that reposed upon the sleeper's breast.

At first he had thought the corpse to be a woman. Then he realized that the metal breast-cups upon its chest were not such at all; they were really the two halves of a silvery globe, very like those he had examined so long ago with Chtík p'Qwé in the Temple of Eternal Knowing in Béy Sü!

The third object lay between the engraved and inlaid gauntlets covering the arms.

It was a golden hand, palm up, the fingers together, neatly pointing up at the corpse's masked chin. From where he stood he could make out the column of Llyáni glyphs as easily as though he knew them by heart.

He had the golden hand and one half of the globe before any of the others could react. Simanúya scooped up the other silvery hemisphere, however.

"Give me that!" Hársan reached for it.

"Now, priest, you'll not be greedy, eh? Not deprive your comrades of some profit!" The man stood tensed and ready. He had probably survived similar situations before.

"No matter of greed. Take all the rest – the jewels, the gold!"

"Hársan, let him have what he would…" Tlayésha interrupted plaintively. She did not know and could not understand.

"He can strip this poor corpse as naked as one of Dlamélish' temple-boys – become rich as the Emperor in Avanthár! Give me the sphere – it is all I want."

It had taken Táluvaz only moments to size up the affair. "Glassblower, you have no use for that object. Come, surrender it. Take what you like of the rest – take all our shares!"

"Something so valuable that all of these baubles are no more than dross?" Simanúya asked in bitter tones. "Something of sorcery, of ancient power? Something we could sell to our pursuers in exchange for our lives?" His voice rose to a barrel-chested roar. "Something you must then take from me, priest, if you have more than buttermilk in your veins!"

Hársan had lost all thought of himself. He began to sidle around the sarcophagus toward the glassblower. The other inserted his free hand into his vest, and a short, triangular dagger appeared. It was a wicked thing, a hollow glass blade. Bluish liquid sloshed to and fro within it.

Simanúya sensed Miruré approaching from his right. He glided back around the sarcophagus, put beefy shoulders against the wall. The silvery hemisphere he carefully laid upon the coffin rim before him. He menaced the girl with the dagger and thrust out splayed fingers to fend off Hársan on his left.

"So you would cheat me?" he snarled. "Pious chatter about despoiling tombs and the dead? Chá, how you priestly hypocrites raise the whore's price after you've seen her dance!"

"Look you here, man," Táluvaz said. "None would rob you. It is as Hársan says. All is yours. All! Save for that sphere-thing."

He gestured sharply, and as Simanúya's one good eye followed his hand, Miruré leaped.

Hársan moved almost simultaneously. He collided with what felt like a stone club, the glassblower's fist. Momentum carried him on to crash into Simanúya's brawny shoulder, and an arm encircled his back to crush the life out of him. He hammered Simanúya's jowly chin with his free hand, but he could not see what transpired behind. Violent motion erupted there by his ear; the glassblower cursed, then shrieked. The arm fell away.

Hársan dragged himself free to see Miruré's blade, scarlet to the hilt, gliding back out of Simanúya's ribcage.

The wound did not even appear serious, a red-lipped slit no more than a finger's breadth long; yet Simanúya's good eye rolled up and began to glaze, and breath bubbled raggedly in his lungs. He opened his mouth to speak, waved a hand, and knocked the silvery hemisphere spinning and rolling out into the room. He wheeled toward Hársan. Slowly, with the face of a man who already knows he is dead, Simanúya crumpled, joint by joint, to the floor.

Tlayésha was beside Hársan. There was no time to explain. He made himself thrust her aside and scrambled to seize the other half of the globe before Táluvaz or his N'lüss woman could retrieve it.

Neither paid him any attention. Táluvaz knelt beside the warrior girl, eyes wide and stricken, his black and red tattoos vivid against the pallor of his cheeks.

"It is only a little cut, my Lord," Miruré said in her soft, foreign voice. A line of red showed against the smooth curve of her breast where neck and shoulder joined.

The Livyáni reached for Simanúya's dagger. Its tip was gone. He sniffed, and his head snapped back from the acrid odour of what the weapon had contained.

"Physician —?"

"I have nothing with me," Tlayésha moaned.

"What is the poison? How long —?"

"*Ajúra*, I think. A swamp-fruit, common in Púrdimal…"

"What does it do?"

"I — I am not certain, Lord. It immobilises, numbs, almost at once. I do not know if it — kills — or how soon. I am not even certain that it *does* kill. Many merchants use it to ward off footpads…"

"At least it is not instant." Táluvaz clenched his fists, beat them upon the stone floor. "We — we must surrender — call for terms. — No, we cannot!" He clutched at his greying hair in anguish. "If only —"

Tlayésha supported Miruré, let her lean against her shoulder. The N'lüss girl seemed dazed, confused. Beads of perspiration showed upon her upper lip and her forehead. She tried to smile but slumped dizzily instead.

Hársan came to stand before them. He said, "It is quite all right, Lord Táluvaz. There is no exit through the sarcophagus. I am willing now to surrender. The game is done, and you may summon Lord Vridékka and his minions. But be assured that I shall bargain them a good bargain for your woman's life."

They goggled at him uncomprehendingly. Hársan held the globe, both halves joined into a perfect sphere, in both hands. His face appeared as though lit from within, but by what strange emotion perhaps only Lord Táluvaz Arrío could guess.

"Come, call to those outside. Let them break down the portcullis. Your Miruré must live — and I shall take Lord Sárku's servants to the Man of Gold."

Chapter Thirty-Eight

I t took longer than expected. Miruré was only semi-conscious when the slow, skeletal *Mrúr* battered down the portcullis and hauled the last fragments out of the doorway to admit Jayárgo and a handful of copper-helmeted temple guards. Táluvaz Arrío refused to let them touch Miruré, and he and Hársan together carried the stricken girl out through the smoke-smelling anteroom to one of the shafts where ropes and a leather swing-seat dangled. Soon they stood once again in the upper cavern of the domes. More of the Undead and another half dozen guardsmen milled about here, together with two *Qól* and a miscellany of smaller creatures of the Underworlds that Hársan could not identify.

There were others, too: five warriors, their leather tunics innocent of any clan colours or insignia, squatted on their haunches apart from Vridékka's followers. They were visibly uneasy though just as unmistakably allied – or neutral – to Lord Sárku's contingent. With this latter party was the man Tlayésha had known as a tanner and whom Hársan had once named a Mihálli. He sat, unconcerned and aloof, upon a fallen stela next to his assistant, the same vulpine-faced little rogue who had slain the young nobleman upon the *Sákbe*-road platform. Tlayésha touched Hársan's arm and pointed.

He was looking at other things. The flaring light of torches and bronze lanterns silhouetted a party of *Mrúr* and their *Jájgi* overseer. The creatures were collecting bodies, obviously dead; these they passed to others of their kind within one of the domes. What better hiding place than the bottom of a tomb-shaft? Armour glinted beneath a bloodied cloak: a military cuirass, Hársan realised with astonishment. The mantle, too, had a soldierly look about it, and it was scarlet with more than blood: the colour of Lord Karakán and Prince Eselné's legions! These, then, were the opponents Vridékka's monsters had defeated while Hársan and his comrades hid in the tomb chambers below! From the look of it, the Yán Koryáni had been the allies of the Worm Prince's servitors, too, and for the moment at least, they were clearly working together. He noted that Táluvaz Arrío also had not missed this connection.

Vridékka came bustling up. He took the Globe of Instruction from Hársan but tossed it aside when he saw that it was blank and empty. The golden hand he ignored: a religious relic from an age much later than that of the Man of Gold itself.

"Well, priest Hársan?" he said. "Good Jayárgo here treats your warrior girl, whilst we make a quick tour of the further depths, eh?"

"First the treatment, then the trip."

The older man motioned indifferently to Jayárgo, who went to kneel beside Miruré. "Agreed, priest."

He looked beyond the girl to Táluvaz Arrío. "We must pay our respects to this noble visitor as well. What possesses a high envoy of a foreign land to overstep his welcome and explore our labyrinths at such an hour of the night?"

Táluvaz gave him a small smile but said nothing.

Vridékka eyed him narrowly. "Surely not a love of archaeology? Not a desire to make sacrifice at the tomb of some noble ancestor? Not the lure of funereal treasures – which you seem to have found aplenty." He glanced down at Miruré's face, empty and childishly innocent now as though she lay asleep. Jayárgo touched her throat, applied an ointment, ran his long fingers over her temples, and cast a minor spell of healing magic.

The N'lüss girl stirred and opened her eyes.

All of the Temples used healing sorcery, and in spite of its theological preoccupation with death, the Temple of Sárku was no exception. Such spells, Hársan knew, worked by drawing power from the Planes Beyond to cleanse the body of poisons and inimical substances, speed tissue and bone regrowth according to some mysterious blueprint inherent within the physique of the patient himself, and rebuild lost strength and energy. Whoever had devised this magic, long ago during the Latter Times or before, had possessed greater skill than all of the modern physicians and sorcerers of the Five Empires put together.

Vridékka spoke again. "Your comrades are also unsuited to such a venture: a fugitive priest of Thúmis for whom there is an Imperial warrant, a slaver's physician doxy, a sometime glass merchant and tomb-robber, now deceased, and one poor N'lüss warrior-girl as bodyguard! Really, my Lord, it appears that you were drawn into this affair by accident, as unready for your adventures as one of Lady Dilinála's virgins for a harem! – At least I think it politic for us to say so. When we are done here, you will be escorted back to the mansion of the Livyáni Legate in Púrdimal – and you should consider making an extra sacrifice to your Shadow Gods that you are out of it so easily."

Táluvaz still made no reply.

There had been no mention of Morkúdz. Hársan bit his lip to keep from blurting out the question. Nor had Ítk t'Sá been named, but their pursuers must surely know that she had been with them and that she was dead. Yes, dead. He still could hardly think the word.

"– Ah? Ah. So. There will be time later for more of this one-sided discussion. – Yes?" Vridékka broke off to engage in a whispered and apparently acrimonious conference with the Yán Koryáni tanner.

"No, there will be no handing over of any of our guests!" he said with finality. "They remain together – and will be so taken above. All but this priest here, with whom we have our business."

"And to that I say no!" Hársan interrupted. "Where you take me, you take them. Else you may well slay them once they are apart from me!"

"Crude fancies do you no credit!" The mind-seer sounded sincerely offended.

"It will be as I desire. You know that my secret is sealed to you, and you cannot come to it, save with great difficulty and waste of time."

"Let me –" the tanner began.

"– And keep this scarlet-eyed shape-changer far from me – from all of us! Else I shall use my powers to put my own head 'around the corner' and destroy my value forever! Nothing can be elicited from a corpse whose skull is lost in the raw energies that flow in the Planes Beyond!"

He had no idea whether this was so, or even whether he could accomplish this feat if he chose. He only hoped that the ancients' seal upon his mind was thorough enough to camouflage this bit of bravura.

Tlayésha said, "We are slain in any case, Hársan, once we have given him the thing you conceal." She shuddered, and he was suddenly conscious of her still-damp garments and of the fatigue and terror she had endured.

"I think not, love. He cannot dispose of a high Livyáni emissary without trace, and you and I are only insignificant pawns once my secret is gone. The Worm Prince is ruthless, but he is too clever to be selfishly vengeful. There is no reason to annoy my temple – and certain others – by killing us." She surely suspected a lie, and he squeezed her hand to keep her silent.

"Agreed, agreed, priest! It shall be exactly as you say. No need to plough the furrow after the seed is sown!" Vridékka waved the Yán Koryáni tanner away irritably. "When we are finished here, priest Hársan, you and your comrades shall all go free. Return to your monastery, pick *Tetél*-flowers, travel to Tsámra with this particoloured foreigner – or go whithersoever your Skein takes you." He took a staff of white *Ssár*-wood from one of the waiting Undead. "Are you ready, Jayárgo? Let us depart. The cold saps my ancient legs, and the sooner done the sooner out."

Miruré stood up, leaning first upon Jayárgo's arm and then pulling away with distaste when she realised whose it was. She moved uncertainly towards Táluvaz, her mincing, faltering steps very unlike her usual stride, and he opened his arms to her. He would have fallen under her weight had it not been for Tlayésha and Hársan. The temple guardsmen surrounded them, together with Vridékka and Jayárgo. Some of the Undead and the *Qól* took the lead and the rest followed. The Yán Koryáni party brought up the rear in wary silence.

The way was not long, but it was convoluted. Hársan realised that he never could have found it by himself, for it led downward through passages and intersections that they had overlooked or had passed all too hastily, into galleries and corridors where several possible exits opened yawning mouths, and eventually into an echoing, hoary cavern filled with more of Lord Vimúhla's frozen fire-stone. Vridékka paused to catch his breath while the *Mrúr* attached a rope to a ring set in the floor and raised a thick stone slab. There were stairs there, cut into the bubbled, ebon rock. At the bottom they came to an open gate still hung about with the remnants of lead seals inscribed with the flamboyant, graceful script of the Engsvanyáli Priestkings. Beyond was another corridor, its walls not of stone but made of blackish, age-corroded metal.

"This much has been told to me by our Temple, but from here I know not," Vridékka muttered. "Hói, Jayárgo! A light – and some guidance!"

The tall priest picked his way forward. "Lord, there is a larger chamber ahead."

"And beyond?"

"We know not. Our creatures feared the guardians of the ancients too much to dare more."

"Guardians? What guardians?"

Jayárgo rubbed his bald pate and consulted with the skull-faced *Jájgi*, the cleverest of the Undead. "None, Lord. But bravery is not the hallmark of our comrades here. Those who have died once are not keen to surrender what passes for life a second time."

Vridékka made a humphing noise in his throat. In truth, though, this section of the Underworld was awash with an indefinable miasma of foreboding. The air was stale and dead, its smell reminiscent of the chemicals in an apothecary's shop. No ornaments adorned the walls; they were as darkly blank as the surface of a stagnant pond. There were no glyphs, no murals, no friezes and dadoes and carven pilasters. This in itself was ominous, for all of the Five Empires and all of those kingdoms and states that had preceded them back to the Latter Times were prone to flowery garniture and architectural embellishment. This place was alien. What manner of men – if men they had been – could live in a bare box?

The hall Jayárgo had mentioned was similar, but larger and cluttered with the flotsam of the unknown world of the ancients. Cylindrical tubes of metal stretched up out of sight toward the unseen ceiling, and housings, like *Chlén*-carts shrouded in grey robes, lined the buckled, littered floor. Other explorers had indeed dared to enter here; many of the cowled things along the walls had been torn open and artifacts removed. Fragments of metal and glass and bits of various softer, lighter, many-coloured substances lay strewn about amidst the rubbish.

"Steel –! A fortune in metals!" Jayárgo breathed in tremulous tones.

"Not so," Vridékka chuckled. "I have watched a smith heat and hammer a bar of this stuff for hours with no result whatsoever. If the thing is not already shaped to your needs, then you may as well throw it away. All that was usable is likely already gone, pillaged by those of the Latter Times, the Llyáni, the Dragon Warriors, the Engsvanyáli, and a dozen others since."

The other was unconvinced. He paused to lay a cautious hand upon a great metal plate from which protruded studs as thick as his thumbs. Then he peered into the enigmatic innards of a container as big as a small hut, felt of the brittle tubes of red and blue materials inside, and was rewarded when these casings crumbled away to reveal fine strands of red copper: the sacred metal of Lord Sárku himself! He turned to debate further with Vridékka, but a glimpse of Hársan's face stopped him in mid-syllable.

The youth was trembling. His eyes were shut, and his fingers made tentative, sorcerous movements in the air.

Jayárgo was no stranger to spell-wizardry. He had a magic-damping counter-spell up before Hársan could complete his own incantation. The young man continued his puzzling finger-gesturing nevertheless. From behind, Jayárgo heard their Yán Koryáni ally exclaim, "He still has the shaking sickness! He should have recovered…!"

Hársan opened his eyes. He let his hands hang open at his sides. "Not so," he said. "I am no longer prey to your tampering, shape-changer, nor am I in need of spells. I am directed by a thing of the ancients, as Master Vridékka knows well – a truly unsettling experience and one I could wish you both to suffer sometime – and this place is included in the instruction. Just now I was – commanded, oriented, by the Globe of Instruction. I know where I am, and I can now take you to the Man of Gold."

Vridékka signed to the temple guards and to the Undead, and these closed up around their captives. "Guide us, then, priest Hársan," he replied softly. "It seems that we are strangers in your house."

Passages, corridors, shafts with oblong metal rungs, more rooms, all were traversed quickly. Twice they were forced to turn back and seek other paths because of the collapse of ceilings and the buckling of doorframes. Once they entered a chamber filled with frozen fire-stone, and Hársan spent long minutes searching for some way that did not end at a charred and blackened wall of solid rock.

The Undead cleared away obstacles as Hársan directed. Eventually they opened a hemispherical metal hatch in the floor of one of the small chambers. This gave upon a cylindrical shaft that once must have been vertical but was now tilted and twisted, here crushed and squeezed as a boy twists a hollow reed, there ripped asunder to reveal charcoal-hued volcanic ash and layers of compressed rock. Then they were there.

The shaft ended in a circular chamber. A tall, rectangular, double-leafed door barred their way, but Hársan went to this and touched the locking mechanism as the second Globe of Instruction had said to do.

Beyond was a hall of wonders.

No tomb-robber had ever set foot in the gritty dust upon this floor; nor had any party of explorers laid eyes upon these marvels since their last owner – some unknown lordling of the time of Llyán of Tsámra himself – had put his unreadable seal upon those doors and departed to face whatever destiny the Weaver of Skeins had chosen for him. He had not returned, but the treasures he had cherished still waited, exactly as he had left them so many centuries – millennia – ago. That owner had probably had nothing to do with the original building of this cache; no, that was likely the work of some still earlier possessor, one of the wizard-princes of the Latter Times.

In any case, the petty warlords of the Three States of the Triangle had not reached this place, nor had the Dragon Warriors. The rulers of the First Imperium had found the secret, and they had passed it down from generation to generation until it ended, lost and buried, partially in the tomb in which the first Globe of Instruction had been discovered, and partially in the sarcophagus Hársan and Simanúya had opened. The Engsvanyáli and those who came afterward had indeed pillaged the upper chambers of the labyrinth, but they had not come upon this cache! All was untouched, pristine, as though just set down by servants who know that their master will come to see his belongings and caress them one more time with his loving, greedy hands before going away.

Cases of seamless grey material leaned against the near wall. Roundish black globes, each as large as a man's skull, lay piled carelessly nearby; one of these had strayed out into the central aisle as though some careless servant had left it there. More chests and boxes and fat, tubular casks of metal filled the shadows beyond. Things that might have been works of art – or weapons, or implements, or spare pieces for mighty engines – occupied a bay to the right. Glass shimmered red-gold in the lantern-light; metal that was still bright after all of the intervening ages – uncorroded and probably uncorrodable – gleamed amidst spheres of coloured, transparent crystal, round plaques of shiny black stuff, angular levers and silvery wheels and bars and cylinders – there was too much for the eye to see. It reminded Hársan of the Hall of Mighty Tongues in the Monastery of the Sapient Eye.

Awed in spite of himself, Vridékka slipped between his guardsmen to examine a creation of many shining rods, and Jayárgo bent to inspect one of the black globes. Táluvaz supported Miruré, but his gaze was wide and rapt, his tattooed cheeks pale with excitement. Tlayésha held tightly to Hársan's arm, their predicament forgotten for the moment. Even the Undead seemed dimly amazed.

"It is like the cache Arundómu hiFershéna discovered under the City of Sárku some fifty years back," Jayárgo breathed. "Perhaps more –"

"More, much more," Vridékka laid a tentative finger upon a graceful handle – and jerked away when it moved under his touch. "Things not from the Latter Times – not some piddling little pot of badly made 'Eyes' and crude copies made by decadent wizards crouching over the last glimmers of ancient wisdom – but originals: artifacts from before the Time of Darkness itself, holy and sacred things, Jayárgo...!"

"We cannot read their tongue – we cannot know ..." Jayárgo pointed to the square, harsh little symbols that writhed across the flattened end of the black sphere he held.

The mind-seer drew himself up. "We can learn. We can experiment. We can study until at least some of it is ours again." He twitched his robe away from contact with a delicately designed couch. He was too late; the fabric crumbled away to dust even as he did so. Soft, sighing, tissue-tearing sounds from farther off told him that the air currents they had brought with them were doing similar damage elsewhere.

"We know a little," the Yán Koryáni tanner – the Mihálli – spoke for the first time since leaving the hall of domes. "These caches of the ancients contain things of danger, as well as of great benefit. The rulers of the Latter Times secreted whatever they could salvage – whatever was important to them – from the age before the Time of Darkness: weapons, of course, but also tools, machines to shape the elements, others to feed and heal and construct – to fulfil most of the needs to which you humans are prey. Even to prolong life – perhaps for centuries....Your Llyáni collected them, stored them, but they knew too little, your later nations still less. Yet we Mihálli possess some skill in these matters. We can aid you – in return for the right bargain."

Vridékka shook his head so violently that his grey locks flew out about his cheeks. "You remind me of our business. None of this is yours! None belongs to your master in Yán Kór! I claim these relics for the Temple of Sárku – and for the Seal Emperor of Tsolyánu!"

The last clause sounded suspiciously like an afterthought.

"Enough, mind-seer," Hársan said. "Squabble over your spoils later as you please. I tire of this game and would hand over your prize and be gone from here. Let me introduce you to the Man of Gold!"

"Guard him!" Vridékka cried. "He must know of traps –!"

The temple guards nervously hastened to obey, halberds and copper-trimmed armour clattering. The *Qól* glided forward.

Hársan raised both hands, palms out. "Ohé, here are no 'Eyes,' no talismans, no magic wards, no demon guardians! Here is but a poor pawn who cannot for a moment stand against your master's spells."

He ignored the soldiers, brushed past Jayárgo, still cradling the black globe, the Mihálli and his rodent-faced little henchman, and all the rest. He strode down the long aisle toward another door dimly visible in the gloom at the end of the hall.

"Come and reap the harvest of your labours!"

Vridékka himself seized a lantern and scuttled after him. "Priest – priest, you value my powers too little! Not only can I bind you with spells, but I am able to see through any snares you may have learned from the Globe – or aught else you foolishly plan! Touch that door and your brain will be as curdled as milk left all day in the sun!"

"Lá, my Lord, touch it yourself. Test it with your magics. Open it. Have your Undead do it for you, or better yet, let your expendable Yán Koryáni comrades risk the throw!"

Vridékka glared but halted in frustrated indecision. He signed to Jayárgo, and the younger priest came to examine the door. The Mihálli shut his scarlet-glowing eyes, wavered between human form and the tall, furred thing Hársan had glimpsed beneath the Tólek Kána Pits, and did something as well. Both shook their heads.

"You are satisfied? Open it."

"Hold him! Bind him!" Vridékka snapped. He waited until this was done. "Kill the physician girl if he moves." He backed away cautiously.

Two of the *Mrúr* were brought forward to run skeletal fingers over the portal. At a gesture from Vridékka they pulled upon the plain, silver-gleaming handle. It swung open as though it had been oiled only the day before.

Light, bright and sunny, sprang up within the room beyond. Something sighed and purred to life within the walls, and a breath of fresh air came to them, as clean as though newly drawn from the forests of Dó Cháka's Inner Range.

In the centre of the chamber, upon a raised dais, stood the Man of Gold.

Chapter Thirty-Nine

Whatever Hársan had expected, the Man of Gold was different.

He had thought to see a towering statue: the wise, solemn image of Lord Thúmis in the Temple of Eternal Knowing, or the awe-inspiring colossus of Hejjéka IV, "Restorer of Dignities," the forty-fifth Seal Emperor, in the square before the governor's palace in Béy Sü: something glorious of visage, crowned and anointed, bearing the insignia of divine authority and of omnipotent power over the mundane world and even over the Gods.

He was disappointed, for it was not so. The thing was indeed golden, yet it was squat and only vaguely manlike. Two thick, cylindrical columns did bear a semblance of legs, but the torso was a gleaming, featureless box, as massive as the body of a *Chlén*-beast; the arms were short, stubby, and covered with glittering spurs and knobs and coils of silvery cable that bore no similarity to hands and fingers. There was no head, just a sleek, streamlined ball of dark glass from which tendrils and helixes and flat plates emerged in all directions. At the base, between the legs, a rounded metal housing extended out upon the platform. This resembled nothing so much as a gigantic phallus, like those the priests of Dlamélish wore on festival days to amuse and excite the worshippers of that Goddess. Hársan suppressed an impulse to laugh: the Man of Gold reminded him of one of the language models in the Hall of Mighty Tongues – and aesthetically not a very pleasing one at that. The aspiring scholar who submitted it as a Labour of Reverence might be promoted to the next Circle, but it would be a near thing!

One of the *Mrúr* held him. His wrists hurt from the tight leather belt with which he was bound, but he wrenched himself about, nevertheless, and sought Vridékka's face. The old man waited by the door, nervously rocking from one foot to the other. One of the grim *Qól* had Tlayésha there, a saw-bladed shortsword in its tentacled forelimb. Hársan shot her a glance of reassurance, but whether she saw or not he did not know. Táluvaz, Miruré, and Jayárgo were visible in the midst of a clump of guardsmen behind her. The Mihálli and his companions moved into the chamber and spread out along the rear wall.

"Here you are, my Lord," Hársan cried. "Ask your Man of Gold to speak! Order him to walk with you to your temple! Inform him that his new master is mighty Prince Dhich'uné, fourth son of the God-Emperor of all Tsolyánu! Make him bow to your Worm-Lord! Introduce him to your new northern friends – if such they be! He awaits your command, mind-seer!"

Vridékka peered about. The entrance was not large enough to permit the thing to be removed. A second door to the left was still smaller. The walls, too, were clearly not meant to be shifted or opened; they were covered with huge, overlapping scales of dull, silvery metal. The ceiling, from which a ball of yellow radiance depended like a miniature sun, was seamless and smooth.

"A problem, Lord? Your Worm Prince must make a pilgrimage hither to meet his servant, not the reverse!" Hársan felt giddy, almost as if he had drunk strong wine or again tasted deadly *Zu'úr*. A myriad tiny voices sang in his head, whether from fatigue or from the effects of the Globe of Instruction he had no idea.

"Ask your dead things to accompany me," he cried, "and I shall lead you upon a tour of your new domain."

"I have warned you well, priest!" The older man stepped carefully into the room, stained brown robe flapping at his ankles. "You – and you – search this place. There must be guardians – wards."

The soldiers and the others made a cautious sweep of the chamber. They returned to report nothing.

Vridékka approached the dais. The front of the metal housing displayed a series of slanted panels, placed invitingly as though for the comfort of a seated human operator; there was no chair. Each panel was covered with round glass plaques, black knobs, and little wheels of metal, all made to be manipulated by human hands, all unknown and un-guessable. The middle panel somehow conveyed an air of special importance: a round hole occupied its centre, and a black bar or handle protruded portentously just below this.

The mind-seer squinted down into the hole, looked all around the dais. "The key, priest Hársan. There must be a key – a rod, a staff of metal – or glass – or some other substance."

Hársan did not answer, but Vridékka saw his eyes flicker toward the second, smaller exit from the chamber.

"Take him and the girl to stand before that door. Anything that emerges will slay them first."

This was done; then one of the soldiers prodded the door warily with his halberd. It swung open, and light swelled up within the room behind.

Unlike the bare and featureless hall of the Man of Gold, this place was a nest of opulence. Soft draperies, thick cushions of red and burnt orange, an expanse of dark russet carpet, tasteful tables of translucent ruby glass, ewers and flagons and statuettes of crystal and gold – all were visible for a moment before the air currents began their work of gentle decay. The tapestries whispered down into dust; the cushions slumped and lost their colour; a figure of carved black wood crumbled upon a bird-necked stand of topaz glass, bringing both chiming down into final ruin. The carpet rustled and rippled and seemed to move. What had been elegance became crumbled rubbish.

Hársan had just time to glimpse two more things. The first was a shining box as tall as a man and perhaps twice as wide in the middle of this room. As he watched, this changed from dark to light, and five figures swam up from shadow within it. The second thing was a row of glittering golden warriors against the far right wall, silent statues each more than a man-height tall, each with a pair of hands that ended in odd-shaped tubes and claws.

"*Ru'ún* – automatons!" Vridékka's voice cracked upon a falsetto note of warning.

A metal-shod boot kicked Hársan's legs from under him. He fell – and contrived to take both Tlayésha and the *Qól* who guarded her down with him as he went. Shouts eddied overhead, but all he could see was a chaotic view of the *Mrúr's* rusty greaves and grave-stained leather tunic. A stench of death mingled with the *Qól's* dry, snake-like odour made him gag.

Light – raw, naked, blinding – ravened and crackled above him. The mind-seer – or perhaps Jayárgo or even the Yán Koryáni – doubtless possessed an "Eye" or some other of the weapon-tools of the ancients. The players had equipped their pieces – their blues and blacks – well!

A smell of burning and wisps of blue-grey smoke drifted down. Bony fingers dug into Hársan's shoulders and hauled him erect. Tlayésha pulled herself up to lean against his arm; she panted and shook her head as though she had been running. The *Qól* would have grasped her, but she dodged aside.

Vridékka gestured the creature away. He actually seemed pleased. "So this was your trap! Clever little priest ! – Nay, clever princeling of the Latter Times! Four *Ru'ún* set to guard this chamber! Let the intruder into the outer hall, let him find this room of treasures, let him be lulled into avarice, and then let the automatons slay him!"

Beyond a swirl of dark cloaks and brown-lacquered armour Hársan glimpsed the ruins of the golden warriors. Tiny flames spurted from the breast of one; a second lay kicking feebly on its side; the abdomen of the third was rent open to reveal a blackened tangle that still glittered and popped. The last of the *Ru'ún* stood as before, but its carven, calm, inhuman face was empty and vacant. There was a ragged hole in its torso.

The box, too, was charred but not entirely destroyed. Inside, against a backdrop of scarlet-flowering trees and green shrubbery, a tall, elderly man stood gazing out at them. A woman sat upon a blue-veined marble bench before him, and two children squatted at her feet. A portion of another, a youth in a tight-fitting suit of glittering amber fabric, was visible as well, but the right side of his body wavered and flashed with eye-dazzling jabs of light. A voice, fuzzy and strangely drawled, spoke words in an unintelligible tongue. The older man's lips moved; he smiled and extended a beringed, gracious hand.

"A picture-box," Vridékka said. "The first lord of this place and his family, mayhap, as they lived during the Latter Times. How long after they had become dust did the savants of Llyán of Tsámra find this place, and how long after that was the secret of this treasure hidden within the Globes of Instruction?"

The man in the box gestured and pointed in an authoritative fashion. The words dragged on, not at all matching the movements of his lips. He reached to take some unseen object from a stand beside him.

"Jayárgo –!" Vridékka shrilled. "No –!"

The balding priest held something small between his fingers. Even as Vridékka cried out, a bolt of radiance sped from this to turn the images into flying, flaming shards.

"He may have had a weapon, Lord – another trap!"

"Such picture-boxes are harmless!" Vridékka tore at his beard in despair. "A thing that has survived for aeons becomes useless trash in a moment because of your gutless, illiterate fear!"

"Master ..."

Vridékka whirled to face Hársan and the rest, fury etched in every line of his skinny frame. "As the Corpse Lord knows, men today are ill-trained – ignoble: naught but wet anuses dribbling childish terrors and superstitions! Thus is knowledge – history, science, the world of the ancients – lost, never to be regained!"

The voices in Hársan's brain sang an angry hymn of hatred now.

"There is no help for it," Vridékka shook his white staff at them all. "Listen, the rest of you! Destroy nothing else as you value your witless heads! Search the inner chamber for a rod that will fit the slot in that panel there. Open everything, look everywhere. It must exist. Unless we find it, our work is as futile as death without Lord Sárku's afterlife!"

He left them to stride back toward the Man of Gold.

Táluvaz Arrío and Miruré came to stand beside Hársan. Neither had been bound, and the soldiers set to watch them seemed inordinately fascinated by the loot their comrades were finding within the room of the picture-box.

Resignation and fatigue stained the Livyáni's patrician features. He gestured anxiously toward Miruré, but his words had nothing to do with the N'lüss girl.

"Priest Hársan," he murmured, "not even a felon upon the impaler's stake appears as hopeless as you do now. Nor do I believe that you have suddenly been converted to the faith of the Worm Lord to cooperate so gallantly with our foes. You must have yet another string for your bow. Confide in us. Let us aid you!"

"Can you loose my hands?" Even as he spoke, he felt calloused, familiar, feminine fingers touch his wrists behind his back. Something tiny and very sharp sawed there briefly, and he knew that he was free. This Miruré had more daggers secreted about her person than a *Zrné* had teeth!

"And now? Tell us." Táluvaz touched Miruré tenderly, embraced her, made as though to support her. Had their guards paid heed to him, they would have known this to be a sham! The girl was a head taller than Hársan himself, making the slender, aristocratic Livyáni seem almost a child beside her. She must be sufficiently recovered to act on her own.

Tlayésha took a strip of her tattered skirt, dabbed at the N'lüss girl's forehead, and whispered something. No fool she, either.

Hársan said, "I know not. I swear I speak the truth, as Divine Thúmis knows my soul! Yet I feel elated, courageous – almost intoxicated, Lord Táluvaz." He stopped, unable to say more.

Something really *was* happening to him. The wash of tiny, fluting organ voices sang louder in his brain; the room dimmed and stretched and shrank. His vision blurred, and he sat down abruptly.

Pain rushed in upon him: little round spots of agony, as though a skilled tormentor of the Legion of Kétl plucked with pincers at each nerve strand. Breath fled out of his lungs – and was just as sharply sucked back in again. A fist closed around his heart, and his ribs became a ladder of aching flame. Was this a brain-stroke, such as had slain old Gnésumu, one of his preceptors at the Monastery so many years ago? He did not know, but he did not think so. Vridékka? No, the mind-seer was far away, marshalling his followers from the dais. Jayárgo was not in sight; he must be searching the inner chamber and wondering how to redeem himself in his master's eyes. The Mihálli was there indeed, but he and his men stood grouped by the door, inspecting some discovery or other.

Tlayésha's face, lined with concern, swam before him. It coalesced with the sharp, bluffly pretty features of the N'lüss girl, shaded off into Táluvaz' tattooed brow.

Voices gabbled, the air quivered and twinkled.

Then the pain was gone. Hársan raised sweat-smeared palms to clutch at his temples.

Tlayésha was saying, "– Some sort of seizure – the spell the Mihálli worked upon him – strain, weariness, lack of food –"

One of the skull-helmeted troopers asked gruffly, "What's to do with him then?"

Hársan himself replied, "Nothing – nothing now. – My – instruction… Summon your master. I have a thing to give him."

Vridékka met the soldier half way. Hársan got shakily to his feet to await him, weak but still unaccountably jubilant. The mind-seer looked him over with a dubious eye and cast a spell.

He recoiled. "Your iron buckler is stouter than ever, priest," he snapped. "You leave me no choice but to prod your willingness, twist your loyalties, give you more of what you endured in Lord Arkháne's dungeons. The girl, then, Cháishru…"

One of the troopers moved toward Tlayésha, but Hársan held out his hands.

"No need, Lord Vridékka. No need to harm her or any other. No more prodding or pushing or threatening!" He felt warm, excited, as full of wild joy as must a priestess of Hriháyal who achieves the climax of the Thirty-Second orgiastic Act! "Your questioning of Helé'a of Ghatón was incomplete, Lord – shoddy for one so skilled as yourself! Lá, did he not tell you of the other relic I had put 'around the corner'? Not the Globe of Instruction which you pried out of me, but something other?"

"What? – No –"

Hársan brought his brows together in fierce concentration. All else he thrust aside, all thoughts and feelings and emotions. He shut out the sights and sounds and smells of the great hall of the Man of Gold, let the alien tendrils of Other Planar power seep into his consciousness.

He groped in the dark that was not dark. Something lay there.

"Why, then, here you have the key, Lord!" he gasped. He held out his hands. The mind-seer instinctively held out his own in return.

An object, white and shapeless, dropped from nowhere into Vridékka's palms. Wisps of vapour arose; the thing actually smoked! A wave of deadly cold smote them all.

It was the silvery-blue rod, all coated now with ice!

Vridékka shrieked, flailed, fell backward. It seemed that he could not let go of the thing! He howled, danced, waved the rod like a glittering sword, and stumbled into one of his guardsmen. The noise brought everyone in the hall around to stare.

The nearest soldier snatched at Tlayésha. "This girl dies –" he snarled.

She reacted in a way Hársan could never have guessed. Instead of struggling, she threw both arms about the man's neck, drew him close, and held up her face almost as though she would make love to him.

She opened her eyes wide.

"Ohé, man, would you then slay one who wears the curse of the Goddess Avánthe!" Her eyes were very blue in the light of the artificial sun of the hall.

The trooper yelled wordlessly and jerked aside to sketch the protective sign of the Worm Lord in the air with two fingers. He fumbled for his weapon. Two very hard hands pulled his head back from behind, and Miruré's powerful, practiced, leather-shod knee snapped up against his spine just below his copper-trimmed backplate. There was a satisfying crack, and he crumpled. She had his sword almost before he struck the floor.

The Mihálli raised his blue-glowing ball, his men fanning out beside him. Vridékka knelt upon the pavement and clutched his hands to his breast in a contortion of agony. There were shouts from the inner chamber, and Jayárgo appeared at the door there to stare forth openmouthed.

Soon – soon, now ...

He realised that he had no idea what was to happen "soon."

Hársan reached "around the corner" one more time. Had not Chtík p'Qwé said that other sages had experimented with this strange place, stored their secrets, their artifacts, and possibly their victims therein? He let his mind swim in the unimaginable tides and eddies beyond his own bubble of familiar reality. Another object emerged to drop upon the floor in front of him: a round ball of blackened ice within which he glimpsed the shrivelled remains of a body, a creature that had many limbs and a face more grisly than any demon carven upon Lord Sárku's temple walls!

He lacked the power, magical or physical, to throw it. But a kick sent it skittering and smoking across the floor to scatter the agents of Yán Kór like goblets from an overturned tray.

Unperturbed, the Mihálli lifted his blue globe and sighted.

A thunderous roar from the room of the picture-box made the creature miss. The beam of twinkling blue light snapped soundlessly over Tlayésha's head. Both Hársan and the Mihálli turned to stare unbelievingly.

Soldiers, the Undead, the remaining *Qól*, a half dozen of Vridékka's small Underworld monsters – all came boiling out of the narrow door. The living fled toward the anteroom, the *Mrúr* stumbled and rose sluggishly to fall again under the feet of comrades behind; the *Jájgi* was visible for a moment, and then it, too, disappeared under the press. Jayárgo dragged himself free to scramble up by the wall just outside of the inner chamber.

Something brown and huge loomed just within the door to the room of the picture-box. It flowed forth, a low and massive wave of crusted, stained reddish leatheriness borne along upon a myriad tiny greyish cilia – a thing like a many-legged flatworm, but with a thousand wetly gleaming, soft tendril-legs for every one that any normal worm possessed! The upper integument was smooth, undulating, glistening russet – like a great carpet carried along by a horde of *Drí*-ants.

A living carpet, Hársan thought.

Yes, that was it! A carpet! The brown carpet he had glimpsed within the chamber of the picture-box! The thing must be some sort of guardian!

Táluvaz Arrío shouted in his ear, "A *Ngoró*!"

"A what?"

"One of the beasts of the ancients – kept to guard their tombs and treasures!" The Livyáni seized Tlayésha's wrist, pulled her and Miruré back around behind the dais.

"Hurry," he panted, "for it slays all! In Livyánu –"

324

Hársan did not wait to hear what a *Ngoró* might do in Livyánu. He must stop both this monster and Vridékka. A glance told him that the old man was no obstacle now. He was either dead or unconscious – perhaps he had used some trance-like spell to prevent his mind from feeling pain. His hands were white and shrivelled, as though long immersed in ice water.

Hársan bent. A jerk and he had one of Vridékka's scuffed leather sandals in his hand. This he used to scoop up the silvery-blue rod, still streaked with moisture and lacy white crystals.

Whatever else, whatever the consequences, he had one more thing to do. The cold of the rod made him curse, but he staggered across the chamber and up onto the dais.

He thrust the rod down into the hole in the central panel.

The black handle moved this way and that under his hand. He felt it engage, and sensed the throb of ancient power building somewhere inside. Many tiny lights sprang up to dazzle him with reds and blues and yellows. Hársan fell to his knees and prayed that the Man of Gold still operated, that it would do what the Globe of Instruction had claimed against the Goddess of the Pale Bone, "She Who Must Not Be Named."

He prayed that it would somehow make all of this death and blood and pain worthwhile.

The organ voices poured forth again within his brain, rose to a crescendo, then dulled to barest audibility. The spots of pain reappeared upon the inside of his eyelids, but they were not as excruciating as before. Indeed, there were words written within each pulsing circle, words in a script that he could not read, words that shifted and changed to vocal, musical notes within his mind. He knew that they had nothing to do with the Man of Gold.

He understood the words.

"Our duty." The organ voices sang. "Our task." A cascade of trebles and basses and shrieking flutings poured over him.

He sensed rather than saw the sweep of the great carpet-creature – the *Ngoró* Táluvaz had named it – as it rolled inexorably forward over the Undead, over the *Qól* and the others, and towards himself.

"Our duty," the organ rumbled in a lower, minor key. "All those who come without permission. All –"

He could see nothing now but the tiny circles of light, glowing orbs that had no colour and no substance.

"Who –? Why –?"

"Our duty," the mighty orchestra boomed in measured cadences that shook Hársan's universe. "Placed here to guard the secrets of –" There was a name, but it did not translate into sound. "To slay those who disrupt the house of him with whom we are allied…"

"We did not come – we are not –"

"So it is. You brought the key, the rod. You could not have that unless you have permission. That is why we strive to speak to you, to read the patterns of your mind." Hársan felt the vibration of the creature's ponderous movement through his shins, pressed against the floor of the dais. "Death must come to those who are here but who are not with you. They are interlopers. Wait."

Hársan dared to open one eye. The sweeping brown carpet filled one side of the hall. There were lumps and unidentifiable objects beneath it. Jayárgo cowered against the wall nearest the door. The Mihálli, his bandy-legged assistant, and two of his bravoes crouched in the opposite corner. The blue globe flashed and flashed again, and seared black spots appeared upon the surface of the carpet-thing.

It flowed forward, swept down upon them.

"Priest, priest!" the Mihálli howled. "Call it back! Stop it!"

"I cannot, even if I wished," Hársan cried.

"If they are friends, followers, servants," the organ blared in his head, "then are we empowered to spare them."

Hársan hesitated.

"Priest –! Oh, Hársan!" It was Eyíl who stood there, terrified, nude save for her flashing blue jewellery, her high, dark-tipped breasts heaving in terror. She was lovely. A pang of yearning struck him.

"No friends of mine!" Hársan snarled.

The russet carpet reared, a great ocean wave, oily-smooth, brown as dried blood on top, red-grey wriggling cilia beneath.

A muscled, snarling, many-fanged *Zrné* rose to face it; then a snake-like dragon-thing; then a furred, feline beast – the same that Hársan had glimpsed before.

The carpet swept over them all. There were screams and crunching sounds.

Hársan blinked; his eyes told him that the Mihálli had vanished just slim moments before the carpet-thing struck. If the creature had the skill to transport itself out along the lines of Other Planar force into some other bubble of reality, then so be it. Something – the *Ngoró* or his own mind – told him that it would not return.

Ponderously the *Ngoró* reversed itself, turned, and made for Jayárgo. The skull-faced priest gaped, then fumbled within his ochre robe. He drew forth the black globe he had picked up in the anteroom.

He clawed at the device, mewling in wordless terror. Something inside the globe clicked, and the top came off. Jayárgo drew back his arm and hurled the sphere at the *Ngoró* as a soldier throws a fire-pot from a wall!

It landed directly before the carpet-creature, rolled, and stopped. A black-brown ichor oozed out upon the floor.

The stuff was very like the grease the carter clans used to lubricate the axles of their *Chlén*-carts. The *Ngoró* rolled on, undisturbed.

Jayárgo squawked, threw up his arms, and fled back toward the anteroom.

The *Ngoró* began to pick up speed, rolling toward Táluvaz and the rest of the knot of figures just below the dais.

"No –! Friends! Not them!" Vridékka, who was certainly no friend, lay there too, but he was still immobile, a sprawled and ridiculous heap of stick-like limbs and ragged brown robes. Miruré stood over him, sword in hand.

The carpet-thing halted. "You who possess the key – your body is like those others, but we are unsure. Within you we perceive differences." The organ notes were wistful, restrained, as though yearning for an excuse to complete the work of slaughter.

"What?"

"We see you as a four –limbed-one, a human. But your mind shows one who has six limbs, a segmented tail…" Hársan sensed confusion and a threatening surge of hostility.

"No, I am no Pé Chói! Look again! Look into my mind – see, I open it to you!"

The answer was an indescribable ruffling: a shaking, sifting sensation reminiscent of an old pedant shaking out a dusty scroll. He found himself on all fours upon the dais.

"You are not. But yet you are." The *Ngoró* humped and rustled. "In one form your thoughts are muddled: this 'Man of Gold,' the many objectives of your species – too much and too disordered. In your other shape you bear a message…" The deep-throated chorus became one of wonderment. "A message – for the 'Underpeople' – for those who dwell in thrall to humankind, your other, original species…?"

Ítk t'Sá! Somehow she still lived then, within him! She had impressed him with her mission, however she had managed it.

The *Ngoró* reared up, a full two man-heights tall, rust-hued cilia coiling and twining beneath its sleek upper surface. "Return to the Pé Chói, then, you who are both! Tell them that some there are who dwell with humankind but who are not 'Underpeople'! Nay, some are 'Overpeople,' if you like either of those two terms! We have lived amongst the soft four-limbed-ones by choice, and we do as we will. None holds us in slavery, none is our master – he whom we served here paid well and in coin of our own choosing for the services we render."

"You would not come forth – to live upon the surface of Tékumel, to dwell in places of your own?" The words were not Hársan's but Ítk t'Sá's.

"Not so. Not all who inhabit the world of mankind are downtrodden, yearning to be free – and 'free,' indeed, of what? We do not covet your forests, nor are we eager for the sight of the sun and the moons. We dwell in *our* chosen places; you in yours. We are not pleased by the nearness of many fellows, by edifices, by the elaborations of manners and customs and societies that busy your minds. If you seek the will of us, the *Ngoró*, then know that we seek only solitude, the privacy of our own company. Know that we are not one entity; we are composed of a million, a billion, tiny minds, all alike, all with the same needs and goals. We are already a community, a polity, a metropolis in every sense of your word."

"Do you never desire the nearness of other species? Communion with beings different from yourself – selves?"

"That we have aplenty – within our own bodies." The organ sang down to a final dark, wailing chord. "We know too much – we have seen too much, and we have wandered too far. We no longer possess that one quality which gives you younger races your life, your animation…"

"And that is…?"

"That which no spell, no mage, no revolt or conflict or new confrontation can revivify: curiosity. The desire to experience more."

The music died away to a last whispered echo of Hársan's own heartbeat. Then it was gone entirely.

The creature flowed around the central dais toward the room where the shattered picture-box lay. It left a trail of broken helmets, weapons, armour, bits of clothing, and bones.

"The – the Man of Gold," Hársan called. "Tell me what it does! Why – how? The reasons for it…!"

"You have set it in operation already. As to what it does, you should have waited for him to tell you – he whose instructions and picture-box your fellows have destroyed." The *Ngoró* humped up again, folded itself, pushed through the door into the inner chamber.

There was little sign of its passing. Debris here, stains there. A gentle slithering noise from the inner room sounded like the opening of a wall-panel. There was probably some secret exit from that room through which it could go to feed – upon what, one could only surmise.

Hársan rose upon aching legs and went to the console. Winking lights welcomed him: a row of red dots, circles of yellow, square boxes of glowing green within which tiny lines merged and diverged to create alien patterns.

Nothing made any sense.

He looked up to find Tlayésha and the others beside him. They had heard nothing, not one word of the telepathic conversation between him and the *Ngoró*. He related it to them briefly.

"You have done more than any wizard since the Time of No Kings," Táluvaz said admiringly when he had done. "Not Súbadim, not wise Thómar, not Chirené Bakál – no mage or hero of the epics could match this." He gazed about the chamber enviously. "These boxes, those mechanisms – whatever the Man of Gold may do, it will be a century before all of this can be studied and put to use! I only wish this place were in Livyánu! Oh, I should have made Prince Eselné include a share of any finds –"

He broke off, embarrassed. Hársan pretended not to notice. The Livyáni began again in urgent, businesslike tones. "Come away, young man. Still must we find a path out of this labyrinth."

"Jayárgo? The Undead? The rest?"

"Crushed or fled." Tlayésha touched his forehead. He was hot and feverish. She looked at the lights and knobs and wheels with undisguised awe – and not a little fear. "What does it do, my love? Does it live? Will it march forth to destroy demons?"

"The 'Weapon Without Answer' of Yán Kór…?" Táluvaz added anxiously.

"I do not know," he answered. He concentrated, but the voices within his brain were mute now. He frowned, and puzzled over the flat panels for many minutes. Tentatively he touched the controls. Then he kicked the metal console, slapped a hand down across a row of black buttons. He was rewarded by a dance of coloured lights.

"I see nothing; it does nothing. I command it to rise and take us hence from here, but it does not reply. I tell it to go forth to slay the Yán Koryáni and – and a certain terrible Goddess and Her *He'ésa* – but it does not move." He knit his brows and concentrated again until perspiration dripped down into his eyes. "Nothing. Oh, it makes pretty designs – a veritable treasure trove for a jeweller or one who delights in magical playthings! Our learned priests could exhibit it to awe the gape-mouthed rustics on feast days. Perhaps it is broken – too old. Perhaps –"

"You saw nothing – sensed nothing?" Táluvaz urged. "No powerful forces, no beams of light? No pressures upon your psychic self?"

"Nothing! Nothing! The carpet-thing, the *Ngoró*, either did not know or would not tell me! The Globes of Instruction said only to do this much! I have done it. As you can see, this much is nothing at all. It glows and twinkles. It does not even make a sound."

"This does not mean that it does nothing. The ancients –"

"Thúmis hurl the ancients into the Unending Grey! See for yourself, I have enough psychic sense to know when the powers of the Planes are active close by – and so do you, I warrant, Lord Táluvaz Arrío! Some of its parts must have corroded away or become defective over time..."

He kicked the Man of Gold again in frustrated disappointment.

Miruré climbed onto the dais to report that Vridékka still lived but remained unconscious. Either the freezing wounds dealt him by the silvery rod were more terrible than they appeared, or else the mind-seer's trance-spell was very powerful indeed. Tlayésha joined with the N'lüss girl in suggesting that they cut the old man's weazened throat before he could awake. Táluvaz urged that they bind him tightly instead, blindfold him so that he could not cast spells with the power of his gaze alone, and leave him to be collected – or to die – later. If they could send a party back for him, Prince Eselné would be very grateful for a scholar as learned in the inner workings of the Temple of Sárku – and as knowledgeable in the doings of his brother, Prince Dhich'uné – as Vridékka. The Concordat did not hold down here, and what had happened tonight would not bear scrutiny in the light of day. No, the Skull Prince would not dare complain to the Petal Throne over the disappearance of his house-wizard.

The others wrangled on, but Hársan paid no heed. Whether they lived or perished here was unimportant. Damn the Man of Gold! It might be arrogant to think oneself a blue or black piece upon the *Dén-den* board, but to win through to the Sun Circle and then find that one's crown was no more than gilded paper! To use one's hard-won powers only to discover them as impotent as a child's toy sword! It was more than one ought to have to bear!

A mighty mage, a hero of epics indeed! Chá, it was enough to sour the sweetest wine!

He smashed his hand down again and again upon the black buttons, turned wheels, pressed knobs. The Man of Gold made no response. It did not speak as the picture-box had done: it emitted no sound at all. The flicker of coloured lights and the wavering lines within its many little transparent panels told him nothing.

At last he put his head down upon the cold metal of the console and wept.

It was thus that Prince Eselné's scarlet-armoured soldiers found them a *Kirén* or two later. They had Jayárgo, bruised and much chastened, with them, and to the surprise of all, Morkúdz. The little Hehegánu babbled out a tale of using a spell of invisibility – really a sort of camouflage that worked best in semi-darkness – to befool the Undead in the tomb chamber. He had then pretended to be a corpse, his greyish skin and lumpy features enhancing that masquerade greatly. When everyone had gone from the upper cavern, he escaped. His adventures amused the others, but they were lost upon Hársan; he had gone once more to kick the Man of Gold and to urge it into life – something, anything, that would make all of this meaningful.

Nothing availed. Tlayésha and the others almost had to drag him away from the glittering console. They bore him forth, still cursing the poor Skein the Weaver of All had woven for him.

Chapter Forty

Arjuán hiDaránu of the Clan of the Victorious Globe was neither young nor handsome. He was certainly no match for the likes of Mríka, his new wife. His clan-elders had warned him against the marriage: the girl came from Hekéllu in the far northeast, as far across the Empire from Tumíssa as one could get, and her own Clan of the Barren Peak was unknown here. It was possibly not even a decent Tsolyáni clan but one from the barbarous mountain tribes of Jánnu or Kilalámmu. Not a proper marriage at all, they said. But then Aijuán thought to detect a tinge of jealousy in their objections, just the sort of mix of envy and respect and recognition that made him suddenly stand out, no longer a balding, faceless scribe in the Palace of the Realm in provincial Tumíssa, but someone to whom pretty women were attracted, a man whose talents were not all to be seen on the surface.

His clan-brothers told him he was a fool to wed one so young and so pretty. Mríka was *Aridáni*, and once she had settled into Tumíssan society – and tired of Arjuán – she would certainly go on to marry other, higher-placed, better looking, and younger husbands. Arjuán had no illusions; he was only a stepping stone – a fact he knew would one day cause him great pain. For now, however, Mríka was indisputably his bride. Men looked after them and whispered admiringly. They attracted attention on the street, in the official receptions of the Palace of the Realm, in the temple of Lord Thúmis, and everywhere they went together. For the present he was happy to have her.

Perhaps, just perhaps, this marriage might revive Arjuán's ailing career. Like an old and tattered scroll that is taken from its pigeonhole and given a new coat of shining varnish, he might still rise in the Palace of the Realm and be promoted to High Copyist when Genému hiNayár, his superior, retired. (Already the old man had three young apprentices to clean up the blots and scrawls his aged fingers left behind!) With Mríka as the cynosure of all eyes, Arjuán could go on to Béy Su, even to a post within the Chancery at Avanthár itself. A dream, indeed, but no longer just a fantasy to be yearned for in the grey hours before the *Túnkul*-gong called him to his morning chores at the scriptorium. The Weaver of Skeins might yet have a golden thread or two to spare for Arjuán hiDaránu.

Arjuán rattled the door-clappers. Mríka had not been well these last several days. Some depression, some nagging worry, had darkened her mood, and she had taken to lying abed longer than was her wont. Some slight by the gossiping, clacking wives of Arjuán's colleagues, some female problem – he did not know, and she did not say.

The hook beside the door was empty; no *Méshqu* plaque hung there to inform visitors of the current disposition of the occupants of the house. Strange. No, worrisome. He fumbled with the latch and the door swung open. Mríka had not bothered to drop the bar from within.

The outer chamber was dim with the murky shadows of late afternoon. The acrid smells of inks and chemicals vied with the warm fragrances of reed-paper and *Hmélu*-parchment. Underlying all of these were the pleasantly remembered redolences of meats and spices and savoury cooking.

Arjuán left his sandals at the door and padded across to the dais upon which they sat to eat and rarely to entertain. It had only three tiers, as Mríka repeatedly reproached him, but was that not enough for a middle-level copyist of Imperial documents? A three-tiered dais was all they required to show respect to their social equals and to his immediate superiors; he could no more expect anyone higher as a dinner guest than he could hope for the company of the Lord Governor himself!

The silent room was oppressive. He stopped, hesitated in the middle of the floor, and bent to pick up a document. The scarlet and black scrollwork illuminations of the Temple of Lord Karakán were still not quite dry upon it.

The parchment drew his attention. What was it doing here? Mríka –? No, she had nothing to do with his work, and she was always tidy. She never asked, never pried, never read any of Arjuán's tediously accurate accounts and records. He squinted. The paper was a requisition for scholars and materials for some projected voyage to Livyánu, and portions were in cipher – which Arjuán copied laboriously without knowing their contents. It bore the seal of one of Prince Eselné's privy chamberlains. This was not at all the sort of thing one should leave lying about!

Concerned now, he went around the hearth to the door of their sleeping room. It was shut. More, it was barred from within, and no little *Méshqu* plaque hung here either to tell him Mríka was sleeping or indisposed. He tapped thrice upon the panel, but there was no response. Again, louder. Then he tried the latch, but this time it was locked.

Was Mríka ill? Did she sleep so deeply, then? Worse, his little internal voice asked, had she left him? Was this the day he dreaded? He pounded on the door, then spent anguished minutes fishing for the latchstring with the key-rod that he kept hidden under the hearthstone.

The door opened upon blackness. Mríka always kept the one window covered against the midday blaze. She did not like sunlight and, like many girls of the lower clans who longed to be pampered aristocrats, strove to keep her complexion as pale as possible. It took more time for his eyes to adjust so that he could see what lay inside.

It was the smell that struck him first, however: an odour of milk gone bad, of spoiled food, of garbage left too long on a muddy riverbank. There was a huddled form beneath the clean *Firyá*-cloth sheet upon the sleeping platform. Mríka must have been terribly sick, vomited perhaps, and then passed into unconsciousness.

He ran to draw back the sheet.

What he saw was so unexpected that he could make no sense of it at all. The fabric was stained with a greyish, milky mulch that stuck to his fingers. Beneath, scattered roughly in the shape of a human body, were objects, things that he could not recognise, strange lumps and wetly shining bluish-white blobs of a substance that resembled spoiled cheese! They stank, and they lay in a pool of pallid, oozing wetness.

Revolted to the core of his being, Arjuán thrust himself away, furiously wiping his hands upon his ink-stained kilt. He gagged and staggered from the room. When he could think again he found himself outside upon the hot flagstones of their clanhouse veranda, clutching his stomach and still vomiting into Mríka's neat bed of *Naludla*-flowers.

His thoughts whirled round and round but always came back to the one logical conclusion. She had left him. She was gone. Certainly that was not Mríka there on the sleeping mat!

What else was possible?

Yet why? Why not tell him, at least? Why this awful affront to his dignity – the hideous, insulting mess upon their sleeping mat? He might not have been the most ardent of lovers, but that –! The humiliation was unbearable. He flung back his head, cursed, groaned, and beat his fists upon the damp stones.

Their neighbour, Betkánur hiFashán, found him thus, took him inside, cooled his brow with a damp cloth, gave him strong *Dná*-grain beer, and sent his little daughter scampering to the Temple of Lord Keténgku to summon the physicians.

By evening the tale of Mríka's vanishing had spread. The city watch came with questions for him, and his superior, Genému hiNayár, also arrived with a priest and two senior scribes from the Palace of the Realm. What had happened to Mríka was riddle enough, but these worthies were even more concerned about the copies of various documents – some important – in Mríka's handwriting concealed within her gaily painted cosmetics box by their sleeping mat. And what was the amulet they found there, too? An amulet made of some pale, bone-like substance, covered all over with spidery writing in a tongue no one could identify? The script, opined one of Genému's colleagues, was clearly nonhuman, but it was not of the Ahoggyá, the Shén, the Pé Chói, the Mihálli, or even the dreaded Ssú.

Arjuán hiDaránu denied all knowledge of the affair. He begged them to find Mríka, but no one heeded him much. The priests, soldiers, and later a blue-and-gold uniformed officer of the Omnipotent Azure Legion only pestered him with serious-sounding inquiries about such matters as spies and agents, Yán Kór and Mu'ugalavyá, and the like. He did not care. He pleaded ignorance, and eventually they all went away.

He curled himself into a ball upon Betkánur's unfamiliar sleeping-mat and wept.

❧ ❧

The drooping *Já'atheb*-tree fronds sketched a ballet in silver silhouette above the Shadow Gods' ponderous temple pyramids. It was not yet dawn, and the city of Tsámra still slept, although Síyuneb could hear the yawning, querulous voices of servants from the labyrinth of buildings and gardens below. The palace of her master, Lord Kétkorez Tanákku, was awakening.

She rose, as supple as a spray of *Já'atheb*-blossoms herself, to wash away the telltale signs of their night of pleasure. The flower-filled pool that occupied a quarter of this, the topmost terrace was cool enough to sting her golden skin and drive away the fumes of the evening's wine. Between the ornate columns, the pre-dawn breeze fluttered the *Thésun*-gauze draperies, brought from distant Tsolyánu, like the wings of little birds, and made the glass-chimes twitter and tinkle upon their tall poles at the corners of their couch.

Soon the sun would stride forth from the Halls of the Underworld to strip away Síyuneb's illusions of youth and beauty. It were best if she were gone before then. The slight thickness beneath her chin, the delicate web of lines at the corners of her eyes, the too-ripe roundnesses of hips and thighs, all would be laid bare by the merciless glare of Lord Qame'él's ball of pale flame.

Síyuneb slipped out of the filmy garments Lord Kétkorez had chosen for her. She bathed completely and washed the sparkling *Níritleb*-powder from her hair. She also washed the curious implements that enhanced the joys of their coupling. With these – and with the arts her body knew – she could hold Lord Kétkorez for yet another year, two at most. After that she did not want to think. He might never reduce her to the ranks of the serving maids, but to live on in solitary comfort in some back apartment of the palace, to pass her days in gossip and idle make-work tasks, to grow old and fat and raise the children of some chamberlain or guardsman, was no life for one who had slept upon her master's High Terrace!

Oh, there were other fates: she might become a priestess of Lord Qame'él: a functionary within one of the temples, glorying in each exercise of petty power; she might take the jewellery and gifts Lord Kétkorez had bestowed upon her and purchase a villa in some remote – and inexpensive – seaside town; she might become a courtesan, a shop-assistant for one of the mercantile clans – many things.

It took a great deal of self-control for her to bring herself back to the much more enjoyable present.

She stretched and spread her black mane to dry. The insect-netting was still closed; her master slept. Síyuneb sat down cross-legged upon the marble balustrade and ran the golden comb Lord Kétkorez had given her through damp-tangled locks. The lines of red and blue tattooed *Aomüz* upon her wrists caught her eye. She was not allowed the symbols of an aristocratic clan and a high position within the temple hierarchy, mayhap, but her present status as First Concubine was not without its rewards. It was a far cry from her peasant forbearers, she thought: better the lady of a great aristocrat than a farmer's wife with no tattooing other than the mud of the fields and the wrinkles of a life of toil.

She was awakened from her reverie by Chákkunaz, the least obnoxious of Lord Kétkorez' body-servants. He was both young and well-made, and his infatuation for her was no secret. Her master was not unkind; he turned a blind eye to an occasional dalliance, and she had wheedled more favours from Chákkunaz than even Lady Láilueb, the Chief Wife. Certainly Chákkunaz was more to her taste than Esúdaz or Qelyúz or any of the other chamberlains. She carefully refrained from comparing him, even to herself, with Lord Kétkorez. Her master might be as young, as learned, as mannered, and as well turned out as any noble in the Five Empires, but he lacked a certain fire; he was a trifle cold, indifferent, and hard to arouse. He had been thus, the old crones of the palace said, ever since he had turned eighteen, after some sort of undiscussed accident in the mountains near the city of Dlásh. Lately Lord Kétkorez had seemed preoccupied and even less susceptible to her wiles than usual. It was this that made Síyuneb's array of special implements so necessary.

"He is not awake, lady?"

"He has not moved since I arose. The wine and the drug-powders and all of Rétumez' greasy cooking last night…"

Chákkunaz pulled the netting aside. He bent over the sleeping figure on the dais, and the red-dawning sun upon his muscled shoulders awakened desire within her. She would have summoned him and whispered of an assignation later, but his stance gave her pause. The young chamberlain stood frozen, astonishment – shock – apparent in the lines of his back, even though she could not see his face.

"Síyuneb," he called softly. "Come here."

She did not protest the use of her personal name as she might otherwise have done. His tone told her that there was something very wrong.

She obeyed. He had pulled back the coverlet, and at first she thought that Lord Kétkorez was not there at all, that he had risen and departed in the night. Then she saw what lay on the patterned mat: glistening mucus, a heap of chalky, yellowish-bluish-white wet things. A parody of a human shape, a mass of garbage – what was it? A prank? Lord Kétkorez never played pranks, nor did she ever recall seeing him smile spontaneously.

"Lady, what occurred last evening?" Chákkunaz backed away. He held his nose.

"Naught unusual. We made love, we feasted –"

"Nothing else? No one came? No sorcerer visited here?"

"No – He was moody and wanted no guests. Why?"

"There are stories afoot in the quarters – tales of others who vanished this very night. A general of one of the legions, a merchant from the Plaza of the Diadem of White, a priestess from the temple of Kírrineb, a pair of traders in the Foreigners' Quarter, servants, clansmen – at least a dozen…"

"What? Like this? Is that – is that – stuff – Lord Kétkorez?"

"The Gods know. It is the same elsewhere. So run the wagging tongues."

"Call the guards –!" Síyuneb started toward the staircase that led down from the terrace. There would be a squad of soldiers on duty below.

"Yes – no! Wait. You were the last to see him before – before this. The *Vrú'uneb* will take you to the temple. You will be questioned – as many others have been already."

"What to do?" A knot of panic was forming just under her heart. "I know nothing. I swear – I had naught to do with it – with this." The sight and smell of what might have been Lord Kétkorez made her queasy.

Chákkunaz straightened up. "You must take what you can and flee." His tone was hard and crisp. "Get your jewellery, all of your money, the best of your things – I will accompany you as far as the harbour. There are ships there for other lands – Tsolyánu, Mu'ugalavyá – even the nations of the Shén."

She began to quake. The horror of her situation was only now beginning to seep into her limbs, a dank and deadly feeling, like a bath in cold oil. The disappearance – or death – of a great nobleman, and she his sole companion, the last to see him alive…?

"You – would you go farther – come with me?" She lacked the courage to go alone.

He gave her an appraising look. "I – might. – Yes, why not? What have I here? And we have – cared – for one another."

She knew him all too well. He might be as greedy as Demon Prince Origób himself, but she thought she could manage him. She must have someone!

Chákkunaz came to her and embraced her easily. "Do not fear, lady – my love – for I shall protect you. We must move quickly and with all of the circumspection of the gods themselves!"

Frantically, shivering with a terror she could neither explain nor master, Síyuneb allowed herself to be led down to her apartments within the palace. A bundle of clothing, her money, and her jewels were all Chákkunaz let her take. Then they departed by the back gate, ducking between the lumbering *Chlén*-carts full of the day's supplies for the palace kitchens. The leather-kilted cooks and naked slaves paid them scant attention.

The *Vrú'uneb*, the ever-efficient arm of the Livyáni theocratic state, the iron dagger beneath the silken coverlet, apprehended them just after they had purchased passage on a round-hulled merchantman bound for Jakálla.

Síyuneb never saw Chákkunaz again, nor was she told what had become of him. The heavy coins he had carried for her vanished as well. Yet she herself was treated with all the deference due a First Concubine, and no one touched the jewels she wore. A cold-eyed captain and a trio of ebon-robed hierophants questioned her politely but at length. Hours, days – months? – passed; she had no idea of time within the blind walls of Lord Qame'él's inner temple. Her interrogators advised her not to return to Lord Kétkorez' palace, not to meddle, never to seek to learn what had occurred. She should go back to her village in the Tláshte Heights and find her clansmen. Her gems would buy a little house, a patch of garden, and a decent husband; then she must make her peace with Lord Qame'él, devote herself to His worship, and grow old as gracefully and inconspicuously as possible.

That was all. She was free.

One thing she remembered from the dreary, anxious hours of her interrogation. It was just a word, one she did not know: *He'ésa*. Her questioners asked her repeatedly and interminably about that, but she could only shake her head.

What was a *He'ésa*? She never dared to ask.

❦ ❦

In Jakálla the city watch reported that one Dlámu hiTranúkka, a rascal who dealt in gems and other curios, had disappeared. Only his much overworked staff thought to ask what the mess was that someone had thrown down upon the floor of his strongroom. He had no strong clan affiliation, no family, and hence his presence was not much mourned. His wealth, on the other hand, proved most useful: it provided the barristers of the Palace of the Realm with cases, claims, and counter-claims for years to come.

❦ ❦

Three scribes who served General Kadársha hiTlekólmü, of the Tsolyáni Imperium's Legion of the Searing Flame, vanished as well. They were serious, conscientious, unassuming workers, and he briefly mourned their loss. He mentioned the matter to his master, Prince Mirusíya, one of whose adherents he was, but the Prince only remarked that some of his own people had suddenly become ill and died, too, quite unaccountably. General Kadársha's physician and sometime house-wizard, Eylóa, consulted his tomes and suggested the possibility of a new form of the terrible Ailment of Arkhuán Mssá. For several days thereafter Eylóa appeared more than usually grim and morose, which was odd even for an eccentric philosopher such as he.

Several servitors of the Vríddi clan of Fasíltum perished mysteriously, as did a half dozen subalterns and junior officers of the Legion of Victorious in Vimúhla, one of Mu'ugalavyá's elite units. An Ahoggyá village chief in Salarvyá, a Shén egg-layer in Mmatuguál, a handful of Pygmy Folk in the subterranean den-city situated on the eastern border of Yán Kór – all did the same. In Yán Kór itself, the clever young master of the Clan of the High Spires of Rüllá was found to be missing, and the matriarchs of the clan hastened to marry his plump widow to his younger cousin, a simpleton far more amenable to decent female management than he had been!

The Lord Staffbearer of the Palace of Effulgent Radiance in Saá Allaqí discovered raddled garbage, like the intestines of an animal, in the beds of three princelings of the blood. Frightened, he reported only that these youths had fled, perhaps apprehensive of some plot by their siblings. The *Ssaó*, King of Saá Allaqí, sent forth a summons to the other thirty or so of his offspring – as many as he could remember. All responded save the Princess Vrísa, perhaps twenty-fourth in line, who was off seeing the world somewhere and could not be reached.

Although no count was ever made, the diligent scribes of the Palace of the Realm in Béy Su estimated that, all across the Five Empires, perhaps five or six hundred (a thousand, whispered some) persons – human and nonhuman alike – died during the Night of the New Ailment of Arkhuán Mssá. There was anxiety for a time, but when the plague ceased and did not reappear, the matter was filed away. More important doings were afoot, and only a few of the presumed victims were anybody important anyway.

Eventually the Omnipotent Azure Legion presented a thick sheaf of reports to Lord Cháimira hiSsánmirin, the High Prefect of the Chancery at Avanthár. In turn, that worthy laid these before the Servitors of Silence, who guarded the Emperor in the Golden Tower. An edict was subsequently issued commanding greater sanitation throughout the cities of Tsolyánu. A council of scholars and priests and physicians was later called into secret session, nevertheless, in the Hall of the Petal Throne itself.

The results of this conference were not made public.

❧ ❦

A hundred lumbering *Chlén*-beasts pulled the wagon. The dust of their passing was a dun-coloured cloak spread over the sere wastelands of the western marches of the Desert of Sighs. Upon the cart rode the Baron's "Weapon Without Answer": a cube the size of a small house, swathed all in black cloth. Worked upon the fabric in silver and green were the insignia of Yán Kór, of the Gods of the north, and of the promise of death to all the Baron's foes. Ten pairs of wheels, each two man-heights tall and a quarter of a man-height thick, groaned and screamed and jolted upon the rough stones. The wagon was far too large to travel upon the *Sákbe*-road that ran from the city of Hlíkku in Yán Kór south-westerly to Khirgár and thence into the rich Tsolyáni heartland. A full thousand masons and carpenters and labourers toiled in advance of the column beside the road to make a way for it.

Two contingents of green-clad troops flanked the march: the elite First and Second Legions of Mighty Yán Kór. Three more Legions preceded the grumbling wagon; still others followed. An auxiliary Cohort of Hláka scouts, the little flying nonhumans from beyond Kilalámmu in the distant northeast, swooped and soared overhead, their ribald chittering drifting down the wind.

From a vantage point upon the highest level of the *Sákbe*-road one could see all of the long serpentine columns: the scurrying insects around the ebon block that was the "Weapon"; the dark squares beyond that were phalanxes of marching soldiers, arms and legs flashing in jerky unison; the hordes of camp followers; the *Chlén*-carts laden with arms and supplies and waterskins; and the smaller bodies of scouts and stragglers and local tribesmen, all the way to the horizon; all rolling inexorably on toward Khirgár as the sea-tide rolls up onto the sand.

The central column, that containing the "Weapon," had halted. No one yet knew why. The flanking contingents continued to trudge on by, and clusters of officers and aides and General Ssá Qayél's elite guardsmen leaned down from the *Sákbe*-road parapets to see.

The ponderous wagon that bore the "Weapon" now stood immobile in the drift-ing dust, surrounded by swarms of soldiers, *Chlén*-handlers, and hangers-on. The sub-altern who had clambered up to the third tier of the *Sákbe*-road to fetch Lord Fú Shi'í shouted, mopped the sweat from his brow, and waved his pennoned lance, but the crowd only milled about, muttered, and gawked. Their numbers grew by the moment.

Lord Fú Shi'í pushed aside the flap of thick cloth that concealed the entrance to the little chamber within the "Weapon" and came out to stand upon the little platform at the rear of the great cart. His expression was bland and pleasant as always, but lines of strain showed around his clean-shaven mouth, and his eyes were cold and furious.

The officer behind him in the passage held a corner of his mantle over his nose. He said, "Lord, the damage? Shall we summon General Ssá Qayél and Lady Mmír? The army —"

"Not yet. Go away. Leave me to assess the matter – Yes, halt the legions, bivouac here for the night, and get rid of these people."

"There is no water here, Lord. We had planned to reach the village of Tnéktla by sundown."

"Sink the village of Tnéktla into the sand! Do as I say. And send me the scribe Truvársh. A report must go this very day to Baron Áld in Ke'ér."

The man sketched a tired salute and climbed down the ladder into the crowd. His emerald crest remained visible above the cylindrical helmets of the troopers for a time, like a beetle surrounded by a horde of *Drí*-ants. Lord Fú Shi'í stared after him, then went back within.

The damage was certainly done. It was far more serious than the legion captain could have suspected. Beyond the still-smoky outer corridor, in the control chamber that lay within the heart of the "Weapon," were five heaps of grey-white putrescence, puddles of thick mucus, and a smell that made Lord Fú Shi'í gasp. Worse, however, were the silence and the darkness. The soft humming of the "Weapon" had ceased. The banks of little purple lights, so deep in colour that one could hardly say when they were lit, were black and vacant. Some were charred. Sadly, Lord Fú Shi'í touched a slender hand to a lever, as those who had supplied the "Weapon" had instructed. Nothing resulted.

"Lord." It was the scribe, Truvársh.

"Come within. We summon a conference."

"Others may see." The man's eyes glinted ruby-red in the hot light reflected from the vestibule.

"None dare enter here. And we will not be long."

The scribe wavered, flickered, and became a furred, long-snouted creature, a Mihálli. It drew forth a translucent sapphire sphere from within its mantle a "Ball of Immediate Eventuation," the special other-planar tool of its race. It concentrated.

They stood upon a glassy plain.

The sky was of no colour, the landscape flat and weirdly foreshortened. Myriad pale tendrils, vines of white that bore no fruit and had never known sun or rain, emerged from a single point beyond the horizon to writhe across this plain and disappear here and there into what might have been the ground. Every one of these filaments was withered, shrivelled, curled, and dead.

"Not here," said Lord Fú Shi'í, a trifle sadly. "Not where 'Those Who Are Seen and Yet Remain Unseen' have perished. The vines that bloom as men on other Planes are gone."

The Mihálli nodded and bent over its globe again.

They stood in the place that was not a place, where little beads of light darted to and fro like fish within a turgid pool. A figure glowed before them, its edges brightening first, then its centre filling in with colour and detail, as dye seeps into a length of fabric. A second appeared.

"My Lord Prince. Lord Baron."

"Four of my personal staff are gone. Others are missing," Prince Dhich'uné said curtly. "This means that the priest-boy has won through."

"So it is. Half a dozen of my people are piles of rotting curds too – not even the *Dlaqó*-beetles will eat the stuff." Baron Áld sat down upon the dais that the Mihálli produced before him. He wore no armour but a hunting costume of green leather.

Lord Fú Shi'í shrugged, gracefully. "All of the Goddess' minions, her *He'ésa*, are severed from our Plane. Without the umbilical cord that sustains them from Her Plane, they perish. The Man of Gold has wrought as its ancient makers intended. We came to the feast tardily and brought too little food." He carefully forbore from mentioning that this had been the decision of his master.

"Our agents – my Vridékka?" Prince Dhich'uné asked.

"We have heard nothing," Lord Fú Shi'í cupped a hand and turned it over, a sign that any player of *Dén-den* would recognise as one of surrender. "Our Mihálli in Púrdimal – gone beyond this Plane, out of reach of contact. All of our people there as well. Some must be dead, others taken."

The Baron spat a string of crackling oaths in his own fierce northern tongue. "And my 'Weapon'?"

"Cut off as the *He'ésa* were, master. All of the Goddess' entrance points are gone, sheared away as a butcher cleaves the head from a *Hmélu* with his axe. No force penetrates now from Her Plane into ours."

"Chá! What's to do?"

Prince Dhich'uné said, "Continue to advance the 'Weapon,' of course. Who is to know that it — temporarily — no longer functions."

"All too many know, mighty Prince. Half the army saw the smoke billowing from the door. The officer who entered it to investigate will tell his tale. It will be old gossip by nightfall. Spies in the camp — Tsolyáni, Milumanayáni tribesmen, and others — will carry it to Prince Eselné within the six-day."

"Repair it. Restore the access points." The Baron clenched brawny fists upon his knees.

"That can be done, master. But it will take time to find another path through the Planes Beyond, one that the Man of Gold does not block. Then will come the work of building connections, replacing the key people with the Goddess' *He'ésa*, as was done before."

"Do you tell me that it will again take as many months — years — as it did to progress this far?" the Baron thundered. He leaped to his feet, and the place that was not a place trembled and quavered. The Miháli looked over at him in silent reproach.

"We can still defeat the Tsolyáni," Lord Fú Shi'í murmured silkily. "We have the troops, the military skill — your own great skill, Lord — and your high determination."

"Gull me not, man! It was risky enough with the 'Weapon,' but well you know that the Tsolyáni have thrice the legions we can muster — older, better trained, more cleverly generalled! Serve me no Ahoggyá piss in place of wine!"

Fú Shi'í bowed his sleek head before his master's wrath. This, too, would pass.

"And what of me?" Dhich'uné broke into the brittle silence. "What of our plans — your promise to relieve certain of my siblings of life? Who now will smooth away my opposition in the *Kólumejàlim*? Well you know that I cannot face my half-brothers in all of the tests that comprise the 'Choosing of Emperors!' The *He'ésa* were to —"

"The Gods know that you cannot surpass even your silly half-sister, Ma'ín Krüthái! Not even if the sole contest were to get yourself successfully sodomised by a Shén!" The Baron paced to and fro. He threw off the fingers Fú Shi'í laid upon his arm. "Go! Resign the 'Gold'! Hide in your worm-riddled City of Sárku! Forget the Petal Throne or else learn swordsmanship and agility and those other arts that will be tested! Hire champions —!"

He snorted. "Cheat!"

The skull-painted face was unreadable. "I will hear no more, barbarian. Now will I let Eselné and Mirusíya crush you, defeat your puny armies, and skewer you upon a pole, just as General Kéttukal's man Bazhán did to your foolish fish-wife Yilrána! My half-brothers will slay you, and you will weaken them just enough to allow me to come forth again as the heir to my father's Empire! When you are done chewing upon one another like an arena-pit full of *Mnór*, I shall be there, Baron, to claim my patrimony."

Baron Áld would have drawn the steel dagger that hung at his belt, but there was no substance here in this place that was not a place. He turned his back to conceal his rage.

Prince Dhich'uné gestured and was gone.

"And you!" Baron Áld fixed his baleful gaze upon Fú Shi'í. "You are correct at least in one matter. Turn the 'Weapon' around, back to the City of Hlíkku! Call up more troops, order the manufacture of weapons, build me more armies. My vengeance will not be gainsaid. Time it may take time aplenty, yet indeed we shall defeat the Tsolyáni, and it shall be by the victory of our arms alone! No more of these magical meddlings, no more pacts with slimy things from beyond our Plane! A pox upon the Goddess…!"

"As you decree, my master." Lord Fú Shi'í sighed. Halting the army and trudging back along the dreary road through the barrens to Hlíkku would be a thorny conundrum in logistics and supply. There would be problems of politics and diplomacy as well. But there was no help for it.

More, both he and Baron Áld knew that Yán Kór had little chance of defeating the ponderous might of the Seal Emperor. Armies? Weapons? A Tsolyáni torrent against the petty rivulet of Yán Kór!

No, now he must hone another sword, work another plan, set a different snare. His own masters, those of whom he did not like to think even in his sleep, would not be pleased, but they were more patient than this thick-brained *Zrné* of a man.

They would wait.

He signed to the Mihálli, and once again the place that was not a place was empty of all life – or at least of that which men might recognise as such.

Chapter Forty-One

And still you are unhappy?" Tlayésha chided.

She leaned upon the sculpted marble balustrade, thoroughly aware of her newfound elegance, like Lady Avánthe herself, Hársan thought, in the simple tunic of sapphire *Gúdru*-cloth she had chosen, her new veil of creamy *Thésun*-gauze draped most gracefully over one shoulder to be tucked into her girdle of embossed silver plaques. Even now, even here, she must hide her blue eyes; people were superstitious, after all. The spray of *Khéshchal*-plumes in her hair set off her oval face and the dark waves of her tresses. It was as though Tlayésha had always belonged here, a princess herself, in mighty Avanthár.

Hársan hesitated. To be honest, he could find no reply to her question, not one that really satisfied him.

"'A hungry man eats whatever the tree bears,'" he quoted, a little wistfully. "I am not sure – I shall never be sure – whether I have given my discoveries over to the best – the noblest – of the players of this game. At least Prince Eselné will use the cache for the good of Tsolyánu – as he sees it."

"And the Man of Gold?"

That, alone of all, was the bitter rind to the fruit. He could not answer her.

The damned thing had not worked! Oh, Lord Táluvaz had suggested that it might somehow be bound up with the New Ailment of Arkhuán Mssá that had so recently and mysteriously ravaged the land. But was that not most likely a sop for Hársan's feelings? Who had ever heard of a device of the ancients that slew a victim in such a way, like a ghastly disease: randomly, with no purpose, one here, another there, as far away as Jakálla, Tsámra, Ke'ér, or Tsatsayágga in Salarvyá?

Alas, so much for visions of glory...

He pulled at his chin. "Why, let it stand there and blink its pretty lights for another aeon or two. High Prince Eselné may peddle it to Prince Dhich'uné – or to the Yán Koryáni – for a basket of rotten *Dlél*-fruit for all I care! Old Vridékka is worth more in trade than any Man of Gold! To the Unending Grey with it!"

Tlayésha gave him a sidewise smile. "It got you here, to Avanthár."

"Not really. The cache of relics did that. They are more useful."

They turned to look down the stair. Below the landing upon which they stood, arches set at angles to one another bore the staircase on down until it was lost to view in the amber twilight of the lamps and the coiling smoke of *Vrés*-wood incense. Above, from whence they had come, were the aureate Gates of Sublime Visitation, the antechamber of the Hall of the Petal Throne itself. The warm, honeyed air pulsed with the cadenced chanting of praises to the God-Emperor, sung day and night throughout the centuries without end. When one venerable singer in the Gallery of Adorations tired, another was there to take up that self-same note. Thus, men said, not one syllable of the Paean of Exalted Glory had been missed for over a thousand years, not even when the armies of Mu'ugalavyá had besieged Avanthár some three hundred years past. Continuity, custom, and tradition: these were the bonds of the Tsolyáni Imperium. They were more lasting than any mortar or cement.

The blue-veined marble balustrade was cold and slick under his hand, polished by reverent fingers for over two thousand years. Each ample step was adorned with golden bosses and mosaic petals of chalcedony and malachite, like flowers strewn upon the threshold of a bridal chamber. At each end of every step stood pairs of guardsmen resplendent in the blue and gold livery of the highest sanctuary of the Imperium. Wealth, opulence beyond any dream of avarice, lay everywhere: carnelian, porphyry, other semi-precious stones, and the omnipresent gleam of gold. Gold, gold, like honey upon a cake!

Tlayésha was looking at him, but Hársan had lost himself in some reverie of his own.

They awaited Prince Eselné. He and his priests and officers had not yet come forth from their audience before the oblong, lacy screen of translucent green-white jade high up in the far wall of the throneroom. This screen hid the Petal Throne from view – or, as some said, it was a part of the Petal Throne itself. A single lamp was lit behind that screen to signal the presence of the Emperor, Hirkáne Tlakotáni, styled "The Stone Upon Which the Universe Rests," the sixty-first Bearer of the Seal of Tsolyánu.

Hársan had been within, too. The chamberlains had ushered him inside to prostrate himself before the God-King: the goal of every Tsolyáni, the fantasy of his lonely childhood, the epitome of all desire. He had heard the Speaker cry his name aloud before the Petal Throne, and his head still reeled from the decree that had come forth from behind the screen: membership in whichever clan of medium rank he chose, promotion to the Fifth Circle of the Temple of Thúmis, money – he did not remember how much – and mention with honour in the Sacred Book of the Leaves of Azure…!

It was all at Prince Eselné's behest, ostensibly for discovering the cache of artifacts below Púrdimal. There had been no mention of the Man of Gold.

The Gates of Sublime Visitation were opening. Prince Eselné himself appeared, followed by Lord Táluvaz Arrío and the senior members of their retinues. In the rear, a head taller than the rest, came Miruré. Her broad, sharp-boned face was nearly invisible beneath the headdress of saffron-dyed *Chlén*-hide scales that marked her as the personal bodyguard of a Livyáni Legate. Only Hársan and Tlayésha had seen the red and black glyph the tattooers had already placed between her high breasts: the *Aomüz* of the proud Arrío lineage of Tsámra.

Prince Eselné wore the glittering court-armour of a High General of the Empire, appropriate to his role on the western frontier. The plumes of his flanged, garnet-inlaid helmet trailed behind him, almost to his feet, and these he thrust back with a brave gesture. His broad, bluff, heroic features were flushed; he was in high good humour.

"Hói, priest Hársan!" he called. "Are you satisfied with my divine father's generosity?"

He was. But his inner reservations still persisted. He made no reply but bowed low instead.

The Prince took his hand. "Come, there are many who would meet you – clanmasters eager to adopt you, sorcerers who would consult you about your musty relics, ladies yearning to test your manhood!" He smiled, a mite too handsomely, at Tlayésha.

"Mighty Prince —"

"Not now, not if you are still too addled. But one there is who will not wait."

The Prince led the way down the staircase, through pillared corridors, into a portico of many arches and columns. Beyond was the night sky. A score of man-heights below, the Thri'íka River flowed beside the western cliffs of Avanthár, a mumbling torrent in the blue-velvet dusk. They were far too high for the spray to reach them here, but Hársan welcomed the moisture-laden breeze; it blew away the somnolent thicknesses of incense and lamp-smoke and perfume from his brain.

Avanthár rose from the conflux of the Thri'íka and the Missúma Rivers like the prow of some gigantic ship, two hundred *Tsán* north of Béy Sü, in the midst of the eastern foothills of the Kraá Range. The citadel was the hollowed out mountain itself, pavilions and gardens and the Golden Tower adorning its summit like a crown. High, arched galleries opened out along its precipitous flanks from the labyrinthine halls and chambers within, and the only entrance was the Water Gate somewhere out of sight beneath them on the south-western side. To the rear, where the long promontory had once sloped down into the mountains to the north, a single mighty fosse had been cut away from one river gorge across to the other. Avanthár had defied all besiegers since before the Priestkings of Éngsvan hla Gánga, before the arrogant masters of the First Imperium, before the ravaging Dragon Warriors from out of the northwest, and, indeed, who knew how many aeons before that. There were no records of the building of Avanthár. This Emperor or that had added to it, dug another gallery (though now the architects warned against this), and embellished it with ever-greater wealth and the spoils of captive nations. Yet no one knew who had created it.

Avanthár was unique; it was Avanthár.

A slight, elderly man sat upon a mat beside one of the casements. Hársan did not know him, but the pearl-grey mantle and ornate canonicals of a priest of Thúmis were familiar. A complex headdress of opals, moonstones, and slate-hued plumes lay upon the mosaic floor beside him, obviously too heavy and uncomfortable to be worn once one had escaped the solemnities of the Hall of the Petal Throne.

"Greetings, priest Hársan. I am Dúrugen hiNáshomai."

Hársan knew the High Adept of his temple by name. He made obeisance as Zarén had taught him so long ago in the Monastery school. He had never imagined he would have a chance to use this bit of etiquette!

"Don't bother. Your bow is three decades out of date. And we don't require the Engsvanyáli salutations any more." The High Adept chuckled.

He motioned to a mat beside him. It lay upon a dais two finger-breadths lower than his own, as was proper. A plate of *Másh*-fruit and spice-scented *Dlél*-fruit glimmered next to him, their vivid yellows and blues reduced to pallid white and sooty black by the moonless darkness. He reached to select a *Dlél*-fruit with a sure, delicate hand.

Hársan looked about for Tlayésha, but Táluvaz and Miruré had steered her off to another of the arched window-alcoves overlooking the river. Prince Eselné sprawled against the scalloped stone railing. The two of them were alone with Lord Dúrugen.

"What clan have you selected for yourself, priest Hársan?"

"I – I do not yet know, my Lord. – The Grey Cloak, if they'll have me. Or the Scroll of Wisdom."

"Either would be pleased to take you, a contributor to knowledge, indeed a hero of the Empire! The epic-singers are already scribbling verses in praise of your deeds!" Lord Dúrugen's tone was faintly ironic. Hársan could not see whether he was smiling.

"Sir, I do not mean to push – to force myself upon anyone –"

He really meant that. At first he had tried hard to convince his comrades and his rescuers that he was no hero, no Hrúgga, no Girl of the Age. Táluvaz and Miruré had been no help, and Tlayésha had been entirely too worshipful, as behooved a pretty girl whose mate has just unearthed the sensation of the century and set all of the sages and sorcerers by their ears! His story had been politely heard, but his protests were taken as no more than youthful humility – true or false, who cared? He suspected that much of this acclaim was motivated by politics rather than otherwise. Somebody – Prince Eselné, the Imperium, the hierarchy of Lord Thúmis – needed a hero, and he had happened along to play the part. It all left a rather dark taste in his mouth.

"The Grey Cloak will take him in all right, eh mighty Prince?" Lord Dúrugen grinned over at Eselné. "They'll make him a clan-brother. Aí, they'll drum up a proper genealogy for him and give him the pick of their lineage-names! Not strictly 'historical,' perhaps, but satisfying, very satisfying, to everybody concerned. This Hársan is now famous – he can be Hársan *hi*-anybody-he-chooses. He'll have to fight off their clan-daughters with a quarterstaff!"

"Whatever my father commands is – or rather, becomes – the will of the Gods," Prince Eselné said. He, too, seemed amused.

"'Noble acts raise even the lowest soul to become divine,'" Lord Dúrugen quoted piously from the Scrolls of Pavár. He sighed and settled himself against the parapet. "What a kettle of stew you have overturned, boy!"

Hársan was taken aback. "Holy Pontiff?"

"Chá! Do not pretend ignorance, young man! Already our delegates are sharpening their tongues for a battle over the custody of your fine black globes and polished silver devices – oh, and your Man of Gold, of course! That too. Now as a priest of Thúmis upon an authorised mission, you are the logical claimant; we, the Temple of Thúmis, are thus the proper owners. Prince Eselné here thinks otherwise. He, acting for the Imperium – or mayhap for the Temple of Lord Karakán, or possibly for his friends in the Military Party – would have his own scholars retain your booty in the Palace of the Realm in Púrdimal." He cackled. "Even the Temple of Sárku has had the amazing nerve to claim that what you did was done in service to them!"

"Next we shall hear demands from that grease-tongued Livyáni," the Prince growled.

"Then it begins all over again," Hársan muttered glumly.

"Thus it has always been, ever since the Gods fought amongst themselves at the Battle of Dórmoron Plain. There can be no real progress – the establishment of 'noble action' – until we ourselves alter our own natures; that is why the Lords of Stability provide a better goal and a greater challenge than do the Lords of Change." Lord Dúrugen inspected a slice of Másh-fruit, and, gratified, popped it into his mouth. "Whatever the disposition – and it may take years – the whole affair redounds to the credit of Prince Eselné here. Not, you understand, to that of Prince Surundáno, the erstwhile protégé of our own Temple of Thúmis. Had you come to us in Púrdimal, boy, we might have had the Hmélu by a different leg!"

"There were reasons, great Lord," Hársan began, a trifle lamely.

"Reasons?" the old man snapped. "What 'reasons' could possibly take precedence over your own Temple? Because of you, Prince Eselné and his Military Party fly up like pretty Sahulén-birds into the favour of our divine Emperor's eye, and poor Surundáno gets not even a straw of the credit!"

"A straw? Chá, a dollop of bird-dung upon the pate is all he deserves," observed Prince Eselné wryly. "Advise your clerkly little Surundáno to give up the 'Gold' and leave the rest to me! With the aid of the three champions allowed me in the Kólumejàlim, I shall become Emperor as surely as Lord Karakán's sword is sharp! You know that brother Rereshqála is near to resigning his claim. I can marry Ma'ín Krüthái – or slay her in the contests if she stays stubborn. Mridóbu is no problem: a master of ink and paper, intrigues and officials, but without substance – a fine lack of nobility. Dhich'uné, for reasons unknown, has gone off to sulk in the City of Sárku. He sees no one but his own priests and sorcerers, and it may be that he will pass up the Golden Tower for a lifetime of worm-kissing and smelly rituals with his Undead catamites."

"And Mirusíya?"

Eselné looked down, his handsome features lost in shadow. "You have found the one jewel in the chaff, my Lord. He and I may have to have it out one day, though some say he is too much the man of action to want to live mewed up in the Golden Tower with the Servitors of Silence and a gaggle of concubines. As for me, I have been trained all my life for just that fate, and I am ready for it when the time comes." He rubbed his cheek thoughtfully. "Yes, I may offer Mirusíya the rule of Yán Kór and the northlands once we have taken them – my father has at last given permission for him to take a major army and advance up through the Pass of Skulls to invest Sunráya, you know. Mirusíya may like that."

Lord Dúrugen felt about on the mat for a knife to peel another *Másh*-fruit. "What of this priest Hársan here, then? Now that you have glorified him and well nigh turned his head around with all these dignities – taking credit for yourself, naturally – we would have him back. He is of the Temple of Thúmis and rightfully belongs to us."

"So that you can use him as your claimant in the matter of the artifacts? Lá, dear Lord Dúrugen!"

"Just as you would employ him as your instrument, if he were added to your staff! Ohé, Prince Eselné!"

Hársan could endure no more.

Slowly, but with increasing vehemence, he said, "And what if I do neither? What if I resign from this game of *Dén-den*?" He warmed to his words. "What if I refuse to bear witness or play the advocate for either of you?"

They both stared at him as though he were an *Akhó* "the Embracer of Ships," risen up out of the stone flagging.

"What, then –?" Lord Dúrugen put down the little knife.

"My Lords, I am a scholar, a student of languages and wisdom. I am no politician, no hero, no courtier to mince about palaces, no barrister to slice arguments and pare clauses!"

"There, now, young man," Lord Dúrugen soothed. "You shall not be forgotten! You shall have access to the things you discovered – perhaps be made Chief Examiner in charge of them –"

"Stuff the relics – and the accursed Man of Gold, which is neither a man, nor gold, and which does not work anyway – into an Ahoggyá's furry arse, throw the temple libraries in after them, and set the lot afire!"

Hársan had astonished even himself. His fingers shook, and he felt a sudden dread of losing control and becoming as he had been under the Mihálli's awful spell. He wiped his lips with the back of his hand.

Lord Dúrugen sat speechless, for once shocked into silence. Prince Eselné straightened up, and for a moment Hársan feared that the next words he would hear would be a call for the impalers and their stake.

Then Eselné began to laugh.

"Hái, a *Zrné* cub leaps snarling upon its foes, no matter their size!" he chortled. "Ah, priest Hársan, would you assault Avanthár and lay waste to the temples of the Gods – and both on the same afternoon? Would that my soldiers were as brave as you!" He choked, broke off to spit a *Másh*-seed out into the night, and gasped for breath.

"What would you have then, boy?" Lord Dúrugen inquired with ominous gentleness.

"Only a place in some peaceful temple – a monastery, an academy of learning, I care not – somewhere. A place in which to work, to fulfil my Skein of Destiny, to study, to learn. No more."

"Aha, Lord Dúrugen!" Eselné crowed. "Oh, let us grant him this – agree to accept his written deposition regarding the relics, find him such a post, and trouble him no longer! His courage demands it."

The High Adept's face was stiff and cold. "Easy for you, mighty Prince, who possess the artifacts and the Man of Gold, whatever it may be. Easy for the Imperium, but not so for us. We have a right to this youth; we took him in, nurtured him, trained him, gave him the skills he would now bury in some rustic shrine!"

"Nonsense. He will warble the tune your Grey-robes taught him. But not, mayhap, exactly as you and I would have him sing! Release him – a noble act upon our parts, and noble action is the sole salvation of all creatures, as the Scrolls of your Priest Pavár say, though I am damned if I can recall just where!" He gestured out beyond the railing, toward the world that slumbered there in the darkness. "Do you not have a temple post someplace, the sort of thing this priest Hársan wants? Let us not be too harsh with our taskmastering!"

Lord Dúrugen's face wore the expression of one who has just bitten into a pebble. "No – yes – oh, have it your way. I suppose so. If you insist. There is a librarianship in Penóm –"

"A stinking city, a sinkhole of swamps and insects and disease!"

"Thráya, then. A teacher died there recently, of that new plague."

"Too remote – and not the sort of place where real research is done. The Monastery of the Sapient Eye, dear Lord Dúrugen! Prior Haringgáshte grows no younger."

"Well. Well," Lord Dúrugen cleared his throat, coughed, and made to rise. "An Imperial Prince decrees. So be it."

"Would you return to the Chákas, priest Hársan?" Eselné inquired.

Before he could reply, another voice asked, "Or may I suggest yet another Skein?" Lord Táluvaz Arrío stood there. No one had heard him come up in the darkness. They all turned about to look.

"And what might that be?" the High Adept asked in sceptical tones.

"Livyánu, great masters. As a member of the venture sent jointly by the Temples of Lord Thúmis and Lord Karakán to explore the southern continent. – Or perhaps a post with your expeditionary force in Tsoléi?" He glanced down at Hársan. "New things, learning, the ancient seat of Llyáni wisdom – doors that only I can open for you within the archives of our temples! No threat to the interests of the Temple of Thúmis or to those of Prince Eselné, either one. Out of harm's way: no Skull Prince threading needles of revenge. No more of players and games."

He gave Hársan a meaningful look.

Here was a possibility, a new idea. What Táluvaz Arrío offered did promise knowledge, adventure, and excitement. More, it would give him peace from the storms that had cast him up upon the shore here at Avanthár.

But then longing for the sweet, green canopy of the Chákan Inner Range welled up within him: the Monastery of the Sapient Eye – Zarén – his Pé Chói friends – his home. Too, there was Ítk t'Sá's mission, embedded within his heart like a gem set in a ring.

He was torn.

He considered for a moment. The others watched. Then he drew a ragged breath and said, "The Chákas, my Lords. – Thank you, anyway, Lord Táluvaz."

The Livyáni bowed. Prince Eselné lumbered up to his feet, very much like the *Chlén*-beast with which the palace wags compared him. So, even more stiffly, did Lord Dúrugen. Káshi had risen, and its ruddy moonlight transformed the sculptured columns of the gallery into a jungle of tangled ochre vines. It was time to go.

Tlayésha met Hársan and took his hand. She said nothing, but he thought that she must have heard.

The great citadel still rippled with life and motion, even at this hour of the night. The *Túnkul*-gong of the Temple of Lord Ksárul sang down through the arched halls and high-vaulted ceilings, calling the faithful to the Service of the Investiture of Indigo. Every sect had its own shrine here, and each of the ten Gods and ten Cohorts was served in accordance with ancient custom and ritual. Throngs of courtiers swept up and down the staircases: nobles on their way to an entertainment, stewards intent upon privy missions, foreign emissaries gawking and gaping at the wonders displayed, soldiers, servants, lackeys, scribes. A hundred, a thousand, meetings and assignations and whispered trysts in the golden, lamplit shadows.

The statues in the Hall of Eminent Rememberings were dark-looming colossi above them as they passed: noble Emperors whose blank stone eyes looked beyond the world to gaze upon the Gods, heroic generals, stern ecclesiastics bearing the cryptic symbols of their sects.

Prince Eselné halted. A young woman had detached herself from a crowd of chattering comrades and was coming toward them. She wore a skirt made of strips of emerald and purple, a collar of green beryls, a silver tiara from which iridescent *Khéshchal*-plumes drooped down to sweep the floor behind her. Delicate silver chains glittered at her wrists and ankles, and her intricately coiffed tresses were powdered with silver as well. Her full, rounded breasts sparkled with artful patterns of dusted gold.

"Lady Misénla," Eselné said heartily.

"Mighty Prince, Lord Dúrugen, my Lords." The woman was little more than a girl, yet her face struck Hársan as old, clever, and altogether too lovely to be believed.

Lord Dúrugen saluted her brusquely, bid his companions goodnight, and stalked on by. The Prince motioned Hársan and the others to stay.

'My Prince, highest one, who is most dear to all of the Empire, let me introduce you to certain new friends." The priestess' eyes glowed yellow topaz in the lamplight. "General Kadársha hiTlekólmü; his house-wizard Eylóa; General Karín Missúm – men say that his ferocity in battle makes him truly 'The Scarlet Death,' as his nickname denotes; Lord Kútume; Lord Shénesh…" She went on to name several others.

"Some I know already." Prince Eselné waved a hand to include them all. They were Prince Mirusíya's "New Men," companions of his army days drawn along to the zenith of glory by Mirusíya's own advancement. If Misénla had befriended these, then there would be more realignments and subtle shifts within the kaleidoscope of Imperial power.

Hársan, however, had eyes only for one in Misénla's entourage.

Eyíl.

She stood in the rear of the group, in conversation with a shaven-skulled, gigantic soldier Misénla had called Lord Shénesh.

Eyíl was staring at Hársan. Neither moved.

Misénla raised one artful brow. "Oh, lá, I had forgotten that your friend there — what is his name? — knows this lady, the priestess Eyíl hiVriyén."

Hársan could smell the fusty cushions of Eyíl's litter upon the road to Béy Sü, the scent of her limbs, the perfume of her hair. It was as though no time had passed at all.

"Hársan…" Eyíl said.

He moved toward her. He could not help it.

"Mighty Prince, I had meant to bring her to your quarters tomorrow," Misénla was saying. "She had so wanted to see this priest, this hero of yours. Something about a useful connection between her clan and his new one. Is it not to be the Clan of the Grey Cloak?"

"I — we have not yet quite decided," Hársan managed.

"I am sure that he would be happiest in that clan," Eyíl murmured. Her eyes never left Hársan's. "My clan and the Grey Cloak are old friends, though we differ upon various minor religious matters."

Small, urgent fingers reached through from behind to encircle Hársan's arm. Tlayésha said, "Even so, perhaps your clan and that of the Grey Cloak are too far apart for easy joining, my Lady. As for Hársan, he has chosen to return to the Monastery of the Sapient Eye in Dó Cháka, and will likely spend the rest of his days buried under a heap of scrolls: a scholar, a researcher, a teacher. — As he himself desires. I doubt whether his Skein will include much of the dazzle of courts and high temple ceremony."

Eyíl's long eyes flicked up and down, just once, over Tlayésha. "One who has been named before the Emperor in the Hall of the Petal Throne is no nonentity, my lady, no mere scribe, no scruffy village schoolmaster to parse Llyáni sentences for peasant boys. My clan-elders would be honoured to meet him, to discuss — alliances."

Her nearness was overpowering. She thrust one smooth, copper-gold thigh forward through the swinging purple and green strips of her skirt. Her lips were parted, her eyes ashine.

Hársan said, "Ah, much remains to be resolved. Later, when there is time…" He was as tongue-tied as ever he had been in old Chnesúru's slave coffle.

"As you say, love." Eyíl laid delicate stress upon that last word. "Your Monastery is not far from Tumíssa, which is home to me and to my clan. The great temple of Lord Thúmis in our city contains books, artifacts — even a clockwork simulacrum said to have been constructed by the wizard Thómar himself. A fine place to study and to work. To settle."

"Oh, yes, of course. But all for the future —"

"We are to be married, lady," Tlayésha let her words fall as firmly as a smith's hammer strikes upon iron. "Once we have reached the Monastery of the Sapient Eye."

This was the first Hársan had heard of it. In Tsolyánu it was not unusual for a woman, an *Aridáni*, to broach the subject of marriage to a man, but at least it was customary to inform the husband-to-be before proclaiming it to all the world!

Tlayésha and Eyíl confronted one another. Where Tlayésha was curved and voluptuous, Eyíl was tall, lissome, and much more the elegant lady. Eyíl's face was the more perfect, but Tlayésha's showed greater charm and animation. One could even become used to her startling blue eyes, ill-omened though they were! Yes, Eyíl was the more polished, but Tlayésha was warmer, earthier, and more worldly-wise. Both were women of poise, determination, courage, and intelligence. People would respect them, and any normal, hot-blooded young man would doubtless write poetry, fight duels, or commit murder for either one!

Hársan discovered, not very much to his surprise, that he loved them both — and for quite different reasons. How had he been fortunate enough to deserve their affections? More to the point, how could he choose between them?

Eyíl gave Tlayésha look for look. "As Hársan says: all remains for the Weaver to weave."

Prince Eselné had grown tired of waiting. He grinned down at Misénla who had come to lean into the crook of his arm. "Oh, come, priest Hársan," he said in his brave, powerful voice. "'One pillar cannot hold up a roof.' Marry them both and raise yourself a dynasty!" He yawned hugely. "Aí, marry both these ladies so that we may be off to bed! And this you must take as an Imperial decree!"

"Great Lord Prince —!"

"Chá! It is good for your clans, for your faiths, and for me – it gives me a chance to make you two wedding gifts instead of one, priest Hársan. Thus it must be. I'll hear no more of it."

He saluted Mirusíya's officers, nodded to Lord Táluvaz, and let Misénla's deft fingers twine his own about her slender waist. He turned to depart.

Hársan gazed after him in open-mouthed dismay. What would happen if he obeyed the Prince? The two women stood appraising one another from no more than a man-height away. Tlayésha did not seem in the least put off by Eyíl's superior height: Lord Vimúhla against Lord Ksárul, two gladiators poised against one another in the *Hirilákte* Arena, a pair of female *Zrné* tensed to fight over a tasty, trembling *Jakkóhl*, Hrúgga against Hásfodel the Purge in the epics….Further comparisons were both unnecessary and unpleasant.

He would require all of the help of the Gods indeed, were these two ever to combine against him!

Hársan stared wildly around. Lord Táluvaz Arrío caught his eye.

"I have reconsidered, my Lord," he announced. "Livyánu is indeed the place for research, for the study of Llyáni, for – for all that you said. I accept your offer! Other matters can – must – come later."

Eyíl smiled, licked her full lower lip, and said, "Why, of course, love. Tsámra is old, sophisticated, a city of culture and fashion and pleasure and beauty. A place created by the Gods for just such as we."

"There are schools of medicine there," Tlayésha's arm linked him to her as firmly as any chain of steel. "Physicians, techniques, a whole pharmacopoeia of medicaments little known here in Tsolyánu – there is much in Livyánu that I would learn."

Lord Táluvaz sighed. "You are more than welcome, priest Hársan. I am glad that you have changed your mind. We have much to show you – and Miruré and I would keep you close to us." He could not repress a chuckle. "– And your two lovely wives, of course."

There are times when even the Weaver of Skeins can make an awful tangle of a perfectly simple tapestry.

The End

About the Languages

Tsolyáni, Mu'ugalavyáni, Livyáni, Salarvyáni, and Yán Koryáni – the languages of the Five Empires – belong to the Khíshan linguistic family. They trace their descent back to Engsvanyáli (the tongue of the Priestkings of Éngsvan hla Gánga – or Engsvanyálu, as some modern Tsolyáni call it), thence to Bednálljan Salarvyáni (spoken by the rulers of the First Imperium), possibly through the little-known tongue of the Three States of the Triangle, and eventually to Llyáni. Before that, no one knows.

Of the Khíshan languages, Yán Koryáni is the most different from the rest; it is in turn related to the languages of some of the other northern states: e.g. Ghatón and Milumanayá. Miruré's N'lüss dialect belongs to the N'lü'ársh stock (as does Pijenáni and the ancient tongue of the Dragon Warriors, from whom the N'lüss are descended), and her speech is thus as distant from Hársan's Tsolyáni – or Táluvaz Arrío's Livyáni – as Arabic is from English.

Tsolyáni is not really difficult for English speakers, although it does contain a number of unfamiliar sounds and combinations. It is important to note that each letter always has just ONE pronunciation: e.g. *s* is always *s* as in "sip" and never *z* as in "dogs"– or *zh* as in "pleasure." This is true both of consonants and vowels.

The following consonants are pronounced much as an English speaker might expect: *b,d,f,g* (always "hard," as in "go"), *h, j* (as in "Jim"), *k,l,m,n,p,s,t,v,w,y,* and *z.*

The *q* is a problem; it is a "back-velar k," as in Arabic "Qur'an" or "Qadi." Those unfamiliar with this sound may pronounce it as an ordinary English *k*-not a *kw* sound, as in "quick" nor "quote."

The Tsolyáni *r* is like that of Spanish "pero." When *r* is doubled (i.e. *rr*), it is trilled: Spanish "perro," or as *r* is "rolled" in Scotland. Kurruné, for example, is "koor-roo-NAY."

The glottal stop (') is common between vowels, especially in Mu'ugalavyáni, which, in "English spelling" might look some thing like "moo-'oo-gah-lahv-YAH-nee." The glottal stop also occurs after consonants, as in Dhich'uné (i.e. "theech-'oo-NAY"). In some languages, too, it glottalises the following consonant: e.g. N'lüss. In these cases, this "catch in the throat" is a bit difficult for those not used to it.

The digraphs (sequences of two consonantal letters used to represent just one sound) are: *ch* as in "chin"; *dh* as in "thee" or "this" (thus keeping it separate from *th*; see below); *gh* as in Arabic "ghazi" (a velar voiced fricative – English speakers can get by with an ordinary "hard *g*"); *hl* is a "voiceless i," as in Welsh "Llewellyn" (the other *h*-initial digraphs all represent pre-aspiration: e.g. Hnálla is "h-NAHL-lah"); *kh* as in Scots "loch" or German "ach"; *ng* as in English "sing" (and *ng* can occur at the beginnings of Tsolyáni words!); *sh* as in "ship"; *ss* is a retroflex voiceless sibilant found in Sanskrit but not in any modern European language: the tip of the tongue is turned up to make an *s*-sound against the back of the alveolar ridge; *th* as in "thin"; *tl* as in Aztec "atlatl" or "Tlaloc"; *ts* as in "fits" (again this is found in word-initial position); and *zh* as in Russian "Zhukov" or English "pleasure."

Other sequences of two consonantal letters are pronounced as written; this applies to two identical consonants as well: e.g. Llyán is "l-LYAHN," Mmír is "m-MEER," etc.

The vowels are likely to give still more trouble, but this is due more to the confused writing system of English than to any fault of Tsolyáni. There are NO "silent letters" (e.g. the "*e*" of "above"); *EVERY* letter – vowel or consonant – is pronounced. The vowels, with one exception noted below, are pronounced as in Spanish: *a* as in "father"; *e* as the "ey" in "they"; *i* always as in "machine"; *o* as in "no" or "oh"; and *u* as in "flute" or "Zulu." In English spelling, these might appear as "ah," "ay," "ee," "oh," and "oo." The vowels of "cat," "above" (either one), "pet," "pit," or "law" are not found in

Tsolyáni, although Yán Koryáni has some of them. There are two common diphthongs: *aí* as in "I" or "bite," and *au* as in "cow" or "how." Other vowel sequences (e.g. *ua, uo, io*) are all pronounced as written: e.g. Arrío is "ahr-REEOoh," and Arjuán is "ahr-joo-AHN."

The non-Spanish exception is the *ü*. In western Tsolyánu this is the "umlaut ü" of German "für" or "über," while in the east it is pronounced as a high-back (or central-back) unrounded vowel not found in any European language, but which does occur as the "undotted i" in Turkish. Some practice is necessary, therefore, to pronounce Hrü'ü properly; an English-speaker might get by with something like "h-roo-'OO." Béy Sü is approximately "bay soo."

Word-stress —"accent," as some may call it – is important in Tsolyáni, just as it is in English (which confuses everybody by not writing it at all: compare "PER-mit," the noun, with "to per-MIT," the verb). Properly speaking, this feature should be shown by an "accent mark" upon the stressed vowel, but this may detract from some readers' enjoyment of the story. In Tsolyáni it can't be helped. A person learning English cannot guess from the letters alone whether to pronounce "syllable" as "SILL-uh-bull," "sih-LAH-bull," or even "sih-luh-BULL." In the same way one cannot tell whether Dhich'uné is "THEECH-'oo-nay," "theech-'OO-nay," or "theech-'oo-NAY." The last is correct, but without diacritics there is no means of knowing. (Since EVERY vowel letter is pronounced, it CANNOT be "dheech-'OON" to rhyme with "tribune." The final "e" gets its full value, as in the French word "soufflé.")

The names used in the story cannot all be listed here, nor will every reader care whether it is "HAHR-sahn" or "hahr-SAHN" (the former is how Hársan himself would say it, the last syllable rhyming with "swan" and not with "span" The name is Chákan, and thus one also hears "Hahr-SAHN"– Harsán – in the central Empire.). Some, like Dhich'uné, are stressed on the last vowel; e.g. Miruré is "mee-roo-RAY," Avanthár is "ah-vahn-THAHR," Eselné is "ay-sayl-NAY," Ahoggyá is "ah-hohg-GYAH," and Eyíl hiVriyén is "ay-YEEL hee-vree-YAYN." The prefix hi- "of" is pronounced "hee"; it is equivalent in Tsolyáni lineage-names to German "von." (It is never pronounced like "high.") Another example is Dúrugen hiNáshomai: "DOO-roo-gayn hee-NAH-shoh-mai."

Other words have the "accent" elsewhere: Tékumel is "TAY-koo-mayl" and Simanúya is "see-mah-NOO-yah." Thúmis is "THOO-mees," and Vimúhla is "vee-MOO-hlah." Táluvaz Arrío is "TAH-loo-vahz Ahr-REE-oh," and Tlayésha is "tlah-YAY-shah." Tsolyánu is "tsohl-YAH-noo," and

Livyánu is "leev-YAH-noo." These are easy, but some words are stressed in odd places — for English speakers: e.g. Mu'ugalavyá is "moo-'oo-gah-lahv-YAH," Salarvyá is "sah-lahrv-YAH," and Aomüz is "ah-oh-MOOZ" (with the "umlaut ü"). The adjective-forms made from some of these are more as an English-speaker might expect: e.g. Salarvyáni is "sah-lahrv-YAH-nee" and Tsolyáni is "tsohl-YAH-nee."

There is also a "secondary stress" in Tsolyáni: a vowel that is less loud than that which bears primary stress, but which is still louder than others in the word: e.g. kólumejàlim, which might be represented as "KOH-loo-mayl-JAH-leem." This can be ignored by all but the language scholars-and for those few lonely people, a grammar and dictionary of Tsolyáni have been published (but are now out of print, alas!).

Several languages have word-tones, like Chinese. This is especially true of the otherwise unpronounceable Pé Chói tongue. Since Hársan is the only human who ever learned to pronounce Pé Chói anyway, this will not matter much to anybody. The other peoples of the Five Empires struggle along with the clicking Pé Chói names as best they can.

And NOBODY can pronounce anything in the tongue of the Ahoggyá!

For those with an interest in the linguistics of Tekumel, a grammar and dictionary of Tsolyáni were published in 1981 by Adventure Games, St. Paul, Minnesota. The sourcebook for Tékumel, originally issued as Volume I of "Swords and Glory: Adventures on Tekumel" by Gamescience, Inc., Gulfport, Mississippi, contains further information about the languages and scripts of the Five Empires. Several of the ancient scripts have also been published as individual articles as Netbooks; cf. tekumel.com. [Many of the original source materials and game products for Tékumel are currently available through DriveThruRPG.com or RPGNow.com; look for "M.A.R. Barker's World of Tékumel."]

As a personal note, I make no apologies for the languages of Tékumel. The world is not Earth, although the humans of Tékumel did come from Earth — in a time immensely far in the future and as irrelevant to modern English as the languages of the Neanderthals are to us. The world is as complete as I can make it, and its unfamiliarities must just be endured by the reader who is exposed to it for the first time. I can only hope that those with little interest in languages will bear with me. Many readers pay little attention to foreign names in a story in any case, I am told, and simply recognise characters and places by the "look" of the words. There is thus no reason to worry about "spellings" unless one has the "linguistic bug." Ignore them in the interests of the narrative! One often finds that people who are not daunted in the least by computer languages, quantum physics, and calculus are terrified for foreign languages, while I, alas, am just the opposite. I feel the same awe and apprehension over the mysteries of addition and subtraction that many people suffer when confronted by Spanish or German – let alone Arabic, Urdu, or Chinese!

Or Tsolyáni...

About the Author

M.A.R. Barker (1929-2012) created the world of Tekumel, the setting for his novels and games. Inspired by Indian, Mayan, Aztec and other non-European mythologies and cultures, Barker wove these together with his own ideas to imagine an amazing science-fantasy setting. A Fulbright Scholar, Barker went on to teach at McGill University in Montreal and then at the University of Minnesota. A long-time historical game player, in 1975 Barker created a role-playing game, Empire of the Petal Throne after playing Original Dungeons & Dragons. After that, he wrote several novels, including The Man of Gold and Flamesong, both of which were published by DAW Books in the 1980's. His work is available again through the efforts of The Tekumel Foundation, established in 2008 to preserve Barker's creative legacy.

About the Publisher

The mission of the Tékumel Foundation is to encourage, support and protect the literary works and all related products and activities surrounding Professor M.A.R. Barker's world of Tékumel® and the Empire of the Petal Throne. To accomplish this, the Foundation was formed in 2008 as a nonprofit corporation. The Foundation works to preserve Prof. Barker's archives, licenses other entities to produce material for Tékumel, and promotes the world of Tékumel by publishing new material for it. This book is an example of the Foundation's efforts.

To contact the Tékumel Foundation, visit www.TekumelFoundation.org.

For more information about the world of Tékumel, visit our website: www.Tekumel.com.

For more information about the fascinating world of

The Empire of the Petal Throne,

visit M.A.R. BARKER'S WORLD OF TÉKUMEL at
DriveThruRPG.com.

Here are just some of the articles and
source material products related to
THE MAN OF GOLD
– many more are available:

The Temple of Lord Thumis
The Temple of Lord Sarku
The Tsolyáni Language
The Pe Choi
Empire of the Petal Throne